I0822301

THE RESURRECTION OF SJ

A SELAH ERA STORY

ANN CLARK MCFARLAND

The Resurrection of SJ
A Selah Era Story

Cover by Alice Briggs at Kingdom Covers, www.kingdomcovers.com
Original artwork for cover by Krista Averani and pelican interior art by Isabella Bianchi

Paperback ISBN: 979-8-9859412-0-3
Ebook ISBN: 979-8-9859412-1-0
Hardcover: 979-8-9859412-2-7

Library of Congress Control Number: 2025909013

Published by:
Realm Trek Press
Port Lavaca, Texas
www.realmtrekpress.com
info@realmtrekpress.com
Author website: www.clarkmcfarlandbooks.com

DEDICATION

For my husband Tim and our five,
William, Daniel, Elise, Rebecca, Bethany,
and their families and all the generations yet to come.

"Sacrifice for what you want or what you want becomes the sacrifice."
SJ's Motto

"Logic and reasoning conquer every contingency."
Cole's Mantra

"The thief comes to steal, kill, and destroy."
Evie's Warning

CONTENTS

PROLOGUE

August 2151
Upper Campus, Vossart Development School, Capital City, Meritus

SOFI'S FEET CLATTERED on the monkstone pavers as she hurried across campus. Light from the rotating trilladome bathed the hillside in a twilight glow and cast long rippling shadows on the megawall. She'd lost track of time while researching Nicholas and Iris Satanopoulos, her soon-to-be host parents, and hoped Mermer would understand.

Her heart fluttered as she swiped her hand across the security screen outside the Counseling and Nurture building. With a quiet swish, the basalt doors slid apart, and she entered, passing through the scanners. Hoisting her bag higher on her shoulder, she sprinted the rest of the way.

Bursting into the office, she ran up to Della, Mermer's assistant. "I'm sorry I'm late. Is she still here?"

Squinty steel eyes peered at her. "You're cutting it awfully close. She's about to call it a day." Della stood and smoothed a tuft of wiry gray hair behind her ear. "Wait over there." She pointed to the kids' corner and then marched off down the hall.

Sofi laughed and called after her, "I'm not a kid anymore."

Della's voice came back to her. "Then don't act like one."

Sitting in one of the larger chairs, Sofi pictured past days—Mermer across from her at their small table, offering playthings to act out and resolve life's difficulties, and a smile touched her lips.

Her gaze drifted upward to the Universe United banner on the wall. Under the large red ankh cross entwined between two steel-gray Us, she had known protection, as did all Meritus citizens.

Created in a test tube, born from a professional surrogate, raised in Vossart, and guided by Mermer, her life was meticulously designed, unlike that of a child born a century ago, when Earth refugees had first arrived on Meritus, and gangs, drug activity, and the severe decline of education had become the whipping end of freewill parenting.

Universe intervened and ruled on all matters of conception, birth, and child-rearing. Meritus's new society of contributing adults would be carefully planned and not left to chance. Child development schools provided the bulk of all education, and regulations limited parenting to host parents, individuals who completed approved training. Even then, host parents were only permitted to match with young people aged twelve or older.

Warmth seeped over her as she watched information about host parent classes scroll across a screen under the banner. For thirty-two months, Iris and Nicholas had attended something similar, and now their day had arrived. Her match to them meshed perfectly with her greatest dream, to share life with people who loved the medical sciences as much as she did.

A hand tapped her shoulder. "She's ready for you." Della stood towering over her.

Sofi nodded, tore down the hall, and pushed through the slightly opened door of Mermer's office.

"Wondered if you were coming." Mermer pushed her cat eyeglasses up on her nose and then plopped her face in her hands and leaned forward with her elbows on the desk. "Tell me what I want to know."

"Yes. Absolutely yes. They are perfect." Sofi scooted onto the chair across from her. "I want to sign everything."

"Everything? Even the name release?"

"Of course. Why not?"

With a sigh Mermer sat back and tugged on the sleeves of her gray wool cardigan. "I guess you can always change it back, although it would be a process." Her face softened, pushing away the frown on her forehead. "But I don't blame you. Moving forward with the name they pick will streamline many things."

"I wish I had matched with them four years ago. I've been waiting a long time for this."

Mermer shook her head and chuckled as she handed a stack of papers to Sofi. "Sixteen? You have your whole life ahead of you."

"I know, but it's so hard to get into the institute." Placing the pile to one side, Sofi picked up the first one and searched for her ID number. "It's his school too, you know."

"You would get in either way, because you have worked so hard for this. But it will be nice to have your debts paid."

Sifting through the pages one by one, Sofi signed each blank spot paired beside her ID number. At birth, test-tube babies were identified by a temporary name staff made from an alphabet number code corresponding to the last four digits of their ID number. The temporary name carried them through lower and upper development school days, until their Name Day when they could choose to keep it or pick another one or sign away the option to a host parent.

Task complete, Sofi stood. "When will I meet them?"

"Two days. They've just returned from an Earthland vacation. I believe they spent time in one of the newest jungle parks."

"Really? That's amazing. I want to go. Maybe they will take me."

Moving from behind her desk, Mermer held out her arms, and hugged Sofi. "It's a wild, wonderful world over there, but I'll stick with my routine here on Meritus."

They walked down the hall together and met Della at the door. She punched in a code, and the door swished open

"Don't be a stranger. We are here to help with anything you need." Mermer's voice had a catch in it, and she gave Sofi another quick hug.

"She's not gone yet," Della grumped. "We have her for two more years."

Sofi giggled. "She's right. I just won't live on campus."

"Of course, and I'm so happy for her. She's just growing up."

Stepping across the threshold, Sofi took a few steps and then turned around and waved at the two women standing in the glow of the only home she had ever known, a counselor's office. Kate always said Della and Mermer were like father and mother to them, and she and Kate were the children.

Kate.

Her roommate and best friend was waiting to hear her good news, and at the thought of this, Sofi began to cry. Despite the joy of her host family match, leaving Kate behind broke her heart.

CHAPTER 1

March 2175
Region Eight, Sector Seven, Capital City, Meritus

THE TIGER IN the shop window paused its pacing and stared at SJ. Both dead and alive all at the same time, it was the latest conjure in pet memorials. Big or small, your beloved deceased feline companion could be expertly stuffed and then robotically animated to move at the whim of your heart and the motion of your hand controls. The crude resurrections, if you could even call them that, amplified the goal she hoped to achieve, to be the first person to medically resurrect human life.

It was all in her grasp except for one thing. She'd run out of money. Her lab had been cut from the fund list, and now the bank towering above her, in whose shadow she stood, had just refused her a loan.

There was only one thing left to do. Call Cole. He was her plan B. Turning her back on the tiger, she set up the meeting before she lost her nerve. Then, she tapped out a request for a car on her wrist screen.

When it arrived, she got in and entered her destination on the dash screen. Nausea swept over her as the vehicle moved onto the speedrail. Her fledgling relationship to a man who controlled empires would soon be made or broken.

Cole had insisted the partnership would be all business, but his flirtatious attention whispered otherwise. All she could do was set her boundaries and see where it led.

Her route took her through the center of the city and past Blue Brick, an urban renewal Smart Zone. Named for the blue-tiled mirror domes that crowned each reclaimed apartment building, the residences were known for their exotically themed roof parties. The tiny units appealed to young entrepreneurs and offered the latest in techno building design.

As she neared the Triad, the parking icon on the dash screen flashed red, indicating full slots. She let out a sigh. When it came to parking, Smart Zones defied their name. She'd take the ample parking and more spacious accommodations of the older medical district where she lived any day.

It was just as well. A short hike to the foot of Josiah's Formula for Life statue would steady her nerves. She messaged Cole about the meeting place change and climbed out of the car at the drop-off zone.

Pulling her collar up to shield against the wind, she set out for the statue.

The fragrance of nearby eucalyptus filled the air. Perhaps the clarifying scent would give her answers.

Was she doing the right thing?

Her assistant, Kate, wouldn't think so. Seeking money from an outside investor like Cole, especially one with no track record in the science arena, would be the basis of her argument. Still, a permanent investor would clear the horizon for their work. Endless worry over finances had left them both drained and out of focus. Cole's proposal for a trial period before finalizing the deal was a good contingency plan, even if the parameters were a bit fuzzy.

When she reached the top of the hill where the statue stood, she picked a bench in the sun and sat. The bronze, ten-foot-tall professor dressed in a lab coat held a book and pointed forward toward the Abide. Dedicated to the professors who discovered the Life Formula, the sculpture first appeared in the Commons. Later, when MeLee Morgue was renovated to become The Institute of Tissue Recovery and Implantation, the statue was moved to the Triad.

While the Institute housed tissue research groups and clinicians from all over the world, the Abide provided shelter for the waiting dead in cylinder vaults that only approved medical staff could access.

Access.

She sighed, sending frosty breath spirals into the air. Facts were facts. She'd lost her funding status, because she'd openly opposed the new Access Agreement. How could she support it? For decades anyone who wanted to be prepped for future resurrection received a dose of Rejuvacatin, but now ordinary people were being denied the drug. Council cited the limited body storage capacity at the Abide. But it was more than that. The newly developed Access Agreement proposed merit criteria to determine a person's eligibility for resurrection. Of course, John Does would serve their purpose as preliminary test candidates, but after successful trials, only candidates deemed valuable to society would be on the list.

She unclenched her gloved hand and spread her fingers. Was she doing the right thing? Letting Cole into her business? Her father had often warned about commercial funding and the strings that came with it.

A crisp breeze lifted her hair then settled it back on her shoulders. *Sacrifice for what you want or what you want becomes the sacrifice.* Her father's motto. Of course. Do whatever it takes to keep the lab afloat. That's the important thing. Besides, Cole's perspective on business didn't seem too far from her own view. He had built DCN, his mega million-dollar company, on the idea of making products available to every man and not just to the elite. Access for everyone.

A blackbird scolded from a nearby tree, sending a squirrel scampering toward a man headed her way. He seemed to have materialized out of nowhere. In his hands were two cups. Sunglasses shielded his eyes, and a scarf covered his lower face. Cole? A second figure blended into the shadow of a large elm. A bodyguard?

The man approached and placed the cups on another bench nearby and gestured to the statue. "What does our professor say?"

Before she could answer the code phrase, the man unwound his scarf and removed his glasses. He rubbed a wrinkled cheek, and his ashen skin melded, and tightened into the tanned chiseled features of Cole. Dark, laughing eyes drew her in.

"Yep. It's me. Can't meet here without a disguise. Protestors would have me for lunch." Cole peeled away the transparent facescreen and tucked it in his pocket. "Pretty good simulation, don't you think? The art of masking has come a long way."

She nodded, and her heart thumped in an exotic rhythm when he flashed his famous smile. Sacrifice? More like a thrill she could get used to. She closed her eyes to the cliff and jumped. "The professor says I should accept your offer."

"Good." Cole sat beside her and placed his arm across her shoulders.

The beat of her heart shifted to high alert when he tried to draw her close. She resisted and stood to her feet. "Before I agree completely, I need to know exactly what kind of partner you will be and what you expect of me."

Cole picked up something from the ground. When he opened his hand, a butterfly staggered across his palm and flexed its wings. "The main thing you need to know about me is that I am a businessman. Some say I make ruthless deals, but others ..." He paused and stroked the creature's wing.

"Others find my arrangements quite agreeable and even delightful. Either way, everything I touch turns golden. You and I will be unstoppable." He shook the creature off and picked up a cup and extended it to her. "Coffee?"

She nodded and accepted the brew, hoping to drown her own butterflies.

He patted the bench.

She hesitated, but then sat, moving as far from him as possible.

The corners of his mouth twitched. "Am I really that bad?"

"I just want to keep things professional."

"Ouch. Maybe I should tell you more about myself, and perhaps then you will better see my merits." He then launched into a speech listing all his great achievements.

She listened without interrupting, a trait she had cultivated when gathering facts, but the more she heard him expound the more she became convinced he was working hard to sell her something.

When he came to a pause, she jumped in. "I believe in your success. I just want to know what you expect from the lab in exchange for the funds."

"I don't need your lab." Cole cleared his throat. "I need you."

The back of her neck prickled with heat. What was he suggesting?

"I need you to pose before the world as my life partner."

She placed the coffee cup beside her and stood. "I don't get it. And I'm not sure you do either. I thought this was a business arrangement."

"It is. You play a role, and you get the funds you need."

"But why do you need me to pretend to be your life partner?"

"I'm expanding my supply distribution into traditionalist regions. Leaders in those sectors respond better to a family man, which I have no intention of becoming anytime soon so I need a life partner without strings attached."

Before she could speak again he signaled, and a willowy man dressed in a python-patterned tracksuit emerged from the trees.

The poker-faced man nodded at her.

"My driver. Let me take you home. Think it over. You can give me an answer when you are ready."

She gulped. "Cole, I'm just not sure—"

"Don't tell me now. Think about it." Cole turned and followed his driver, who led them to Cole's black Aquilos, parked nearby in a Premium Park unit, a benefit for those who belonged to an exclusive parking club.

Wishing her doubts would take a back seat, she climbed into the car and exhaled. Every fiber of her scientific mind questioned the odd arrangement. How had money come to rule over her life to such a degree? To the inclusion of such a risk? The answer made no difference. What else could she do to get the money? She'd run out of options, and the bills were stacked high.

Turning her focus to the purple-gray skies of the late winter day, she listened half-heartedly to Cole's almost constant narrative about the buildings and ventures he'd been a part of.

"Look at those." Tapping on the window, Cole gestured to the dull, endless lines of identical buildings extending as far as the eye could see. "Another example of the benefit of partnering with me. Construction is almost complete, and my company delivered the supplies that built all these."

"There's certainly a lot of them."

"And there's a good reason for that. All those people relocating from other sectors will now have adequate housing because of DCN and Universe United."

"Your company seems to have a hand in many ventures."

A smile came over his face. "We do. I'm a firm believer that any problem can be solved through combined effort."

She nodded. "I agree." His concept of problem-solving meshed with her own. Perhaps the nagging voice in her head regarding the partnership came from her own tendency to overthink.

When they had parked in front of her house, Cole reached over and covered her hand with his. "My lawyer will finalize the details and set a signing day as soon as you say the word."

Heady knowledge stomped down her fear. *I can do this. I'm saving the lab.* She clenched her teeth and offered a plastic smile. "I'm looking forward to it."

He moved closer. "I'm so glad to hear that."

Her heart jolted, and she pulled her hand away. "I've got to go."

Cole frowned. "What's the rush? I could come in. We could celebrate." He tapped on a panel beside him. It retracted to reveal a waiting bottle of champagne and two glasses.

"That's very nice, but I have work to do."

His eyes narrowed. "You said you were taking the day off."

"I am, but only from the lab. I'm running my monthly GenCom surveys. It's my side gig." She leapt out of the car, almost knocking over Cole's driver who held open the door.

A car door slammed on the other side, and Cole walked around the back of the vehicle. "I'm certain I pay better than your side gig. You know what they say. All work and no play. Makes for a dull life. I think you need to add a little color."

Looking for a distraction, she pointed to the driver's red athletic footwear. "Like his?"

The man snorted.

Cole laughed. "Serpens knows how to live, don't you, buddy?" He patted his driver on the back. "We have grand history together."

Serpens upper lip curled. He gave a half smile and got back in the car.

Cole turned to her. "You've got to do better than that." A warning flashed in his eyes.

"What do you mean?"

"You have to act the part. The part where you are eager to be with me. The adoring girlfriend. Everyone has to believe it. Is that too much to ask?"

"Not at all. But we said—"

He took her by the arm and pulled her to him. "You need to trust me." His breath fell in her ear. "Everyone has to believe our story. My business expansion depends on it. And so does yours. You act. You get the money. That's the deal."

She twisted free of his grasp and managed a smile. "I've got it. Thank you for the ride." She pushed past him and entered her house and then locked the door.

What had she done?

CHAPTER 2

FROZEN ON THE other side of her door, SJ waited with her hand over her thudding heart until the rumbling of Cole's big black beast of a car faded away.

She exhaled. It was all going to be fine. So what if he was demanding? She could handle it. She just did. In time she'd get the hang of it and give a seamless performance. Anything for the money. Her work was all that mattered.

Stopping in front of the hall mirror, she pushed back her hair. Thick and straight, it tumbled constantly over her glasses. Gathering a bunch of it in her hand, she held it up in the back. Time for a cut. Something more sophisticated if she was going to play the romance interest of Cole Magnus.

Ignoring the clanging bell in her head, she marched to her closet, found some joggers and changed, and then moved into the kitchen where she punched in a request for a peanut-berry yogi bar on her Savor machine, upping the peanut count to avoid an insufficient protein warning on the nutrition panel. While the yogi bar printed, she selected her dinner meal—roasted squash pupusa melt, a tube of pickle slaw, and a side of lentil soup. All would be ready at six.

The bar dropped into the receiver tray. She took it to her office and sat in front of her motion-activated desktop screen. Nibbling on the crunchy edges of her treat, she leaned over the glass and made faces. The surface remained dark. She sighed and brushed away crumbs. An upgrade was long overdue. She patted vigorously on the upper right hand corner. A buzzing sound ensued, and then a welcoming flicker, and the whole surface illuminated. She adjusted the tilt for ease of access and the brightness value to mesh with the afternoon light.

Chomping on the last bites of her yogi bar, she entered her passcode. Seconds later, her GenCom—Genealogy Communications account populated the field. As part of his exploration on all aspects of death, her father designed the program to capture participants' final words and conversations—their end messages.

When she took over the project, she enhanced the research by distributing end tablets so video recordings could now be made. She also organized the database to sort the end messages by topic. Communications generally separated into ten categories. End messages might express or request that long held secrets be spilled. Some asked for forgiveness or gave it. Others conveyed love, invoked a memory, offered directions for work or family, or presented a life summary. Sometimes a person's last words communicated emotions of fear, sadness, or anger. Less often, and mostly from much older participants, there were end messages that spoke of gods or an afterlife.

While she waited for the monthly review to generate, she initiated a Life Clock scan. The result came immediately. The death rate of Region Eight had climbed to 17.49. Increases showed across all global regions. Superbugs, incurable disease, food shortages, and natural disaster casualties still held the upper hand. The birth rate remained at a steady 10.42, a surprising feat considering that parenting was restricted to only those individuals who had received the required thirty-two months of approved child-rearing training.

A chime indicated the monthly report was complete. She tugged her finger across the desk surface and selected a new date file.

A knock came at the front door.

She paused her process and tapped her security cam icon. Her neighbor Bea, a heavy woman with dark corkscrew hair, stood on the porch shouting something unintelligible.

She rushed to the door and flung it open.

Bea gulped at the air. "I think … it's the end."

SJ grabbed her arm. "Are you all right?"

Bea nodded. "I'm fine. It's Pete. Can't find … his injector."

SJ slid her bag off the hook by the door and followed Bea across the street. Passing through Pete's quirky garden of oddly shaped dirt mounds and potted plants, they reached his home in his sister's backyard, a converted utility shed.

Bea jiggled the door handle, and it opened a crack. Then she leaned on it, and the gap widened onto a debris-strewn floor. "Watch your step. I haven't been able to clear out anything since he's been stuck inside."

Towers of boxes filled with broken electronics and damaged tools cluttered the room. SJ followed Bea into the maze. She understood her neighbor's ever mounting problem. When Pete was well, his fantasy garden distracted him, and Bea could take a load of his junk in her car, promising Pete his things would benefit some charity. All of that stopped when charities became stricter, and more declined to accept his broken things. "Pete? Petey? I'm back." Bea's gentle but urgent tone reflected her deep love for her brother.

A moan came from the corner.

Using the wall for balance, Bea and SJ staggered along the edge across mounds of paper until they reached the far end of the room.

There they found Pete, asleep in a disheveled bed on the backside of a barricade of boxes.

When Bea approached the bed, a black furry head popped out of the covers.

"Come here Jingles." Bea's tone shifted into full command, and she reached for the cat.

The fluffy feline hissed.

Bea pulled back her hand.

"He don't want you, sis." Pete's jaundiced eyes, now open, reflected how much the cancer had taken.

"It's not good for you to let him stay."

"Doesn't matter anymore." Pete stroked the cat's ears. The black cat yawned and stretched. "We're saying goodbye. Until my return. You be good to him, you hear?"

Bea sat on a broken-backed chair beside the bed. "Petey. About that. I can't find it. I've looked and looked."

"You've got to …" Pete struggled to raise his head and then flopped back. "I've got to come back. Jingles needs me, and the garden's not done."

Bea gestured to SJ. "She's here to help us."

"Sure, Bea. Tell me where to look." SJ studied the room.

"Never mind that. I'm sure you can get him a new one." Commander Bea pointed to SJ's wrist scanner. "I tried already. They wouldn't listen to me, but I know they'll listen to you."

SJ gulped. "I'm not certain there's time."

Bea pulled back the covers, unbuttoned Pete's shirt and slid out his arm. "Let's find out." She pressed along his bicep. "Scan it. Right here."

SJ initiated the biochip program on her wrist scanner and then held the device over Pete's arm. Bea wouldn't understand that her credentials would not be enough to request another injector for Pete. Why? Because Pete was a nobody according to the new Access Agreement.

The scan came back. Zero hours. Twenty-nine minutes and forty-two seconds.

SJ showed Bea the screen. "Not enough."

Bea put her head in her hands. Her shoulders shook.

SJ reached for her bag. "Bea, I have a plan."

Bea raised her head. "What is it?"

SJ pulled out her injector. "We'll use mine. The stock numbers are matched to me, but you can tell them you stole it from me. You were desperate. When they notify me, I'll act shocked. But I'll tell them I'm not pressing charges. You'll get a fine, but I'll pay it."

Bea jumped up. "Oh, my goodness. Thank you. Thank you." She launched into an energetic hug that almost toppled SJ to the ground. But then she stopped and held SJ at arm's length. "I'll pay you back. But what about you? Will they give you another dose?"

"I sure hope so." Of course they would. She had Cole. He'd not only promised funds but the lead role on the Resurrection Team, and that should count for something. She'd just have to stay alive until a replacement came. Restock had been slow lately.

"Did you hear that, Petey? Bea shook her dozing brother. We've got an injector." She shook him again. Pete did not respond. His breath came in slow, shallow draughts. She motioned to SJ. "Now, please."

SJ opened the injector and secured it to Pete's wrist and pressed start. The green light flickered and then stayed lit. It would dispense the preliminary resurrection drug, Rejuvacatin, into Pete's body over the next five minutes.

The best opportunity for future resurrection meant a person had received the drug as close to the time of death as possible, either before or after the event.

Together, they watched as the medicine ran in and Pete slipped away.

When the injector light turned red, SJ pulled up the covers, unsettling the cat who jumped to the ground.

Bea kissed her brother's forehead.

SJ reached for Bea's hand. "I'm so sorry. Life Preservation and Resource will be here shortly. Remember to tell the LPR worker what I said."

Bea nodded through her tears. "Do you think he will be exactly the same? Or will he be different?"

SJ reached down to pat Jingles, who meowed at her feet. "We don't know. Time will tell."

CHAPTER 3

THE NEXT DAY, SJ worked on the speech she would give Kate.

"It's all for our good, including yours, dear Phinny." She placed the lab-bred pelican on the thermoscan table and examined his lifeless body.

Two more tail feathers came off in her hand. She set them aside and inspected the bird's skin through her opti-loupes. It showed no signs of discoloration. If resurrection was affecting the molt, then there would be vascular anomalies.

The recycle nature of her experiment with Phinny unsettled her heart, but all labs were deep into their second species test. Her request for a single bird had taken Genetics months to design and complete, and the cost had been astronomical.

Most of the other labs, including Birch, had settled on monkeys, but she held a different perspective. Resurrection success depended on tissue viability, and tissue health depended on oxygen uptake. Birds modeled the greatest efficiency in that process.

She stroked Phinny's form with gloved fingers and then picked up the feathers and touched each to her heart for luck as she had done as a child before placing them in a drawer with the rest. She kept the collection as a reminder that every little thing should be accounted for before testing resurrection on humans.

The door alert sounded. Kate entered the lab and then disappeared into her office. Minutes later, she emerged with her dark curls barely confined under her cap. "Phinny up yet?"

SJ shook her head. "It's too soon."

Kate pulled the flex light closer to the bird's iridescent plumage. "Such a waste. Why would the Department of Genetics alter a breed that's been around for millions of years to look more like a peacock?"

"You're right. It's unnecessary." SJ spoke in soothing tones, hoping to buy grace later.

Kate grumbled and left the bay.

SJ glanced at the clock above the table. It blinked out the time, simultaneously narrowing the margin between death and life and conflict and peace.

Since the council's preliminary decision, a dark cloud of defeat hung over the lab, but Kate's despair hurt the most. They were as close as sisters, bonded together by a lifetime of shared experiences, which was why she knew Kate would see her choice to accept Cole's offer as reckless.

A chime alert sounded. Phinny's exposure to the resurrection drugs had been optimized.

Kate returned to her side. Together, they placed Phinny on his back and massaged the injected tissue.

SJ talked to the inert form as if it could hear and understand. "Your colors will be the cause of much bias and sentiment," she whispered. She only allowed Kate to witness her deep affection for Phinny. The bird was as close to a child as she ever expected to have, and Kate was her only family—her Designated Kin.

She checked the time again and then cupped the bird's torso in her hands.

Kate nudged her. "Prayer time?"

"Nope, but okay." They always followed the same pattern of action, but today Kate's request seemed more ridiculous than usual. Neither of them believed in a god. No sensible person did anymore. But Kate liked to call to the universe each time they beckoned Phinny back to life.

"Please help our sweet boy to return. Amen." Kate adjusted the inhalator and turned up the flow speed.

SJ blew into the opaque open eye. "Up and at 'em, big boy."

The dark orb swiveled.

"There's our brown-eyed wonder." Kate grabbed a flailing, webless foot and spread open the limp talon. It took another twenty-two seconds for the inner membrane of Phinny's left eye to retract. "He's back."

The two partners worked in tandem to complete the routine. SJ manipulated the bird and checked reflexes. Kate recorded the findings. After a third set of satisfactory vital signs, they released Phinny.

The bird struggled to stand, wobbled a few steps and then sat. SJ held up a fish chunk and moved it back and forth in front of his head. The bird did not respond. She tried moving it slower and closer to his beak. "Turn on the media wall. He always gets excited when he watches the others."

Kate set the wall screen to display a live view of pelicans diving into the surf for fish along a sunlit shore.

Phinny flapped his wings but then lost his balance and fell over in a heap.

"Something's different. He's not even looking in the right direction." SJ repositioned him.

"Come on, Phinn. Hop up here and greet your pals." Kate patted the counter across from the bird. In the past, he would flap-hop to the other side, but today he made no effort. He stayed hunkered down on the thermal bed.

SJ picked him up and held him close. The bird stretched his neck and then waggled his head back and forth before resting it on SJ's arm.

"I'll test him again after a while." Kate pointed to the clock. "Don't you have a meeting with the council?"

"I've rescheduled." SJ took a deep breath. "I've accepted a partner."

Kate's eyes narrowed. "You promised to let me weigh in."

"I'm doing what I have to do to save our work."

"I'm surprised you're using the term *our work* at all," Kate snapped. "You're the one making the decision."

"You're right. And this decision was mine to make." SJ spoke in careful tones and stroked Phinny's wrinkled bird skin.

"Fine. Choose Birch. It's a logical choice, but I wish you'd told the truth when you said we'd decide on a partner together." Kate snapped the lid onto the feed bucket.

"Silly goof. It's not that kind of partnership. It's Cole. He's asked me to be his life partner, and I accepted."

"You did what?"

The distracting sound of squawking, scuffling pelicans filled the screen.

Kate switched off the media wall and glared at her. "You hardly know him. What's it been? Two very glamorous dates, and now he's your mate for life?"

SJ turned away and weighed Phinny. She carried him to his bio unit while Kate followed close behind voicing her objections.

SJ didn't want to fight. She wanted to win. She needed things to fall into place, because someday, somehow, if she and Kate kept going, their work would pay off. Successful human resurrection would inspire hope amidst the unending surge of deaths across the regions.

"Can't you see I'm doing this for us—for the lab? I've found a way for us to survive." SJ poked a fish chunk into Phinny's beak. The bird thrust his neck out and swallowed.

"By being Cole's life partner? It just doesn't make sense."

"You know he's famous, right?" SJ stroked Phinny's head. "Cole's life is on constant display. Many of the deals he makes are with traditionalists. Eastern leaders still favor a family man. He said our life partnership would just be a show for them. In exchange, I have access to all the funds we would ever need."

"Would you have to stay at his house? Who he is in private could be very different. He might be a murderer or an evil, torturing abuser. You have no idea." Kate aimed a stream of water from the wash tube at Phinny. The pelican squawked and gulped.

"Honestly, Kate, your imagination is out of control. Cole's seldom alone. His staff are always around. I understand that you want to protect me, but it's my life. How hard can it be to pose as the life partner of someone as rich and famous as Cole?"

"This is insane." Kate slapped a towel into a laundry bin and then whirled around. Her eyes sparked with fire. "You barely know him."

"You should be focused on the benefit this is for our lab. Besides, I've agreed to it because of your suggestion."

"My suggestion?"

"You said I needed to find someone powerful to influence the council."

"I did. But I didn't mean you should become life partners with a stranger. Besides, why would he have influence over the council? He's not involved in research. He's in the supply and delivery business."

SJ rubbed the sagging skin under Phinney's beak before shutting him inside. "Rest well, dear boy. Aunt Kate will be back to harass you later."

Hoping she'd triggered a hint of a smile, she faced her friend. The flush of red on Kate's cheeks and downturned mouth spoke otherwise.

She took Kate by the arm. "Come." She pulled her assistant into a data cubicle. "I need you to listen to me." She pointed to a chair. "Sit."

Something flickered in Kate's expression, but she obeyed.

SJ crossed her arms. "You're not getting the point. Cole's well connected. His company supplies all the labs. He conducts business with the heads of every Universe region and sector. Meritus depends on DCN products and delivery. His influence is huge, as well as the amount of money he plans to invest in our project."

Kate crossed her arms. "And you're not thinking this through. Resurrection is not a product, and your life isn't payment."

"My life is mine to spend as I please. I got us into this mess, and I'll get us out. With Cole at my side, our lab will never lack funding."

"And you don't see any danger in this crazy idea at all?" Kate's sarcasm filled the cubicle. "Do you really believe posing as housemates with Cole the Magnificent is all he wants in exchange for his blessing?"

Voices on the far side of the lab indicated the arrival of other staff.

"Yes, I do. Cole has reason for resurrection to succeed as much as I do. We both have fathers waiting to be resurrected. Every new day brings more illness and disaster deaths."

"Did you tell him human resurrection is still at least a couple of years away?"

"I didn't discuss specifics, but he's on the same page. He believes our partnership creates opportunities for his company. His specialty product line grows wherever innovation grows. Resurrection is his new frontier. Ikar Lab's reputation will help minimize public doubts over his involvement."

"Amazing logic." Kate stood. "But too good to be true." She left the cubicle.

An ache filled SJ's heart. Why couldn't Kate be happy?

She mixed up a fresh bowl of Nutren pellets and returned to the bio unit. The pelican resisted her coaxing and offered no enthusiasm when she placed it inside and mounded fresh bedding.

Kate reappeared. Sweat glistened on her face and neck.

SJ offered her a towel. "Kate, we've got to get this sorted out."

Kate took the towel and dabbed at her neck.

That's when SJ saw it—the revealing bruise at Kate's hairline. "Is there something you're not telling me?"

"Yes. There is." Kate tore off her protective gown. "I didn't want to say anything at first, but now you've guessed. Everyone's getting them. All over the world, they say. Anti-relocation sympathizers trying to create chaos. The news calls it the 'Five Hoax.' No one respectable believes there's another world of people out there."

"Okay. Slow down. I know about this, but what does it have to do with me?"

"You got a message." Kate dug into her pants pocket and pulled out a long loop of paper and pushed one end of it into SJ's hand. "This one."

It was the kind of paper that came out from their thermoscan print slot when a user error occurred.

Keeping hold of one end of it, Kate backed up, stretching the strip smooth between them. "Read it."

SJ scanned the words. It seemed to be a letter. She dropped the end of the strip. "You're right. It looks like one of those hoax messages. Someone managed to hack into our thermoscan to send it."

"Then we agree you've become a target. Plus, it accuses Cole."

"Of what?" SJ shook her head. "You know what? It doesn't matter. I'm not changing my mind because of a nonsense message. I'm going through with the partnership."

"Just read it. Please." Kate never begged, but now she sounded practically hysterical. "I'm certain someone in the resistance has singled you and Cole out, and not in a good way. Sure, the words are crazy, but that's the point. The person behind them might be even crazier. Whoever it is has a grudge against Cole, and they want to retaliate. We don't need this kind of mess connected to the lab. I wasn't even going to show it to you, but your decision changed everything."

"Okay. I'll read it." SJ took the printout from Kate's hands. "But you'll have to calm down. You've been under too much strain. That bruise on your neck? Have your symptoms returned?"

"I'm fine except that my best friend is about to jump off into the deep end." Kate wadded her discarded gown and shoved it into a waste bin. "For your information, the bruise came from a collision I had with a stubborn cabinet door." She stormed off.

SJ spread the printout on the counter and read.

Error Log Date: 3/75

Dear SJ,

This is not a mistake. I'm writing to warn you. Although we've never met, we're related. My name is Evie, and I was born May 5, 1998. You are my great-great-great-granddaughter. There is much I want to tell you. I'll start with the year I turned twenty-three and got a job halfway across the country to avoid being near my mother.

Work was all I cared about. I believed a generous salary would get me everything I wanted. My new job ended shortly after it began, because of the economy. After I was let go, I lied to my mother and explained how I couldn't come home for Christmas because I was too busy at work. She'd called to tell me her doctor was sending her back to the hospital. I knew she was hinting that she wanted to see me, but I did not want to get stuck living like her.

I hurried to end our conversation when I heard someone knocking at my door. When I opened it, I saw a package lying on the threshold, but no one was in the hallway.

I picked up the parcel and noticed the word "self" handwritten in black letters across one end. The return address was from a familiar clothing store. Inside was an expensive sweater I'd ordered for my mother for Christmas. The company sent the sweater to my address instead.

I remember tearing apart the box and specifically shredding the weird part that said "self." That night, I struggled to sleep. Worry over my predicament haunted my mind. I came to a conflicting conclusion. My selfish lifestyle had only made me unhappy. Perhaps by living unselfishly, I could be happy. So I spent all my savings on a ticket to fly home.

That's how it began. With one package.

Suffice it to say that I saw many more package deliveries over my lifetime. I was one of a few (there were others) who could see the odd handwriting and catch the warnings on the box labels.

Many deliveries became channels that turned the recipient's life sour. The deliveries whispered of a false life. People believed that their value came from the things they acquired.

Most people never noticed the bait and switch. The deliverymen—not the human ones but the true thieves—were invisible enemies who appeared to bring improvements to life but instead hijacked the core goodness of life.

My perception skills grew until I began to see not just the words but the thieves at work all the time. My talent seemed both a gift and a curse.

Eventually I became a resident of Five—the name of the place where I now live, and the realm from where the delivery thieves are banished.

None of my story matters, only that you know the truth about the deliverymen thieves—the existence of Fol, whom you know as Cole, and his band of robbers.

They must be stopped.

You'll hear from me again soon,

Evie

"The thief comes to steal, kill, and destroy. I come that you may have life to the full." Book of Wisdom 43. 10. 10

The story was quite inventive, but SJ saw no motivation except perhaps a creative prankster's intent to disrupt, or maybe one of Cole's disgruntled employees or an anti-relocation sympathizer riled up by the resistance. The worldwide group protested the mandates which required people from disaster-prone sectors to relocate into other sectors with greater resources.

Kate returned, coffee cup in hand. "Well? What did I tell you?"

SJ put the message aside. "It's no use, Kate. These ramblings mean nothing. If her story is true, then Evie would have to be over one hundred fifty years old, and so would Cole. It's like you said—part of the Five Hoax. Something to get people upset and confused. I'll do what it takes to save this lab and our work."

Kate placed her coffee on the counter. "I'm committed too." She picked up the paper. "Which is why I'm begging you to find another way to fund the lab. Hoax or not, the message accuses a man named Cole and says he must be stopped. If a crazy person is obsessed with stopping Cole, then how long before you become a target too? Or this lab?"

SJ tapped on her wrist screen and waited for the tally. She held up the search result so Kate could see. "There are 89,346 people registered in this century who have claimed the name Cole. My Cole isn't a thief. He's our savior."

CHAPTER 4

March 2175
Five, a parallel realm ruled by supernatural beings.

THE SNIP, SNIP, snip of garden clippers broke the quiet stillness of the rose garden.

Martha stood on the ladder and tugged on a budding shoot. “See. It’s come back even fuller. When we cut off dead blooms and canes, the plant has more energy to pour into new growth. Pruning also helps keep fungus and disease from settling into the bush.”

She handed Evie the clippers. “Your turn. Find a withered bloom and snip below it, but just above the next closest leaf set. Cut it off at an angle.”

Evie took the tool, picked her target, and made a cut. The severed piece fell at her feet. She retrieved it and dropped it in her basket.

“It’s all for the good,” Martha said. “Like everything is here on Five. I’m sure if the rosebush had a brain, it might look at the clippers and see harm, but we know the good we are doing.”

Evie laughed. “Sometimes I wonder if the plants on Five do have a brain. Everything grows amazingly well.”

“Well, almost everything. I’ve heard the heralds talk about a blight that is appearing on trees in The Wilds, but they have a plan to take care of it.”

Evie handed back the clippers. “Isn’t that near the sheep pens?”

“Yes. It’s the uninhabited side of Five. There are no gardens there, just natural plant growth. Only heralds and herdsmen know their way around those parts. Long ago, there used to be an orchard but—” Martha paused and pointed.

Evie turned around.

Rays of prismatic light danced on nearby foliage. The source of it poured through the garden gate and then moved along the path toward the women.

Martha came down from the pruning ladder and stood beside Evie.

Above the whisper of rustling leaves, a melodious voice called Evie’s name. When the radiance diminished, and the atmosphere readjusted, a messenger herald materialized before them.

Dressed in the trademark tea-with-cream colored linen suit and standard issue white cufflink shirt, the herald produced an envelope from his lapel pocket and offered it to Evie. “Soul Evie. You have a lesson today. Come to the dais by the sea if you accept.”

Bracing for the transfer of heat, Evie took the envelope. A jolt of intense warmth ran up her arm. She winced and stepped back. “How should I prepare? Do I bring anything?”

The herald’s smile enlarged. “As always, only your presence is needed. Everything else will be provided.”

“Yes, herald.”

“There’s one more thing. Today is your birthday. It’s a special occasion. One hundred seventy-seven years of life is important to celebrate.”

“Thank you, herald.” Evie struggled with the number trying to understand. Somehow, her time on Five seemed shorter.

The messenger herald nodded and then turned and retreated back down the path. The atmosphere shimmered around his presence until he disappeared.

Evie sniffed. “Why do they always smell like that?”

"Like what?"

"Bergamot."

"Does it bother you?"

"Not in the least." Evie giggled. "It reminds me of tea." Evie dropped the envelope in her clipping basket. "Do you mind cleaning up without me?"

"I will if you don't open the invitation before you leave." Martha's eyes sparkled, and she snatched up the envelope.

Evie took it from her and gave a half smile. She turned it over and slid her finger under the flap, breaking the wax seal. She pulled out the invitation. A grand lesson. In the three years she'd been awake on Five, she'd only attended basic lessons. *Why was I chosen?*

"He's wrong, you know."

"About what?" Evie stared at the elegant script.

"Your age."

"Perhaps. But I don't exactly remember."

"You're one hundred forty-seven. I count from the day we arrive, but I guess he's using herald time, which starts from birth. Don't you remember? Our boats landed the same day."

"I remember in fuzzy bits here and there."

"Oh, my goodness." Martha touched the invitation. "Look at the words. It's a grand lesson. You're required to wear white."

Martha's obvious excitement conflicted with the feeling of dread that suddenly rolled over Evie like a tide.

Martha prodded her. "It's going to be great. You always do well. Remember, nothing here can harm us. Everything is for our good."

Evie nodded but did not move.

Martha hugged her and then gave her a little push. "Go. It's going to be wonderful."

"I guess so."

As she headed for the baths, Evie replayed Martha's words in her head. *Nothing here can harm us. Everything is for our good.*

Pristine grass parted slightly ahead of her footsteps, indicating the path Evie should follow. She glanced behind her. The meadow looked as if she'd never passed through it. The miracle of it always amazed her. Paths revealed just at the time you needed them and then melded back, leaving the beauty of Five unmarred by foot traffic.

Soon, soft grass gave way to clumps of wiry beach turf, and ruby sand sifted between her toes. A pink dragonfly buzzed past her going the other way. She longed to chase after it—away from the ocean.

She usually avoided traveling along the beach. Martha found the surf invigorating, but Evie discovered it wielded an opposite effect on her. Her first glimpse of the ruby red sand against the turquoise water, which then deepened to emerald and dark navy at the horizon, crippled her with fear and caused her legs to become useless. Martha had to summon a herald to give her a tonic so she could walk home. He explained how making new memories sometimes collided with old emotions, but his words brought little comfort.

All residents of Five had crossed the sea to get there, but none of the other souls she encountered seemed troubled by it.

Martha advised patience. "Each of us is different. Time will help you with this. You'll see."

The sea separates you.

The contrary whisper came from nowhere. Evie pressed her hand against the pounding in her chest. *Nothing here can harm me. Everything is for my good.* But there was no use denying it. Dread surged against rational thought. The heralds would sense her struggle if she arrived at the lesson burdened with fear.

She had to wait. Waiting was the first skill residents learned to utilize on Five.

Lifting her skirt free from her ankles, she sat on the sandy ground. The fabric of her gown shimmered in the light. Soft yet substantial, her dress fit perfectly. It reminded her of all the goodness on Five.

Sifting through a mental list of delightful things helped calm her fears. Every day she discovered new treasures for her tally. She closed her eyes and remembered. An easy choice was the food. Always bountiful and arranged beautifully. Nourishment that filled her but never too full. Another amazement was her body. She never felt pain, and her occasional clumsiness caused no marks, bruises, or scraped shins. It was as if an invisible buffer protected her.

Yet, somehow, she knew fear.

She opened her eyes. The shadowy idea had come unbidden, interrupting her exercise. Similar hauntings had begun to infest each new day. The presence of them alarmed her. Martha had theorized that if Evie could name her plaguing shadows, then she would be healed.

Evie spoke in a loud stern voice to the inkling. "You cannot have me."

A cheerful bird twittered back.

Only goodness had a rightful claim on her. Therefore, if only goodness was permitted on Five, then the whispers dealt in false claims and powers. No dreaded thing could harm her here. There's nothing to be afraid of.

Calmness returned. A light breeze fingered her hair. She heard the whisper, "You are loved."

Her heart soared.

She stood, brushed off her skirt, and took off running along the beach, normal speed at first but then lightning quick—speed running—a body feature she'd come to understand and manipulate since living on Five.

Soon she reached the shoreline directly in front of the dais, a high rock plateau jutting up from the dunes. Stopping to catch her breath, she discovered a path ambling off into the sandy mounds. It came to a dead end in front of a large, rugged boulder. It seemed odd that the trail did not circle around the rock, but again, she waited. No law prohibited her from finding another path on her own, but the habit of waiting always brought extraordinary results.

She patted the boulder encouragingly. It wiggled slightly and then rocked sideways back and forth, as if gathering momentum. Then it moved. Passing beside her, the heavy weight of it caused the ground to tremble.

Giggling, she caressed the boulder's warm granite surface. "Thanks," she whispered. The marvel of rocks, trees, and fields—all gloriously animated on Five when the right moment came—always delighted her.

The path beyond the boulder rose up a steep slope. She began the climb. The turquoise rolling water held back by ruby sand called for her fearful attention, but she refused to look at it. Instead, she focused on the path and putting one foot in front of the other.

When she reached the top, she clambered onto the flat expanse of the dais and headed straight to the center where others were assembled. The confidence of the crowd buoyed her spirit.

Closing her eyes, she exhaled and imagined the sea breeze blowing away her last flecks of worry. Goodness reigned.

A voice boomed above the surf noise. “Souls, gather to me.”

She opened her eyes.

An arch herald stood on the edge of the dais, three times as tall as any she had ever seen. His robe billowed behind him like a great white cloud reaching toward the sea. When the wind lifted the hem of it, she saw battle boots, a fitting match for the scabbard hanging at the herald’s side.

Unease came over her at the sight of the arch herald’s weaponry. Her mind filled with fuzzy details of a memory or past dream. She recalled a man with massive arms who lifted her from a boat and carried her to soft grass and offered her something to drink. Then, she remembered him fiddling with a small silver dagger. As she watched him move the blade in and out of an ornate leather scabbard on his belt, she choked so violently on her drink that her rescuer, who turned out to be a herald, had to fly with her to a healing house, where she received a tonic to relieve her stricture.

Pressing against the lump forming in her throat, she swallowed.

Don’t be afraid. The voice came soft and clear, yet from no one near her. She found the source. The arch herald’s gaze seemed to be impossibly directed at her. Again, the phrase came. *Don’t be afraid.*

He knew.

When he turned his great head away, she moved deep into the crowd until she could squeeze in no further. Everyone around her chattered. Several mentioned the arch herald’s name, Thomas. All hushed when he spoke again.

“Souls, you are chosen for this lesson because of something you all have in common. What that is, is not important to know today, but my instructions are.” Thomas’s voice echoed in a strange way. It sounded as if the wind carried it across the water to the horizon, and then the sky bounced it back from every direction.

People near her seemed pleased. Discussion broke out about what might be the common denominator. She thought of nothing but her shame and fear. Surely, the heralds had made a mistake in picking her.

"Remember, you do not have to participate. It's a choice. The lesson offered is for your good. As always, nothing will harm you on Five, but I will warn you, this lesson will bring pain."

Murmurs came from the crowd. Her mind filled with questions. A choice that would hurt? How was that not equal to harm?

"But with this lesson, much healing will come." The resounding voice continued.

She wanted to be cured of her fears, but there had to be a better way.

At that moment, Thomas pulled out his sword and brandished it with great flourish in the air.

Cries of surprise came from the crowd when the invisible paths carved by the herald's sword formed letters and words. "Eye hath not seen, nor ear heard, nor mind conceived what is prepared for those who are loved."

The word phrase materialized in shimmering gold dust. It gleamed momentarily above the crowd, held its form, and then broke apart, spilling away into the wind.

She knew the words. They came from the Book of Wisdom. The beauty of seeing them glistening in the air took away all her fear.

She would participate.

"Here's the lesson. First you must dip in the ocean. Go under once. Make sure your head is covered by the water. Then come back onto the beach and write." Thomas's voice thundered out the challenge.

"What will we write on?" A man near her raised a question.

"Your words will be marked in the sand. You will make them anyway you can."

An auburn-haired young woman shouted, "What should we say?"

"You will know after you dip in the ocean. If you accept this lesson, from this day forward you will be forever called a scribe."

"You said this would hurt but that we would gain healing. What exactly does this mean?" A dark-skinned man with an accent spoke aloud Evie's concern.

"The part that causes pain will be the memory that returns temporarily after you dip into the water. But it is the same memory that will guide you about what you should write."

"Who are the messages for?" A familiar garden worker standing near Evie asked the question.

"The messages will appear to people in a world filled with endless knowledge but no wisdom. They have lost what is most important." The majestic herald spoke in sorrowful tones. Then he bowed his head and became motionless.

Evie began to doubt her decision. She had no special knowledge. If she did, she would have solved her own problem with fears.

As her uncertainty grew, the wind stopped. Nearby gulls landed and hushed their cries. Everything became still. Even the motion of the sea ceased.

Finally, Thomas lifted his great head. His tangled veil of thick hair tumbled aside.

Evie had to shield her eyes from the unbearable glow now emanating from his face.

"Souls … the words you write in the sand will reappear to someone important to you. On Five, you have been shielded from memories of family and knowledge of their existence, but they do exist. If you accept this lesson, your words will be seen by one of them. Tell them what is best. What is true. What helps. What persuades of the good life you now live. But above all, tell them Who Love Is."

After the echoes subsided and the gulls took to the air again, people began to move off the plateau and down to the beach.

Evie stayed. As she listened to the endless roar of the ocean, her parched mouth longed for water, but she hesitated to leave until Thomas disappeared. He must not know of her cowardice.

When the opportunity came to make her escape, she rushed off the same way she'd arrived but stopped in her tracks when she spied him. He sat on the same boulder that had moved aside for her when she first came for the lesson. He was still dressed in the white robe, but now his feet were bare and dangling, and he seemed deceptively like any other resident of Five. Radiance no longer filled his face. Only his stature referenced his greatness.

Evie wanted to hide but realized that she'd rather face him than take a dip in the ocean.

He beckoned to her.

She approached but stopped several yards short of his presence and waited.

With his massive hand, he picked up a small chalice sitting on the stone beside him and extended it down to her. "For you."

Her thirst surged, but fear rose too, barring her from taking the refreshment.

Her benefactor pulled back the offering. "Soul Evie. You should know something. The opportunity you have touches the life of your great-great-great-granddaughter."

Trembling but curious, she asked, "What's her name?"

Thomas slid down from the stone. "She's known by two letters. SJ. She refuses any other address, but her name is . . ." He paused but then continued. "Her name is SJ. That's enough for you to know for now."

She nodded and stared at the amber liquid in the cup, her thirst unbearable.

"Will you drink it? It helps with courage."

"I will." She put the cup to her lips and let the cool sweetness roll down her throat.

Evie dog-paddled into the swells. The sand soon gave way, and her feet no longer touched bottom. As she swayed in the ebb and flow of the ocean's dance, the gulls called out encouragingly, "Keh-keh-keh-keh."

Nothing here can harm me.

Minutes later, her baptism came. A large wave crested over her head and pushed her underneath the churning water. Images and voices mingled around her. The water cleared, and she stood in front of a familiar door.

Someone knocked on the other side. She opened it but found no one. At her feet lay a package with the word *self* hand-scrawled along the side.

She picked it up. Memories returned, and from the doorway, familiar sights and sounds streamed by. Occasionally, the movie-like sequence slowed, and the scene enlarged. One character in particular loomed prominent. The thief. Vignettes played on until she could no longer stand it. A tearing aching pain erupted in her chest. Fear, sorrow, and anger swelled inside her throat, and she began to choke.

She needed air.

With frantic clawing effort, she broke through the water's surface. Even as her coughing and sputtering continued, she staggered onto shore and wasted no time using her finger to trace words of warning in the warm ruby sand.

When she finished writing, she could no longer feel her fingers, and her arms ached. The other scribes had left. Only the arch herald remained on the beach. He faced the water, leaning on a rock about one hundred yards away. His white robe appeared to be soaking wet, the weight of it unyielding to the breeze that shaped the turquoise water into graceful, rolling curls.

She shielded her eyes against the evening sun. Thoughts of the thief muddled into an indeterminate shadow. Her struggle to access details, which minutes before had been so clear, left her feeling unsettled. How could this be part of her healing?

Her head spun when she attempted to stand. She slumped across the gritty surface, bent over like windblown grass. Above the roaring water she heard the herald's advice.

"Next time, write only what is necessary. Your messages are numbered. Today is your first."

Motivated to adjust the words, she scrambled to her feet, but only her reference to the Book of Wisdom remained. The rest had been washed away.

CHAPTER 5

THE SONG DRILLED on, relentless.

"Life is overrated.
Work is such a dread.
Learn to find escape, dear.
Sleep only when you're dead."

SJ fumbled for the headboard control. 1:00 a.m.? She groaned. Why was her alarm going off and not even playing her usual song? She hated the dark-humored howls of Skullwag, the same group Kate loved. Seconds later, the answer to the musical riddle pierced her foggy brain. She tore back the covers and ran to the media wall.

No. Please, Kate, no. It had to be a mistake. Or one of Kate's practical jokes to get her attention. Her heart thumped as the song surged. She entered Kate's security code onto the wall control. It took several attempts to get it right. When the live view of Kate's living room appeared, she yelled into the receiver, "Come on, Kate. This isn't funny. Are you there?"

A man dressed in an LPR uniform appeared on the wall screen. "Unless you're designated kin, you'll need to close this connection." The man tapped something on his forearm screen.

"I am. I'm SJ. Kate's designated kin. "Has something happened to her? Is she …" She refused to say it. She took a deep breath and spoke as authoritatively as possible. "Tell me what's going on."

"As soon as we confirm your kinship."

She slid back her sleeve to expose her shoulder.

The LPR worker pointed his data scanner in the direction of her arm from his side of the screen. She kept still while he scanned her biochip.

The man nodded. "Verified. But with one exception. You must declare your full name. Initials are not allowed."

She bristled at his request. "That's not true. My initials are my legal name. I paid the fee to have them on record. You've no right to request otherwise."

The man's face filled the wall screen. Fierce eyes, colored a genetically rare shade of blue, glared back at her.

She softened her tone. "Please. I need to see my friend."

"Full name. What is it?"

The sound of her full name spoken aloud always made her cringe, but she forced out the words. "SJ—Satan Junior."

A smirk crossed his face. The man gave a solemn whistle. "The Satan? Satan Junior? Offspring of the late, great Dr. Satan himself? The illustrious founding father of the resurrection formula?" He delivered the tribute in a mocking tone.

Heat flooded her cheeks, and she cut to the core. "Yes. It's me. My raising father loved mythology and had a warped sense of humor. He shortened our family name from Satanopoulos to Satan, pronounced like the cloth."

The man chuckled. "Satan's not so bad. It's truthful. Seeing that we all have a little devil in us. And that's not a myth."

She clenched her jaw. Despicable man. "Can we get on with it? Where's Kate?"

The worker disappeared off-screen, and a draped gurney rolled into view.

The song, triggered to play on SJ's alarm sound system when Kate's biochip temperature reached ninety-five degrees Fahrenheit, continued its obnoxious rant. Kate would have loved the spectacle. Kate wanted the alert so that SJ could ensure she received her dose of Rejuvacatin.

This couldn't be happening.

"Hey," SJ yelled into the screen receiver. "You need to know what happens next."

The LPR worker popped back into view. "Yeah? What's that?"

"I get the full details of cause of death, and Kate's not going under. She's a resurrection candidate. It's all in her declaration. Look in her bed cabinet. Top drawer. Next to her Rejuvacatin injector. Please check to see if she's used it."

"Already checked. Not there. But her declaration was on the floor beside her." The man lifted the drape. "Initial assessment. Probable cause of death due to advanced stage of biomalism. Her blood indicators exceed elwinde stage. You'll get the full report in forty-eight."

The ashen, plastic-skinned clone of Kate on the gurney looked too real. The worker confirmed Kate's biometer number and temperature reading of ninety-five degrees. SJ's breath seized in her chest, and she sank into a chair. This couldn't be happening. Kate was in remission.

She did the calculations based on the temperature. Kate had likely been dead three hours.

SJ closed her eyes, pressing back tears. *Oh, Kate. Please tell me you took it.*

"I'm sorry, S."

Her eyes flew open at the sound of the bass voice. Cole's Apollo-like face filled the screen.

"What are you doing at Kate's?" Before she could get her answer, he disappeared, and the LPR workers came back into view. As they moved the gurney out the door, the lump in her throat expanded and threatened to choke off her air.

After a few seconds, Cole reappeared. "My driver called it in. Kate's annual home restock shipment was scheduled for delivery today. When my driver arrived, he found her stock unit open. He went to advise her of this and saw her on the floor. House door was open. Our data file showed she worked at Ikar. Who is she?"

"She's everything. My best friend and lab partner."

Cole looked over his shoulder, and then back at her. His dark eyes flashed as he held up something.

She enlarged the focus to capture details. An injector. "Is that hers?"

"No." Cole pointed to the ID number. "It's mine. No injector was on her body or nearby. LPR wasn't too happy that I jumped ahead before they arrived. We've been here a while sorting things out."

"Thank you."

Cole nodded. "I've got to go. We'll talk soon."

Gratitude filled her heart. Cole's initiative gave Kate a better chance at resurrection success.

A voice boomed offscreen. "Dr. Satan, we didn't find her injector, but it seems Mr. Magnus read her declaration and found her signed resurrection intent. He then used his own injector to carry out her wishes." The LPR worker's face reappeared where Cole's had been. "Mr. Magnus will be issued a new injector. Also …" The man held up a comm device. "We found this. There's something on it. Not sure if it means anything."

The Ikar Lab insignia on the front identified the device as an end tablet.

Tears flooded her eyes. She wiped them away, but they kept coming. Kate had written something. She must have known she was out of time.

The man synchronized the end tablet with the media wall and left the room.

SJ enlarged the text and read Kate's words on the screen.

"Believe and live. Book of Wisdom 43.11.25."

No. The words were wrong. They couldn't be Kate's final communication. Kate knew nothing about a book of wisdom. But a resistance hacker? Yes. And likely the same one who'd generated the first message.

She reset the media wall to the expanded room view of Kate's apartment. Whatever the truth, she vowed to figure it out. The culprit who spewed riddles and robbed her of Kate's precious last words would pay for their actions.

After the LPR team left Kate's apartment, SJ went to her desk, opened her GenCom program and typed in the message from Kate's End Tablet. "Believe and live. Book of Wisdom 43.11.25." After a few seconds of searching, the result came. "No match." She set up new parameters and selected the advanced search feature.

While she waited, she initiated a request for a replacement Rejuvacatin injector for herself. Kate's untimely death reminded her that no one could predict their final moments. Death was a villain, and so was the person who stole Kate's last words. She would get to the bottom of the fake message.

Another "no match" popped up onto the screen.

I'll figure it out. The truth always comes out.

Her chest heaved, and sobs resurfaced. Whether she uncovered the culprit or not, it made no difference. Kate was gone.

Shutting off the database, she returned to the couch and curled up against the arm. Perhaps if she fell asleep, she'd wake up in a world where her best friend still lived.

She closed her eyes, but all she could think about was their last conversation and how upset Kate had been about Cole's partnership. Then there was the cause of death. How could it be true? Advanced biomalism? The terrifying secondary illness plagued those who survived the global virus outbreak of more than ten years ago. Many died from the deadly platelet deficiency caused by the disorder, and the fatalities increased due to bone marrow transplant shortages.

The condition could remain dormant for years and then suddenly surface out of nowhere. Kate received her diagnosis a year ago, the same time as the newest bone marrow stimulation drug trials had begun. Kate had entered a promising trial, and her last set of blood indicators measured within remission parameters.

SJ tossed and turned until she could no longer stand it. She needed noise to cancel the mounting clamor inside her head.

She jumped up and selected World News Broadcast on the media wall control. Images of resistance protesters gathered in front of the Division of Equity and Trust center filled the space. A red-faced man shook his fist and led a chant. Protest signs against the universal government read, "Unfair United!" or "Re-home no more!"

Kate always said that people wanted equality until they had to personally give up something to get it.

The protesters objected to the mass relocation mandates. Equity defended Universe United's strategy. A spokesperson explained how Sector Thirty-One's severe population decline from disaster and disease resulted in unsustainable per capita expense for supplies and infrastructure. Moving everyone was the solution. Sector Twenty-Eight became the logical relocation destination.

SJ muted the sound of the angry debate and remembered Kate's passion—how her friend believed in resurrection and the good purpose it served, reconnecting families and returning to the world those individuals whose life work and contribution to society had proven invaluable. A different kind of relocation, from death back to life.

Like you, Kate. Back to life. You deserve a second chance. "Please let it happen." She whispered the request aloud. Kate would call it a prayer. Perhaps it was, if prayer was a wishful-thinking-sometimes-spoken-aloud-somet imes-silent-set-of-nice-words-to-make-you-feel-better speech.

SJ fell asleep, dreaming in fits and imaginings centered on Kate.

A strange whirring sound woke her. The wall screen indicated five a.m. The news feature read, "Update on possible source of mysterious messages." She unmuted the sound and enlarged the screen view, hoping to see details of the odd communications.

An official with Universe United's Department of Global Safety gave a report in front of a crowd urging them to stay calm and recognize the messages as part of the elaborate Five Hoax. "Nothing about the communications is true. The idea that your dead relatives are still alive somewhere is ridiculous. Someone with access to DNA records is playing a game to sow distrust and disrupt our lives."

The strange whirring noise sounded again, but it did not come from the wall.

SJ got up and searched the room. Her wrist scanner vibrated on a table nearby.

She picked it up. A missed call appeared. Someone had tried to contact her from Kate's apartment two hours ago.

CHAPTER 6

SJ SWITCHED THE media wall screen from the news to room scan feature and logged in to view the darkened interior of Kate's apartment. A snoring noise came from Kate's no longer symmetrical couch. Kate's favorite zinnia-patterned comforter lay stretched diagonally over a mounded lump that overflowed the sofa.

She punched digits to alert security. How could there already be a squatter?

"Don't do it." The baritone voice came from the couch, and the lump shifted upright. "I'm here on legal business."

She paused, hand hovering over the control.

"Good girl. There's no cause to alert anyone. I'm here to transfer Kate's belongings." The figure's features remained hidden in the shadowy room.

"Turn on some light," she said, wondering if she'd found her hacker.

When the person complied, Kate's zinnias hit the floor.

In the light, every crinkled detail of the trespasser's leathery, sun-ravaged skin indicated a man, an Ancient—someone who refused scientific reversal of their aging condition. Khaki pants hung loose on the man's gaunt frame.

Certain that she'd caught a slick con artist who normally slept outside, SJ kept her voice fierce. "Who are you?"

"Transfer Agent Frank Gordon." The tall man seemed amused.

"How can that be? I'm Kate's designated kin. I didn't call for a transfer."

"Kate did."

"Kate couldn't. She's dead." She waited to see the man's reaction.

The man grabbed a paper and brought it close to the screen. She recognized the document as a transfer contract, an official form filled out by someone planning to have their belongings moved to a new location. Dated from the previous week, Kate had signed her possessions over to be sold at auction, and her signature authorized Frank and his company to do the transfer.

The details stunned her. Kate hadn't mentioned she was moving.

The man placed the transfer contract aside and picked up the comforter.

"Nope." *No way, Ancient.* She refused to call him Frank. The name, more likely an alias, spoke of honor and forthrightness, and the intruder seemed to be made of neither. "I'm not buying it. It's going to take more than your paper to convince me."

The man shook the blanket, and something fell out. He leaned over and picked up a green object and waved it in the air. "She asked me to keep up with this. Her exit pager."

It made no sense. When did Kate get an exit pager? Why would she give it to a stranger and not her?

She shook her head. "No. You're not from our transfer unit. Your base is nine. It says that right on the paper."

"Look missy, I'm here as a favor to Kate. That's why I didn't need you to let me in. She gave me the door code. We met last week at the Driftwood. Kate said our encounter was destiny, because I had the forms and expertise."

"So hanging out in bars is your idea of work?"

He scratched his head. "What? No. I'm on standby. Waiting to be called to Sector Thirty-One to help with the relocation mandate. My base may be nine, but I'm an authorized Universal Agent."

Pressing her lips together, she rubbed her aching temples.

"Kate told me about your presentation and didn't want you to be distracted. She was really proud of you." The Ancient raked back his thinning hair.

Tears flooded her eyes. She grabbed her empty coffee mug from the end table and held it to her mouth and took a fake sip. Once composed, she continued her interrogation. "Here's the thing. I still don't believe you. Why were you sleeping on the couch? And if you knew I was Kate's kin, then why didn't you contact me just as soon as you heard of her death?"

"She said if she died, you'd know it happened even without the pager because of her biochip alarm. When I got the alert, I requested an assignment delay and then hurried to her place. I knew she wanted her belongings removed right away so the unit could be sold."

"How do you know all that, and how did you get in?"

"With the door code she gave me. Kate wanted you to use the money from the sale for lab funds. Look. It is her pager." The Ancient brought the pager close with the screen facing her. "And I apologize. I didn't mean to fall asleep. I sat down to rest and must have dozed off."

She squinted and read the programmed message. The log showed Kate's name as the owner and the date of activation and time.

How did Kate plan so many details without her knowledge? Why did a stranger know more than she did? The Ancient could just as easily be the hacker trying to come close to Kate, so he could plant messages for SJ.

She'd catch the trespasser at his game. "I need to verify something. Will you kindly take a seat?"

"How about a seat on the throne? I need to use the bathroom."

She hesitated. He could slip out the window in Kate's bathroom, but common sense told her the maneuver would be impossible because of his size. She yielded but commanded, "Don't go anywhere else."

"Nowhere else to go," he growled. He turned and caught the edge of the lamp table and lunged to grab something before it hit the floor. He held up Kate's end tablet. "Have you seen this?"

"Leave it. It's none of your business."

"But it is. Kate wanted to be sure you got it. She talked about it and said if I came to get her stuff, I should give it to you. It's her last words. Don't you wanna know what it says?"

"I already do."

"It's a weird message." The Ancient moved his fingers across the surface and seemed to be ignoring her wishes.

"So was the other one." She watched his face for a reaction.

"Don't know about any other message. Only this one." The man placed the tablet back on the lamp table. "It's been a long time since I've seen a reference to the Book of Wisdom." He turned and headed in the direction of the bathroom.

"Stop! So you know about this book?"

"Yep. Look, how about we chat some more in a minute? I've gotta go."

"You'll go when I say so. The security team will be on top of you as soon as I press the button. I've every right to call them. It will look as if you've taken advantage of a dead woman's goodwill and slept in her place."

The Ancient stormed the wall screen, waving both his hands. "All right, all right. What now?" His deep-set eyes seemed to pierce the wall and reach into her soul.

She stood her ground. "Tell me, Frank Gordon, what do you know about the book?"

Frank's fierce gaze softened. "I memorized a few quotes from it back in the day."

"Is it a virtual book?"

"Nope. It's way older than anything virtual."

"Do you know where I can get a copy?"

"Can't say that I do. Even in my day, I seldom saw an actual copy. Just heard some good quotes every now and then. Most people considered the text too religious and unrelatable."

Her heart sank. His words confirmed it. The message hacker belonged to some unwelcome remnant of religious fanatics. She hated the idea that Kate's last words or even her fake last words reflected anything about religion.

"How about you?" Frank's head filled the screen. "Sounds like you know something about the Book of Wisdom."

"No. Not really." *Keep your distance, old man.* "I'm not sure I want to."

"That's too bad. If you did, then it might make Kate's words clearer."

"I have a program that researches end messages, but there's been no match."

"Well, I guess you'll have to figure out some other way." Frank left the room.

She at least had a start. The quote from the Book of Wisdom matched the style of the message from the lab printout, proof that both were part of a contrived scam composed by the same hacker. As for Kate's actual spoken last words? Their plea wouldn't stop playing in her head. Postpone the partnership. Find another way. *Oh Kate. Are you sure?*

CHAPTER 7

FOR DAYS, SJ feasted on her cowardice and guilt. Every morning she vowed to talk to Cole about delaying the partnership, but the day would pass, and any energy not consumed by work became mired in grief. When her door clicked shut at night, she refused to switch her media wall view to seascapes or birds flying in range of mountain foothills, her usual nighttime lullaby. Instead, she stared at the dim view of Kate's empty living room and closed her eyes. Her ears strained to hear Kate's snorting laughter, the sound that erupted every time she told her corny jokes.

Oh sure, Kate's body was still intact, preserved in a cylinder storage bank in the Abide along with many others, all waiting for their resurrection day.

She'd known Kate since their child development school days. As far back as she could go in her memory, SJ could find Kate. Even after SJ left to live with host parents, Kate had kept in touch. Kate always wanted the best for her.

In contrast, she'd been a shabby friend to Kate. A transfer agent knew more about Kate's final week of life than she did. Not only that, she'd lied to Kate. When Kate begged her not to go through with Cole's deal, she'd avoided telling her that the partnership date was set. The omission haunted her.

When her partnering day finally came, she could no longer put off the task. She dressed in her red Atlatigo suit with pressed gold trim and arrived at the hexidome two hours before their scheduled signing and celebration dinner.

She chose the private entrance directly leading to Cole's office. He was not there, but his wall screen showed him at a company rally, standing in front of a large gathering of workers in the side portico of the building. She turned up the volume and sat in an executive chair beside his desk.

His compelling voice surged through the air. "Throughout the ages and despite great hardship, our company has remained the most successful and innovative single-source distributor of all products and supplies."

He flashed a captivating grin. "More recently during the efforts of the Great Reversal, our alliance with Universe United has helped strengthen the communities of this world. Religious fanaticism, natural disaster impacts, and incurable disease are the villains we seek to conquer. It's only through human innovation, unencumbered by gods, that we will save our population."

Cole's ease before the crowd belied her concerns. No one in their right mind turned Cole Magnus away. As his designated kin and life partner, she'd never have to worry about money or power. With him at her side, she could do anything.

Her apprehension drifted as she drank in his physical attributes. His chiseled face, athletic stature, and tousled black hair resonated perfection. His mesmerizing voice expounded on details she knew by heart.

The crowd cheered. Cole tugged on a cord, causing a drape to slip away from a sculpture.

"Here's our new company logo. The symbol of our future." He patted the side of the fixture twice his size. "See how it shines? DCN. Delivery Conquers Need."

Crossing to the other side of the emblem, he stood with his back to the crowd as if admiring it and then turned around. "Years ago, my father envisioned a delivery service that would transport supplies to all regions and sectors." He smiled and stepped close to the crowd, shaking hands and talking as he went. "We've succeeded, and we are the best. Wouldn't you agree?" The feed displayed closeups of the faces of people nodding in front of him.

"I've been asked many times what is the secret to our achievement . . ." The view expanded as Cole moved away. "And my answer is always the same. Our customers."

He bounded back to the logo and tapped the side of it. "We do best when we let your needs and those of your neighbor dictate our actions. There's no one more powerful than you. Not religions, nor Ancients or Rulers—just you and our supply network. We work for the good of everyone everywhere."

The sound feed roared with enthusiastic clapping.

Cole stopped pacing, stood square to the audience and interlaced his fingers, a trademark stance he often held until complete silence returned.

She watched as the crowd hushed.

"I have big news. In our quest to give people what they want—what they need, our research team has been experimenting with the safe harnessing and construction of household fusion energy generators. Our achievement is now complete. DCN is set to be the single source supplier of these generators in a quantity that can satisfy worldwide demand and eliminate energy constraints for all time. There will be a great reveal coming soon."

The crowd, including the attending media, went wild, and Cole bowed.

Relief flooded SJ. She slid back in her chair. Cole loved media attention. Frenzied coverage over his big energy news might eclipse her small request to delay their partnership.

When the noise died down, Cole held a finger to his lips. "*Ssshhhh.* There's more. A reveal of a more personal nature."

Her heart flip-flopped as his eyes pierced right through the wall screen at her.

"To celebrate this day of new beginnings, I've taken a fresh step of my own. Today is my partnering day. I've chosen Dr. Satan Jr., head of Ikar Lab, to be my life partner."

CHAPTER 8

SJ GRIPPED THE arm of her chair. How could Cole do this to her?

The crowd of workers on the wall screen applauded Cole's declaration of their partnership, and the cost of her procrastination increased a hundred times.

"Kind of makes you wonder if my brother's even capable of seeing the benefit of subtlety." The unexpected voice came from a shadowed corner of the vast room. The diminutive speaker rose from a corner settee, stepped forward, and extended a child-size hand. "I'm Rumi. Cole's my brother."

SJ marveled at the fierce grip of the slender, androgynous person. The surge of crowd noise coming from the media wall made it impossible to respond until she muted the sound. "I'm sorry. I didn't realize Cole had a … sibling?"

Laughter, surprisingly deep but ending in a trill, came from the person who returned to the settee and patted the cushioned seat. "Come sit by me here. That way we'll be out of view range when Cole returns with those media mongers."

SJ tried not to stare at Rumi's hair. In proximity, the cropped silver-white strands with black tips, expertly faded into patterns resembling feathers, reminded her of Phinny.

"You like?" Rumi brushed aside her bangs. "I'm a rare bird."

Warmth flooded SJ's face. Rumi's awareness of her scrutiny made her feel ashamed. "I'm so sorry. It's very beautiful. The feathering seems almost real."

"No shame. Beauty is for looking. I'm used to stares, but I can see that my existence is a surprise to you. Cole asked me to come. He's using my logo design as his new company emblem. I'm guessing he planned to introduce us but just hasn't gotten around to it. My brother is full of surprises. The two of you really couldn't be any more different from each other." Rumi laughed.

SJ wondered how a person she'd just met knew such truth.

"Cole tells me everything, so let me make this fair. I'll tell you all about myself." Nodding as if confirming with someone, Rumi shut her eyes.

"That will be fine."

"The first thing you should know is I want to be referred to as a female, but I am not one." Rumi opened her eyes and patted SJ's hand. "And as a scientist, you'll see the irony of my history." She released her grip and stood.

"I'm a genetic invention of a parent's dream, an all-grown-up designer baby. A set of host parents requested a gender-neutral DNA fertilization, the genetic fad at the time I was conceived." Rumi turned from side to side as if displaying a designer's latest fashion gown.

SJ nodded. "I remember hearing about the option. Did you and Cole have the same host parents?"

"No. Before my surrogate had even birthed me, they died in a horrible accident." Rumi's singsong voice turned fierce. "My surrogate mother had the first option to keep me, but she said she did not want an eligeren child, the name they gave our kind, so officials placed me in an Orphan Rearing School. No one believed I'd be requested. But then one day, a man the students called 'Beast' arrived at my school and asked to become my host father."

The details matched what SJ knew. Eligerens were a gender-neutral novelty of human life, now banned for almost a decade because of the Life Preservation Act. Scientific strategies for arresting the downward spiral of living humans prohibited genetic crafting of anyone who did not have the anatomy to procreate.

"Shall I continue?" Rumi pulled at the wrist cuff of her blouse.

"Yes. Please. You said a man named Beast is your father?"

"Cole's father too. He got his nickname because each week when he came to my school and read stories aloud, he roared and stomped when narrating the villain."

Rumi moved across the room and picked up one of the miniature grotesque figurines from Cole's bookshelf and balanced it in the palm of her hand.

An uneasy childhood memory pushed into SJ's mind. Although the formed details of it remained fuzzy, she recalled an important man labeled an animal by several teachers because of the conflict he caused in her rearing school. The outcome resulted in the dismissal of a superintendent.

Rumi placed the figure back on the shelf and turned to SJ. "You know something about my father."

"What? No." SJ lied to soothe her rattled thoughts. *Is she a mind reader?* "Please continue."

Rumi returned and sat beside her. "Beast named me Rumi. It means beauty. He said the world would someday worship my 'pretty little head.'" She gave a sly grin and brushed her hand across the velvet settee surface between them. "But he said my fame would come from my creativity and perceptual genius, not just my looks."

Right. SJ ignored the peculiarities of Rumi's story and focused instead on their similarities. "The aspirations of a father. Sounds familiar. Yours could be kin to mine."

Rumi's eyes widened. "Do you think so?"

"Just a figure of speech but, yes, my host father also wanted great things from me." SJ clamped her mouth shut before she thought or said more than she intended.

Rumi leaned over and patted her hand. "Your father would be proud. After all, you are the one who will bring us resurrection." Her voice reflected the odd tone of reverence that SJ often heard when people mentioned her work.

SJ gave her usual protest. "Several labs are working on the prospect. When human trials are approved, the council will appoint a team. That's important to remember."

"So it is. So it is." Rumi laced her fingers together in a gesture that reminded SJ of Cole. Then she became motionless. Her gaze seemed to fixate on the muted media wall which featured the last of the crowd dispersing. Cole stood off to one side with a Universe leader, who appeared to be in terse conversation with another leader.

Any minute he would plunge through the door. SJ's stomach churned as she anticipated the discussion. Perhaps she should wait until they were alone. It seemed Rumi had a close connection to Cole, although he'd never mentioned a sibling. Why the secret? Were there other family issues she should know?

"So … your host father …" SJ attempted to continue the discussion of fathers to distract from her mounting anxiety.

Rumi turned her head and gave her a vacant look.

SJ plunged on. "Your host father took you out of the school and brought you home and ..."

"We don't refer to him much as father—just Beast." Rumi unlaced her fingers and seemed to be studying them as she spoke. "Since his death, Cole and I reclaimed the name for him. A father he was not. It's not that he ever hurt us, but he was driven. That's where Cole gets it, I'm sure."

An awkward silence ensued, but then Rumi clapped her hands and pointed to the screen. "There. It's done. Cole has greeted the director of operations. That means he's made the circuit and will be back in this office before you know it."

Acid flooded SJ's throat. She stood and forced a smile. "It was nice to meet you. Cole's lucky to have you."

Rumi gave her a quizzical look. "I'm the lucky one, and you are too. Cole protects his family." She smoothed the trousers of her meticulous suit and then held up her hands as if inspecting for flaws. "In my case, he buffered my relationship to Beast."

"Sounds like that's a good thing."

"It was. When I turned eighteen, I was supposed to pick my gender and have surgical amendments to accomplish it, but I rebelled. I refused to pick either gender. Beast became very angry. He'd wanted to be one of the first to host-parent a DNA gender neutral child and offer an unbiased environment so they could choose for themselves. He said people would mock the experiment because of my decision. To his everlasting dismay and Cole's delight, I remained an eligeren."

"I can see Cole means a lot to you. But I don't need that kind of protection. We have a business arrangement, and I'm not sure he can—"

"Keep it straight? Maybe his ways are different from what you are used to. Don't assume …" Rumi paused and looked away. "Here's the thing." Her gaze returned to SJ. "I can't say I'd wish my life on anyone. There are constant expectations and assumptions about me. My life would be a very uncertain existence except for Cole's protection. He makes everything possible."

Voices shouted Cole's name nearby. The iron door flung open, and Cole rushed in.

CHAPTER 9

DCN GUARDS HELD back a throng of reporters. Cole stepped inside the room and slammed the door on the crowd.

He moved toward SJ, but she sidestepped his embrace and pointed to Rumi. "Look who's here."

Cole gave SJ a sour look but then turned to his sibling and pulled her to her feet and kissed each cheek. "Dear one."

Rumi pushed him away. "Don't dear one me. Your behavior is very bad. Making a public announcement when she only wanted a quiet one." She spoke as if she was in charge.

The boldness surprised SJ and so did Cole's response when he bowed his head and appeared contrite. Then he sat at his desk and gave SJ a bemused stare. "I'm sorry, S. I don't know why I said it. I know we were going to keep it under wraps, but I just couldn't stop."

She took a deep breath. "I forgive you, but you'll show your remorse by treating me to dinner at Empires and a show at the Esplanade, and I'll need you to make excuses over our delay in the matter. I want two months before we make it official on paper."

His expression darkened. He snatched a file from the top of a stack and handed it to her. "It's too late for that."

She opened the folder. Sifting through pages of the life partnership agreement form, she got to the last one and discovered two signatures at the bottom. One looked like her own. She sank into a chair. "How is this possible?"

He whisked away the file and muttered, "It's what you wanted, right? I got it done earlier. They know me at the registry. I told them you hated publicity."

Everything slowed, and blood pounded in her temples. She caught sight of an odd expression on Rumi's face and sensed a secret communication had passed between the two siblings, and she didn't like it.

When the world returned to normal speed, panic set in. She grabbed her jacket and stood. "You had no right to do this. The choice was mine to make. Do you think you can control everything?"

"He does." A loud gravel voice exploded the air.

When she turned her head to look for the source of it, everything moved in slow motion. Walls bent and undulated as if under water, and the entire room's interior became distorted and shrank. What seemed like a giant plane of glass shot across the space in front of her. When the motion stopped, she touched the illusive surface and found it solid. The plane separated her from Rumi and Cole, but she could see the small versions of them talking and moving in the office. It was as if she viewed them from a great distance.

Small Rumi picked up an even smaller figurine from the shelf and held it out to a diminutive Cole. The statuette resembled a creature with the body of a leopard, feet like a bear, and mouth of a roaring lion.

Cole pushed Rumi's hand away, and the same gravel voice bellowed, "Not now!"

Light exploded. SJ rubbed her eyes to clear her vision and found the room normal.

A full-size Cole stood in front of her. "You've made yourself sick over this. Too much worry for no reason, which is exactly why I signed the papers. I wanted to spare you. Now you have nothing to do but imagine your life with the world at your fingertips. Is that too hard? I'll give you everything I've promised and more."

She couldn't believe his audacity.

He pulled on his coat and held out his hand. “Come. I’m tired of all this. Let’s go out and greet the world.”

She jerked away from him. Her stomach and throat had become one gnawing lump.

His gaze held fire. Then he turned away. “Rumi? Won’t you join us?”

Trilling laughter filled the air. “Not on your partnership day. That would be truly disastrous.”

“But when else will you have time to tell her everything you know about the Book of Wisdom?”

Cole’s unexpected question penetrated SJ’s fog.

Rumi turned away and made a hasty beeline in the direction of the door.

“Rumi? The book? You will tell her. Won’t you?” Cole’s voice carried the weight of a demand.

Stopping in her tracks, Rumi replied, “It won’t happen today, dear brother. There’s not enough time. I’m sure you’ll need whatever’s left to finish your confession.”

SJ’s heart thudded loudly in her ear. What else could there be?

Cole grabbed SJ’s arm. “Rumi’s being ridiculous.”

SJ snapped. “Is she? What’s wrong with you? What game are you playing?”

From the doorway, Rumi laughed. “Manipulation. And he’s the worst at it.”

“What is she talking about?”

Cole let go of her and lunged at Rumi, who extended her hand, palm out, as if to push him back. “You need to make things right with her. It’s what partners do. Tell her about your mission to resurrect our father first.”

The words toppled SJ into a bottomless abyss. When would the surprises end? She’d been such a fool.

Rumi left the room.

When Cole turned to face her, SJ willed the fire in her eyes to reflect his. “I can’t believe the game of secrets and flamboyant disclosures you are playing. It’s so childish.”

“It seems to me that you are making a mountain out of nothing. Really, dear. Your anxieties are quite tedious.”

Wanting his father resurrected was not what bothered her. It was his presumption about everything and the fact that he only revealed his intentions when they were forced out of him. "I may be tedious, but it's exhausting contemplating someone with such a great need to control."

"Just look in the mirror darling. That's why I picked you."

"What do you mean?" Her temples pounded and her neck prickled with heat. "Are you talking about my research? That's how it's supposed to be. Science methods are precise processes. Controlling variables is the only way to get to the benefit."

"Exactly. And that's the same reason I do things the way I do. For people's benefit."

"No, it's not. You say that, but you don't have the slightest idea what that means. Even in little things. I told you about my search for information regarding the messages, but you failed to mention you knew about the book until just now, when it suited you. Kate is all the family I have. Why did you keep this a secret?"

"Because the messages are a hoax. I'm trying to help you. But you just won't quit. What you need to do is to stay focused on your work. That's your role in this partnership."

"My best friend just died, and your fixation is on my research?" She swallowed back the acid building in her throat.

Cole stood with feet apart and arms crossed. "Is that so wrong?"

"Yes, and it shows your complete selfishness. Your effort to broaden the success of resurrection for the world is not anything but a guise for your own agenda. You want to ensure that your father is resurrected and that he be the first."

"Someone has to be first. Why not him? Kate could be second." He tilted his head as if weighing the notion. "Yes. We would make her second. My plan is not entirely bad." He sneered at her.

Her heart sickened at his shallow lure. How could she be so blind?

"Don't you see, my love? It all fits. Energy supply is going to be the hot button for this next election. People are angry over the shortages. Once resurrected, my father can be the spokesperson who pushes DCN energy products in all the sectors. Think about it. How persuasive will it be to have the voice of assurance coming from the scientist who first discovered how to harness fusion for personal use? He has a reputation for getting things done."

"By force and scheming like you?" She hit low, and she didn't care. "I'm done with this conversation." She slipped on her jacket.

"Don't leave quite yet. There's something you need to see, my dear. You really must appreciate the gain you've received from my scheming." He seemed to be waiting for her response.

He moved back to his desk. "I'd preferred to keep this a secret, but now that you mention scheming with such distaste, I can't resist." He entered something on the media wall control and then gestured at the ensuing image. "It's only because of me that your lab is safe, and my deal-making skills gained you a new position."

"That's a lie. I'm well respected by my peers."

"Peers? Maybe. Power players? Not so much. Watch and learn."

The video feed showed her boss George, Dr. Contrell, Cole, and another man she didn't recognize seated at a conference table.

Cole turned up the sound.

"She's too sentimental at times. She clings to the idea that resurrection is for everyone. And this whole issue over her name. It's only awkward, because she makes it so." Dr. Dionysus Contrell, head of the Life Preservation and Resource Council, spoke to the group. "Her work is thorough, but she has a habit of personalizing the test subjects, and her focus is not as singular as we would like."

"She'll regain focus and fall in line, I promise. I've a calming effect on her." A smirk crept across Cole's face on the screen.

The shaming words filled her ears. She wanted to run, but her feet seemed to be made of lead. "You've made your point, Cole. Turn it off."

"Almost finished."

She grabbed for the controller in his hand, but he waved it out of her reach.

"We need to do what's best for the project, and Birch Laboratory has been with the research program for many years." Dionysus turned to George who remained silent and seemed unhappy. Then Dionysus nodded at Cole. "Dr. Birch also agrees that your father should be the first candidate for the resurrection process. Of course, only after success with the John Doe trials."

The Cole on the wall screen stood. "You've got one thing right, gentlemen. My father will be first. But here's the rest of the deal. Birch is not the man.

SJ will take charge of the Resurrection Project and lead the team. I've got the support and the money." He produced documents from his briefcase and handed them to George, who glanced at them and then pushed the stack over to Dionysus and the other man.

Cole continued. "It's all there. The council stands to gain significant backing from world leaders. All are cooperating with me in support of the trials because they won't have to spend a dime. Birch Labs keeps their funds, but Ikar Lab takes the lead. SJ will do well enough, and Birch will be there for back up. I'm done discussing."

The media feed of the meeting ended, and Cole clicked off the wall screen. "There's the benefit of my skills, dear heart." He sat in his chair and bowed his head as if being humble, but a smirk played on his mouth.

SJ wanted to scream at him, but only her breath raged. Untangling their partnership would definitely tank her lab for life and bring more scrutiny than she could bear. She saw no safe way out. Suffocating from the weight of it all, she shoved a chair out of her path and headed to the door.

"Where are you going? You asked for dinner and a show." Cole's voice, slick with insincerity, posed the question behind her.

She whipped back at him. "Dinner would make me sick, and I've already had a show." She yanked the door open.

"At least stay for a toast." His mockery continued.

She turned and watched him grab a partially full glass from the bar behind his desk and hold it high.

"To us, my dear. Congratulations. Life partners."

She left before he could take a sip.

CHAPTER 10

COLE THREW THE toasting glass. "Abaddon!" His roar shook the room. Glass shards danced along the floor.

Four tiny grotesque figurines slid forward on a bookshelf. One tumbled off the edge, transforming from statue into life as soon as it touched the floor.

The towering figure swept his arm to the side in an exaggerated motion and bowed. "My liege." Snarling features, half hidden by rivulets of black unkempt hair, along with bulging muscles, impossibly restrained by a shredded leather vest, compelled fear in the strongest of minds. A sledgehammer hung at his side, completing the effect.

Abaddon's conversion from figurine to form always entertained Cole. But not today. His heart seethed over SJ's rejection. She had undermined his authority. She would pay for her mistake.

He beckoned to the broken glass on the floor. Scattered pieces reassembled into the goblet and flew back to the minibar.

Abaddon laughed. "Love's got you broke into pieces."

Cole exhaled sharply and slammed his fist on the desk. "Quiet! The power you have can be taken away. I've scores who would jump at the chance."

Behind the jokester, a second figurine fell from the shelf and transformed into Snake, aka "Serpens," wearing yet another version of his endless collection of python-patterned tracksuits.

Ignoring his master's command, Abaddon prattled on. "She's gotten the better of you, Cole."

Cole raised his hand, and a sound like metal grinding against metal escalated.

Abaddon cowered and covered his ears.

"Had enough?" Cole sneered at the quivering thug and then winked at Snake, who appeared indifferent to the sound.

"Apologies, my liege. I spoke without thinking." Abaddon bowed his head.

Cole lowered his hand, and the noise faded into a dull groan and ended on a final grinding clank. "You must remember, Abaddon, your skill is destruction. You're no good at thinking or speaking. For that we have our gifted spin maker, Snake." Cole signaled to the thin man, who stepped forward and extended his trembling hand.

Grabbing it, Cole grinned. All spirits but Snake generated heat upon touch. By contrast, Snake's sensitivity to it was notorious. Snake grimaced, and Cole released his hand.

Cole pushed his chair out from his desk, stood, and then moved to the bookshelf. "What's taking them so long?" He poked at one statuette until it fell. When it hit the floor, it exploded into a ball of light and rolled about.

"Lucas travels from the relocation effort in Navana, and Morbid returns from securing the connection between our transfer allies in Region Twenty-Two." Snake spoke in soothing tones while edging sideways toward Abaddon.

"Stomp on him, Abaddon. I'll not be kept waiting." Cole pointed to the sputtering light ball still rolling around on the floor.

"Really, my liege? Is Lucas to be treated so?" Snake moved between him and the light ball, but Cole waved him away and motioned to Abaddon.

Abaddon clumped forward cautiously and raised his iron boot over the light orb, but it scooted out of his reach into the corner and then shot upward. Close to the ceiling, it wavered illusively for several seconds. Then it opened and spilled down like a waterfall, solidifying into the eclipsed form of Lucas. His light-pierced outline remained as much a feature of his form as his dark shadowy shape.

"You're late." Cole addressed Lucas but focused his effort on the final statuette perched on the shelf. It toppled before his touch even reached it.

Morbid materialized. He wasted no time shaping into a hunched figure of a man with withering skin and gaunt eyes, leaning on a cane filled with pock holes, each housing a writhing worm. In the confines of the room, the transformation process placed Morbid's wispy-haired head just under Cole's chin.

Cole stepped back to avoid the stench of decay.

Morbid smiled slyly, bowed halfway, and mumbled, "Your grace." He then gave an almost imperceptible nod to Lucas.

Cole saw the disloyal gesture but chose to ignore it and moved instead to his media wall, where he illuminated the Generations Timeline. His officers gathered around him.

"Fiends." In the dim light reflected from the timeline, Lucas's outline, and the final efforts of the sun at dusk, Cole searched each face. They seemed attentive. "Mortar is on the loose again. The messages arriving from Five are his doing. But someday, the One Who Holds All Things Together will discover there's no one left—no one to bind with. If we work hard, Meritus will house only those of my kingdom."

"So let it be." His henchmen spoke in unison.

Passion swelling, he pointed with light he emitted from his fingers. "Each fleeting generation has given me increasingly more territory to rule." He circled boundary lines as he spoke but then paused on the last. "But this …" He drew an X. "This is my most valuable generation. The Contingency Generation. They've no concept of life or power aside from their own. Because of this, they are most suitable to me. Blind to everything but their natural world, they've worked the hardest to control uncertainty. I'm gaining access to everything, because of their reliance on self-will."

"But what good does it do? The messages say their world's time is ending soon. What about that?" Morbid hobbled toward a chair.

"It's of no concern." Aggravated, Cole aimed his fingers at the chair and scooted it further away from Morbid.

Snake snickered and stepped closer to the timeline.

Cole enlarged the chart to reveal only the last five generations. "Mortar has always claimed the end of man is near, and so with it, my territory concluded. But the clock still ticks. With human resurrection, our kingdom rule will be unstoppable. Imagine it with me."

Cole closed his eyes. "The Great Reversal turns in our favor. Mortar will be tempted to delay the end once again, because he'll see new numbers of pitiful souls he could save." Cole chuckled and peeked at Morbid, who stood shifting back and forth on his ancient feet. He sent the chair sailing into his crusty crony, and the withered man plunked backwards into the seat. "He's weak like you, dear Beed."

Morbid's lips curled into a sneer revealing his gap-toothed mouth.

"Careful, Beed. Unlike Mortar, who stumbles over his clinging attachment to humans, I'm not partial to any of you."

Cole gestured to the timeline. "Back to business. Mortar never factors into account the attachment people have for us and our delivery system. We hold the ticket to all human loyalty. It's their hunger for satisfaction. Once they think they have it, they want more of it or they shift to desiring something else. Our system disguises what they need and delivers what they want instead. This makes them ours to control."

Cole smiled as he contemplated the glory of humanity becoming his own.

"But the matter of free will for them to choose Mortar remains. What about this?"

Cole's eyes whipped open to view the naysayer. The perpetrator sat in the window seat. "You really are a downer, aren't you, Morbid? You've simply got to get a better perspective. Our supply network is beyond what anyone has ever seen. This generation truly does have everything available to them. Complete fulfillment is at their fingertips. Why in heaven would they choose him?"

"You mean why in the world would they choose him," Snake said from where he stood by the wall screen.

"That's what I said." A burning sensation swept into Cole's feet. He pretended to be focused on the display and not their unsettling observations.

"No, you said 'why in heaven.'" Lucas spoke coolly and moved to the window as if to sit by Morbid but then paused and took Cole's desk chair instead.

"A mere slip of the tongue." Avoiding the bait, Cole kept his course and amplified the display until only the current population appeared. "There is, of course, another delicious and even better opportunity if this new frontier of human resurrection succeeds. I've thought about it quite a bit. I believe when the resurrection moment comes, we can have a demon spirit prepared to slip inside and take over the resurrected body immediately. It will be more efficient. A human instantly loyal to our kingdom is much better than having to concentrate influence on them for the rest of their lives."

"That's completely absurd." Lucas rocked back in Cole's chair. "You really think Mortar would allow life to return without a soul?"

"I guess we'll find out, Lucey." Cole knew he hated the nickname.

Snickers sounded around the room.

Cole cleared his throat. "The important thing is to expand our territory as quickly as possible on all fronts." He turned off the media wall screen and plunged the room into darkness. The others would see the fiery glow of his skin as he seethed and be reminded of his power.

"Will we invade Five too?" Lucas's outline radiated and grew to an even greater degree, expanding and contracting with each noisy breath.

"You guessed my very thought. It's as if we are one mind." The slickness of the question, a thinly veiled act of commandeering, sent Cole bounding for the light control. "We'll start the persuasion on Five after my father is resurrected. You will prepare the influence process. You may leave at once."

Lucas stood, and Cole exhaled. Giddy waves of relief poured over him as his chair emptied of the one who would eagerly usurp his rule if it weren't for his father's decree.

"And Dr. Satan?" Snake lifted the partnership paper from Cole's desk. "Little Satan, Junior. So aptly named." He sneered and let go of the paper, and it fell to the ground. "The fall made them little devils, just like us."

Cole snatched it back and sat in his chair. "Except she's human and will remain in the dark about any of this. I leave her in the expert hands of Rumi to convince her of my love and concern for her."

Abaddon puckered his lips and made kissing noises.

Guffaws bounced around the room.

Cole roared. "Enough! All of you. Go! Snake, you and Abaddon stay on top of the messages. As long as they keep appearing in their technology, they'll be seen as a possible hoax. That's what we want. If the messages appear anywhere else, then make sure they are discredited."

Snake and Abaddon moved to the door. There, they changed into their human apparition form, both clothed in DCN uniforms to convey the appearance of deliverymen. Abaddon's hair reassembled into a neat ponytail.

"And me?" Morbid rose from his chair and pulled his cloak around him.

"Return to the process of connecting our allies."

The old man shuffled to the door.

"And Morbid … do try to look more youthful."

"But I'm not. For that matter, neither are you or any of us. Why should I look otherwise?" The old man seemed genuinely puzzled.

"Youth is their comfort. They feel safe and more fulfilled around youth. Acting as an Ancient will only jeopardize their trust."

Morbid nodded and sighed. Cole watched as he passed through the door and transformed into a blond-haired, genetically manipulated, blue-eyed executive wearing the latest designer suit.

Their compliance brought relief. All were still a treacherous lot, but he had ruled over them since forever and knew how to use their weakness to keep them in check.

"What about the resistance in Navana? Do you have a correction plan for this?" Lucas's tone challenged Cole.

"Leave Navana to me. That is all." Deliberately Cole turned his back and busied himself with sorting papers on his desk. He did not watch Lucas leave. *Let him think I am fooled.*

When the door clicked shut, Cole went to the shelf and picked up the remaining figurine. He spoke softly, cradling the small leopard with bearlike feet and open lion mouth in his hands.

"Father, they've all gone now. Speak to me. Rumi is gone too, but you'll be glad to know her powers continue to develop. As long as she doesn't get any new ideas. You will see what I have done very soon. I've taken a partner. A woman. She and I will be as Adam and Eve and create a kingdom from resurrected humans. A kingdom to rival Mortar's kingdom. We will rule." Cole bowed his head. "Speak to me, Father …"

CHAPTER 11

SJ FLUNG HERSELF onto the seat of the transport car, and it took off onto the speedrail. How could she have been so stupid? She'd held no illusion about her partnering day. Except for Cole's proposal, she'd never seriously entertained a life partner offer with anyone. When she'd imagined such a day, she'd envisioned a time of mutual respect and celebration. Cole only wanted a pawn.

She had to end it. After entering Kate's address as her destination, she closed her eyes and pressed her hand to her heart in a useless attempt to stop her raw soul from bleeding. She needed an exit plan, but Cole's power overwhelmed her.

After the car exited and then stopped at an intersection near the complex, she switched the drive gear to manual and found a parking spot behind Kate's unit.

At the door, she swiped her wrist scanner across the lock to enter. The affirming click brought relief. She still had access.

Blank walls and cold tile greeted her. Frank had done his job well. Still, she would comb through each room for a remnant of Kate's life.

After a fruitless search, she stood at the kitchen window. Tree branches dipped and swayed under darkening skies. A single plant dwindled in a large pot on the patio. She stepped outside and looked for something to use for digging. A gap in the fence revealed a rotten board. Snapping off a piece of it, she picked the sharpest end and used it as a makeshift spade to dig up the fragrant leafed plant. The large pot always housed multiple herb plants which Kate grew to make remedies. Kate once boasted how an Ancient taught her to use plants to cure almost anything. Except for biomalism. Why wasn't there a cure for that monster?

After loosening the root mass, SJ hunted in the storage shed and found a box to hold the plant. The word "shelf" labeled the top. The "h" was mostly rubbed out. "S elf." She considered it a sign. With Kate gone and her disastrous decision now made legal by Cole, she'd need to do a better job of looking out for herself. Her cheeks grew hot as she meditated on her monstrous miscalculation, her secret notion that despite what she'd told Kate, Cole had made the offer because he was in love with her or that he might love her someday. She had to have been under a spell. People like Cole did not love. They ruled. She would not make the mistake again. She would ignore any impressions of love. Stick with facts. Her trusty ally.

She marched back to the pot on the patio. A few steps away, the ground rolled and pitched her forward. She tried to stand. The ground heaved again. She fell against the pot, and it split apart. She struggled to her feet. An earthquake? Her hand throbbed. Blood dripped from a gash. She applied pressure and studied her surroundings.

Something poked through a crack in the dark dirt beside the broken pot. She cleared away the dirt and looked closer. It was a grapefruit-sized stone, and it had an inscription on it. "Love is. Book of Wisdom 43.3.16."

She scrambled to her feet. Trembling took over her body. *It's impossible. Just a coincidence.* A message in stone meant nothing. She needed to get hold of herself and get moving. Earthquakes often came in multiples, and tremors in Sector Seven had been escalating for months.

She scooped up the plant and placed it in the box. If this was another hoax message, then the stone might hold a clue to the person who wrote it. She dropped to her knees and tugged on the stone, wiggling it back and forth until it loosened completely. Then she placed it in the box along with the plant. She carried her treasures back through the apartment and out the front door.

She paused outside Kate's apartment and whispered her goodbye. Under the moonless canopy of sky, she walked to her waiting transport car and placed the plant and stone inside it and powered on the auto console. She climbed inside and waited for warning details regarding the quake's likely epicenter to appear on the screen. While she waited, she ticked down a list of positives.

Kate's neighborhood rose high above the city. From her vantage point, she could see the main speedrail, where traffic seemed to be moving smoothly along the course of it. The valley below glowed with light, which meant the power grid must be intact. Everything seemed normal.

She jumped at the sound of rapping on the window beside her.

Rumi's delicate face peered in at her.

She lowered the glass.

"Cole sent me to check on you."

"Did you feel it?"

"What are you talking about?"

"The earthquake."

"I didn't feel anything," Rumi said.

"I was in Kate's backyard. It threw me against a planter." SJ stepped out of the car and retrieved the stone marker. "This turned up in the dirt."

Rumi took the stone and tilted it toward the car light. "Where did you say you found it? Show me."

"Kate's yard. I was rescuing one of her plants when the tremors hit."

Rumi handed back the stone. "I didn't experience anything like you describe. No tremors. Nothing." She pointed to a red Morenci parked by the delivery alcove. "That's my car. I followed you here. I've been sitting in it the whole time."

Rumi moved toward the apartment complex.

SJ placed the stone back in the transport car and followed Rumi until she caught up with her.

"Which one?" Rumi asked.

SJ led Rumi to Kate's door. They entered and passed through the interior to the back yard, where SJ discovered the planter intact and the ground smoothed around it. "This can't be right." She touched the pot surface. "It was broken. I'm certain." She turned to Rumi, who stood gazing at the sky with a strange look on her face.

SJ tapped her foot on the dirt. “I found the stone in this spot.” She raised her voice. “I fell on the planter. And the stone was right here. Covered by dirt.”

Rumi shrugged and left the yard.

SJ waited. The night breeze soothed her face. But her mind raced. Everything was true. Her dirt-stained fingers and gash on her hand proved it. She trudged back inside and found Rumi ending a call on her wrist scanner.

“I can’t figure it out.” SJ brushed some leaves off her skirt. “I know what I felt and saw.”

“It’s okay. That was Cole. He said to bring you to The Nest.” Rumi ran her hand through her feathered hair and frowned. “Listen to me. Cole may seem pushy when he makes a deal, but his obsession is his way of caring. I should know. Without his help, I’d never have survived. If you want your lab and resurrection to succeed, then you’ve got the right partner to get it done.”

“You might be right, but I can’t stand to be manipulated.”

Rumi smiled. “There are ways around that. Meanwhile, you don’t need to let go of your dream. Cole can make it happen. You’ve got to trust him. He wants everything you want, and he can deliver what he’s promised.”

Everything? Sure, she wanted her lab to thrive and resurrection to be a success. But she also wanted respect and for Kate to still be alive, although Cole had nothing to do with that. Or did he?

Rumi headed toward the door, then stopped and came back. “One more thing, and I’m not criticizing. I’m just stating facts. I’m guessing you can’t call off the partnership, because you don’t have another funding source. It’s not a complicated decision. It might work better for you to call it a sacrifice.”

Sacrifice. Her quest-for-success word. It was true. What else could she do? “All right.” She pressed her lips together and swallowed. “I’ll do it with one condition.”

Rumi turned and faced her. “Okay?”

“No more manipulation or deception. He has to be up-front with me.”

“Then tell him that. Your partnership is straightforward. Think of it this way. You both use each other for mutual gain. Cole’s gain right now requires a unified front, which includes acting as amiable new partners celebrating life together at The Nest for the romantics who want to see a fairy tale.”

SJ swallowed hard and then nodded. "Okay. I'll try. If Cole wants a show, then I'll put on a show. We'll play at life partners before the world, as long as he keeps his end of the bargain and agrees that I carry out my own decisions."

"Good girl. I'll send the transport car back to the station. You can ride with me." Rumi left the unit.

In the doorway, SJ whispered, "I'm sorry Kate." Then she locked the door.

Back at the car, Rumi offered her a towel. "You've destroyed your suit."

The beautiful crimson fabric had snagged at the hem. Dirt streaks stained one sleeve. SJ wiped at the damage as best she could.

Rumi retrieved the plant and stone from the transport car. "It's an odd inscription. But not as strange as your outfit." She laughed and placed the plant and stone in her Morenci.

"Yeah. I've made a mess of myself," SJ said.

"Your appearance fits the destination theme Cole's picked for your stay at The Nest."

"What theme?"

"It's supposed to be a surprise." Rumi giggled. "Survivors on a deserted island."

Her mind eased a little over Rumi's amusement. Perhaps she could master the game of appearances with her help. The lab was worth the effort. She had an inclination to test the water of Cole's goodwill. "Did you tell Cole about the stone?"

"I did. He wants to see it." Rumi patted the hood of the elegant vehicle. "Get in."

SJ settled onto the sumptuous seat.

They left the parking area, and the car surged onto the speedrail in one smooth transition that defied the jostling of ordinary transport cars.

She surveyed the surroundings for signs of an earthquake, but nothing seemed out of place. "It's so strange."

"What?"

"I can't prove the tremors, but the stone—at least that's real. Cole said you know about the Book of Wisdom. I know it's banned and part of religious writing, but have you seen a copy?"

"It's more like an elaborate fairy tale. I know some of it by heart. My father—Beast—kept a collection of banned books. I often snuck into his library to read them. One day the copy was gone. Cole told me Beast had thrown it out."

"Do you know what the message on the stone means?"

"Not the exact words but something about … to live is to love."

"Really? That seems useless." Disappointment filled SJ's mind. The phrase sounded like two ignorant school children arrived at a dull conclusion after discussing matters in the dark.

"You're right. It's not very profound. But that's religion in a nutshell. A premise of promises that never quite deliver. Unlike our dear Cole, who always brings the goods. Stick with him and you'll find a god like none other."

SJ heard the echo of truth. Cole's company, DCN, maintained a worldwide presence which gave Cole universal power, not unlike a fictional deity. What was she thinking? Who wouldn't want to be partnered with someone as influential as that? With Cole, her sky had no limits. Her strategy to keep Ikar funded and on top couldn't get any better.

CHAPTER 12

TWENTY MINUTES LATER, their car passed through the gated entrance of The Nest.

Rumi offered SJ her coat. "Wear it to cover your suit."

The wide sleeves slipped over easily and hid the dirt stains, but the length fell short of SJ's frayed hem.

Rumi smirked. "Not that your outfit wasn't gorgeous before you fell, but the publicity hounds lurking in the lobby are just waiting to make something out of nothing."

"I'll just tell them I fell."

"Nope. You'll end up saying more than that. They're experts at getting newly minted celebrities to gush upon arrival. I'd tell them to mind their own business, but my brother is another story. He'll want to show you off. Next thing you know, your photographed head will appear all over the world speaking nonsense."

"Don't worry. I'm not so easily tricked." SJ's chest tightened as her heart mocked her quick answer. Her skills of fact-finding had recently failed to uncover Cole's true motivation.

The car stopped behind other elite vehicles in front of the gleaming pyramid structure. A uniformed man signaled to a valet.

Rumi patted her hand. "Move quickly through the ranks of misquote captains. If Cole runs into us before I can smuggle you away, then your public exchange becomes golden. My brother plays with publicity like a man plays with a fish on a line. It's you who'll get caught in a net because of your sincerity."

Rumi's wariness set SJ on edge, and so did the resort, an ethereal pinnacle of exquisite design sporting unmatched luxury. SJ stayed close to Rumi as they moved through the glamorous lobby. Throngs of costumed characters and society posers parted as they pressed on to reach the shuttle chateau. From there, they took a turquoise and pearl studded tram to Cole's selected theme space.

Enticing exhibits of destinations materialized on the tram window screens. The Nest, advertised as "a dream world with everything the heart desires," offered many unique escapes to work-weary citizens. Wealthy ones of course. The dream life began when a guest entered their assigned lodging. There, a seamless experience of their choosing unfolded with few clues to indicate any other reality.

When they arrived at Cole's suite, the destination theme for celebrating their partnership became apparent. A flawless impression of a secluded bungalow with rustic window views of a tropical garden, waterfall pool, an aviary against a white sand beach, and distant turquoise waves beckoned to SJ.

"Isn't it glorious? The only things real are the furnishings, food, and drink." Rumi placed the plant and stone marker from Kate's yard in a corner and then went about touching things in the room. She seemed delighted when the details fooled her. "Isn't it great?"

"I guess so, but saying so implies I like being tricked, and I don't. I'm more a fan of what's real." SJ swallowed her apprehension and wandered off to the bedroom. The floral and leaf motif embroidered on the bed cover and carved into the majestic sandalwood suite echoed the nature theme throughout the bungalow. On the table, a card welcomed her with her initials. At least Cole had sense enough to get that right.

Her discontent gave way to awe when she found the dresser stocked with clothing in her size, each piece beautifully designed for warm tropical days.

Rumi invaded the room and oohed and aahed over the collection. She helped SJ pick a late dinner outfit—a gold caftan edged with red embroidery—and then wished her goodbye. "Cole will be here any moment. Remember, he wants to help you, and you and the world will be better for it." Rumi clapped her hands, and music played from somewhere in the suite. She swayed back and forth to the beat a few times and then scurried away.

SJ returned to the sitting room and plopped onto an opulent sofa. The fake waterfall tumbling into the pool seemed more real than before. She closed her eyes and woke up with Cole's face hanging over her. She jerked upright.

Cole laughed. "Surprised? I am. I figured you'd run. But I'm glad you stayed. We need to trust each other. Our partnership is perfect. We'll both get what we want."

She turned his words over in her mind. "Just for clarity's sake, exactly what do you think I want, and what do you want from me?"

"We've been over this. We want the same thing. To lead the world into the first human resurrection. After the John Doe trials are successful, then we will resurrect my father. His return will be the most public and creative landmark of your accomplishment."

"You do know that our trials aren't ready to advance to human subjects? We're still working with birds."

"You're naturally cautious, my dear, but I believe the time will come sooner than you think. And this ..." Cole retrieved the stone marker from the corner and placed it on the lead glass table in front of her. "This is what I don't want. You can't get caught up in a hoax. Your fixation must stop."

He reached into his black leather bag and pulled something out and placed it in front of her. It was a stone, similar to hers. "No more distractions over messages. They're nothing but fake gibberish created by resistance protesters, or in this case, a factor of coincidence."

She traced her finger over the identical inscription. "Where did you get it?"

"Rumi sent a picture to me. I ran it through our delivery network. Two sectors responded with positive matches. I had my team pick up one. Several years ago, Icthus manufacturing produced various stones for home garden projects with options for personal inscriptions."

"I don't believe it." She turned the stone over.

Cole pointed to the fish emblem on the back. "Facts are facts. Same message. Just a coincidence. And the other messages? Clever but meaningless delivery of ancient writings by eccentric rebels. None of it matters. Their future belongs to the authorities. Your future lies with me and the success of resurrection. We do this together. Otherwise, things will get complicated."

They already were.

He extended his hand. "How about dinner? Our show must go on."

She took his hand and shut her mind to the warning in her heart.

It was time to sacrifice.

CHAPTER 13

EVIE TOOK THE pen from Logos, the Word Keeper, and signed the agreement. With the Book of Wisdom in front of her, she'd be able to compose the perfect message.

Logos adjusted his tiny spectacles higher onto his nose and gestured to an armchair. "Wait over there." Then he shuffled behind the counter and disappeared through a doorway.

She sat on the tattered seat. Everything about the vault seemed old, including Logos. His ancient appearance, unlike that of any herald she'd ever seen, surprised her. No one on Five ever looked old. In fact, she'd forgotten everything about aging until her recent adventures as a scribe. Her dips in the ocean brought back memories. Random fragments of the past now littered her consciousness like seashells washed up on a beach. Thomas, the arch herald of scribes, said the memories of her life before Five would diminish over time. She hoped for the same effect on her new and unexplainable fears.

The last two days had been unbearable. She'd been too anxious to go back to the beach, let alone think of what to write. Her stomach stayed in knots, and she choked every time she tried to swallow food. Thomas said her cure would come soon, but he'd sent her to the Word Keeper's vault for good measure.

Eighteen minutes passed. No sign of Logos. She stood and leaned over the counter, trying to catch a glimpse through the open door. Perhaps she could scoot under the marble top, but that seemed undignified.

Returning to the chair, she sat and closed her eyes. Powerful things happened when she waited. Seconds later the door slammed shut and she jumped at the sound. Curiosity overpowered her. She crawled under the counter and stood before the door Logos had gone through. She pulled on the door handle. Then she pushed, leaning against it with all her might. It might as well have been part of a wall.

A familiar whisper nudged. *Knock and it will be opened unto you.*

Tapping at first and then pounding more firmly with the heel of her hand, she knocked. She paused to put her ear to the door but jumped back when she heard a snapping click. A scuffling sound followed, and then a thump.

She pulled on the handle again, the door swung open. On the floor lay a package. She picked it up and placed it on the counter and then stood in the doorway, straining to see inside the cavernous space.

Lines of flickering lanterns hung in sparse rows above endless shelves filled with books. Cool air from the vault brushed her cheek as she crossed the threshold. Stepping to the nearest shelf, she stopped and picked up a book. The title flooded her heart with warmth.

Beside it was another copy and another and another, all carrying the same familiar title. But none of the book's copies were exactly alike. Some had worn edges while others were newly bound. Color details and even language varied from one to another. Some were big, and some were the size of her hand. Every one of them as unique as a person.

She tried to open one, but the book remained sealed. The leather cover bent, but it would not yield. The next copy did the same. After several more attempts she gave up, and sadness poured over her like rain, because the books refused to open. Hundreds, thousands, and maybe even millions of the word vessels stood on the shelves, all containing the water she needed to drink—the power that would quench the driest of thirst. Her yearning became unbearable. Tears blurred her eyes.

Stumbling back through the vault door and under the counter, she rushed outside. "Soul Evie." Her name reverberated, loud as thunder. The sky had turned dark, and lightning came in constant staccato. Had she imagined it?

A strong wind spun the hanging veil of a nearby weeping willow. Blossoms from an adjacent pear tree scurried across the cobblestone path.

"Soul Evie." This time the sharp crack and boom of the voice came directly beside her.

She whirled around and found Logos.

He handed her the package. "You left without this."

Touching the smooth paper covering, she felt the hard rectangular shape underneath.

"It's yours. The others didn't belong to you."

Great, floppy drops of rain began to splatter around her, and Logos beckoned her to follow him back to the vault. They made it inside just before the sky split open and dumped torrents.

Placing the package on the counter, she tore off the paper wrap and flipped open the familiar cream cover. Notes and dates of occasions filled the margins of the printed text. She held the collection of words to her chest and exhaled. Relief brought new tears.

Logos offered a handkerchief.

Reaching for it, she dabbed her eyes, and the comforting scent of bergamot filled her nostrils.

"Stay a while. Sit by the window and read. It will do you good." Logos's gentle voice held healing.

Hours later, she tucked the book under her arm and said goodbye to the wizened herald.

Buoyed by her time in the book, she practically skipped down the cobblestone path. She followed it along until it reached the woods, where it ended. She stopped and breathed in the raw scent of dirt washed new. Overhead branches still echoed with the tap, tap, tap of dripping rainwater. Thinking of all the new message possibilities, she waited for her route to reappear.

But instead, a shadow drifted over her, settling in like a cold damp cloak. She clutched her book to her chest and refused to give in to ominous thoughts.

Nothing here can harm me. Keeping a vigilant eye on her surroundings, she turned in a circle looking for movement.

Relief came when a small tree sapling twitched just ahead and then another, and another swooped to the side. Then feathery grass followed suit. Her pathway through the grove had emerged. She exhaled and smiled.

The revealed trail led her through mounds of pine needles and zigzagged around low places made sloshy by puddles, until it came to a place where the canopy thinned and stopped. Pausing in the sunlit glade filled with green-and-white striped hosta plants, she stooped to admire the adorning droplet jewels clinging to each leaf. Behind the hostas, the purple and pink blossoms of fragrant peony bushes appeared in vivid contrast to all the greens.

She'd reached the end of the forest. Ahead of her stretched an expansive field of manicured grass. To the west lay the Majesty Rose Gardens. A din of crowd noise came from beyond the entrance. Letters on a fluttering flag nearby proclaimed, "Rose Festival Today."

After her recent stretch of sleepless nights, she wondered if turning east toward home would be the better choice, but festivals on Five always entertained and usually concluded with a feast. She made the decision. Her stomach gnawed with emptiness. It would be food today.

Just past the arbor entrance to the garden, she found a man making crown wreaths. A typical one made of bay laurel rested on top of his flowing red hair. More elaborate rose headpieces of all shapes and colors lay stacked in a pile beside him.

Using cut rose stems, which grew thornless on Five, he worked on fashioning his next crown. "Greetings, Soul Evie. Have you come to compete today?" He singled out two coral tea rose stems from a bucket of cuttings and placed them side by side on his worktable.

"I'm not much of a racer. I've come to watch."

The man nodded. "I see." He was most certainly a herald, since he knew her name even without looking at her.

She guessed the wreath headpieces must be for the race participants. When the wreath maker said nothing more, she turned to follow the outer path to the spectator stands where she'd join other non-participants in the role of cheer giver.

She paused at the base of the first bleachers and scanned the noisy, happy sounding crowd. All but a few seats were full. Just then a trumpet sounded, and the crowd quieted.

A voice boomed out. "Souls, the Rose Race is about to begin. If you are a player, please take your position." The announcement came from an arch herald dressed in a lavishly embroidered overcloak who stood in centerfield.

Participants stepped forward, all adorned with glorious head wreaths. Half were dressed in blue caftans and the other half wore white. Each team lined up. One by one, they ascended short marble capstones that stretched in two parallel lines down the open center of the garden to the throne pergola at the far end.

Her heart fluttered at the sight of the throne. Author Perfector would be in attendance. His presence gave cause for great enthusiasm, which the crowd already seemed to radiate.

On the sides of the contestant field, cook staff and food bearers assembled the feast. Evie shielded her eyes and looked for the drink stands. Her mouth watered for a lemon verbena smoothie.

"Soul Evie." A voice beside her spoke her name. It was the wreath-making herald. He held out a headpiece made of coral tea roses, maidenhair fern sprigs, and miniature red sweetheart buds. "Your crown."

"It's stunning. But I can't accept it. I'm not participating. Remember? I'm only a cheer giver today. But thanks for considering me." She knew the gesture was an honor, but her recent struggle with fear and doubt made her feel unworthy.

Pennant bearers suddenly appeared and began encircling her. The crowd noise swelled. It seemed they'd mistaken the herald's presence with her as an indication that she was a contestant.

Evie waved gaily to the crowd but shook her head firmly, "No."

"It belongs to you." The herald held the floral wreath high and then placed it ceremoniously into position. The crown shifted on her head. Her hair strands responded and intertwined with the rose stems, forming a bond that only a herald could undo.

She patted her new headpiece. "Please. I've been unwell and thought it best that I watch today. I'm afraid this is a mistake."

The wreath-making herald smiled. "No. No mistake. You are chosen."

"But I received no notice."

"You just did." His eyes twinkled.

Without graceful alternatives, she accepted. As with every challenge, she took comfort in silently saying the mantra. *It is best. It is good. All will be well.*

She handed her Book of Wisdom to the wreath maker for safekeeping.

He smoothed the tattered cover. "Everlasting. Beyond withering grass and fading flowers, it endures." He spoke in reverent tones.

"It's my life," she whispered. "I've only just discovered it again."

"I'll take the best care of it."

She nodded and entered the contest field.

CHAPTER 14

TRUMPETS ECHOED IN vibrant tones signaling the start of the race. When the last note faded, an arch herald, bathed in a golden glow, stepped out from the throne pergola at the far end of the field and moved to a center position between the stands.

"Contestants, may I have your attention." His voice resonated above the noisy crowd. "The Rose Race will begin after a few reminders."

The arch herald waited while two other heralds, each carrying a footed silver bowl, entered from opposite sides of the pergola.

"First of all, the petals used in the relay are symbolic. Do you know what they represent?"

"Words of wisdom. Words of wisdom. Words of wisdom." The crowd chanted the phrase repeatedly. Many waved and gestured with the beat.

The arch herald held up his hand, and they became quiet. "You're correct. Not just any words, but words from the Book of Wisdom." He gestured to the bowl-carrying heralds, and they held up their vessels heaped high with rose petals.

Exuberant crowds started chanting again. The arch herald held up both hands, shushing the crowd. "Your enthusiasm is splendid today." The energetic hollering died down and he continued. "As you know, the goal of the race is to blanket the walkway leading to the throne with your petals.

"Your petals are supplied from the bowl, and you must scatter them by hand from your capstone. When you are satisfied with your effort, pass the bowl of petals to your closest teammate so they can repeat the process. We'll give a little demonstration."

He motioned to the heralds holding the bowls of petals. One of them placed his bowl on the ground and then took a stand on a capstone. He accepted his partner's bowl, grabbed a handful of petals, and tossed in each direction from his perch. Then he handed back the bowl.

"See? That's how it's done." The arch herald nodded at the bowl heralds and they hurried off one to each side of the field. "You will get more than one turn unless you get tapped out for a fade, martyr, or team loss. This action of spreading the petals symbolizes the passing of the Book's words of wisdom to the next generation. The team that does the best, covering the longest and widest territory with rose petals in the time allowed, will receive the prize."

He made a fist and blew into it, and the trumpeters blew four long blasts. Then he held his arm high. "At this time, could I please have some cheering for our two teams?"

The crowd roared generously as both teams waved. Twelve heralds entered the field dressed in colors of the two teams. They spread out as two groups of six, one in front of each of the viewing stands on either side of the open grass area. When all seemed situated, the arch herald stepped away from the pergola, raised his hands, and then bowed his head.

The structure behind him filled with light and the sound of a rushing mighty wind. The fragrance of roses intensified. When the wind decreased to a gentle whisper, the arch herald turned and prostrated himself before the throne.

Evie joined her teammates as they stepped off their capstones and fell to their knees. She raised her voice in choral unison with the crowd.

"Abba Father,

All praise, glory, and honor to You.
To the One who is, will be, and always has been.

Our hearts and voices cry out,
Giver of life,
Revealer of truth,
Sustainer of all living things,
To the One who is, will be, and always has been,
We remember your words today.
Forever and always,
Amen."

At the end of the tribute, colorful birds flew to the sky and warbled an echoing song. The effect was glorious. As the last twitter faded, people rustled about, rearranging themselves in the stands, and team members retook their positions.

The arch herald resumed his stance. Facing the crowds, he bellowed more instructions. "For those who are new to the race, there are some additional variables. All actions of dispersing the petals are to be done in a forward motion, reflecting the passing of time. Don't pass the bowl to the team member behind you."

He signaled again, and the trumpeters blew six short blasts. "When you hear that, it indicates the end of an intermediate time span, and all petal tossing must cease. At that moment, the team with the best petal-covered walkway will receive an extra bowl of petals to disperse when the new time span begins. The team that is behind will lose a player, leaving a gap in the line."

In slow fashion, the arch herald turned in place as if taking in the scene, and the crowd hum grew louder. One of the line heralds came up to him and spoke something in his ear. The arch herald straightened and clapped his hands. "I've just been reminded. I have to tell you about tags. Each team will be subject to martyr tags. Three of them will occur. If a herald tags a player as a martyr, then he must step off the capstone and end his play. There is a team benefit to receiving a martyr tag. With each one, the team also receives an extra bowl of petals to spread."

The field herald nodded and returned to his place in line.

"And a final challenge." The arch herald's voice boomed. He clasped his hands together, and his glow dimmed. "There is a fade tag. This obstacle symbolizes a person whose life ceases to include words of wisdom from the Book. A fade tag is called only when a player holds the bowl. If tagged, three handfuls of petals will be taken out, and the player must cease to play and step down. The event becomes a setback for the whole team."

For a few brief seconds, the crowd stilled as the arch herald held his hand against his heart and then bowed his head in an exaggerated display of distress.

The only motion in the garden came from the wind.

Then the herald threw up his arms. "But that is not the end. As long as there are petals and final time is not called, the race is not over."

The crowd cheered.

"We are set to begin after the bell toll reaches thirty-three." The arch herald paused to consult with a seraph, who now sat covering the opening of the pergola with its wings. After their exchange, he nodded to a herald waiting on the sideline. The herald waved a white flag and at the signal, a herald perched atop the pergola ran across the long edge of the roof and climbed into an opening in the bell tower.

The count began.

One … the solemn sound reverberated in the air, reminding of the dear life long since given to save all others.

Two.

Three.

Four.

Five …

Evie stood on the last capstone at the end of the white team's line. She patted her rose headpiece and then turned to gauge the distance to her nearest teammate, a tall woman with dark, wavy hair. The woman seemed to regard her with a similar focus.

Evie smiled at her. "Hi there. Is this your first Rose Race?"

"Yes. It is. I just arrived. My herald said it would help me. How about you?"

"I've witnessed them before and been a cheer giver, but I've never been a participant. So, I guess I should say, yes, and no."

One of the heralds carrying a large, silver-footed bowl of rose petals had reached the end of the line where Evie stood.

The bell continued to chime.

Eleven.

Twelve.

Thirteen.

Fourteen.

"Are you ready?" The herald holding the bowl spoke in a low voice beside her.

"I'm ready." She adjusted her ankle-length skirt to loosen the folds.

"No. You're not. You've not sought the name of your teammate." He nodded toward the young woman who had just exchanged conversation with her.

Warmth flooded Evie's cheeks. Exchanging names was the custom when meeting for the first time on Five.

Twenty.

Twenty-one.

"It's not too late. There are twelve more tolls." He adjusted petals in his bowl.

Evie glanced at the woman on the nearby capstone. Her attention seemed focused on scuffing the surface under her feet. "Do you need any help?"

The woman straightened and beamed at her. "No thanks. Just smoothing away some pebbles. I don't want to slip."

"Good idea. My name is Evie, by the way. When the race is over, would you like to join me for a lemon verbena smoothie?"

"That sounds so refreshing. I'm Katherine, but everyone calls me Kate. I'm under healing restrictions, so I'll have to check with my herald. He says fear is a factor, but he doesn't say why, and I can't seem to figure it out. I know that everything on Five is for our good and nothing here can harm us, but somehow, sometimes, I get afraid. Do you know if that's a common problem?"

Touched by Kate's open admission, Evie seized the opportunity. "I might be able to help, but we'll have to visit more later. The final bell is almost here."

Twenty-nine.

Thirty.

Evie glanced at the bowl-carrying herald. He had a sly smile on his face. "You knew," she whispered.

He nodded.

"Do heralds know everything?"

"Of course not. Only Author Perfector does."

Thirty-two.

Thirty-three.

The crowd roared when the last toll sounded.

Evie reached for the overflowing bowl of petals. Grabbing handfuls, she tossed them and watched them settle like confetti across the path. She repeated the process in the direction toward Kate. When she felt satisfied, she held out the bowl to Kate, straining to bring it as close to her reach as possible. Kate leaned over to receive it but lost her balance and came off the capstone.

Evie held onto the bowl. "Don't worry about it. It's not a problem. Just step back on and continue the race. Falls are expected, but the race must only progress from the capstone position you've been given."

Kate got back in position and then tossed multiple handfuls of petals across the path. When she finished, she passed the bowl to the next teammate.

A hand tapped Evie's shoulder. The wreath maker stood by her holding another bowl brimming with petals. "Each petal is a word from Him who paved the way. Everlasting. Beyond withering grass and fading flowers, it endures. But for now, you do not. Your role play has ended."

She nodded and stepped down.

"As promised, your team gets extra petals because of your martyr tag." He walked over to Kate and handed her the extra bowl and then returned and held out Evie's book. "It is safe."

But she was not. An unexplainable sense of doom swept over her. She took the book and clutched it to her chest as she watched the path of blood-red rose petals expand toward the throne. A more beautiful and fearful sight seemed unimaginable.

CHAPTER 15

A STORM LOOMED, SPEWING a cold breeze across the beach. Evie shivered. Her morning reading from her Book of Wisdom had helped, but nothing completely eliminated the battle of will and emotion that came with each breath she took.

As the clouds amassed and spread thick fingers across the sky, her uncertainty grew. Where are you, Kate? Thomas had told her there would be no more messages after this one, and Kate had promised to be with her.

A distant shimmering prism on the sand signified an approaching herald's presence. Soon, the shimmer appeared only a few yards away, and Thomas emerged. Evie waved. *Bravery is not the absence of fear. It's going on in spite of fear.* Thomas's words from the last time they were together encouraged her heart.

Still. Kate had promised. Evie left her book on the rock and scrambled to the top of the dais to scan the field on the other side for signs of her friend.

Thomas called from the beach below. "Soul Evie. It's time. You can't wait any longer."

Evie climbed down and noted the herald's battle garb. "Are you fighting today?"

"No. I'm winning." Thomas's face crinkled into a radiant smile.

Evie handed him her book. He took it and walked with her to the water's frothy edge. As the spray hit her face, a tremendous wariness swooped over her. Even the wind coming off the ocean pushed her back, calling for the safety of the shore.

"What is it, Soul Evie?"

Evie struggled with her questions and finally blurted out her concerns. "What if it hurts too much? Will my words even be enough for SJ to know the truth? Will I truly be healed when this is over?"

"It is enough. You are ready for this. Author Perfector wrote all that is necessary for this day before you even took your first breath. Now, within his image, you write too." Thomas sheltered her under his arm until she stopped shivering.

When he released her, she looked up, hoping to find blue sky, but the heavens still brewed, ominous.

"Remember, nothing here can harm you. All you encounter is the memory of an experience that no longer exists." The arch herald patted her shoulder.

Evie nodded and then stepped into the warm water. The soft sand cushioned her feet but soon gave way, and the water crested over her head.

When the bubbling cleared, Evie stood looking out a window at the secondary school in Yerwa, her mission home when she was thirty. Her students, all girls, talked excitedly beside her about the van that had just parked on the street in front of the school gate. The long-awaited supplies for the new semester had arrived. A man stepped out and loaded boxes onto a cart.

When she opened the door to greet him, the sound of yelling came from across the street. A gang of thieves that had been plaguing the neighborhood came running around the corner.

Evie quickly pushed the girls back inside and locked the front door, but the sound of breaking glass in the kitchen informed her that an intruder had already gained entry.

A figure dressed in military garb and a balaclava mask appeared in the dining hall.

The girls screamed and ran to huddle near Evie.

"Don't be alarmed, little ones. I've come to rescue you." The intruder spoke in a tone a father might use and moved around the first table.

The girls' bodies pressed against Evie, and she had to pry Myra, her littlest student, off her legs to move toward the man. She whispered to Sasha as she passed, urging her to lead the others away and make a run for it.

"You must come too, Teacher Evie," Sasha pleaded, even as Evie pushed the young woman away. Evie knew the others would follow Sasha. She waited as Sasha led them into the corner where the smaller girls huddled down and hid their eyes with their hands. When violence came, it was all they knew to do.

Evie turned her attention to the unwelcome visitor. "You're not here to rescue anyone. You're a thief." She spoke sternly, as if talking to an errant teenager, which the intruder undoubtedly was—a youth of seventeen or eighteen years of age carrying out his first mission.

"Ah, but that's not true. It's you who rob, and you must pay for your crime." The bandit pulled out a long sword, carved it through the air, and then stabbed it into the wooden tabletop where the blade stuck until he pulled it out. The girls screamed, and Sasha tried to quiet them.

Evie did not take her eyes off the man but instead eased away from the girls toward the kitchen, where she kept a small collection of defense weapons. Surely, neighbors would arrive any moment, as they'd done in the past. She only needed to buy some time. "Why do you say I am a thief?"

"You steal girls' minds and replace them with lies."

"That's not true. I teach them to read and write so they can learn."

The villain did not follow her but instead moved back to the other side of the table, closer to the corner full of whimpering girls. "Hush," he told them, holding his finger against his mouth. "I'll prove to you girls that it is your teacher who steals. I will ask her questions, and you will hear the lies she tells. Then you will know the truth."

Sasha boldly stood in front of the little ones and spread her arms to block them from running. The thief raised his sword over Sasha's head, and Evie quickly called out a diversion. "Ask me any question, and I will tell you the truth."

He whirled to face her. "All right. Let's make it a game. With each lie we tell, we take a step. The person asking the questions continues to ask until a truth is told. If we tell the truth, we stand still. I'll begin."

Evie nodded her agreement, hoping to stall until help came or the girls got away.

"Here's my first question. Do you believe there is one God?"

"Yes." Evie's heart sank. The game would not be about math and science.

"That is a lie. You worship not just God, but Jesus too. You may take a step."

"But Jesus is a part of God. God is God the Father, God the Son, who is Jesus, and God the Holy Spirit. Just as I am one human, but I have a body, soul, and spirit." Evie prayed her words rang true to him.

"A lie, dear girls." He looked over at Sasha, and she crossed her arms as if in defiance. His focus returned to Evie. "There is only one God. You speak of three. Since you won't take a step, I'll take it for you." He moved toward her and continued his interrogation.

"Do you say that Jesus is God even though he was born from a woman, and lived on Earth, and died on a cross like a man?"

"Yes." Evie whispered.

"Louder please, so the girls can hear."

"Yes."

"Oh dear. You simply must take a step for that lie."

"I will not."

"It isn't right to play a game and not stick to the rules, is it, girls? Your teacher keeps saying what is false, yet she will not play the game right. She's supposed to take a step if she tells a lie."

Evie knew the man would soon reach her. Poised to run, every muscle fiber screamed for release, but her feet stayed planted.

"Oh well. I guess it's up to me. I will take her step for her." He brandished his sword and kicked a chair out of his way.

"Is your Jesus still God even though you say he died as a sacrifice for the sin of men?"

"Yes." Evie tried to remember her martial arts training about how to throw a person off balance.

He took another step.

Two pace lengths stood between them. Out of the corner of her eye, Evie caught the image of more masked faces staring through the window. *God help me.* I will fight them all. David slew the lion. In His strength, I'm able.

"And do you say that God condemns all men unless they believe in Jesus?"

The question came from far away, because nearby, music and singing had filled the air. Evie relaxed, and her words tumbled out freely. "I say God loves all men, and if He gives them an opportunity to hear the truth, then they must believe the truth, or they will not have eternal life."

The thief did not move. It was as if he listened to the music too.

The song reverberated, but then he roared, and it stopped. "Did you come here to teach our children how to read and write?"

"Yes."

"That is a lie! These girls tell me that you came to give them an opportunity to believe in your Jesus God. Right?" He turned and terrorized the youngsters by swishing his sword at them.

Myra began to wail, but Naomi put her arms around her.

Evie called him back. "It's my answer you want. Not theirs." She picked her next words ever so carefully. "I came to teach these girls the things they do not know."

He leaped onto the table, and then with a second jump, his breath fell on her face and his sword pressed into her neck. "Will you choose to believe your truths even if I kill you for them?"

Evie closed her eyes. But the music returned and compelled her to look beyond the blade to the dear, sweet faces. She managed a whisper, "Dear Jesus!"

"Tell them you have lied. Choose this, and you will live. Say it to these children."

"No. I've always told the truth. I do not lie."

"Then you will die for your choice."

"Yet I will live eternally because of Jesus." She spoke the hope aloud, boldly, because she knew the words would be her last gift to the girls.

Razor sharp pain pierced her neck. She began to choke, and her shell cracked wide open.

Raging foam swept her over the edge of dark. The tossing and turning took away her sense of direction, and she no longer knew which way was up. She willed her arms and legs to propel her, but nothing happened. She grew increasingly tired and drifted, hoping for the end of consciousness.

Strangely, it did not come. Instead, aided by unseen hands, she shed her broken shell with the ease of a child slipping off play clothes at bedtime.

She moved, weightless and cold, through navy depths that eventually lightened to cobalt and turquoise foam. Water turned to air, and warmth enveloped her. Her watery lullaby yielded to the solid hum of earth, and her sight filled with a spectacular evening sun splitting apart a canopy of dove-gray skies. Her view rolled ever so slightly, and the sky shot out a stain of red that met with crimson sand.

Voices babbled nearby. Two heads appeared. The dear faces belonged to Kate and Thomas.

"Don't be afraid, Soul Evie. Nothing here can harm you." Thomas raised her up, and she sipped from a cup Kate offered.

"Lemon verbena tea," Kate whispered.

Evie finished half and watched as Kate placed the cup beside her. She tried to smile at her friend, but her effort felt disconnected. "Do I have a face that smiles?" Her voice came from her but also sounded far away.

Kate laughed. "You do."

"Feeling connected to your body will take some time. Coming back through The Passing is strange." Thomas spread a blanket over Evie's now trembling limbs. "A scribe's last dip in the ocean is the worst, because the soul reconnects to the memory of the circumstance when their life before Five ended. Their death."

Evie struggled to sit. *Death.* Her fear had a name. It was a word she'd long forgotten, but still, somehow daily, she'd walked in dread of it.

"And in your case not just any death, but violent death at the hand of those who would extinguish the Word of Life. Perhaps you recalled I spoke at the Grand Lesson about a common factor among those chosen to become scribes. It's"—he pulled something out of his robe and held it out to Evie—"martyrdom. It's what all scribes have in common."

Evie touched her Book of Wisdom. Welcome strength poured into her hand and tingled all the way up her arm and into her shoulder. She knew the power did not originate from the book itself but from the words it contained. The words of Author Perfector lived on the pages.

"It's time to finish your assignment." Thomas scooped her up, and Kate carried the book and the blanket. They took Evie to the base of the dais. There, they propped her up between two boulders, and Kate sat beside her to block the wind.

Thomas stood with his back toward them and held out his arm. He raised his hand as if stopping an unseen foe. His voice boomed above the noisy sea. "Take all the time you need, Soul Evie. The sun will not go down until you are through."

Evie opened her Book of Wisdom to the place she'd marked. Before this day, she'd devoted many hours to strategies about what her final message for SJ should be. "How would you decide?"

"Perhaps it's harder for you. I've not been told who will see my messages as you were." Kate patted the book. "Also, I don't have one of these."

Thomas's voice rumbled above them. "Even if a generation is without a Book of Wisdom, Author Perfector still calls to His creation. The recent appointment of martyrs as scribes to send messages indicates His latest call."

"But if the Book of Wisdom is gone from people, then what good is giving a reference to it?" Evie caressed the pages of her priceless treasure.

"What other words bring healing?" Kate stood. "Since my arrival on Five, I've been told that all words of Author Perfector hold power, and death bows to even the shadow of His words."

Kate's answer made it clear. Evie's final message would lift up The Choice and the power it had over death. After all, because of it, she'd exchanged her own death for new life on Five. The Choice had secured her future. Evie wanted the same for SJ.

With Kate's help, she carved her final message in the sand. Then, while Thomas built a fire to keep them warm and cooked fish to eat, the two friends sat and watched the waves roll in and the stars come out. Eventually, they all climbed to the top of the dais and looked down on the beach. In the moonlight, the washed out words of her message written in the sand looked somewhat like the outline of a butterfly.

Transformed was the word that came to Evie's mind. Her fear was gone. The absence of its weight practically caused her to float home.

CHAPTER 16

AFTER HER PRETEND honeymoon at The Nest, SJ returned to work and brought doughnuts. She placed the treats on the counter in the break room, pulled out a blueberry cake one and munched on it. Several workers entered and left without joining her, mumbling excuses about diets and too much work to do. She finished only half of her doughnut and tossed the remainder.

Back in her office, she discovered a gift on her desk with a congratulatory note on her partnership from one of Cole's business connections. The box contained a set of gold-edged drinking glasses. Her flush of excitement gave way to a gnawing pain in her stomach. The warm gesture from Cole's camp only exaggerated the cool reception of her team.

Pushing the gift aside, she sat at her desk screen and initiated a quick scan of her intake file. Seventy-eight notices—mostly about study data, but one title in particular caught her attention. It was a communication from the council, forwarded to her from George.

She opened the notice. It seemed the council had agreed on a temporary assignment of two third-year Testing & Research Interns under Medical Programs, or TRIUMP workers, who would work combined part-time schedules to fill Kate's vacancy.

Tears welled in her eyes. Kate was really gone. She dabbed at her face with a tissue as she read George's explanation about his request to the council, including the fact that he'd already approached existing lab team members, and nobody wanted Kate's job.

Pressing her hands to her temples, she closed her eyes. Kate's negotiation skills had kept the team working together. In the past, when Birch Labs tried to hire some of Ikar's best workers out from under her, Kate had intervened and renegotiated with the employees to keep them at Ikar. Now it was all up to her to keep them united and afloat. The staff needed to know about Cole and the funding she'd secured. Confidence would come when she clarified this achievement.

She called a team meeting and delivered the news but omitted any mention of her promised lead role on the resurrection team. Only a few from Ikar could accompany her, and the current state of fragile egos suggested a need for more recovery time before that conflict came to light.

Her good news about funding brought a subdued response. She asked for feedback, and comments around the room revealed another focus—Phinny's progressive blindness. The affect meant the pelican could no longer be a test subject. Some felt the bird's sight loss came from disproportionate oxygen uptake. Others wondered if resurrection left residual amounts of degenerated tissue, which in turn led to the blindness.

In the middle of the discussion, she received a message from George requesting a conference. Slipping away from the staff's avid debate over blindness causation theories, she breathed a sigh of relief. It seemed that the staff's lukewarm reception over her return had more to do with their worry over Phinny than her partnership with Cole or funding.

She returned to her office and pulled up George's recent correspondence in preparation for the conference. As her liaison to the council and appointed oversight manager regarding her research, George treated her more as a mentor and friend than a regulatory enforcer. She wondered what he truly thought of her partnership with Cole, but her best approach was to play it cool and give no indication of her knowledge of Cole's influence over her position. George would not have her turn away money, and he certainly didn't believe Birch would be a better candidate to lead the team.

On her media wall control, she punched in George's code. A gigantic image of his bald head and ear appeared. "Morning, George."

"Morning, S."

"Something's off with the feed. I'm gonna work on it a bit."

"Do it, but I'm kinda in a hurry." His head dropped out of camera view.

"I'll be fast." She reduced the zoom factor and worked to center their connection using the wall picture of his daughter Laura standing under an arbor of wisteria blooms in front of her home. The image always reminded SJ of George's resilience. He left the project after a rare tunnel accident took Laura's life. The extensive tissue damage made her body unsuitable for resurrection. George was devastated and took a year off from work, but when he returned, he threw every ounce of influence he had as liaison to the council to promote Ikar's stance about bird research.

"There. That's better, I think. Look up and let me see."

George lifted his head.

His gaze seemed fixed on something beside her. Unaligned image connections never bothered George, but they aggravated her sense of perception. Media walls were capable of exact transmission, as if two people were in the same room face to face, instead of miles apart on each other's wall.

"Enough." George's face contorted. "It will have to do. On to business." As always, his attempt at a smile had more in common with the toothy grimace of a gorilla. "I trust your honeymoon gave you some much needed rest?"

"It was an amazing place. Have you ever—"

"Glad to hear it."

She waited while he scribbled some notes. Then he looked up again, and this time his focus seemed directly on her. "I have big news."

"Okay. What is it?"

"Animal trials are over. We're moving on to homo sapiens. Council wants to initiate phase two of the Resurrection Project." His eyes shifted off to the side.

"We can't. We are not ready. We need more time." SJ enunciated the words of her protest in an exaggerated effort, less so for George and more for the ears of the hidden audience she was certain stood out of view in his office. It wasn't the first time George had to deliver a decision from the council with a concealed representative present.

"We can't run bird resurrects indefinitely." His voice crackled. Being virtually present at the same time but physically distant at eight thousand or more miles apart muddled the wall feed and display capacity.

She dialed down the screen magnification even further. “It’s bad timing. Oxygen uptake in the bird’s circulatory system differs from humans. We need to establish contingencies.”

“No. We must make a leap of faith. John Does donated their bodies for the benefit of others, and their families received the approved compensation. No matter what happens, we’re covered. We have no liability.”

“That’s one way to look at it but not what I’m concerned about. We have no consensus on the final adjustments required for human circulatory recovery, and circulatory variations can lead to a wide range of impacts.”

“There’ll always be something more to adjust when it comes to perfection, but we’re close enough. It’s time. The council’s appointed you to lead the trials.” He swiveled his chair around, and the arm knocked a stack of papers to the floor. His head ducked below view.

“It’s too early.” Whoever was distracting George off screen needed to know exactly where she stood. She took a deep breath. “We don’t have our best corollary. Even the primate studies are premature. Avian circulatory recovery will always be less problematic due to their enlarged heart structure and more advanced oxygen uptake abilities. We have to account for this.”

“So do it. Factor it in. But don’t make it an excuse. It’s time to move forward.”

Heat crept up the back of her neck. “Refusing to experiment with human subjects because we have not solidified our circulatory approach is not some random justification. Returning life to a human subject is a complex mingling of body systems. Any miscalculation could cause human candidates to experience immense discomfort, possibly even to a greater degree than any pain they may have had upon their initial death.” Fire flooded her veins as she laid out her justification. How could anyone accept such a risk?

“Under proper sedation they won’t remember or even be cognizant of anything for quite some time.” The voice that spoke below view sounded noticeably un-George-like.

George popped back into view and wore a sour grin.

That confirmed it. An invisible audience stood at the helm. She pretended the media wall connection had botched up and she spoke especially loud and with exaggerated enunciation. “I’m not certain you heard me, but you already know what I'm going to say. Sedation is speculative. We are still in significant uncharted territory. Everyone seems to forget this."

Whoever drove the meeting was not George. In the past, he'd shared her frustration when power players shoved aside intelligent research to push along their own agendas.

"George. Are you hearing me? I won't jump ahead just for the glory of it." She prodded again for good measure.

"It's not for the glory, Dr. Satan, but out of urgency," the not-George voice said. "Surely, you've heard the unsettling news from Sector Thirty-One? Forty-eight percent of the population now test positive for the Rochelle factor which means biomalism is advancing beyond predictions."

"Whoever you are, you know I can't see you. But you should know that the blood factor connection is not fully proven."

George grimaced, mouth closed, and then he slumped back in his chair.

"Who I am is not important. But the new direction the resurrection trials must take is vital. I'm afraid it appears nothing can be proven enough to satisfy you, Dr. Satan."

Who was talking? The voice sounded female and oddly familiar. She began to wonder if the defiant spokesperson saw her at all. Shifting the screen mode to Room Reflect would reveal her concern. High-pitched static filled the room. Maybe saying nothing would draw out her opponent.

Sure enough, seconds later the sound feed cleared, and the irritating voice returned. "The Institute of Medical Plausibility has compiled studies showing that the occurrence of the Rochelle factor in the blood is an indicator that biomalism symptoms will follow in ten years or less. If we cannot resurrect successfully soon, then there will be no way to stop the rapid population decline."

"Except for babies." SJ watched for clues on George's face. "We can always get more babies. DNA co-ops took care of that."

"Yes, but successful women like us are not interested in the birthing and rearing process. Only those without resources agree to be incubators, and they are often the same ones most susceptible to biomalism."

Whoever spoke was obviously a snob, and her words stung. Kate had wanted offspring someday. She'd completed the government-required child-rearing training but had not had time to match with a surrogate.

"The decision is made." The presumptive person spoke again. "The Institute of Medical Plausibility believes research proves a readiness to progress to human trials, and the council has appointed the team you are to lead."

George nodded but his gaze remained averted.

I'm too old for this treatment. SJ flipped the wall switch to Room Reflect, but her screen instead went dark. That meant the audience on the other side of her screen had not set their view to see her at all. The setting was for sound only, so she would give them sound.

"Here's the thing, whoever you are. Plausibility is a joke. They've been inept for years. We're forced to dump our data into their sham of a database and endure their direction. We've spent years on research just to watch their gurus, straight out of diapers, make a mess out of everything. They're famous for this. Intelligent life on any planet knows Plausibility moves only on the political winds of the day. They've nothing to offer but the glory of gain by palm greasing."

The screen view returned and featured George, bustling with activity as he stacked papers on his desk. The corners of his mouth twitched.

"I was wrong. It is important that we meet, Dr. Satan, so you can see who you are arguing with." The not-George voice sliced the air with each word.

The female fiend wanted to engage. Bring it on. SJ smiled.

George rolled his chair back and stood. After a moment a face appeared on the screen.

It was Kate.

It couldn't be.

Before SJ could speak, Kate held a finger to her lips. SJ recognized Kate's government-issued masking identifier code in the screen corner. Kate had managed to abate the mask of whoever she impersonated to allow her own face to appear instead.

"Meet Dr.—" George's introduction crackled and wavered. The name blurred indistinct, but the title, "new CEO of Medical Plausibility" broadcast clearly.

The fragmenting connection lasted long enough for SJ to witness a glimpse of the intended impersonation. When Kate's facemask finished transforming, SJ saw a stranger's face. A well-kept woman with fierce gray eyes and shoulder-length blonde hair glared at her. Then the screen went dark.

What was going on? SJ reattempted the connection, but the report indicated insufficient signal. She couldn't believe it. Was Kate alive? The art of masking was strictly forbidden except in the entertainment world. Kate would never agree to any form of illegal use. Maybe she'd been kidnapped and forced to use her skills.

Static sounds popped in the air and then cleared.

"Sorry about that, S. Although you should be grateful it cut out after your rant." George's voice connection came back, but the picture feed remained blank.

Did he know? She tested the water. "I need to see her."

"Who? The CEO from Plausibility? That will be difficult."

"Why?"

"They spliced her in from somewhere. Not from headquarters, either. They said she's on a world tour drumming up consensus."

"So she wasn't in your office?"

"No one here but little old me. Technology's amazing, isn't it?"

"Yep. It's a trick." She tried to piece things together.

"Are you still there?"

"Yes. I'm here." She worked with the settings to bring back the screen view.

"I need you to understand me. I'd rather not move ahead until you're ready, but as you just heard, I'm not in charge of the timeframe. They want to start John Doe trials. The resurrection team meets in the morning, and you're taking the lead."

"Got it. I know it's out of your hands." *But there's more to this than you think.*

"So, everything's clear. Right?" George's sweaty face reappeared on the screen.

"Right."

"Okay. We'll talk again tomorrow after the team meets."

She turned off her wall screen. Nothing made sense, and she needed answers. She sent Cole a message to ask if he knew the CEO of Plausibility.

Cole's answer came back quickly, but he offered no help. "Plausibility is in charge. It's not up to you. Do as you're told, and all will go well. I'll see you at lunch."

No, you won't. Dead or alive, I'm going to find Kate. Then we'll see who's who. She sent back her response. "Working through lunch. We'll meet up later."

CHAPTER 17

SJ HURRIED TO the Abide. A young agent, perhaps even a girl playing dress up in a security uniform, greeted her at the staff entrance and waved her data scanner over SJ's arm. A mechanical voice came from the device. "Access denied."

"Try again. I have clearance."

The girl agent gave an exaggerated sigh and rolled her eyes. "It's never wrong." She swiped her scanner over SJ's arm again. "Access denied."

"Can I talk to your supervisor?"

She shrugged. "Not sure my boss is available. Could take a while."

SJ unclenched her jaw and spoke with exaggerated calm. "I've got all the time in the world."

The young woman frowned and radioed for a replacement guard who appeared almost immediately. After a brief exchange between the two of them, the girl agent entered the Abide.

SJ crossed the walkway and sat a few feet away in the central plaza where she could keep an eye on the entrance. Proof of whether Kate was alive or dead lay on the other side of the door. She had no problem camping out all day. She'd seen Kate's dead body and the final report listing advanced disease conditions that caused Kate's death. Yet less than an hour ago, her best friend's animated face had appeared on her wall screen.

Which is it, Kate? Are you dead or alive?

A cloud of TRIUMP interns swirled past her. Dressed in their standard blues, they moved as one undulating wave. Their carefree demeanor contrasted with the intermixed flow of more somber pedestrians, relatives of those stored in the countless cylinder vaults at the Abide.

Storage of the dead had become a huge and intricate business. Space exploration glory days had at first yielded no other planet but Earth capable of sustaining human life.

But now Meritus had become an alternate refuge for the extinguished but reusable offspring of earth's nurture, and just beyond the sublevel doors of The Abide, the fully prepped, tallied, and cataloged resurrection candidates awaited revival.

"Dr. Satan?" Her persistent gatekeeper ambled toward her.

SJ got up to meet her but not fast enough to elude the stares and whispers of several nearby interns.

"Well?" SJ glared at the interns who seemed to take the cue and hurried off. "Do I have clearance?"

Girl Agent frowned. "It seems there's a problem." She twisted a wavy blonde hair lock that had escaped her olive beret.

"What kind of a problem?"

"Protocol restrictions limit vault visits to authorized medical personnel and council approved designated kin. Your departmental At Will clearance remains denied. If you'd like to set up an appointment for a future visit, I can ask—"

"I'm here in the capacity of council-approved designated kin. I'm not making a department request."

The woman's eyes narrowed. "You are the designated kin of who exactly?"

"Kate Auburn Rigsby." SJ held out her wrist scanner to show the confirmation. "Here's my kinship confirmation."

The security guard backed away as if SJ had begun hemorrhaging. "I'm sorry. I have to see matching confirmation in our system." She tapped on her own wrist scanner. "Nope. I'm showing a designated kin by another name."

"Whose name?"

"I'm sorry. I'm not at liberty to reveal that. You're welcome to chat with my superior and see if there's been a mistake." She spoke in a mechanical, rules-and-regulations voice.

"Of course there's a mistake." Heat flooded SJ's face. "I'm Kate's only kin. Your system is as bungling as you are."

"I'm sorry—"

"Stop saying that. If you were sorry, then you'd clear my visit so I can pay my respects to my dearest friend."

An alarm tone came from the security guard's belt. She switched it off and seemed torn between the duty of the call and SJ.

"Go." SJ barked the command, and the young woman practically jumped to salute her.

SJ softened. "Go do your security stuff. I'm no threat. I'm merely a harmless woman wanting to visit a dead friend. Let's call it a truce. I'm hungry, and our little chitchat has managed to consume most of my lunch break. I'll grab a sandwich while you run away."

Maintaining her stance but now looking uncertain, the woman did not budge, so SJ sauntered toward the café. After a few steps, she turned around to shoo at the agent and the woman took off. SJ took a few more steps toward the café then turned around and spotted the olive-green beret of the guard bobbing along with the crowd. The woman eventually disappeared in a throng of interns headed to the north exit.

"Smart girl. She took your offer and ran. Perhaps I can be of assistance?" A gap in the crowd revealed the source of the deep, slow-paced voice. A man with shockingly red hair, strapped upright in a bot chair, rolled toward her. Dressed in TRIUMP blues, he had a bemused expression on his face.

"Sorry for eavesdropping, but it's not entirely my fault. My hearing adaptive is wonky and amplifies far beyond the usual range." The man's clouded eyes and drifting focus indicated visual difficulties if not complete blindness. He held out his hand. "The illustrious Dr. Satan, I presume?"

"Yes. But I prefer Dr. S, or SJ." Not wanting to be rude, SJ grabbed his extended hand, and a strange heat sensation crept up her arm.

"You can call me Ben." His mouth formed a half smile. The warmth coming from his touch became intense and seared the top of her shoulder. His grip revealed unexpected strength. He let go and glided back a few feet. "I'm cleared for all Abide entrances. I can escort you anywhere you need to go, if you want my help." He swiveled in a half circle and then rolled off in the direction of the Abide.

"I appreciate the offer but—" Caution got the better of her. She wanted to solve the mystery of Kate's appearance on her own.

Ben whirled his bot around and beckoned. "Come on. You told the agent your lunch was almost over. I can help you. But not for free."

"Okay. What do you want?" Surely, he didn't intend to have lunch with her?

He continued to face her as he traveled backward. "I need to settle a question about your father. I'm a huge fan."

Relief came. "Ask away. I'll do my best." Questions about her famous father were familiar intrusions.

Ben turned away from her and rolled forward in the direction of the public entrance. She followed.

They passed through Abide security after Ben's arm scan triggered the confirming Abide logo, a triad of overlapping circles containing three centered flames. The emblem symbolized the hope of resurrection. They entered the lobby, a three-story-high, light-infused sanctuary formed by six converging arches. A larger version of the logo hung in banner form from the ceiling.

Ben navigated around clusters of people huddled in front of specific media wall panels watching film montage tributes of their deceased loved ones.

SJ followed him through the southeast arch into a perimeter hallway.

He stopped under a skylight. "Here's a quiet spot to tell me what I want to know."

"What is it?"

"A little history matter I want to settle about your father, Dr. Satanopoulos. Some say that he will be the first human resurrected in honor of his discovery of the Resurrection Principle. Others say that he refused to donate his body for resurrection purposes, because he found religion at the end of his life."

"The latter is most certainly incorrect." Her father's last-minute turn to religion was a shameful secret she fought hard to keep.

"Then my guess is confirmed. I've read his later works, and they suggest he became less concerned with the existence of God and more interested in why humans believe in one. He also refused to become a resurrection candidate for fear that people would begin treating resurrected humans as mini-gods."

SJ nodded. "You are correct. Society's advance in knowledge, strengthened by more recent decades of scientific research, debunked eras of reliance on religious belief to explain the unexplainable. Had my father lived to see this dramatic shift take place, I believe he would have chosen differently about becoming a resurrection candidate."

Ben beamed and swished his hand through the air. "There. I got what I need. Now, what about you? Is there something more I can do?"

SJ gazed back at the groups of huddled mourners. Should she let him go? He would believe she was there to grieve for a friend. But then there was still the matter of her clearance. Several security checks still remained.

"It was nice to meet you." Ben jutted his hand out in her direction, but she did not take it.

Her heart raced. "I need to get to the modules."

"Okay then." Ben's mouth twitched. "My arm is at your service."

He spun his chair around and moved to a nearby maintenance elevator, which they took to a half floor. From there they entered the Maze, a labyrinth part of the Abide which connected to the bowels of the surrounding medical complex. Zigzagging through a strategic selection of corridors saved time and allowed them to avoid the overabundance of security checks on the major floors. SJ remembered some of the twists and turns from her college days.

Soon they reached the expansive sublevel where the module banks stretched out in rows.

Ben stopped at the end of the first row. "Here we are."

Thousands of cylinder storage machines hummed, drowning all other sound. SJ pursed her lips and whispered, "I'm not sure I should do this, but I need to know the truth."

"Then know. Choose truth." Ben had heard. He rolled down the row. "Living in ignorance is the same as living with lies."

"You're right." She followed him. "What about the cylinder lock?"

"I'll run a thermo test scan. It's part of my job here. I perform them weekly on random cylinders to check proficiency. I can check your cylinder of interest as part of normal routine."

"Why are you helping me?"

"I have my reasons, but foremost, I admire your father." Ben tapped on his bot chair screen and drew up a list of resurrection candidates and their location in the modules.

She found Kate's name. "I should do it. I don't want your position jeopardized. If we're caught, you can claim you simply showed me the cylinder. I asked, and you thought I had permission."

"If that's what you want." Ben moved on.

They passed several rows and headed down a third. When they reached Kate's cylinder, she placed her hand on the cold exterior. "What would you do?"

"It's not my decision, but here's one way to look at it. Either Kate's body is here or it's not. If it's not, then something must be done. I'll keep a lookout." Ben rolled several yards away.

She hesitated but then selected 'thermo test scan' on the control.

The test sequence began. Kate's cylinder cap illuminated. Temperature readings on the dial began to fluctuate. SJ's heart raced. She kept her hand over the reset switch in case errant variations triggered the alarm. Numbers continued to stream in micro increments on the digital display, as calibrations sought consensus.

It was taking too long.

Perhaps she could determine cylinder occupancy another way. She hit reset and looked for something to pry up the cap. A transfer rod rested at the module base. She hesitated.

"Don't. Damage too … my skills … high … regard." The prevailing noise of technology muffled Ben's words.

"What did you say?"

Ben rolled back to her. "I said my skills at lock picking are highly regarded." He smiled.

"Can you deactivate the lock without setting off the alarm?"

"With your help." He came close and held out his hand.

She placed his palm on top of the cap screen and watched as he took control of the process. Without tangible key distinction, the smooth glass screen offered no usable method for a person with limited sight to verify the entry sequence.

Seconds after he started, an icon of a switch labeled *Finish* changed color from orange to green, indicating success. The cylinder cap swung slightly open, and vapor poured out. The air cleared, and Ben reached inside. When he pulled out his hand, he turned and rolled out of the way, gesturing for SJ to step forward.

She approached and reached inside. The space was vacant where the inner cylinder should be. "It's empty." A sick feeling flooded her stomach.

"Yes. I'm sorry about that. I noticed abnormal readings when I started the sequence but wanted to be sure."

Before she could respond, he shoved her aside and fumbled with the cylinder cap. "We're about to have company." He removed something from inside the cap and pressed it into her hand.

Three figures moved toward them from the far end of the aisle. One moved ahead of the others.

It was Cole.

She wanted to run but focused instead on positioning the cap into its fitting seal.

"Act normal. You were only helping me with a test." Ben spoke in a calm, low voice as he completed the reset sequence.

Her chest tightened when Cole came close. The rage on his face spelled caution. "We need to talk." He grabbed her by the arm and twisted sharply.

"Of course we do." She kept her voice congenial. "But first I want you to meet someone." She turned to introduce Ben but found he'd disappeared.

"Move. Now," Cole barked.

Her fingers closed tight around the rolled paper as he pushed her past the two approaching Abide security guards.

"It's okay, guys. I've got her. I'll take her to second level for interrogation."

The guards looked at each other and then nodded and left the area.

At first, Cole's icy demeanor registered as less important than her feeling of panic over what had happened to Kate. God only knew what awful scheme was taking place. Mounting evidence of criminal interference seemed inescapable.

But then something else happened. As she allowed Cole to propel her through the Abide, a new sensation washed over her. It slowed her heart rate and relaxed her gut. Anxious thoughts began to shrink and even seemed ambiguous.

What was it?

Nothing about her circumstances had changed. All her problems still stormed around her. Yet, if she could give the sensation a name, then she would label it "calmness."

Why did she feel calm?

She had no reason to be. The body of the dearest person to her was missing. In addition, Cole's anger and ruling ways pressed in on her.

What changed?

"The word, god."

The odd explanation came as another voice intermixed with her own thoughts.

It was true. She had thought it. 'God only knew what awful scheme is taking place ...'

Impossible. She'd never credit a god for anything, because she did not believe in a god. Yet, no one near her had made the suggestion. Considering the events going on in her life, she should feel panicked. Maybe she'd reached the mental state that existed beyond panic. Insanity.

"No, you're calm." The not-a-voice declared her condition again, and her self-analyst agreed.

Then another statement came.

"Ben is wrong. Knowing answers and pursuing truth are not the same venture. One quest seeks conclusions, and the other harnesses forces with hope and trust. The question is, which pursuit will you follow?"

"Truth." She spoke the answer aloud without hesitation. She'd lived long enough to see how ego and pride delivered many fake conclusions. Discovered or not, proven or not, truth still existed. And for the first time in her life, despite circumstances, she could feel the closeness of it. She suddenly wanted to pursue truth no matter where it took her. "Truth. I choose truth." The phrase fell out of her mouth unbidden.

Cole's grip tightened. His touch burned fiery hot. "Choose whatever you want, dear. It makes no difference. All that matters is that you honor our partnership."

They got off the elevator, but not on the second floor.

"Let's go." He gave her a push, and she staggered forward into the swirl of humanity inside the lobby. Even in their short history together, she'd become accustomed to his temper. She hoped that if she walked willingly, he'd soon defuse.

His vise-like grip remained on her arm as they passed through the lobby and then outside, where a group of anti-relocation protestors chanted their grievance. After clearing the mob, he released her and spoke into his wrist scanner, calling for his car. His black Aquilos moved from a switch rail and into the pickup lane, gliding to where they stood.

Cole opened the back door. Their eyes met. In the moment they dueled, she stood firm. She knew Cole wanted her to feel intimidated, but her silence defied him.

He broke first. “Get in.”

She slid in, and he slammed the door and got into the driver’s seat.

While his focus diverted to the auto controls, she slipped out the paper she’d gotten from Ben. Tears flooded her eyes when she read the words. “Choose truth. Book of Wisdom 43.14.6.”

No human mind could have anticipated her thoughts and placed such a message. She hid the paper and shifted back on the seat, but the movement brought intense pain. She felt her shoulder and discovered an injector stuck on her upper arm. “Stop, Cole. Something’s wrong.” She clenched her jaw and yanked it off her arm. It was empty.

“Yes. Something is wrong. We’ve got to get out of here.”

The car’s acceleration pressed her back into the seat. She struggled to hold up the dosing mechanism. Her vision blurred and then cleared. Propofylozine. And enough of a dose to put a four-hundred-pound gorilla to sleep. She weighed only one hundred forty-five pounds.

A thought floated in and out of her consciousness like a butterfly. Who wanted her dead?

CHAPTER 18

THE AQUILOS HEADED north out of the city. After it crossed the river, Cole switched the drive mode to emergency, and the Aquilos accelerated to maximum allowable speed.

SJ's motionless form remained slumped across the back seat. Was she breathing? He checked the life alert screen. The display showed her biochip readings. Her breaths were in the lower numbers but not out of normal range.

His impatience had gotten the better of him, but drugging SJ was more expedient than constantly having to persuade or manipulate her to follow his plans. Free will was the worst thing Mortar had ever allowed for his creatures.

He was certain of one thing. SJ's preoccupation with finding Kate was likely Rumi's doing. Rumi knew exactly what motivated another human's heart. Her skill rivaled that of any of his heralds. His plan to craft SJ into a tool for his purposes had been foolproof, but Rumi cared little for resurrection and the possibilities it brought to grow the kingdom. She insisted that deceit and manipulation were more trustworthy methods than his plan—planting their kind in newly resurrected humans. She obsessed over proving him wrong.

Anger pulsed in his temples and caused his skin to radiate fiery hues onto the console beside him. Rumi had grown increasingly independent and proud, flaunting her opposition to his plans on several matters. He would have to find new ways to coerce her or remove her from the Conquering entirely.

He fidgeted with the controls attempting to push the speed past maximum.

The car slowed.

Cursing, he hit the control with his open palm.

A warning sounded. "Checkpoint ahead. Option to select or resume."

He selected the connection to the cross-country underground. Maybe today he'd be lucky. Or maybe he'd abandon the sluggish travel of human autorail and travel instead by celestial methods. He longed for the day when who he was and what he could do would be out in the open, and all mankind would fear him.

The car shifted off the autorail and into the long checkpoint line. He seethed and turned over plans of destruction as he waited. When a trickle of smoke wafted across his lap, he startled back to his current reality and discovered the side seam in the chair upholstery had melted apart. He punched in a medic alert on the console. He needed to speed things up.

A traffic worker approached.

"My partner's in trouble." He yelled to be heard above the roar of engines launching into the tunnel. "We're headed to her treatment center."

"You're closer to the Abide. Turn back. You'll get help quicker."

Not a chance, idiot. I need her in my territory. Cole worked on his best composure and managed a reasoning tone. "She's part of a new treatment at Kerioth Medical. Sedation is the only thing that keeps her seizures at bay until we get there." Cole produced SJ's wrist scanner which confirmed him as her designated kin.

"Right away, sir. Let me pull up the connecting exit clearance for you." The young man punched away at his database screen.

A traffic captain appeared and directed Cole to pull out of the line.

Cole fumed about the man's incompetence and whipped the car onto the parking pad.

The traffic captain reappeared at his window. "I'm sorry, sir. Checking the location of Kerioth Medical. It does not appear to have any connection entrance to the tunnel. Perhaps there's an alternate name?"

"Look up SHEOL. It's part of SHEOL, man." He spoke through clenched teeth and gripped the edges of his disheveled seat to keep his hands from strangling the man.

"Sheeool?"

"Yes." Sarcasm set in. "SHEOL. DCN headquarters. Ever heard of the company? It's mine, actually. I'm sure you noticed my title when you pulled up my registration. We operate all the speedrails in every region of Meritus and run the largest shipping and energy infrastructure in the universe. Check again. S H E O L–Subterrain Hub of Energy Offices and Living domains. My headquarters! MY BUSINESS!" He ended up shouting after all.

The captain tapped rapidly on his wrist scanner.

Cole's focus shifted to SJ. Had she moved?

"Good news. It's here." The stupid man thrust his arm through the window to show the destination on his screen display.

Cole slapped the man's arm out of the way. "Of course it's there. Now let's see what else you can jumble up. I need a medic. Does LPR keep a responder at this station?"

"You betcha." The man talked into his data screen. "LPR to park pad pronto."

The checkpoint station door opened, and a tall man dressed in LPR garb approached. "What's up?"

The traffic captain waved at Cole. "This man needs a medic."

"Not me. Her." Cole pointed to SJ in the back seat and stepped out of the car. "Do you have a sedometer? My partner's sedation level is crucial. If she wakes up while we are in the tunnel, her seizures will return. She was dosed before we left, but I need to know if her sed sats are still suitable for our timeframe. If not, I'll need a sleeper for when she wakes up."

"I'll see if we have a sedometer in the station. They've changed outfits, so I'm not sure. It might take a minute."

Cole nodded. "A minute's all you've got. I'll be in the head."

When both men were out of range, he moved to the bathroom dais outlined on the pavement. He had to take the chance. Transmissions turned sketchy underground.

With his feet planted on the marked footprints, he waited for his weight to trigger the surrounding walls. Outside engine noises muffled as the enclosure sealed completely around him, and a grungy commode and sink rose from their designated blocks.

He activated his scanner and input his orders. "Team alert. Initiating Alpha. Repeat. Begin Alpha. SJ to arrive shortly at SHEOL. Prepare for alternate resurrection plan. Confirmation from the Life Preservation and Resource Council by Contrell will follow. Dr. Birch cleared to serve as team leader or assist, dependent on SJ's cooperation. Execute measures necessary to ensure resurrection trials begin in SHEOL as I have instructed."

He paused to review the details and then added, "please confirm receipt of this update." After several seconds, affirmations chimed and showed on his screen except for two, Rumi and Lucas.

"Sir?" Someone tapped on the bathroom enclosure.

He slapped the commode switch and then punched the wall retraction command. Rumi and Lucas' delayed response spelled trouble. Where were they, and more importantly, what were they up to?

The LPR responder stood outside holding a sedometer. "Your passenger is out cold. Might move around a bit, but she won't remember anything. What did you say she was given?"

"I didn't." Cole hurried to the car.

The persistent responder followed him. "The sed rate displayed at the highest level."

"I think it was called Propo something or other."

"Well, her chances for waking up are zilch. At least for a while. Maybe half a day. I'm gonna give you this antidote in case you see her O2 levels drop. The car's life alert stats should monitor that. Do you know how to use the feature?"

Cole stopped and glared at the dutiful man. "Done this before. Several times. As long as she's under, then we're good for the trip." He grabbed the antidote from the man's hand and jumped in the car. He made a show of leaning over the seat to evaluate SJ as any designated kin would do.

The responder walked off.

Despite his relief, Cole's larger aggravation remained. Repeated requests for confirmation from Rumi and Lucas went unanswered. The rest of his band could see this result. Compliant team members usually took action against the ones who delayed their response, ensuring that the whole group performed his wishes.

When his car finally came into first position again at the tunnel entrance, a DCN trainee took his fingerprint and then offered, "Godspeed."

Cole's breath froze. At the undesired salutation, a cough erupted in fierce spasms. Before he could seal the window shut, he heard the traffic captain chide the trainee. "You fool. Don't you know who you are dealing with?"

He savored what he could between hacking eruptions. The captain's acknowledgement showed he was one of his own, after all. A small comfort. But the bumbling idiot reminded him of how quickly delivery expansions had grown. Rapid DCN development had left recruit training incomplete and sloppy. If allowed to continue, the neglect would become a serious weakness in his empire. Morbid would have to step up his game and prioritize the education process.

As robotic mechanisms jerked the car into the darkness, the rumble of pavement noise gave way to the quiet rush of speed. He watched the route progress on the dash screen.

After descending a quarter of a mile into the tunnel from the entry point, the auto veered onto the main route heading west.

Expedient but dull, underground journeys were best broken of their monotony by companions and conversation. Sparring with SJ would be unlikely. If traffic delays stayed at a minimum, then there was more than enough time to travel the eighteen-hundred-mile distance between Sector Seven and SHEOL before dinner.

He reclined the seat and reluctantly closed his eyes. At night, he usually dreamt of nothing. His daydreams, however, were another story.

A familiar chime came from his wrist. He glanced at the screen and read Rumi's response. "All is well." Her beautiful lie spelled trouble.

Cole wasted no time when he got to Kerioth. He delivered SJ, still unconscious, to waiting staff and assigned Morbid to play doctor.

Then, he flew to the spa. The glorious use of his wings soothed his frustration. Alighting on the rooftop of the parlor, he melded through the tiles and settled beside a grate in the ceiling, his window into the salon.

Rumi sat on the serpentine lounger below him and scrolled through fashion news on her data screen. Her latest convert, an auburn-haired model in her late twenties, slept beside her. The scene reflected the image of best friends, but Cole knew the woman rested in a drugged stupor, lured to her choice by Rumi.

Inflicting punishment was all he cared about. He dropped through the ceiling into the shadows of the laundry room and exhaled sharply in anticipation. The air current around him recoiled, creating a vacuum that allowed the unbolted sauna door to swing fully open.

At the sound, Rumi came alive. She sprinted for the sauna and closed the door behind her.

He laughed. "Really, dear? You would hide in there?"

"The deception was Lucas's doing." Her voice reverberated all around. "He said you're misguided. Resurrection is uncharted territory. Soul oppression and possession are our proven strength."

"He is not in charge. I am!" Cole levitated a shelf full of nail polish bottles and hurled it against the door. Dripping color christened the frame. In rapid succession, he sent three more shelves of nail polish crashing against the door. Splintering glass punctuated his roar. "You. Will. Do. As. I. Command."

Destruction usually satisfied him, but today he needed more, and Rumi needed a lasting reminder. He reached for the sauna control knob, and his touch evoked arcing electricity. Tongues of fire erupted and lapped at the wood paneling. Burning was a risky venture. Rumi's mortality provided only a fragile boundary. He withdrew his hand, and the flames died down.

He didn't want her dead. He wanted her cooperation. He seized a lounge chair and sent it orbiting into a massage room. It crumpled against the wall and left a caved-in depression from the force.

The lethargic woman on the couch moved and mumbled something.

His focus shifted to her. Of course. She would pay too. In a sudden swoop, he jerked the couch up by one end and toppled the woman onto the floor. She awoke, half crazed and reached for his help.

Cole laughed as he grabbed her hand. Contact with him would burn her.

Sure enough, the woman winced and cried out, "Why are you hurting me?"

"Leave her be, Cole. You have no right to her!" Rumi spoke from behind him.

He whirled around and lunged to seize her, but instead found himself thrown back to the wall. Her shield was impenetrable. She held the book.

"Why did you do it? Why did you lure SJ with Kate?"

"To prove my point. A beautiful lie is what manipulates. SJ left her work to follow a lie." Rumi caressed the book. "Mortar's words with a twist. A lie worked at the beginning of time, and it will be our success at the end. Your displays of force and power only create fear. Fear is what sends them back to Mortar."

"They banned his book. They don't care about his words." Cole brushed the top of each shoulder causing his wings to meld back into his arms. "They will soon be running to me."

"You forget, dear brother, they are wired for his words. Even when his words are no longer near, he speaks to them in the echoes of their world—the world he created. Now they're hearing his words again in the messages from Five."

Cole pointed to the book. "Put it down. I command you."

Rumi stepped back and shook her head. "You'll only destroy it. Then we'll not be able to twist the truth, which we must do with relentless resolve and ever so carefully, to make them believe our words instead of Mortar. Father predicted your impulsive rage would doom our success if it remained uncurbed. I'll not party with your childish need for power."

Cole roared. He swept his hand through the air, and products resting on shelves around the room became airborne. Then with a quick upward flick of his wrist he sent them spiraling to the ceiling.

The woman shrieked and scuttled to the corner where she crouched in a fetal position and covered her head.

Cole pointed to the ground, and everything fell, smashing down.

Clutching the book, Rumi held her stance and remained unscathed.

Finally, in a false appeal to her mercy, Cole collapsed at her feet, gripped her ankles and groveled, "Please, Rumi. I need this. You'll see. SJ will raise bodies to hold the souls of our kingdom troops, and father Beast will rule again. All will be astounded and easily led."

Rumi bent over, pulled away his hands, and then lifted his chin with one finger.

He saw his prize, the book, melded together with her other hand and arm. Attacking her now was of no use.

She spoke softly as a child. “Mortar will never allow it. His breath alone gives life.”

He stumbled to a standing position. The book’s presence affected his balance. “How do we know that’s true? Maybe life is not singularly evoked by his power.” He brushed glass shards off his suit and tugged at the tattered hem of his jacket. “Mortar declared this world as our kingdom.”

Ducking to catch his reflection in a piece of mirror still attached to the wall, he finger-combed his hair. “We’ll never know unless we try. Science has advanced to this place, and humanity is ready to receive it. The timing couldn’t be more perfect.”

“And if resurrection fails or the ruse is discovered?” Rumi extended a hand to the trembling model, willing her to see only a drug-induced nightmare.

“It won’t. I know how to tell a beautiful lie as well. Besides, who would disclose it? SJ would be considered a lunatic, and no one from our team would sacrifice their position. Tainting DCN’s reputation would affect all our alliances and push our strategy back to the Dark Ages.”

The woman sobbed loudly. “Oh God. Please don’t hurt me.”

Rumi righted a toppled chair and gestured for the woman to sit. Hesitant, she approached, and Rumi picked up a shawl from the floor and wrapped it around the pitiful figure. Then Rumi stepped over the wreckage and filled a cup with water at a broken sink. She offered the refreshment to the woman, who gulped and stared at them, wild-eyed. When the woman finished drinking, Rumi took the cup and rested it on the upended couch. Then she handed her guest an eye mask and pushed her into a reclined beauty chair, all the while soothing her protests. “Sleep. You’re having a dream.”

Cole watched as the skillful persuasion unfolded. Rumi undoubtedly mastered the art. He needed her help, but commanding his sibling had never worked. “Rumi, you’ll have a grand place in the kingdom. All that is beautiful will be under your direction. Think about it. After Father’s resurrection, the Conquering will be certain.”

Rumi stepped into the nearest treatment room. Her voice held firm. "I disagree. Resurrection is a gamble that's unnecessary and only feeds your pride. Why must you keep grasping for the freewill choice of a human? Without use of oppression or possession, it's risky business."

"Mortar does it. They freely choose him. Our side is equally capable."

"You're too proud. You loathe human free will, yet you still want them to choose us without applying influence. Can't you see that without our manipulation, free will repeatedly rises to block our Conquering?"

"Why is my desire to have humankind freely choose our path such an impossibility in your mind?"

"Because of Mortar's words. Because of this." Rumi separated the book from her chest and held it out ever so slightly. "Our words alone, without combining a distortion of his words, do not compel. His words are unmatched."

"That may be true for the past. But now, by my hand and SJ's skill, resurrection will convince the world to adopt our ways without ever again reflecting on his. Our kingdom will surpass Mortar's."

Rumi seemed to be regarding his proposal. If he quickly added one more detail, he knew he could pull her in completely. False apology and appealing to her pride often worked well. "Taking SJ by force was a mistake, but you contributed. I was angry when I discovered your ruse and how quickly she could be led off course. Now, I must concede. You're the expert with the beautiful lie. Please help me delude her again, and then, after Father's resurrection, I promise we'll discuss a plan together. Think of it. We'll be three again. Father, you, and me. United we'll conquer everything, and all for our kingdom. What do you say, Rumi? Please?"

Rumi smiled. His beautiful lie worked.

CHAPTER 19

SJ WILLED HERSELF to see, but eyelids made of stone would not open. Then a curtain lifted, and her view filled with three flickering shapes moving about in front of a tan oblong outlined by light.

"I'll give her more antidote now."

A cool, aching pain crept up her side. She tried to turn her head to identify the voice and instead found ceiling lights. She counted eight fixtures. Her focus dropped to eye level, and she discovered Cole's face and another just above him, a person whose features reminded her of an Afghan hound.

Cole loomed close and picked up the hand resting nearby on the covers. Her hand? The sensation registered as dull, clumsy pressure.

Voices morphed into indistinct mumbles. Her gaze shifted back to the tan oblong wall piece framed by light. She felt certain it held a clue that explained her surreal experience. After a time when nothing identifiable came to mind, she made an attempt to form words. "Where … am … I?"

"Room 106. Kerioth Medical. I brought you to SHEOL after the sabotage attempt."

"Someone … drugged me." She searched Cole's face for a reaction.

"Yes, dearest." His eyes, inky pools of expressionless sight, held no warmth.

She could feel his touch now and managed to pull away. "It was you. You … are ... a … madman." The effort of speaking made her bold.

Cole's eyes rimmed with fire. "You're delusional. Why would I want to harm you?"

A new voice spoke. "The sabotage involved anti-relocation sympathizers in the Abide. Protestors outside the entrance provided a distraction. They are the likely culprits."

SJ followed the sound and discovered Rumi's presence at the end of her bed.

"Kate's cylinder is empty …" SJ struggled to recall.

"Part of the protest." Rumi switched places with Cole. "Authorities discovered several microtherm cylinders shifted around, and some unoccupied. The group taking responsibility said it was symbolic of the cruelty of sector relocation. Authorities initiated a lockout."

"But why … here?"

"For your protection. Medical Plausibility gave orders to extract all resurrection team members and question them for sabotage connections. Because of your condition, they cleared you for transport to a secure location for treatment. Cole brought you here by undersurface connections." Rumi patted her hand and delivered the details as if a newscaster pronounced them.

SJ strained to review the sequence that led to her current state. Kate had appeared on her media wall at the conference with George and then masked herself as the CEO of Plausibility. Then she'd found Kate's empty microtherm cylinder and remembered pulling the injector out of her arm in Cole's car.

Rumi stepped aside, and the Afghan hound face reappeared. He shone a pinpoint of light in her eye, and her throbbing head pain intensified. The dogface person had patches of wispy hair and smelled sour like rotten apples.

"I'm Dr. Morbeed, head of Neuro." The odd man chuckled. Then he proceeded to lift her legs in alternate succession and let them fall. Try as she might, she could not hold them up at his command.

"It's okay." Dr. Dogface grinned at her. "You velly, velly lucky anyway." His expression revealed gaps formed by missing teeth on his right side. "You got shot with neutrino toxin. It paralyzes most of the body's systems. We give you antidote in time. Soon you feel better. Hallucinate some more, but maybe not." He tapped in data onto the headboard chart and then adjusted her Veniflow. When he finished, he unhooked a cane from the bedside and walked hunched over to the door.

Cole followed and exchanged words with him at the doorway. SJ strained to hear the conversation, but all noise seemed to be part of one symphonic song projecting in muffled tones from the room's walls.

The strange hallucination left SJ feeling uncertain about her mind. Tears came. She willed her hand to wipe away the moisture, but the stream continued unbidden down her cheek and gathered under her chin.

Cole returned to her bedside. "I'm leaving you in Rumi's capable hands. She'll take you to Mi Manera when you leave. Remember? I spoke of it. Our home is here in SHEOL. You'll be safe here. We are eighteen hundred miles away from your attackers."

SJ struggled to speak her intention of returning to Sector Seven, but her mouth refused to form coherent words.

The two siblings exchanged nods. SJ sensed the gesture meant something important. Darkness swept over her. She closed her eyes. Lulled by the unseen orchestra that filled the air, she slept.

When she awoke, she remembered everything again. This time her muscles moved at will. Cheered, she looked for someone to communicate with about her progress and found Rumi standing beyond the bed facing the oblong wall box. Her hands moved with the music that filled the air, or perhaps her hands created the music, because the notes grew louder or softer or changed rhythm with her motions.

"How are you doing that?" SJ spoke loud and clear.

Rumi turned and tapped on her wrist screen. "With this. You like? It's my invention. I select a song and conduct a bit of it just once. The next time I gesture, it remembers. I can alter the tempo, tone, and theme with a wave of my hand. The box will even continue to play without me if I want."

As if to demonstrate this, Rumi came to SJ's bedside while the music persisted.

SJ struggled to sit. With Rumi's help, her limbs obeyed.

"See. It's working. I play for your healing." Rumi twirled around, half-dancing and gesturing, and her motions yielded a trombone warble. Then she circled her hand above her head and the effect prompted a flute-like trill to pierce the air, tremble in place, and then finally meld into the more haunting undertones of woodwinds and brass.

When the last chords died down, SJ applauded.

Rumi made a little bow.

"What do you call it?"

"Oh, I didn't invent the piece. It's Symphony Fantastique. I played it often to soothe my father when he lived."

"No, I mean … what's the name of the wall box that the music comes from?"

"It doesn't have a name yet. Cole's spin team names and promotes whatever he wishes, including every beautiful thing I dream up to be in our kingdom." A faraway look passed over Rumi's features.

"So, it's true." SJ grimaced as the dull pain returned to her side. "You two are planning to take over the world together."

Rumi's eyebrows furrowed. She rushed over and grabbed SJ's hands. "Please don't tell Cole you found out the plan from me."

"What plan? What are you saying? I'm only making a joke."

Rumi snorted and laughed with excess energy. "Of course you are. Besides, it takes more than two to build a kingdom. Three is much better. Won't you join us?"

SJ nodded absently but focused on the new melody that now began to play in her brain, the one where truth reconvened and posed a question. If something sounded too good to be true, then it was the opposite. Right?

While Rumi created more music, SJ worked on a plan to free herself from the web of deceit that seemed to be expanding all around her.

CHAPTER 20

EIGHT HOURS LATER, an aide brought SJ her belongings and said she was discharged. SJ immediately began searching her clothes for her wrist scanner but without success. "I was wearing it. Why isn't it here?"

"Everything you wore on admission is in the bag." The aide seemed unconcerned.

"No. My wrist scanner is not. I never take it off. Please check again to see if it's mentioned in my admit survey." She needed it to contact George and retrace her steps. Based on proximity and time selected, the scanner kept a record of the biochips of any people she encountered. Anyone close enough to slap an injector on her when she was leaving the Abide could be pinpointed. She would turn the chip numbers over to the police for identification. Whoever drugged her might also be linked to the messages.

The aide left the room, and SJ dug through her clothing all over again. Nothing. Except for the message. The one Ben handed her after he found it in Kate's empty microtherm cylinder.

She unfolded the paper. "Choose truth. Book of Wisdom 43.14.6." Truth? The truth was, someone had drugged her, and someone had stolen Kate's body, or Kate was alive.

She examined the writing. Any hack could generate a machine message, but handwriting suggested another story. Identifying a group of religious fanatics who referenced an archaic book of beliefs and didn't care for Cole seemed important, but locating her missing wrist scanner took priority. She tucked the message safely away in her jacket and slipped it on.

The aide returned and informed her that no record of a wrist scanner appeared on her admit survey.

SJ dangled the replacement scanner she'd received. "Explain this. Someone attached this to me when I was unconscious. It should show a completed security sync when my hospital records officially started thirteen hours ago."

"The hospital provided it at someone's request as soon as you were brought in, I guess." The aide shrugged her shoulders and tackled her duties of collecting bed linens.

SJ grabbed one corner of the blanket and held firm.

The aide tugged the blanket free.

SJ's head pounded. "That's fine, but no one gets a replacement scanner without syncing from an original. Security protocol. Unless I find the wrist scanner I came in with, I'm stranded. None of my personal data or connections are on this one." She removed the band. "It's useless to me." She tossed the replacement on the bed.

"Perhaps those in charge were more concerned with your treatment." The aide's voice rang with sarcasm. "The admit survey shows that a sync was declined. Apparently, no scanner to sync from. They duplicated the important stuff like your medical data from your designated kin's records."

The aide's theory rang a familiar tune. Cole. Alternate plans were his specialty. As her designated kin, he could supply details concerning her identity. But if he had her scanner, why would he decline a security sync? It made no sense.

"It's a huge inconvenience for me." She tried her best to keep a reasonable tone. "I'm sure you can understand. I need my personal scanner to access my contacts."

"I'm sorry. You can fill out a missing items form, and security will be alerted."

"I'll think about it." SJ sat on the end of the newly stripped bed and massaged her temples. Sharp twinges on both sides made her head spin.

The aide placed the remains of her room stay, including dishes, linens, and medical paraphernalia into the appropriate chutes. "Do you need me to issue a transport request?"

"No, thanks. Mine is on the way."

"All right. Take your time. Just push the discharge button on the wall outside the door so that Room Prep can attend after you leave. Otherwise, the room door self-locks at 17:00. There's no rush."

After the aide left, SJ searched the room one last time. Finding her missing scanner was urgent. Misplaced or stolen, either way, somewhere between the Abide and her arrival at Kerioth Medical, her ability to connect with her team had disappeared. Sabotage contingency measures were put in place when the Resurrection Project was first initiated. However, nothing detailed how she was to proceed after being secretly fortressed in an underground facility miles away from the rest of the team. She needed answers, but all she had were questions.

She pushed the discharge button and left the room. Navigation wall screens illuminated as she passed, as well as many picture windows. Nothing real, of course, only virtual scenery. How could Cole's workers live this way? The fabrications underscored the high regard people had for pretense. Cole gave them what they wanted. Patients at Kerioth Medical and residents of SHEOL could easily forget they lived and recuperated underground. He'd explained the concept of SHEOL when they first met. The unprecedented subterranean architectural gem combined DCN's primary office headquarters with a massive, and entirely robotic, product and energy fuel distribution center. Kerioth Medical was added later so that every aspect of human need could be met on location.

To her, none of the illusion changed the fact that SHEOL remained cocooned inside tons and tons of rock and dirt held back by manmade barriers, all to protect Cole's interests. She should find comfort in this protection, but instead she longed to feel the winds from the sky and the warmth of the sun to keep her frayed nerves in check.

Following the wall screen directions, she descended three stories to reach the lobby. Once there, she pushed past throngs of people standing in a snake-shaped line without apparent end or beginning. Some wore masks and hospital garb.

She evaluated the room for a less crowded corner. She caught sight of Rumi and waved.

Rumi rushed toward her. "Are you ready to leave?"

"What are they lined up for?" SJ gestured to the crowd.

"Resurrection assignment. Cole's campaign to supply you with new resurrection candidates. Isn't it wonderful?"

"No. We already have candidates. At the Abide. Who does Cole think he is?" Her temples now pounded with relentless throbbing pain.

Rumi frowned. "I guess you've not heard. Because of the sabotage attempt, Cole's making a case before the council for the resurrection trials to take place in Kerioth. He's even securing more candidates by offering SHEOL families double the compensation set by Plausibility. Terminally ill workers or family members can sign a waiver to stop medical treatment and sign on as a resurrection candidate. Cole's marketing team explained how the dying process ends disease elements and resurrection brings a fresh start."

"He has no right to execute any of this. I'm the team leader. His actions are unauthorized," SJ barked at Rumi, who gasped and began frantically tapping on her wrist scan device, likely alerting Cole.

SJ realized her mistake. Mustering as much calmness as she could, she changed tactics. "I'm sorry. I didn't mean to snap at you. Cole's so efficient, and I can't even connect to my team." She reached to touch Rumi's extravagant scanner. "May I?"

"Do you like it?" Rumi took the bait and excitedly showed SJ the scanner features and how the tricolor gold casing resembled an object of art, which emulated her design firm's quest to marry fashion with function in order to elevate everyday objects.

"It's beautiful. My own is ugly but functional. Except now its lost or stolen." Or Cole had it. "The hospital gave me a basic replacement from their stash, but it has only general contacts. It will be difficult to use."

Rumi took off the scanner and held it out to SJ. "Take mine. If it helps, I will give it to you. It will have some of the contacts you need, and Cole will have the rest. He will meet us in Mi Manera."

SJ accepted. Without the device, Rumi would be prevented from contacting Cole. At least for the moment, and she needed to buy time to figure out her strategy.

Rumi adjusted the strap. "There. It looks good on you. I'll have another one made for myself. Now that you're family, it's my job to see that you have only the best. Okay?"

SJ nodded, but she knew no amount of gold could erase her frustration. Somehow, she kept missing the truth and had been taken in by lies. She would prove it and escape this deadly pattern.

CHAPTER 21

THE MORENCI FLEW through the main tunnel toward the dwelling structures. If only her life would follow in as straightforward a path. SJ took a deep breath and then exhaled. Nothing made sense. She turned her focus to the blur of a tunnel wall outside her window. Dr. Morbeed insisted clarity would come sooner if she stayed relaxed. Hiding underneath a mountain of rock didn't help. She needed to get back to the surface. Sector Seven. Her lab. Her territory. Perhaps then, she'd discover what she'd missed.

All she had now was a confusing set of facts and questions and no useful answers. Who had drugged her, and where was Kate? Was Cole responsible, or was it another person, perhaps the same one leaving her cryptic messages?

"Are you all right?" Rumi's voice broke through her fog of uncertainty.

"I'm fine." *Mind reader.* She needed something to divert Rumi's keen sense of intuition.

"No, you're not."

"I'm just wondering about something. How do people stand it?"

"Stand what?"

"No sunlight."

"SHEOL workers are used to it." Rumi switched the map to the menu on the car's console screen.

"Aren't they endangering their life quality?"

"Relying on the sun has long been unnecessary. One of the many reasons Cole built SHEOL is to prove this over time. Everything needed to sustain a good life is just a matter of technology." She pointed to a list of musical selections. "Should I play something?"

Remembering how Rumi adored music, SJ nodded her approval.

As a melody filled the interior, Rumi explained how it synchronized with periodic receptors in the tunnel, which then triggered specific displays of virtual outdoor scenery on the walls.

The effect soon developed, and SJ's window view went from stone to famous scenic byways. None of it cheered her because, apart from the occasional illuminated vista, all that brightened the rest of the tunnel corridor was a subdued dusk-like glow from ceiling light strips. Even worse, in places where the lights had burned out completely, the tunnel remained exactly as expected, a pitch-dark cave.

A few minutes later, the music crackled into a jarring sound. Rumi tapped the console screen and fiddled with the signal receiver, but it did not help. The static muffled into a rhythmic pattern like that of cresting ocean waves.

The throbbing hum settled into SJ's chest and pressed against her lungs. It was no use pretending. She couldn't stall what needed doing. "I've got to get out of here."

"What?" Rumi turned down the static.

"I've got to get back to my team," SJ bellowed over the din. "I don't care who's sabotaged the project. I'm the leader, not Cole, and it's up to me to get the Resurrection Project back on track." She pressed the brake on her passenger control console. It worked. The car decelerated.

Rumi tapped the driver lock-out button, shutting off SJ's control access and then hit accelerate. "It's obvious you're suffering residual trauma from the poisoning, which makes you more sensitive to a condition in SHEOL known as Sun Dep D. It's a depressive affect and triggers sudden emotions, and irrational judgment. Your sensitivity factor is probably off the charts. As soon as we get to the dwellings, we'll turn the sun lights on high. You'll feel better in no time."

SJ had never resorted to physical force against another human being in her life, but when she looked at the petite person in control of their route, she wondered about her options. Her heart raced in tandem with her fear. Why was Rumi being so stubborn?

She'd try reasoning again. "Rumi, there's nothing wrong with me. I've just got to get back. If you can't bring me to the surface, then drop me off, and I'll find another way."

Rumi mechanically repeated, "You'll feel better in no time."

The life alert screen illuminated, and two chime alerts sounded, indicating an abnormal biochip reading.

"See?" Rumi pointed to the screen. "Your heart rate and blood pressure are up. You need to rest at Mi Manera like Cole said."

The dumb warning chime continued. SJ banged on the screen. "Doesn't the idiot thing shut off?"

Rumi stared straight ahead.

"Just get me to an exit. There has to be one near here for emergency measures." SJ tried to keep panic out of her voice.

Rumi reached over and patted her hand. "I'll take you to Mi Manera. Cole expects it. Once you're there, everything will seem more normal." Her voice reflected the tone a mother would use to soothe a distraught child.

"I can't imagine that." SJ gripped the door handle and tried to think of a way to convince Rumi to let her out. The speed of the Morenci continued to be an intimidating factor.

Something flashed by SJ's window. "Wait! Slow down. I think I saw a sign."

Rumi turned up the music and crackling sounds roared from the speakers.

SJ switched her passenger screen console to map mode, traced their route, and then tapped on a mini book emblem. The name, L'Ecole Transformante, popped up. "It's a school. Just ahead of us." SJ pointed to the name on the screen. "You have to drop me off there."

Rumi shook her head. "Not happening."

"Yes, it is. I can arrange for transportation from the school. It shows the double U, so I'm certain they'll cooperate. I've teaching connections to all educational facilities affiliated with Universe United."

The car's speed increased, and they passed the school exit.

SJ could think of only one other strategy. *Do I really want to bring this up?* "Tell me something, Rumi. Are you afraid of Cole? Because if he's pressuring you in any way, I'll make him stop."

The speeding car went into a tail-swishing halt. The momentum carried SJ forward despite restraints, and she felt the impact in her shoulder. Alarms from both life alert systems combined into a discordant jangle. SJ looked behind her into the glum darkness for any approaching vehicles. When she turned back, she saw Rumi's head resting against the steering wheel. SJ jiggled her arm and heard a low groan. "What's wrong? Are you hurt?"

Rumi raised her head. "How can you be so smart and so ignorant at the same time? Of course, I'm afraid. You should be too! Don't you know who Cole is?" Rumi's gaze held a wary story.

"Of course I know who Cole is. He's your brother and a famous business tycoon. So what? I'm a famous scientist. But that doesn't mean he has the right to dictate what should happen. I've got a choice, and so do you."

Rumi groaned again and gripped the steering wheel. "You really don't understand."

For a split second, SJ hesitated. She stared through the windshield into the tunnel ahead and wished she could see the future. Then she opened the door and got out. When it closed, the only noise in the vast emptiness of the tunnel was the muffled idling of the Morenci. SJ tapped on her wrist scanner from Rumi to bring up a map.

Rumi's door slammed, and she stood, glaring at her across the hood. "Don't do this. Get in. I'm begging you. We'll be at the dwellings in less than ten minutes."

"Sorry, Rumi. I can't wait there like a bird in a cage hoping for a merciful hand to open the door." SJ squinted into the gloom ahead and thought she saw lights flicker. Did Rumi see them too?

"You can't be serious."

"I am. Dead serious." SJ pulled a safety vest from under her seat and put it on. She punched the emergency switch on the dash, and strobe signal lights illuminated along the rear and front bumpers. The effect would trigger any approaching vehicles to decelerate. "It's better this way. You can tell Cole that I ditched you. He certainly doesn't expect we'd duke it out, does he?"

Rumi sniffed. "He expects us to follow his plan. Are you sure you want to cross him?"

"I have to do this." SJ smiled at her as confidently as she could, considering the insanity of her plan—hitching a ride with a stranger in a tunnel several hundred feet underground in order to find her way back home over a thousand miles away.

CHAPTER 22

RUMI FOLLOWED BEHIND SJ. "You don't have to do this."

"Of course I do. I'm in charge of the resurrection team. I have to get back and sort out what happens next." SJ held up her hand exposing her wrist scanner in the direction of the approaching vehicle.

"This is crazy. You've no idea who the driver is."

"Which is why I'm checking the registration." SJ showed Rumi the result. It was a work van registered with DCN, Cole's company.

"Well, that's a relief. Still, even though it's one of ours, you're better off staying with me. You've just left the hospital after surviving an attack on your life. Running back to your lab is the worst thing you can do."

"I'll be fine." *Or not.* Hitching a ride with one of the company's workers could put Cole on alert. She'd much rather be miles away before Cole learned of her choice to leave.

The vehicle slowed and flashed its headlights. Rumi hung onto her arm as they waited for the van to stop.

The driver stepped out, and a man's voice bellowed. "Do you need some help?" Glare from the headlights kept his features hidden in the shadows. As he drew closer, his wrinkled shirt and muddied pants became apparent.

Rumi tightened her grip on SJ's arm. "He's not wearing a DCN uniform."

The driver removed his cap. It was impossible. SJ pulled free of Rumi and stepped toward the driver. "Frank? Is that you? What twist of fate brings you this way?"

"I asked first. What's going on? Is it car trouble? I've got all kinds of gear in my tool kit. I'll get you fixed in no time."

"Nope. No car trouble. Just a change of plans. I need a ride."

"Where to?"

"The school." SJ turned and pointed behind her. "Not far from here. We just missed the exit, and the turnaround is still a way ahead. I'm headed to the school, but Rumi has somewhere else to be. I insisted she stop when I saw the headlights. Any chance you can take me there?"

"Does the sun rise every morning?" Frank's leathery face crinkled into a wide smile. Then he swatted at his pants, knocking off clumps of dirt below his knees. "Pardon my dust. Didn't expect to play chauffeur today."

SJ snickered. His use of odd expressions made him unmistakable.

Rumi nudged her and spoke in low tones. "You're acting weird. Do you know this guy?"

"Kind of. Sort of."

"Well?"

"We met once before at Kate's place. His name is Frank. He's the transfer agent that took care of her things after she died."

Rumi gave Frank a nod and then muttered to SJ under her breath. "He looks mentally off. Why is he driving a DCN vehicle and not a transfer unit? Why is he driving at all? He's obviously an Ancient."

As if on cue, Frank broke into an odd sort of jig, which involved stomping his boots, likely to jar off more dirt clods. SJ pressed her lips together to maintain composure. Then Frank gave a wink and declared, "I'll be waiting in the van."

SJ pulled her arm away from Rumi's protective grip. "I appreciate all you've done but I'm going to be okay. Frank might seem peculiar, but he's harmless."

"Right." Rumi frowned. "He appears as innocent as a puppy. Are you really sure about this?"

"I am. I know you want me to follow Cole's plan, but waiting in SHEOL accomplishes nothing. I need to get back to my team."

"There's no reason to drive to them. You can stay right here and set up contact when we reach the house. Why are you doing this?"

"I need to reassure them face to face. I need to get to the bottom of this."

Rumi shook her head. "You're as stubborn as Cole." She stomped away and climbed into the Morenci.

SJ got into the van before she could change her mind. The rumble of the Morenci motor jiggled the view screen of the van. Rumi hadn't moved. But when Frank set the route destination for the school and the van pulled away, the Morenci took off like a rocket into the darkness of the tunnel going the opposite direction.

Frank settled back in his seat and draped his cap over his knee. "So, tell me. What kind of doctoring are you doing a jillion miles from your den in this underground noodle bowl?"

He remembered her.

"I was brought here after a sabotage attempt."

"When did that happen?" His tone turned serious.

"Don't you keep up with the news?"

"I do. All the time." Frank selected "media" on the console screen. The message, "unable to access," scrolled across the display. "Except, of course when, I'm working underground, or a solar hatch puts a wrap on it. Like today." He pointed to the weather icon where an illuminated sun storm warning appeared.

SJ squinted to read the small ranking number under the warning. "An X55? It must be a mess out there!"

"Yep. Starting to feel like chaos follows me. Last week everything went down in Sector Thirty-one where I was manning relocation buses. But no solar flare was involved. Some say protestors hacked the main comm center to cause disruption. Anything to call attention to their relocation grievances. I just keep my head down and try to do my work."

"Where are you going today?"

"Actually? The school. My assignment came from Global Safety. I'm picking up the belongings of a known anti-relocation sympathizer, a teacher who disappeared from the school after a small fire broke out in her room. No one could find her, and she never returned to claim her belongings."

"Why isn't someone more concerned with locating the missing sympathizer?" SJ tapped on Rumi's wrist scanner device hoping for a connection. She needed to turn it off soon to avoid being tracked by Cole.

"I don't know. I wondered the same thing. G. S. seems bent on tying disgruntled activists to every bad thing that happens."

SJ sighed. The scanner screen remained blank. "It's all about unity. Identifying a common source of bad keeps sector momentum going the right direction together. One universe. It's the motto we cut our teeth on."

"You got that right. G.S. keeps telling us that fear of the unknown makes people respond in weird ways. So they try to explain everything just to keep the peace. Do you believe that nonsense?" Frank snorted. "I mean come on. Is that really true? Does having a good sense of logic and having heaps of knowledge keep people peaceful and united?"

She pressed her lips together and swiped, tapped, and jiggled the scanner in a frenzied effort for contact but to no avail. Perhaps Frank would take her silence for distraction, and she would not have to say what she thought. Of course, having knowledge increased the odds of a better life, and having a better life brought happiness. It was why she chose her career and why she worked to develop a process for human resurrection—to wield power over the accelerating death rate and lessen people's fears about death. Both were good outcomes.

Frank chuckled. "I can hear you thinking, so I guess I've got your answer."

Heat flooded her face. "I guess you do." She needed to keep the peace until she at least reached the school. Perhaps he'd go for a different subject. "How did you manage to make it to SHEOL with all the power issues?"

"When maglev power is off, I switch to manual and keep my battery charged whenever I have the opportunity. I only had to push once when the converter jammed at an entry switch and locked out my restart. That's where I slipped in some mud and gave myself a dirt bath."

"And there's the bright side. Free spa treatment. Scrubs away the dead stuff when you wash." SJ spoke with exaggerated cheerfulness and patted her cheeks, but her gut churned over the possibility of a breakdown in the tunnelway.

Frank reached over and tapped her device. "Good luck with that." Then he pointed to the console screen. "You've got two strikes against you—the pile of terra firma above, and beyond that, the God of Sol who plays havoc with communications."

SJ nodded. "Of course." She tried to settle into her seat, a design obviously configured for a person with a waist-to-neck ratio much longer than hers.

Frank pushed something on the console, and her seat flew backward. "Oops. So sorry. Just trying to make you comfy. I'm not too familiar with the adjustments. It's a loaner till I can get mine back."

SJ reset her chair just in time as the van veered off the main tunnelway and took the exit for L'Ecole Transformante throwing her sideways and nearly onto the floor. Regaining her position, she latched onto the new topic. "A loaner? So Universe and DCN are working together?"

"Not officially. But power outages make strange bedfellows when it comes to getting a job done. Some guru at Universe figured that DCN's success in moving goods might work to relocate people. But I don't like it. People aren't products, and feeding DCN is like feeding a lion. They're already more powerful than any other business in the world."

The van slowed. Frank attempted to increase speed but without success. "Shoot. The juice is down to a trickle."

Then the vehicle came to a complete stop. Frank tried to switch to maglev power, but the indicator stayed on manual and displayed zero charge. "I bet it's that rinky-dink converter switch again." He illuminated the tunnel map on the console panel and pointed to a landmark. "Looks like the distance from the school to our position is about two miles. You got your walking shoes on?"

"Not really, but if that's our only option..." SJ thought of Rumi and how soon Cole would know of her detour. Maybe that would not be so bad if Frank turned weird on her.

Frank reached over the seat into the back and pulled out a large navy backpack. Then he grabbed some water and tossed her a bottle. "Wha'd ya say? We can walk and swap stories about the futility of counting on the good of the present moment."

"So, you'd rather hold stake in the future?" SJ watched him take a swig from his bottle.

"Nah … past, present, future … none of it matters when you've got no power." Frank recapped the bottle and put two more in his pack. Then he programmed a tether route for the van to the maglev in case the power came back.

SJ stepped out of the van. She slipped her bag over her shoulder, activated a light baton, and pointed it into their shadow world. The gloom defied the notion that high above them a sun storm raged.

CHAPTER 23

THEY'D ONLY WALKED about twenty minutes before pain shot across the bridge of SJ's foot. It throbbed with every step. When Frank stopped and removed his backpack, she welcomed the pause.

"So, what's it like?" Frank adjusted his pack straps.

"It hurts." She balanced against the elevated safety curb and rubbed the top of her foot through her sock.

"Yah. That's what I thought. Makes me wonder if we should even be trying." He slipped his pack back on and continued walking.

What was he talking about? She tugged on the tongue of her shoe to ease the friction burn. Walking to the school was his idea. She'd have been willing to wait in the van for power to return. She'd heard DCN tunnelways included an alternate power supply even if Universal's tunnelways did not.

She tried to keep up with him, limping along just a few steps behind. When the ceiling light strips ended, they hiked in complete darkness except for the light from their batons.

As the pain increased and the distance between them grew greater, she attempted to walk on the outside edge of the sole hoping for relief. When nothing helped, she called out to him. "I'll do whatever you think is best."

He turned around. "What did you say?"

"I'll do whatever you think is best."

"That's great but it's not up to me. You're the one who did the research."

The truth was, she relied on Kate's shoe reviews to know the best kind to buy. She shifted her bag to her other shoulder and hobbled toward him. "Listen. I don't test on my own. I rely on the reports of experts." Why was he bashing her footwear?

The beam of Frank's light baton illuminated the bumps and ridges of the tunnel wall between them as he approached. "What kind of a researcher does that? Expert testing or not, you have a responsibility. If it's uncomfortable, then maybe we're not supposed to be on this path."

His words settled on her like a cloud of biting gnats. The man was clearly a lunatic if he was going to keep fussing about her shoes. "You don't understand what I am saying. I said I'd do whatever you think is best. If you think it's better for us to wait, then I'll wait. I'm fine with letting you choose."

"Nah. You think you would do that, but that's not true. Destiny is your thing." Frank's expression, half in the shadows, reflected an eerie sneer. "You'd always regret not taking it and controlling it. Even if the process hurts, you're convinced it's for the best. Who am I to persuade you otherwise? I'm no brainiac. I'm just a transfer agent who shuffles things about. You, on the other hand—"

"We hardly know each other." Her jaw tightened. "I'm not as committed to controlling fate as you seem to think. Especially if it involves excruciating pain. I'm human, after all. There's a limit." She took a deep breath and exhaled, willing the pain away. "Here's the deal. I'm perfectly fine with waiting a while."

Frank held up a hand. "Hold on a minute. So, you're saying the process causes severe pain?"

"Yes. Of course. Isn't that obvious?" What was wrong with him? Were Ancients always this dense? She began walking again.

"No. It's not obvious. I'm not a scientist, and I've no idea how the resurrection process is supposed to feel to the candidate."

A smile crept across her face, and she pointed her light beam at her feet. "We're not talking about my shoes, are we?" She waited for clarity to sink in.

Frank roared with laughter. He stomped about, snorting, and pointed to her feet with his baton. "Your feet? No. I'm talking about resurrection. Not your foot problems."

She laughed just as hard, and her pain eased a little.

"Do you want to keep walking?" Frank's voice held concern.

"I'm not sure." She stared into the dimness. A thought came to her. Maybe Frank was safe. In the past, she'd confided in Kate alone about her life puzzles. Now Kate was gone, but this Ancient was someone Kate had trusted. Maybe she could trust him too. Maybe he could help her unravel the mystery of events she could not comprehend.

"Take them off."

"What?" She looked where Frank was pointing.

"Your shoes."

"Why? Then I won't have any protection."

"You'll be fine. Leave the socks on if you want, but without shoes, you'll ease the pressure and sense the ground better and move instinctively toward smoother areas. Sure, you'll ruin the socks, but I'm certain we can borrow more at the school."

She tried his advice, and while they walked she told him everything, and in the process, she forgot her foot pain.

When she finished and had answered all his questions about Kate's death and reappearance, the messages, and Cole's controlling behavior, Frank stopped walking and pointed the beam from the light baton up the curve of the tunnelway. "Here's an observation. When something appears to be outside the realm of ordinary life, it's easier for most people to believe that it's a trick than to believe that it's true."

"Then I guess I'm like most people."

"But you're a scientist. You always look deeper. What would it take for you to believe otherwise?"

"You mean what would it take for me to believe the messages are not a hoax?"

"Yes. Exactly. And believe me, I'm asking myself the same question."

"It's not just one thing." She shifted her bag to her other shoulder. "First, I'd have to discover Cole is not who I think he is. Then I'd need proof to back up the first message. The letter from Evie claims another realm exists and that she lives there but also lived on earth many years ago." She paused, second-guessing her choice to confide in Frank. Ancients were known to thrive in the outlandish. She just wanted to uncover the truth about all that had happened.

Frank crossed to the opposite side of the road. When she caught up, he continued speaking. "What if evidence proving the messages are factual is delayed? Could you agree that it's possible that Five is a real place? After all, there are many things in science that were predicted to be true, but at the time, evidence proving them true was still years away."

"You're right, but there are also some predictions that turned out to be wrong."

"Okay. Then how do you, as a scientist, decide which possibilities to accept and which to reject?"

"Some things are just illogical."

"So, based on your logic, you decide what is possible."

"Everyone does that."

He turned to face her but continued walking backward, and with as much skill as a teenage boy. "But what if there's a logic that's higher than what you can conceive? Isn't it a bit limiting to make your own logic the basis for your acceptance of a possibility? For example, consider a child's logic. It expands with his growing knowledge of the world, which is constantly evolving. So, in the beginning of his life, a child does not even know what a parent is, yet parents are very much there in his life and affect most of what happens to him. But in an infant's mind, the parent—as we know the parent—does not exist."

"I guess when you put it like that, I have to agree. Logic higher than human logic could exist. But without proof, I just can't see—" About eight hundred feet ahead, their exit tunnel ended in a cul de sac.

A trio of arched passageways appeared to lead into the school. The white stone of the central arch had an illuminated sign across the top which read, L'Ecole Transformante. Viny green spirals stretched in wavy ribbons from the central arch base to the sign. "Look." She pointed. "The sign is lit up. The power must be on."

"Maybe. But it could be auxiliary. All residence schools are required to have their own backup power." Frank hurried to one of the side arches and beckoned for SJ to follow.

She moved past him to examine the viny tendrils of what turned out to be a real plant. She stooped to sniff a creamy thumbnail-sized blossom and was reminded of the heady scent of Kate's star jasmine, which thrived in the full sun of her yard.

"Come on." Frank waved his arms in frantic swoops.

She pointed through the central arch to a set of wrought iron doors. "Don't we enter through there?"

"Nope. Not today." Frank put a finger to his lips and turned off his light baton.

"I don't see why we can't just go through the front," she grumbled, as she flounced toward him.

He grabbed her by the arm and pulled her into the shadows just as the doors clanked open. A man dressed in a security uniform stepped out onto the middle of the cul de sac. He held a light and aimed it down the tunnel and then across the opening where they stood hidden in the shadows. After a couple more sweeps, he reentered the building.

"Why are we hiding?"

"Didn't want to advertise your presence."

"Why? I thought that's why we're here. I'll have the cooperation of the school because of my Universe status."

"And if you use your status, Cole's security team will discover you. They'll report your arrival back to their boss. I assumed you were trying to avoid him catching up to you."

"I'm simply trying to reach my team. Did you plan to hide me in the van all along?"

"You guessed it." Frank slipped something out of his pocket, inserted it into a small single door in the side passageway, and jiggled the handle.

"So, you're a smuggler too?"

Frank pushed on the handle, and the door swung open to the bottom of a stairway. "Look, Doc, I don't want to be accused of misreading the situation, but Cole Magnus can be a ruthless dictator when people stand in his way. You must believe this, or you wouldn't have taken the AWOL route back to your team in my rig. Why didn't you wait in SHEOL as he ordered?"

His assessment cut through her like a knife. How could a perfect stranger point out the obvious about Cole? She'd been convincing herself that Cole's proneness to take charge came when others didn't or wouldn't assume their responsibilities and that he pressured because he wanted success, but maybe his power plays spelled something more. But what?

She followed Frank up the stairs, and they paused on the landing. Distant yells and shouts came from somewhere on the other side of the stairwell door. Frank looked through the small glass pane and then moved aside. She stood on tiptoe and caught a glimpse of a hallway and an entrance into a recreation room where several children played with a ball.

"Wait here." Frank left the stairwell, and SJ watched through the door pane as he entered the rec room and beckoned to someone. Then he returned and put his finger to his lips as he stood silently beside her. His covert approach set her on edge. Her temples throbbed.

Suddenly the door flew open, and a younger and thinner version of Frank joined them.

The man gave Frank a hug. "Good to see you, bro. I've been waiting for days. What took you so long?"

Frank responded with an attempt at a playful headlock, but the spirited man ducked.

The man glanced briefly at SJ, but then his focus returned to Frank.

Frank took off his cap and held it out to the man. "Yours. I couldn't get away from relocation transfers until just this week."

"Keep it. Maybe it'll help you remember me sooner." The man laughed. Then his look turned serious. "Wait here while I get the box."

After the man left, SJ remarked, "You two seem close."

Frank nodded. "That's Chris. He's my brother."

CHAPTER 24

RELIEF POURED OVER her. "This is perfect. Instead of using the school's Universe connection, I can use your brother's privacy connection to link with my team."

"Really? You think that's a smart move?" Frank looked at her as if she'd suggested they sign up for meal delivery to a lion's den.

"Why is it so hard to imagine my predicament?" Her brief affection for the Ancient turned to aggravation. "The sooner I communicate with my team, the quicker I'll know the extent of the sabotage attempt and how it affects the Resurrection Project."

Frank raked his hand through his thick, white spiked hair. "Cole will likely be watching for any communication to the lab, Universe or private."

"Maybe so, but maybe not. Do you really think he would use his power to scan privacy links?"

Frank sighed.

She nodded. "You're right. He might. But all this delay alters the timetable. I have to let them know I'm okay and headed back. Not communicating stirs up credibility issues. Remaining undercover slows me down." And made her feel like a criminal.

"Aren't you forgetting something?" Frank pointed upward. "Solaris tempestas. I can get you back to Sector Seven long before the solar storm relents and allows your team comm to go through."

"What about your delivery?"

"Global Safety requested that I deliver the missing sympathizer's belongings to the closest GS office. Power issues, being what they are, make the idea of *closest* a relative term. I can make the drop-off in your sector as well as anywhere. Three hours tops."

SJ was about to explain her aversion to reckless disregard for authority, but Chris returned carrying a box with a pair of women's boots on top. The contents smelled of smoke.

"Here's everything. It's all they could salvage after the fire." Chris handed Frank the box. "Who's your partner?"

Before SJ could speak, Frank jumped in. "She's a stowaway."

Chris gave her a knowing smile. SJ got the sense that the two had cooperated in trafficking before.

The men left the stairwell and headed down the hall. She followed close behind. "Look. I'm just going to say it, so you know where I stand. I'm not one for tricks and hiding. I'll do whatever gives me the quickest opportunity for contact. I'll ride in the van if it's available, but surely all this deception is unnecessary. If Cole finds me, so what?" Her heart raced in the daring of her words.

Frank turned around and shushed her. "He's going to find you. But if we're careful and the solar storm lasts a little longer, then he won't discover your position right away."

She swallowed further protest, and immediately her stomach churned. *What's wrong with me?* She'd always been a champion of facts and truth, and yet somehow, she'd allowed recent circumstances to dampen her passion for forthrightness. In exchange, she'd assumed a life of secrecy and deception. The idea of it made her head spin.

Chris's voice drifted back to her. "Look at it this way. You'd really be doing Frank a favor. He has an eccentric reputation to maintain. In the transfer world, he's known as Frank the Notorious. An Ancient who wards off his retirement by engaging in wild and dangerous transfers without a fuss. I figure your mission fits into that category with room to spare."

The lighthearted description brought no relief from the throbbing pain that now stabbed at her temples. Maybe a residual effect of her drugging?

She stumbled and reached to the wall to steady herself. The men moved on to another door, and Frank disappeared through it with the box.

She hurried to catch up and overheard Frank tell Chris she needed to stay hidden while the van was being repaired. Passing through the door, she found the men standing in a well-stocked equipment room. Chris cleared some sports balls off a small sofa. "Here's a quiet corner. No one will disturb you."

Frank placed the box on the floor. "I won't be long, and I'll be back with some grub too. If you lay low, it'll be a lot less complicated."

Too tired to argue, she stayed mute. Maybe silence would become an annoying new habit. After the men left, she closed the door and sat on the sofa and shut her eyes. She replayed the day's events. Just hours ago, she'd been discharged from the hospital, but it felt as if she'd been out for ages. Medical training advised that recovery from poisoning or drugging should be done at a leisurely pace, which would exclude hiking through tunnels and hiding her identity.

Did she look as bad as she felt?

She got up and stood in front of the mirror on the back of the door and leaned in close. She patted the skin under her eyes.

The doorknob turned, and she sprang sideways over a pile of sports equipment to avoid being bowled over by a young girl who rushed into the room. The girl seemed startled.

SJ put her fingers to her lips and whispered, *"Shhh."*

The girl cocked her head. "Are you hiding too?" Strawberry blonde wisps escaped two pigtails, which crisscrossed her head like a crown.

SJ nodded, hoping that if she played along the girl wouldn't give her away.

The girl placed her arms akimbo. "Tell me what you look like."

The command puzzled SJ, because the girl's eyes were open, and the light was on. "Can't you see me?"

"No. I'm blind. But I can feel you." The girl giggled. "Shake my hand."

SJ hesitated. Kate was instantly at ease with children, but SJ always felt awkward in their presence. She never knew if she was doing the right thing.

The girl extended her hand, so SJ reached for it, and the child latched on and began vigorously pumping it up and down. "What's your name?"

"I'm SJ."

The girl grinned. "My name is Bow. Not like hair bow but bow. Like this." She stooped over with one hand behind her back and the other across her stomach. "See?" She erupted into gales of laughter and then stopped. Her freckled face displayed a quizzical look. "What about your name? It's only got two letters."

"It's a nickname."

Bow giggled. "I know *that.* So is mine. Bella Orinda Washington. B. O. W. But what does SJ stand for?"

"Well … it's actually a name that I got from my dad, who was a doctor." SJ gulped, hoping she could divert the full revelation.

Bow squealed. "That's what I want to be! A doctor or maybe a Stick Healer. My teacher told us about the Stick Healer. Do you know about him?"

"I don't think I do."

Bow held out her hand. "Then I'll tell you the story."

Oh dear. Now what, Kate? SJ imagined what Kate would do and allowed herself to be pulled to the couch to sit.

Bow closed the gap between them and leaned against her. "A very long time ago—maybe six thousand years—I like numbers, so I'm gonna say them in the story, but they might be made up ones. Okay?" Bow had a look of concern on her face.

SJ suppressed a laugh and solemnly agreed to the matter. She found herself relaxing as the warmth of the small body beside her seeped into her own.

"And this story was about people living on Earthland, only long before it was called that. Okay?"

"Okay." SJ gave her consent again and watched as Bow wriggled against the back of the couch. The child seemed pleased with her attention.

"So, the man's name was Musa, and he was leading the Torah tent people to their new home when some fire snakes came and bit them and many people died. Isn't that terrible?" Bow tilted her head toward SJ.

"Sounds awful." SJ patted the small hand.

The girl pulled her hand away and fluttered it like a bird flying. Then she smacked it down hard on the couch seat. "Those people got really scared and they asked Musa to please help them, and do you know what he did? He asked the Stick Healer what to do." Her eyes shone as she wriggled about.

"What did the Stick Healer say?"

"He told Musa to make a metal snake and put it on a stick, and everyone had to look at the snake to get healed from their bad snake bites. Isn't that the best story? My teacher told it before she went away. She said it was true."

"It's a great story. Did she read it from a book?"

"Yes. I can tell you the name of it, but let me do a brain think first." The girl put a finger on her temple and pressed.

Just then, the door opened, and an athletic young woman zoomed in. "Oh, my goodness, Bow! We've been looking all over for you. What are you doing in here?"

Bow covered her eyes and pushed up against SJ and giggled. "I'm invisible. Don't tell her I'm here."

The woman gave SJ a bemused look. "You must be the new assistant."

Bow uncovered her eyes and proclaimed cheerfully, "She's SJ, but she doesn't know what her nickname stands for."

The young woman patted Bow on the head. "Oh, you silly thing. Of course she knows." Then she took Bow by the hand and said to SJ, "I'll give you the grand tour just as soon as I get Bow back to Elsa and the team."

"There's no need. Really. It's okay. Chris asked me to wait here."

The young woman gave SJ a sour look. "If you prefer." Then she led Bow out the door.

Bow called back to her. "Goodbye, SJ. I hope you get your name back."

SJ closed the door and looked for something to block it from easily opening again. She found a couple of weights which she placed in position along the bottom. She flopped onto the couch, yawned, and closed her eyes.

"Time to go." A man's voice drifted into her dream.

She opened her eyes and found Chris and Frank standing there, and Frank's eyes said something was wrong. "How long have I been here?"

"About an hour. Follow Chris. Do exactly as he says." Frank picked up the box and left.

"Where's he going?"

Chris grabbed her hand. "No time to explain. I've got to sneak you into the back of the van."

Chris scouted the hallway. Then he beckoned to her to follow. "Are you coming?"

She nodded and hurried along behind him. When they came to a door, he opened it and signaled for her to slip out. The door led to the outside passageway, which they followed to the end. There, they waited in the shadows of the arched opening. She spotted the van and two other DCN vehicles parked outside in the cul de sac. Frank stood laughing in the main entrance with a couple of DCN workers. Most likely their mirth centered on one of Frank's flamboyant stories. Loud music from the van drowned the exchange.

Chris motioned again, and she ran to the back of the vehicle, climbed inside, and then cautiously peeked out. She saw Chris struggling with Bow, who finally calmed down and gave Chris something. He took it and hurried to where she was hiding and handed it to her. "Bow insisted I give this to you, or she would keep running. Running is her specialty."

Chris returned to the child, who remained in place waving frantically. SJ waved back before she remembered Bow could not see.

A DCN worker shouted, and SJ dove for cover. She scooted as far back into the cargo space as she could and then pulled a tarp over her. The cargo doors slammed, and Chris's voice came from just outside them. "We've got a little runner here at the school, and I was just making sure she's not inside."

"Right. Once they start, running is a hard habit to break."

The worker's words summed up more than Bow's predicament. SJ longed to end her stretch of running and settle back into her routine.

CHAPTER 25

PRIDE SETTLED OVER Cole like a regal cape. He wanted to fly, but instead sprinted like a human to the elevator.

Manipulating Rumi to help control SJ was nothing short of genius. It paved the way for everything to be in its place in seven days when his father came alive again. Then the world would bow.

"Which floor?" A young man held the door open.

Cole stepped in. "Base level." The man reminded him of Michael when they first met in the heavenlies.

The door closed.

Cole sniffed. The idiot youth reeked of Mortar's kind. The scent brought back memories of the glorious realm, and an ache crept into his heart. He looked away and clenched the hands of the body he inhabited. *Study the mark. My kingdom will exceed Mortar's.*

Human targets were to be hunted and turned or rendered useless. He tingled with the sense of challenge.

Possession, a talentless and tiresome task that only worked on the unaligned, paled in contrast to oppression, a harassment against those loyal to Mortar. The tactic required Elite skill, and he was by far the elitest of all the Elite even if he was no longer welcome in Mortar's realm.

He gazed slyly at the man who seemed mesmerized by his own wrist scanner. "Are you in SHEOL for business or pleasure?"

The man looked up. "Both, I guess. My business is my pleasure."

Cole laughed. "Ah. One of those. The one who knows no difference. All you see is endless conquest."

"Perhaps."

Cole felt the tug of opportunity. He licked his lips. *Focus. Not now.* Neither a full spree of possession or oppression carried a reward worth his detour today. His time tick-tocked for only one thing. Resurrection.

"Almost there." The man gestured to the panel where floor buttons illuminated as the men descended.

Cole smiled. "Isn't this building amazing?" He could not resist the lure.

"It's incredible." The young man patted his pocket and then pulled out a brochure. "I signed up for the tour. I hear the architect who planned SHEOL also has a home constructed here. Solid gold fixtures and an art collection worth millions."

Cole coughed away the roar of laughter that came to his throat. As always, the glitter of physical accomplishment drew men to praise. Such easy prey.

He swallowed his hunger. Not today. A grander target lay ahead, the biggest wonder to ever grace history. Select notoriety, world leaders, and practically everyone—all moved to gather as witnesses to the first human resurrection, and he had important strings to pull in the matter.

"The truth is …" The young man shoved the brochure back in his pocket. "I don't have time for the tour today."

Truth? The word should be banned. Cole sucked in, and the elevator lights flickered.

"Whoa. Did you see that? The lights dimmed. I hope we make it. There's a sun storm out there." The man pointed up. "It messes with electricity."

"SHEOL has a generator system. Nothing to worry about." Cole willed the light back to normal strength. *Stupid man.* Truth revealed was a far more disastrous event than losing electricity. It was the one thing that time must not welcome. At least not yet. Not until human resurrection had filled his kingdom with souls loyal to him.

"Maybe it won't work. Generators can be tricky."

Cole eyed the imbecile. "Of course it will work."

The man grinned. "If you say so."

The idiot's words once again held sway. Cole's stomach swirled. What was going on? It was his words that always cast uncertainty in a target's mind, not the other way around. A sea of doubt surged. What if it didn't work? His plan. What if it failed? He needed to win. To be greater than Mortar. Then all would be right again.

Heat surged through his body. He fought the urge to incinerate the man right there in the elevator.

The elevator slowed. The Michael look-alike tugged on his shirt cuffs and pushed up his tie. Most likely preening for some trivial meeting.

Cole closed his eyes to the fool in front of him, and a fresh idea came to mind. Even if his demon spirits were unable to enter the bodies upon resurrection, there would still be a positive. If Mortar-made souls returned to claim their resurrected bodies, then the effect would diminish Mortar's soul acquisitions in the afterlife. There would be souls loyal to Beast returning as well. Fresh opportunities all around. He chuckled at these happy thoughts.

"Good joke?"

Cole opened his eyes. The simpering man was still there.

"Come on. You look like you can tell a good joke."

Cole could not resist the compliment. "Just thinking about my callback strategy."

"What did you pitch?"

"World domination."

The young man laughed. "Now *that's* a hard sell."

Cole nodded. Little did the moron know. World domination times two. His father's kingdom and the world.

His lungs filled and his heels lifted. He would fly to Mi Manera and see to it that SJ settled in well at his exquisite abode. With her as his queen, his image was complete.

The elevator doors opened, and Cole stepped out and adjusted his crown.

He flew, but not by wing, instead he sped through the tunnelway by car. Although flying as a herald was a far better way to travel than any human method, his Aquilos brought him places in style when he had to appear human. He took great pride in his deception of living as a human. A very rich and successful human. Only a few knew his real form, and his talented designer, Loki, was one of them.

When he arrived at his mansion, the exuberant man greeted him with a kiss on both cheeks and waved his hand at the newly decorated space. "Voilà. C'est magnifique, n'est pas?"

Cole nodded. "Très magnifique." Loki performed best when his aura remained replete with the affirmation of others.

Loki sashayed away from the entry and led Cole to the kitchen. There, he pointed out the titanium tiles that bordered the countertops. "See how the etchings of woodland birds in the shimmering tile marry well with the white marble and the use of black iron."

"Yes, it does. You are a ceaseless genius." Cole feigned awe over the design element.

Loki clapped his hands, and a troop of staff members paraded into the room. The first one, a portly man dressed in gray trousers and a pristine white shirt, moved to stand by the stove. The rest lined up beside him, all dressed in similar fashion.

Loki waved his hand at the man. "Chef Bosma."

The man stepped forward and bowed his head. His thinning black hair and thick sideburns glistened, and sweat gleamed on his brow. Something about his apparent nervousness pleased Cole.

"Bosma received his culinary degree at Universidad Francisco and worked as a line chef under Jose Adria at Rosados." Loki followed down the line, giving introductions and gushing over each servant's lineage.

Cole couldn't care less where the staff came from or what they'd accomplished, as long as they followed his commands and kept watch over SJ.

After introductions, Loki delivered his usual canned loyalty speech. "If you all do as you're told, then you'll be rewarded with many happy years at Mi Manera, La Casa de Cole."

The designer winked at Cole.

Cole offered only a half-smile. As lesser species, humans should not expect anything but misery, unhappiness, and servanthood. It was his tragedy that his father's unfair fall from Mortar's grace had placed him squarely in the company of these deplorable creatures and their singular living spaces, the habitat realms of morons.

He cleared his throat and grasped for a tone of charm. "As Loki said, your job is simple. Please me. Anticipate well the needs of two people, myself and my partner, Dr. Satan Jr., although she insists on her less formal address, SJ. She will arrive shortly with Rumi, my sibling. SJ has been through a medical trauma caused by a sabotage attempt in the Abide. She'll recuperate here and then resume her highly regarded resurrection work, but only in SHEOL. Due to ongoing security issues, she'll not be returning to the Abide. The change of location will be an adjustment, and your help in maintaining this home is essential to her comfort and success."

Loki shook his head. "Poor lamb. She must be overwhelmed. Her sad world must be transformed. I'm certain she'll find solace in the Cabana Room. You must see it. Come. Come." Loki pranced away, and everyone followed.

The designer stopped at a set of glass doors and clapped his hands. The doors swung open onto a room decorated to resemble the inside of a glamorous beach hut with a spectacular view. "Voilà. The default light setting in this room matches the light of the Caribbean and the scenery of Frigate Bay on St. Kitts back on Earthland. SJ can change the selection at any time as well as the light balance." Loki puffed out his chest and his eyes gleamed.

Several bamboo fans hung from the faux thatch ceiling above the group and gave consistent detail to the tropical theme. Loki sidled over to Cole and whispered in his ear. "The space is an homage to love, to remind you of your honeymoon at The Nest."

Cole instantly hated him. Retching pressure expanded in his throat over the reminder. He stormed through a set of doors off to the side that opened into the aviary. Colorful birds shot upward and settled in a banyan tree.

He gripped the railing that encircled the airy enclosure, a cavernous space filling two floor levels. He'd tried many times to break Mortar's curse over him in the matter, but in the end his inability to love or be loved remained his weakness.

He heard Loki shooing the group out of the Cabana Room and shortly after the sound of sniveling behind him. When he turned around, Loki rushed to him, wringing his hands. "What is it? What have I done wrong? I tried my best to capture—"

Cole cut him off. "Really, you are quite ridiculous. Everything is not about you. I have much more weighty matters to address than your arts and crafts projects. Please advise the staff about the house controls."

Loki's face contorted as if he might cry, and then the morose man darted off.

Pleased with his wounding, Cole headed to his office and sat at his desk. He switched on the house cam screens and found Loki. The staff stood gathered around the designer in front of an alcove in the Mahogany Room.

Cole watched as Loki pressed on the wood chair rail below a wall painting. A portion of the wood trim retracted, and a small screen slid out. The illuminated screen surface featured several switch icons. One, outlined in red, stood apart from the others.

Cole turned on his audio and listened.

"This is the house control panel. As you know, successful adjustment to living underground requires a great deal of light exposure, so this is the most important information. If power fails, this is the main switch that kicks on the generators." Loki pointed to the red icon and spoke in a tone that lacked the bravado of his earlier enthusiasm.

He tapped on several numbered switch icons on the panel, and each enlarged and displayed a room name. "These relate to the media walls in the main rooms and should not be altered from their default setting, which links them directly to Cole's offices. For SJ's protection, Cole must always have access to her presence. Permission for any other linking must be approved by him, as there are those who would trace her location to do her harm."

Cole spoke into his microphone. "The Resurrection Project makes SJ a prime target."

The group seemed startled to hear his voice.

Loki pointed to an intercom screen. "As you just heard, your work here can be observed. It is an important security feature for you and our guests."

Bosma came up and whispered something to Loki, who nodded and announced, "Chef Bosma needs to return to dinner preparations." The designer waved the rest of the house staff back to their duties.

Cole confirmed the hour on his wrist screen with the time on his Cartier Mystery clock which rested on a shelf across from him. He spoke into the intercom. "Loki. Come to my office."

A minute later the dejected man stood in his doorway.

"Where are they? They should have been here by now."

"Perhaps the power interruption at the crossway put—" Loki's words cut off when a rapping noise came from the entry door.

The sound increased to obnoxious pounding.

A view of the top of someone's head in a cream fedora appeared on the entry cam screen. *Lucas.* Rumi was nowhere in sight. Cole rushed from his office to the entry hall with Loki following two steps behind. With one swift yank on the golden handle, the monstrous door swung open.

Lucas extended his hand. "Greetings."

Cole did not match the gesture. "What is it?"

Lucas dropped his hand and shrugged. "I'm here on your sibling's behalf."

"Why?"

"She fears your displeasure." Lucas shifted his feet. "Can I come in?"

Cole did not budge. "What might displease me?"

"Not what. Who. SJ. She chose against your plan and separated from Rumi and makes efforts to communicate with her team in person."

"Why did Rumi let her go? SJ can't do this. It's for her own safety." Cole spoke calmly, contradicting the fire that raged within.

Lucas's face broke into a twisted smile. "As always. Safety first."

"Where are they?" Cole gripped the golden door handle, and it softened in his hand. A liquefied drop of it fell steaming to the floor.

"They're no longer together. SJ left Rumi en route to the dwelling and hitched a ride instead with a transfer agent in a DCN van going the other direction."

"Then you must arrange for the DCN driver to bring her here. See to it." Cole released the handle.

Lucas tipped his fedora. "As you wish, my liege." Then he barged past Cole.

"What are you doing? I don't need you here. Go find the driver." Cole jerked his hand away from Loki, who dabbed at his gold-dipped fingers with a handkerchief.

Lucas disappeared down a hallway.

"Where does he think he is going?"

"With Lucas, it's always a mystery." Loki pressed the cloth into Cole's hand. "Take it. Wrap your hand. The staff must not yet know of your powers. It will scare them."

Cole shoved the handkerchief back. "Maybe they should. Fear is a good motivator."

He tore after his henchman and found the troublemaker in the dining room standing at the head of the table. The gleam of gold spilled off the plates, candles, chandelier, and every perceivable thing.

Lucas whistled. "What a spread. Even you must agree it looks a bit like"—Lucas pointed up—"what used to be." He smiled at the housekeeper, who stopped folding napkins and gawked at the ceiling where he pointed.

"Perhaps." Cole moved to the head chair, and Lucas stepped aside. "But only to those without discernment. You know the expression … all that glitters is not gold. What used to be is nothing compared to what is now. What I have here … for her." He gestured grandly. "The gold, of course, is the purest of pure. Only the best for my true love, SJ."

Lucas snorted. "True love, eh?" He took quick steps away from Cole to the other side of the table.

Rage poured over Cole, filling every crevice of his mind. Only one thing would satisfy. He counter-circled to intercept his mocker, but Lucas broke away and made a dash for the entry. Cole caught up with him in the doorway, but before he could deliver his punishment, Loki rushed up and pointed to his wrist screen. "I've already located the DCN van. Should we send a message to the driver?"

Cole lowered his gaze to the mat under Lucas's feet. "A change of plans, Loki. I've decided to give my message in person."

Lucas stood defiant, arms crossed, but when the flames from the mat lapped at his ankles, he sneered at Cole and took off.

CHAPTER 26

SJ STAYED UNDERCOVER until Frank completed the turnaround into the main tunnel. Then she sat and unfolded Bow's drawing and held it to the light. Above the image of a curlicue snake on a stick were the words, "Be healed." The initials, B. O. W. and the numbers 43, 3, 14, and 15 paraded across the bottom of the paper. More writing appeared on the back.

"This drawing was made for SJ by Bow with a helper. Bow remembered The Stick Healer story came from her teacher's Book of Wisdom, and the book has the same initials as her name. The numbers 43, 3, 14, and 15 are Bow's favorite way to add up numbers to make 75."

SJ gasped at the familiar sequence. Another message? She needed a copy of the Book of Wisdom to decipher the riddle, and because of Bow, she now had an idea where to find one.

Frank reached back from his seat and tapped the picture. "What's that?"

"A little girl's drawing of a story about a healer." She spread the picture out on the console. "I met her in Chris's office. Her name is Bow. She said the teacher read the story from the Book of Wisdom. Can I see if the book is in the box of the teacher's belongings?"

"Help yourself." Frank patted the box resting on the seat beside him and increased the light in the cab. "There's no restriction, since there's no investigation. Global Safety said to just deliver the property."

"It's crazy that no one is worried about finding the teacher." SJ lifted the lid off the box and pulled out a set of boots and set them aside. Then she rummaged through the layers of smoke-scented clothes. "Did your brother offer any details? Were they close?"

"Just co-workers. He said she had a reputation for reading stories to the children from the Book of Wisdom. Someone complained that her actions conflicted with Universe's Freedom From Religion law, and an investigation followed. Her defense was that the stories perfectly illustrated the school's core theme.

"What theme? I assume the purpose of the school is to educate SHEOLworkers' children."

"Nope. Not unless they're disabled. It's a boarding school for disabled students to learn advanced transformation skills. The founders believe that young people who endure certain life challenges are best suited, when properly taught, to become inventors and developers of transformations needed to secure the world for future generations."

SJ reached the bottom of the box and held up the last item, a small, navy suit jacket with the school emblem, a circle composed of four colored wedges. She ran a finger over the raised crest. "What are transformation skills?"

"Advanced adaptive abilities. I call the skill results miracles, even though that description is not allowed. Students achieve giftedness in the miraculous. All science-based of course. Their skills develop in four primary areas. *Conversion*, which is substance transformation, and it allows for new versions of fuel or material. *Multiplication*—a process that implements ways to increase food and water supply. And *Restoration*—studies which yield students who are expertly equipped for maintenance, repair, or healing techniques.

"What about the fourth?" She folded the jacket and heard something crinkle.

"Can't remember … something about service, I think." Frank tapped on the navigation screen.

SJ patted a pocket and pulled out a strip of paper and held it to the light. It looked like someone used it for a math problem. Two columns of six smaller numbers were paired under a large number. Ten was the top number in both columns. The rest were random.

"She was a good teacher." Frank's voice sounded sad.

SJ folded the paper inside Bow's drawing and slipped them both into her shirt.

"The kids adored her. Chris said she cared about them. Officials had no right …" Frank stopped talking.

SJ placed the contents back into the box and closed the lid. "I hope they find her."

"They won't. She's dead."

"What are you talking about?"

Frank frowned. "I wasn't supposed to tell you that."

"What do you mean? You said she'd disappeared."

"There's no real evidence that she died, but Chris believes it. He said the teacher was discovered bleeding and unconscious. The student who found her was an older student and very reliable. When he went to get help and the staff returned, the teacher was gone."

"So what about the fire? Was it a cover-up?" Something familiar tugged at her consciousness.

"Chris thought so. It broke out that same night in the teacher dorm. Her room was the only one affected."

Sudden awareness flooded over SJ. Goosebumps rose on her skin. She pulled out the paper that came from the teacher's jacket pocket to re-examine it and then handed it to Frank.

"What is it? Another drawing?"

"No. It was inside the teacher's jacket. They are the same."

"What's the same?"

"The numbers on this paper match the order of the numbers on the messages I've already received. Except for the first one, which was a full letter, the messages contain short phrases and the words, 'Book of Wisdom,' followed by a string of three or more numbers."

"Are you sure?" Frank handed the paper back.

"Yep." She studied it again and pointed to Bow's drawing and then back to the paper slip. "Well, mostly sure. These two match. The number forty-three is common to all of them. It's the first number in each sequence, and it's at the top of this paper from the teacher's jacket pocket. Not a coincidence. I wish

I could check them to be sure, but my data is on my misplaced wrist scanner or 1,820 miles away in my residome.

"All the more reason to get you back there quick." Frank tapped *display* on the navigation screen and a map popped up. "I at least have Atlas access, just no setting application because of the solar storm." He traced a route on the screen. "The way I figure it, we'll take the Keystone Tunnel to Robert's leg, exit at Grant for a short above-ground jaunt, and dive into the Upper East at Littleton. Speedrail tunnel time will put us across the country in three hours. You'll be snoozing in your residome somewhere around, zero-dark-hundred. Not bad for a journey that takes most mortals twenty-six hours topside."

Her stomach churned despite Frank's assurance. Cole would be angry over the change of plan, but would he hurt her? The nagging question made no sense. He'd wanted the partnership and had exerted his influence to ensure she became the team leader. Heading back to the lab and not hiding out in SHEOL would show how resolute she was.

She climbed into the front passenger seat and exhaled. Their relationship was on a learning curve. She needed to show him how capable she was. Yes, she needed his investment, as many businesses need investors, but her work, the messages, and the mystery over Kate were hers to solve. Not his.

CHAPTER 27

FORTY-SEVEN MINUTES LATER, they passed through the exit at Grant and parked at the Pike Forest waystation hub. While Frank went off to submit his credentials, SJ waited in the van, feasting her eyes on the outside world. No virtual vista compared to the real thing. Tree-shrouded mountains stretched out in every direction.

When Frank reappeared, he stopped to talk to a man with a backpack. The man pointed to a gravel road that climbed north up a slope.

After getting into the van, he made a U-turn onto the same road.

"Where are we going?"

"Just a quick detour. The speedrail will reopen in thirty minutes. Something about a safety shutdown. Large equipment coming off the rail."

"What's up this road?"

"A place I'll bet you've never seen before."

"You'd win the bet. I don't travel much." She sighed. A delay wasn't part of her plan.

Frank lowered the windows. "Smell that?"

She sniffed and drank in the scent of dirt and pine. Cool air prickled her skin.

"Hang on. It's gonna be bumpy." Frank steered the van up the rocky incline. When they reached an overlook, he pulled to one side and parked.

SJ got out and held up Rumi's wrist scanner. "Great place for a signal."

"Are you sure you want to do that?"

"I need to talk to George. I'll switch it off as quick as I can."

He snorted and mumbled something.

"What did you say?"

"Nothing. It's your decision."

She moved a few yards to the right and pointed the scanner in the other direction.

Frank strolled toward the edge of the overlook.

SJ kept an eye on the scanner. It had enough signal to come on, but the connecting icon swirled without result. She gave up and moved to the edge and stood beside Frank. Scattered gleams of light punctuated the darkening basin below them and gave witness to life and home. Across the valley, the last of the evening sun grazed the ridge and outlined the fir trees, transforming the ordinary into glorious. Her anxiety fled in the marvel of the moment.

Frank nudged her. "Stay here." He took off down the slope.

"Where are you going?"

He stopped and pointed. "Down there."

She spotted a lone figure standing in the treeless opening a few yards below them. "I'm coming too."

As they drew closer, the twilight revealed a statue of a man atop a tall, squared-off stone base. Portions of the statue had crumbled away or been knocked off. The man had downcast eyes. Dressed in a floor-length robe, he clutched the edge of his cloak against his chest with his left hand and extended his right hand straight out with the palm facing down. The figure's gesture seemed to speak of peace and humility.

"Amazing." Frank spoke in hushed tones and circled the base.

"Who is it?" She looked for an inscription.

"Christo de los Rockies. A replica or the real thing. Not sure which." Frank took off his hat. "Someone took the trouble to place it here."

"It looks old."

"The original stood in a forest on Earthland and was over two hundred years old."

The sound of an engine and car tires approaching on the gravel road above them interrupted their discovery.

Frank grabbed her hand and pulled her down behind the statue. His reaction triggered a rush of adrenaline. Why were they hiding?

A car door slammed, and footsteps crunched on the slope above them. A light beam swept the darkness but paused on the statue.

"S? S? Are you there? I know you are. I followed you."

Her heart lurched at the sound of Cole's voice.

"Don't let him see you. It's me he wants." Frank spoke in calm tones.

She pulled free of Frank's grip and stood. It was no use. She should have realized that, with Cole's resources, flying under the radar wouldn't last long.

The beam of light found her. Then it widened to include Frank.

"I've come to take you home." Cole held something cone-shaped in his hand and waved at her with it.

She watched him descend the steep slope. When he got near, he moved directly to her side, forcing Frank to step away. He thrust a bouquet of roses under her nose. "Drink of my love. Don't they smell sweet?"

She recoiled. His reliance on cliché romance increased her wariness. He'd often used such exaggerated efforts before to convince others he had feelings for her, but she knew better. Resolute, she set her jaw.

"I've come to ensure your safety. I'm afraid Michael here would put you in great danger." He gestured to Frank who now stood several yards away and appeared inattentive.

"Here's the funny thing, Cole." She met his gaze with her own surge of fire. "I don't need to be rescued. I'm not headed into danger. Didn't Rumi tell you? Frank came along and offered me a ride back to my team. But …" She stopped. The niggling detail seemed important. "Why do you call him Michael?" She gestured to her ancient friend.

As if signaled, Frank approached. Cole backed away when he came near and executed a mocking bow. "Michael goes by many names. Perhaps Frank is his latest invention, but to me, he's always been Michael—the *great* Michael of ages past." A sly smile crept over Cole's face, but Frank's face remained as stone.

Something strange passed between the two men. The air prickled with conflict. She pulled on Cole's arm and led him to the other side of the van. "Really, Cole. You can't keep pushing me and others around. I can handle things for myself."

Cole gave no response but seemed transfixed on something behind her.

She turned to see what stole his attention and found Frank standing on the pedestal alongside the statue. A white blanket, made up of hundreds of doves, covered the ground at the base. Mournful cooing sounds filled the air. One bird perched on Frank's finger, and he smoothed its feathers. Then, he lifted it high, and it flew off. The motion sent the rest of the birds flurrying into the sky, and the sound of rushing wings filled the air. When the last one flew off, Frank jumped to the ground with the ease of a child.

She gasped. Where did all the doves come from? And why was Frank's outline glowing? The trick of light subsided as he strode toward them. She stepped back as he planted himself between her and Cole. "It's your choice." His tone was gentle. What do you want to do?" Behind him, out of the corner of her eye, she saw Cole toss the rose bouquet to the ground.

"I don't know." She wanted to know, to be certain of her direction and make her choice.

When she hesitated, Frank moved aside, and Cole closed the gap. He grabbed her by the shoulders. "She wants to be with me. After all, we're partners."

Her eyes met empty pools of darkness. Intense heat radiated from his vice-like grip and traveled down her arms into her fingertips. She began to protest, but Cole put a finger on her lips. "Sweetheart, I know things have been a bit rough, but continuing the trip is unwise after all you've been through. You'll stay safe in SHEOL until the protests die down. Mi Manera has everything you need, including a sunroom and your very own staff. You're the shining star of the resurrection effort."

"My answer is simple. I'll do what I need to in order to communicate with my team. That's my priority. Driving there is the only logical choice as long as the comm blackout persists."

"But it doesn't. It's over." Cole chuckled. "How do you think I found you? And I come with good news. I've spoken to George. He waits eagerly to communicate with you. You may contact him as soon as you like with this." He dangled her wrist scanner.

"What? Where did you find it? She took the device and swept her finger across the screen.

"At the hospital. I might have a little more sway than you do in some places. If you want to get things done, then stick with me. I've got everything under control. You just have to trust me."

"No, you don't." Frank spoke the caution in a low, quiet voice.

She nodded and pretended to be examining her connections and data fields on her wrist screen to buy time to think. If ill will existed between the two men, then it was all the more reason to send Frank on his way before Cole erupted. Cole's influence was legendary. She did not want to put Frank's job in jeopardy. He had been nothing but kind to her. The matter came down to simple effectiveness. The path that brought her closer to her goal now tied to Cole, and his promise of connection with George showed his appetite for control was malleable. George would make Cole understand once and for all that she was in charge of the resurrection trials.

"I'm sorry, Frank. Circumstances have changed." She followed Cole up the slope. Although she'd reached her decision by logic, her heart weighed heavy. She wanted to explain her thinking to Frank.

"Gather your things. I'll be waiting in your chariot." Cole headed to his Aquilos, parked a slight distance away.

Frank stood by the van and held out Bow's folded drawing. "Don't forget this."

SJ took it. "I hope you can understand. It's not an easy choice. It seems better to go with him. I have to face my problems, and now that I have my contacts, I expect I'll get some answers. Don't you think?"

"What I think doesn't matter. You've made your decision." Frank took her hand and held it briefly to his chest. Bowing his head, he mumbled, "Be with her." Then he climbed into the van and closed the door.

CHAPTER 28

SJ CLIMBED INTO Cole's car. "I want a conference with George as soon as we arrive."

Cole reached over and patted her hand. "Of course."

SJ pulled away and tapped her message for George onto her scanner screen. "I'm letting him know, so he can be ready."

"As you wish."

A stream of concentric circles undulated across the screen. She breathed a sigh of relief when they solidified into a solid blue ring. The transmission was successful.

"Good to see you smile. Your decision to return with me paid off."

SJ set her jaw. "It will be even better when I can get back to my team and the lab. Can you arrange transport tomorrow?"

"Really, dear? You agreed to stay at Mi Manera until the protests die down."

"I agreed to go with you so I could make contact with my team. The timetable was your idea. You don't seem to understand. We're partners, but I'm in charge of my lab and the project."

"Yes. We are partners." The words came as a steely whisper. Cole reached toward the console then pulled back his hand.

SJ held her breath, waiting for the angry reaction that would surely come.

He reached again, tapped '*manual control*' and then '*cloak*' and slid his fingers up the throttle line on the dash. The Aquilos roared, and the tunnel blurred to black.

The acceleration pressed SJ into her seat. Acid flooded her throat. The monster was back.

"As you can see, my dear, I am also in charge, and two at the helm doesn't work for me." Cole pointed to the Atlas indicator on the console. A red square speed warning flashed over their route. "My car wants me to slow down, but I won't because I'm in charge."

Her heart thudded. He wanted a response, but aggression did not deserve a reward. She closed her eyes and felt the car roll into a turn.

An audible alert sounded. "Impact warning. Thirty-six seconds."

The pounding in her head matched her heart's. He was an idiot. She counted. On number twenty-four, the car fishtailed to a stop. She opened her eyes.

"Well done, my dear." Cole patted her shoulder. "You are a worthy partner."

SJ shrugged off his hand. "And you have a death wish."

Cole chuckled and switched off the Cloak setting. A row of lights pierced the darkness.

Her door opened, and a compact man with ruffled gray hair extended his hand to her. "Welcome to Mi Manera. My name is Loki. I'm Cole's designer and jack-of-all-trades."

She accepted his surprisingly strong grip and climbed out of the car. The row of lights turned out to be gold lanterns punctuating the black stone walls of the arched passageway surrounding them.

Loki motioned, and a man with thinning black hair and sideburns rushed up and took her bag.

Cole came around the car and took her by the arm. "Here we are. Home. Safe and sound."

She pulled away from him and stepped in behind Loki, who led the way to a mammoth set of intricately carved wood doors.

Cole brushed past them both and reached the door first. He pushed on the gold lever door handle. It swung open to a white marble entry hall. "What do you think?"

"The grandest of grand." SJ turned in each direction and noted the artwork on each wall. "It's really quite marvelous, but I'm afraid I can't take it all in until I've talked with George."

Cole nodded at Loki. "How soon?"

"Patience, my friend. Surface communications are a delicate matter. In your haste to initiate the format, you reconfigured the parameters. I've had to initiate a reset. This is not something one learns at design school, but in later experiences when one deals with impatient clients. I'll let you know when we're ready to transmit."

Loki's freeness of speech with Cole surprised SJ, but she was relieved. Loki's answer meant Cole had been working toward the goal of connecting to George and that was all that mattered.

The two men exchanged quiet words, and then Loki left, and Cole beckoned to her. "Bosma prepared a late-night refreshment."

He brought her to a massive kitchen, introduced her to Bosma, the dark-haired man with sideburns who had taken her bag.

Bosma pulled out a chair for her at the bar and asked her to select any fruit from a bowl. She picked kiwis and strawberries but insisted on helping. He gave her a knife after much protest.

Slicing away strips of fuzzy kiwi skin, she portioned the juicy green pieces between halves of strawberry on a plate. The methodical process calmed her jangled nerves. When she finished, she carried the fruit to a small table by a window in the dining room overlooking an aviary.

"You should have let Bosma fix the fruit." Cole's voice chided from behind her.

She turned around in her chair. How did he do it—suddenly appear out of nowhere? The expansive room had only two entries from what she could see. The farthest one opened to a passageway from the kitchen, and the nearest one, right under her nose, connected to the aviary.

"Surprised my dear?"

"No," She lied. "After all, you are the architect."

He seemed pleased with her compliment and sat across from her. "But really. You must let Bosma serve you. Having servants is part of your life now. Letting them take care of you is a favor to them. It contributes to their skills. They should pay us for the privilege." He pierced a kiwi slice on his plate with his gold-tipped fork and then speared several slices together and gulped them down.

She pressed her lips together to keep from giving her opinion, which contained a high regard for self-sufficiency and a great dislike of letting others wait on her.

Bosma appeared with fluffy omelets. They'd hardly begun eating when Loki returned asking for Cole's help with the reset process. Cole apologized and left.

She ate one bite of her eggs and realized she was more tired than hungry. Perhaps it came as a residual effect of her drugging, but more likely it was a result of the constant challenges she had with Cole. Parameters regarding the respectful resurrection of the human body had been an effort of research and planning for many years. Cole's rash attempt to line up new John Does by offering resurrection candidacy as an incentive to morbidly ill patients of Kerioth Medical was grossly irresponsible. Sabotage or not, the Abide already had a docket of prepped and screened resurrection candidates. When she returned to Sector Seven, she'd begin the trials with one of those. She knew she could count on George to explain all this to Cole.

She pushed away from the table and stood. A yellow bird inside the aviary darted into a stand of red-leaf banana trees. She marveled at the tropical two-story enclosure carved from a solid rock several hundred feet underground.

Following Bosma's directions, she set off down the hall to find Cole's office. On the way, she passed several vast rooms, each one lavish with antiques and art objects.

When she reached the office, she stood outside the closed door. She could hear George heaping praise on Cole for his assistance in getting her safely to SHEOL. Something about the flow of George's flattery made her uneasy.

She entered the room. "I'm here."

Cole gave a little nod and handed her the media wall control. "I'll leave you two alone to discuss things."

After Cole left the room, SJ asked George for a verification scan to erase any concerns of masking. He agreed, and when his familiar set of digits appeared in the corner, she breathed a sigh of relief. "Did you miss me?"

"I figured you were in skilled hands when I learned Cole had you in SHEOL."

"I lost all my contacts. My wrist scanner went missing at the hospital. I'd hoped to be back in Sector Seven last night but decided otherwise." She sat behind Cole's desk.

"Good call." George shifted her view of him to include details of his office. "The Abide is shut down, but I think security is overreacting. Only a handful of bodies is missing, and most were just moved to a new location."

Lacing his fingers together, he leaned forward. "The theory is, protesters of the relocation mandate rearranged the bodies to send a message."

"How could they get around restricted access?"

"Authorities believe a handful of TRIUMP interns with ties to the sectors being evacuated acted out of sympathy and allowed their Abide worker status to be used for access."

Could Ben have been one of them? Her mind swirled with the possibility.

"And S … I'm afraid Kate Auburn Rigsby is listed as one of the bodies actually missing and not just relocated to a new spot. I wanted you to know."

Although her boss's mouth continued moving, SJ could not hear him. Racing thoughts took over. If Kate's body was truly missing, then her tissue stats might be compromised. If that happened, then resurrection would be impossible. But maybe Kate was not dead. She'd seen her face on the media wall. But Kate would never use her masking skill for false influence unless some malicious instigator forced her.

George's laughter interrupted her scattered focus.

"What did you say?" She leaned forward.

"He always was an early riser."

"Who?"

"Cole's father, Beast. He will be the first official resurrection. But that's a secret to the rest of the world until it happens. His procedure will follow preliminary John Doe trials. If they go well, his will broadcast live. All the trials will be done in Kerioth, for now. Initial candidates have been transported from the Abide. Six days is not a lot of time to factor in many trials, but it has to start somewhere."

"It's too soon, of course. You know how I feel about that." She bit her lip, trying to find words against the insanity of it all.

"We aren't pulling the strings anymore, S. We don't need to fret too hard about the results."

"So … Cole gets his way." She clenched and unclenched her hands looking for strings draped to the sky and held by a giant puppet master. Why had she ever believed Cole could stay on the sidelines?

"Just stay the course. Remember, we are all working for the same goal. The only difference now is that it's to be done with Plausibility's timing and candidates. The Access Agreement originated with them, and they've gone mad as far as I'm concerned. But they and the council are of one mind on this. For now. I'll make sure the fallout lands on their heads and not ours."

"This is happening too fast."

"Listen to me, S. It's not our show anymore. All you have to do is play the game."

CHAPTER 29

THE NEXT MORNING, Serpens drove SJ to the A Complex of Kerioth where the trials were to take place. Everything in her screamed to slow down, but keeping her position as team leader was all that mattered. If she did what was expected now, then she'd be in position for the direction of the project later.

A DCN guard at the security desk handed her a signing tablet and pointed to the family waiting room.

She paused at the doorway when she saw a man and woman huddled together as close as two chairs allowed. Soft sobs came from the woman.

"Jess. Stop, my love. You can't think of it that way." The burly man rested his cheek on the woman's hair.

"I know. But what if it doesn't work? Once they try, then it's over." The woman's voice came out muffled from his chest.

"You're right, but you gotta ask the other question too."

"What do you mean?" The woman lifted her head and wiped her nose on her sleeve.

"What if it does work? Then we have our Natalie back."

SJ turned to leave, but a notification chime sounded from her wrist scanner and gave away her presence.

The man stood. "Hi, there. Are you the Doc? We're Natalie's parents. Steve and Jess." He grabbed her hand and shook it.

SJ shifted her grip on the electronic tablet. "I have some documents for you to sign. If you need more private time, I can come back later."

"No. No. We're ready." Steve took off his tattered coat and placed it on a chair and sat beside his wife. "I guess we best get used to the idea of no privacy, 'cause being kin to the first person to get resurrected is gonna be a big public deal. I've been telling my Jess here that our Natalie will be a star—a shining hope for all that's waiting their turn."

Jess sniffled and her face contorted. Steve dug in his pocket and pulled out a handkerchief.

SJ swallowed back the lump in her throat as she watched him dab at his wife's eyes. She did not have the heart to remind them that Natalie's life might not return despite the best of efforts, and for this reason, Universe did not want the John Doe trials publicized.

SJ cleared her throat. "Actually, Natalie will be our first unofficial human resurrection."

"Unofficial?" Steve's eyes narrowed. "What does that mean?"

"Our program's financial backers have requested a very specific person's resurrection to be publicized as the first. Your daughter's case will be anonymous."

Steve seemed disappointed, but Jess jumped up and hugged SJ. She spoke in her ear, "Thank you. Oh, thank you. I can't bear the idea of turning our Natalie's resurrection into a spectacle." Then she let go and smoothed her bobbed gray hair behind her ears. "Sorry about that. It's just that Natalie is all we have."

Steve stood and wrapped his arms around his wife. "Natalie will always be our baby, even though she lived to be thirty-three. We couldn't afford genome selection to create our own child, but when the Leave a Legacy program offered host parenting, we jumped at the chance. We passed the Universe qualifying exam on the first try and had our baby in our arms a year later."

"That's amazing." SJ's stomach twisted. Their warm nostalgia tore a gaping hole in her plan. If Natalie's resurrection failed, Jess and Steve would experience the death of their daughter all over again.

Robotic frenzy took over. Don't think. Just do.

She motioned to a table where the couple would sign the consents. Then she spent the next few minutes explaining the procedure, the same process which had taken several lifetimes of science to formulate.

When the document signing was complete, Natalie's parents thanked her over and over again. She managed an optimistic response and hurried out of the room.

The hallway blurred through a swimming mess of tears. She stumbled into a nearby coffee corner, brushed the moisture away, took a deep breath, and straightened her lab coat. Natalie's parents wanted their daughter back. They freely chose to take the chance for resurrection, and trials were part of the process. Sacrifice.

She tapped on her wrist screen and located the theater where the resurrection would take place in several hours. After endless walking through connecting hallways, she passed through security and entered the data bay outside the theater. As team leader, she was required to confirm all details concerning the case. She examined the ectogram scan. The report identified Jane Doe #1 as a thirty-three-year-old female, with biomalism listed as the cause of death.

Her stomach tensed. *Her name is Natalie. Not Jane Doe #1.*

She ran her hand down the seamed side of the microtherm cylinder. A recessed break in the seam revealed a string of numbers that must match the report. The same digits were assigned to a cluster of tissue cells conceived in a petri dish from an anonymous DNA collective group years ago. The conception contributors probably never knew, cared, or recalled the embryo by name, but the host parents did.

Natalie.

The digitally identified cluster of tissue was placed inside the womb of a paid government-regulated professional, an anonymous surrogate birth mother who had no inclination to name the blob growing inside her, but the blob's host parents did.

Natalie.

For Jane Doe #1, the leap from performing successful bird and animal resurrections to attempting human resurrection was small. But for Natalie, the leap was too great.

Cole's manipulation of Universe had gone too far. All because of his self-absorbed publicity stunt to resurrect his father. The rush to perform human resurrection created unnecessary risk.

She knew it but did not know what to do about it. None of her years of research and use of assistive technology contained enough sophistication to guide her. If only she could talk to Kate. Somehow their conversations always brought clarity.

Scrolling through pictures of Kate on her wrist scanner, she paused on the last one she took of Kate's supposed end tablet message, "Believe and live. Book of Wisdom 43:11:25."

Then she changed the view to display all five messages she'd received including the picture Bow drew of the snake on the stick. What was the story? The tale told of sick people and their leader, who asked the Stick Healer what to do.

She closed her eyes and whispered her plea. *Tell me what to do. If you are real, then tell me what to do.*

CHAPTER 30

SJ INITIATED A search on her wrist scanner and found Birch's ID activated in the third conference room. She followed the connecting map to the room and stood in the back as a steady flow of staff moved past her and began filling the seats. On the front platform, a lean figure stood waving something back and forth.

Birch. What was he up to? He loved attention, but surely he had better things to do in preparation for the trials. Her stomach churned. She needed his help now, but a public encounter was not part of her plan.

"Rejuvacatin. Our magic elixir." Birch's voice boomed around the room. He held a small object to the light. "This little injector is where our journey begins."

Why was he talking about things as if he were in charge?

"This …" He held the injector close as if inspecting it. "This unique formula, the one we've prescribed for years in anticipation of this day, will now be confirmed."

Stepping close to the audience, he waved it high again. "For those who don't know how it functions, let me explain. Given as close to time of death as possible, this extraordinary substance gets to work interacting with existing ADP, otherwise known as adenosine diphosphate, to form a protective barrier for each cell, similar to how a fetus is bathed in amniotic fluid. This preserves the tissue until the day it can be reactivated. Isn't that remarkable?"

The crowd hummed appreciative words, overtaking her uncertainty with the force of their confidence. Maybe her concerns were just nerves.

"Of course, precise and continuous storage of the body is a critical component too, from the first few hours to years later." Birch raked his hand through his hair. "You know the drill. The mechanical ebb and flow of pressure inside the cylinder keeps the body tissues saturated and suspended in the protective substance until the candidate's resurrection day arrives."

Birch put the injector in his coat pocket and patted it.

"For decades, people have received Rejuvacatin in their final hours. Despite their terminal illnesses or mortal wounds, they held onto the hope of a future life. They trusted in us, that we would someday break through the confines of their death and bring them back to life. And guess what?"

He strolled to the side of the stage and patted a banner depicting the medical symbol of Asklepian, a serpent wrapped around a rod. "Today is that someday. Medicine will accomplish the final healing and bring the dead back to life. Resurrection."

Loud cheers and clapping erupted throughout the room.

SJ's breath stuck in her throat. Everyone wanted this. She had to get out of there. Re-evaluate. Jostling past some latecomers, she pushed for the door.

"Dr. S. Is that you? In the back? By the interns? Come on up here." Birch's voice rumbled from the platform.

She turned around. Heat flooded her face. Several blue-coated TRIUMP interns in the doorway shifted aside so she could pass back into the center aisle.

"She's here, everyone. My great colleague, Dr. Satan, Jr., or Dr. S., or SJ as she prefers to be called, has just arrived. She's the one who will lead us forward to our success. She's recently recovered from a remarkable turn of events and has just now been speaking with the designated kin of our first trial candidate. Please welcome her. I know she'll be glad to answer any questions you might have."

Team members stood and clapped. Her head spun as all eyes focused on her. She felt like an impostor.

On stage, Birch's greeting projected above the noisy room. "Glad you're here. I was just making up stuff till you arrived."

A man in the front row chuckled, and several others snickered.

Birch stepped outside the sound ring, the select space where words amplified to the audience, and spoke to her in private tones. "You were late, so I just started talking. They said you were notified."

"I wasn't." She moved to stand within the ring outline on the floor and waited while the audience settled down.

"Hello, everyone." Sweat beaded on her neck. She hugged the signing tablet to her chest as if it were a shield. "Thank you for your kind applause, but please realize that this event … resurrection of a human life … is very much a team effort."

She gestured to the crowd. "You and your teammates deserve equal credit for all the hours you have put into perfecting our medical skills to make this event possible. Give yourself a hand."

Clapping and cheers broke out around the room.

Swallowing against the dryness in her mouth, she continued. "As you know, each vital organ team … brain, heart, kidney, liver, lungs … will contribute to the process when the time comes. "Our first candidate," she paused, wondering if she dared say Natalie's name. Pressure pounded in her temples.

Birch cleared his throat.

"Is a female in her thirties." She assumed the expected tones of an emotionless clinician. "The woman died due to complications caused by her advanced stage of biomalism. Most of her life she lived with general good health. The hope is … with resurrection—and our studies have shown this—the terminal illness mechanisms will not return, but her good health base will."

SJ paused. Perhaps there were others who had concerns about the rush to the trials. Maybe an appeal to the larger group was the better way to enlist support after all.

She took a deep breath. "We've spent many years and hours getting here, and each medical team held a significant stake in the success of resurrection. But I want to be clear. I would be careless if I did not express my concern that there are still many unknowns. That is why I believe it is in the best interest of ..."

Faltering over her next choice of words, she locked eyes with a vaguely familiar woman sitting in the front row with the press. "That it is important for all of us to stay on our toes during the process that could take only minutes …" She fumbled again, trying to place the woman.

Was she the new CEO of Medical Plausibility? The woman whose face had transformed into Kate's face in the teleconference with George?

SJ gulped. She was. The woman's watchful stare sent tingles up her spine.

Deep breath. Continuing a candid talk with the team now seemed like a bad idea. She'd already clashed once before with the woman. She would have to be more subtle. Gain Birch's cooperation first and then inform George. He couldn't ignore a timeline request from his top two researchers.

"You were saying, Doctor?" Birch called her out of her trance.

"The resurrection process …" Still muddled by the woman's presence, she looked to him for a clue.

"Could take minutes," he prompted.

"Oh yes. Minutes or even days for the patient to gain full recovery."

"Right. So, since we're …" Birch checked his wrist scanner. "Less than three hours away from our first trial, maybe we'd better take some questions now."

The room buzzed with voices, but one distinct question emerged from the right side of the room. "We've all heard rumors that someone famous has been selected to be the first official resurrection candidate after the trials. Do you know who it is?"

Birch nodded at SJ.

"I do know. But satisfactory trials must occur with the John Doe candidates first." She moved to the left side of the ring. "Next question, please."

"Is it true that you refused to sign the proposed Access Agreement? Do you still believe in that decision, or have you changed your mind and now agree that only those who meet certain criteria should be resurrected?" The question came from somewhere in the center of the crowd.

Her tongue stuck in her mouth. Why were they asking these things?

Birch jumped in before she could speak. "I'm certain that what Dr. Satan feels about the agreement is not the topic we need to address, today."

Heat rose in her face. "Actually, Dr. Birch, although we have more specific topics to address, I am able to answer—"

"Yes." Birch stepped to the front of the sound ring. "It is only sensible that selected candidates for resurrection should meet specific merit criteria, given our years of extensive research and work. Fortifying our population via resurrection should begin with the best." He turned and nodded at SJ. "I think this meeting needs to end so we can begin."

The room erupted with cheers and clapping. SJ smiled and waved through clenched teeth. How could she work with such a conceited man? But she needed him. She needed him to stop this runaway train.

She pretended to be focused on her wrist screen and took deep breaths while the room emptied. Entrenched in a cluster of colleagues, Birch moved to an exit. His towering figure made him easy to spot. She followed him at a distance. Little by little, his entourage dispersed. She caught up to him when he stopped at the end of a hallway in front of a door.

"What brings the great Dr. Satan rushing after me?" He spoke without even looking her way.

The flush of heat returned. "I wanted to talk to you." She waited as he pressed his index finger on the lock, and it opened.

He turned to her. "Yes?"

She gulped. "I just wanted to thank you for your rescue. Somehow, I missed the memo about the meeting. A big surprise with the press being there and …" She stopped speaking. A placard beside the door contained his name. "Wow. That happened fast. Do you have an office here? I thought you'd just arrived. Like me."

He gave no answer but instead beckoned her into a helter-skelter office. He closed the door and snapped his fingers. A multicolored geometric image appeared and hung vertically in the air. Colored pieces bounced about inside the everchanging border, and then all but one tumbled out of sight. He reached for the lone piece and pushed it around in the shape-shifting illusion. She'd seen air puzzles before but never had the patience to wrestle with their complex designs.

"You should try this," he said. "It stretches your thinking. Pieces fit more than one puzzle. The sooner you correctly identify the geometric shape of your current puzzle, the higher your score will be. Puzzle shape choices stream across the bottom."

She sat on an orange leather couch and placed her DocU sign device beside her. She had one goal, and the man wanted to play games.

"You never know if the piece you hold is the last one. That's why you guess as early as possible, based on the pattern you see. It's the test of the game." He settled three yellow triangle pieces in what appeared to be a developing heptagon.

His fascination for the sport seemed endless.

"We can't do it, Birch. We can't go through with the trials."

He snapped his fingers, and the puzzle pieces froze in space. Then he sat behind his desk, leaned back in his chair, and gave her a stony look. "Explain."

"You already know. You've read my findings, and I've read yours. My concern remains with adequate oxygen uptake abilities regarding the human circulatory system post-resurrection. We're just not there. Almost. But not quite. We need to postpone."

"We need to begin. The acceleration of biomalism deaths and increase in incurables and natural disasters are wiping us out. You know this, because you've been following the Life Clock stats like the rest of us. Can't you see we must start and deal with the problems as they occur?"

She nodded. "I see the stats. But I believe we're not ready. This rushed timing is only happening because ..." Her stomach tied in knots. Publicity stunt or not, this was about her leadership. Cole's name did not need to be part of this. "I want to postpone because I believe we're stepping across a threshold that needs more consideration."

"Consideration for what? We've long known how life ends, so it's high time we dabbled in the other end of the spectrum. Resurrection is the pot of gold at the end of the rainbow. You should see it as a blessing. We'll finally control the thing that haunts us all."

"But will we?" She asked the question of herself as much as she did him.

"What are you talking about?"

"I confess, I've always believed that nothing existed for a person after they died. So if we control death, then we will have breached the last frontier restricting our lives. But lately I've wondered if there's a realm beyond death."

"And your point is?"

"If there's more, some kind of alternate life after death here, then human resurrection, if successful, will impact a place we know nothing about."

"Look, Satan, if you want to believe there's another realm, then fine. But what's to say that it's good? It could be a horrible place. Performing a resurrection could rescue the candidate from something that's terrible. We'll be thanked doubly. Once for bringing them back from such a horrible place, and a second thank-you for increasing our species numbers."

"I didn't think of it that way."

"Well, you should. I don't believe there's anything else for us after death, but if there is—and by the way, there's talk about you and messages from Five. Some suppose that's why you've been wavering." His words ceased abruptly.

Truth hit her square in the face. He knew something. "Some? Who? Who's been talking?"

His posture straightened, and he spoke as if soothing a child. "Really, Satan. There's no need to be concerned. It's just talk. Mostly from the mouth of Plausibility. I told them I'd step in to finish the task if you still needed time, but they deferred to your partner and refused my offer."

Heat flooded her face. "Cut the cozy chirping, Birch. What are *they* saying?"

"Everyone's been concerned about the sabotage attempt on your life, Satan." His tone grew sly, and he began to play with his puzzle again.

"It wasn't that big a deal," she murmured, biting back the storm boiling inside of her.

"And then there's the disappearance of your friend's body." He got up from the chair and reactivated the puzzle. "So many distractions, Satan." He tilted his head. "Oops, I mean 'Satin.' I keep mispronouncing it."

Heat crept up the back of her neck, and she balled her hands into fists.

"I'm so sorry about everything." He sat back in his chair and the corners of his mouth twitched. "I can't imagine the strain all this has had on you." His false soothing tone grated like sandpaper.

"Really, Birch?"

"Why are you surprised? And I've told them I've the utmost faith in your professional work. Most of the others do too. Of course, there are a few ..." He moved two puzzle pieces into place.

She set her jaw. "You've had your say. Now here's mine. First of all, never again refer to me by the name Satan. I went through the courts to change my name from the childhood joke that it was when my father bestowed it on me. It's SJ. Two letters. Simple and clear to all concerned. Surely your asinine assumptions aren't an indicator that you've also lost your grasp of the alphabet."

His look of surprise shifted to steel.

"Secondly, you can tell your network of doubters not to worry." She glared at him. "If you're good to go, then I'm good to go. I'm fully able to carry out the task."

CHAPTER 31

SJ MOVED THROUGH the medical complex's hallways without thought or purpose, but to put distance between her and Birch. Rounding a corner, she paused to catch her breath, and the blood pounding through her temples reminded her to unclench her jaw. Birch's reaction clarified everything for her. All her minutes, hours, days, and years of work had flowed to this day. Why should anyone else lead the team forward? She'd sacrificed everything to get here.

The dream of human resurrection lay within her reach, and she'd almost lost her place in it because she had let uncertainties fill her mind. What was she thinking? Inklings of doubt accompanied most great achievements. Hers were no different. And Cole? Even if his push to succeed was selfish, it matched her agenda.

She found the nearest doctors' lounge and changed into scrubs. Every vague concern of another realm now seemed silly. She folded her street clothes and closed them in a locker along with her final nagging thoughts. No, Cole did not drug her. It was a hallucination. Something quite common with Propofylozine. And Kate? Authorities would locate her body. She would make sure of it.

Tracing her finger along the wall screen map, she located the resurrection suite deep in the bowels of the complex. Perhaps a twenty-minute walk. Enough time to focus on her one perfect goal. Resurrection. And specifically, Natalie's resurrection.

When she reached the suite, she swiped her wrist scanner across the security panel outside the door. It opened into a scrub hall. A leaderboard above the sinks illuminated current sign-ins. About half the resident team had checked in. She noted the little K and took it to mean they were from Kerioth staff. Relocation of the trials meant support staff would not originate from the Abide. Only the attendings, preselected and known to her as experts in their field, would be familiar, but none were signed in.

Welcoming the small grace of moving about incognito, SJ slid in beside a row of chattering surgical residents at the sinks and completed her scrub routine. Then she entered the arena, found the task log screen, and selected "inventory." A six-digit code appeared when her status cleared. Most prep work was traditionally done by the residents, but she always found the robotic nature of routine soothing.

After a quick survey of the arena, similar in design to those of the Abide, she located the med room, nestled in the corner nearest the lower left side of the treatment table. The mini bay contained the resurrection drugs she would use.

She moved across the floor, sidestepping team members positioning equipment. As she expected, the six-digit code unlocked the med room door and the Lock Cart inside. Rows of red and green vials filled the top tier of the cart. Each red one contained Corpicom, the substance that re-activated body fluids and specifically the dormant blood cells. Each green one contained Verdegan, a cell memory prompter that triggered sleeping tissue cells to reawaken and resume their tasks. She counted the vials and matched their digits with the list of numbers on the cart side panel. When she finished, she selected "complete" on the panel and stepped back into the arena.

The initial chaotic bustle of activity on the floor had been replaced with order. Residents clustered around their specific triage stations and checked off final preparations with their attendant leaders. The leaderboard in the arena now contained only one blank line. Birch. What was he up to?

It didn't matter. The moment was hers. "Good morning, everyone. I'm Dr. SJ. I'm here as your leader for this historic event. Although we are not conducting this trial live before the world, we are recording, so I'd like us to summarize the resurrection process before we begin and as we work."

Motion ceased, and all eyes seemed to turn her way. She knew her friendly tone contrasted with the format of her fellow superiors. Senior staff seldom addressed support staff except for correction or ridicule, but today she needed to dispel fear and create camaraderie for the best chance of success.

"It's okay. Don't stop what you're doing." The nagging thought returned. Maybe they should stop. No. Stop thinking. Just do. Sacrifice. She cleared her throat. "I'll have questions for you later."

Tasks resumed around the room.

"Just as fire requires three things to thrive, so does the human body. An intact physiological structure, transportation of nutrients and waste, and oxygenated air are vital components for human life. Since oxygen is a given, successful resurrection is really only two scenarios away from reality." She paused as her lesser confidence whispered in her head. *Two scenarios? It will take a miracle and every optimal condition in order to succeed.*

Eyes above surgical masks seemed to stare at her. Perhaps they'd heard the naysayer too?

No. The group of professionals all around her exuded proficiency and single focus. There was nothing to worry about.

She cleared her throat again. "We're merely working to reverse a process." The audacious simplification sounded good. "One could say that the day a human is born is the same day he enters the continuum that leads to death. The premise of resurrection science is to rebuild this final portion. Our goal today is to use all that science has taught us about the human body. We will work to reverse and then restart the physiology that gave our John Doe life. By the way, from this time on, I will only refer to our resurrection candidate by name. Our Jane Doe. Natalie. Please call her this."

You claim her name yet plan to perform an untimely act you know is wrong. The voice in her head whispered grievance.

Defiant, she placed her hand on the body cloth that covered Natalie. "Assistance, please."

A heavyset woman moved to her side. Already extracted from the cylinder, Natalie lay face down, warming on the thermoscan table for the preliminary phase.

SJ noted the name and seniority symbol inscribed on the woman's chest pocket. "Macy, what can you tell us about thermoscans?"

"They were invented decades ago, when cryogenics was thought to be the best preservation method for human tissue. Today's machines are much more evolved. Regaining normal body temperature is important at the end of the resurrection process, after initial cell activation and exchange has been present for some time."

"Good history recall. Now let's inspect the skin." With Macy's help, SJ pulled back the body cloth. Natalie's skin appeared to be in pristine condition. "We all know the skin is the largest organ of the body and the first line of the body's defense. Consequently, the first place we reverse the effects of death in the process of resurrection is the skin. If you care to look, the telltale signs of bruising from biomalism are present around Natalie's joints, but research shows that these infectious microorganisms cannot survive the effects of death. The bruises will fade over time once life is restored."

Several in the team came over to observe, and then they turned Natalie over, face up.

SJ sucked in her breath. A small tattoo of a church window featuring a dove in front of a cross with the bannered words "Book of Wisdom" embellished Natalie's neck.

She licked her lips and barked out a distraction. "Class quiz. What is the first step in the process of resurrection?"

A resident at the hepatic station piped up. "A person must receive a dose of Rejuvacatin if it's believed that death is immediately pending."

"Correct. Natalie's resurrection process began when she received her dose, which of course has been verified in her documented history. Now, can any of you tell me what Rejuvacatin does to the body and if it is part of the resurrection drug class?" She circled away from the table. The tattoo was just that. A tattoo. It held no other significance.

"Rejuvacatin is not classified as a resurrection drug. It is a preparation drug." The answer came from a pulmonary team member.

"Can you describe how it acts in the body?"

"It causes cell life to enter into a state of hibernation. Cellular hibernation."

"Excellent. The discovery of how to suspend cell life without detriment became the biggest medical breakthrough of recent decades. Without its presence, we could not conduct our trial. Even if we fail today, our future candidates are preserved because of this drug."

The team member nodded at SJ and returned to the task of attaching oxygen tubes to the cryodome hood.

"Here's the important thing to keep in mind." SJ moved back to Natalie's side. "Existing in a state of cellular hibernation, as Natalie has been, is not the same as being fully alive. We don't call the hibernation state 'alive.' We've adjusted definitions in the science community to reflect this distinction. Can someone tell me anything else about the drug?"

Macy raised her hand. "The drug solves the problem of preserving structure and prohibiting decay, but it offers no solution for jumpstarting the exchange of nutrients and the removal of waste."

"Right. Let me elaborate. Macy's pointed out a critical problem. Human tissue cells must be able to recognize and receive what is beneficial and good, and they must also recognize and discard what is toxic, or bad. The correct exchange is vital. When it's incorrect or missing entirely, the cell dies." SJ paused, noting that the attendance monitor now flashed green, which indicated all team members were present. But the log board still showed Birch had not arrived.

"Thank you for your attention. It's time for all teams to run a final assessment. I will meet with each group to hear your contingency measures should the path of resurrection revert and become unbalanced and threaten vital organ functions."

Pride surged as she circled the room. Her father's studies and now her research stood together in a long line of dominoes, each within striking distance of the next. All had toppled, one into the other, pushing to this day.

With renewed confidence, she signed off on each team. As she completed the last sign-off, someone entered the room, moved to the table, and stood across from her. It was Birch.

"Shall we begin?"

She looked her skeptic square in the eye. "I already did."

He offered no response but picked up a vial and a syringe.

Over the course of the next several hours, careful distribution of the two substances, Corpicom and Verdegan, managed by incremental injections in the five primary locations—the back of both knees, the joints of the elbows, and the base of the neck, paved the way for reestablishing the circulatory system.

Excitement built as the team noted evidence of tissue vitality. The path of the revival process worked from the outside in. Drug permeation near the surface progressed into deeper tissue. The ripple effect commenced. As she had anticipated, human resurrection would take more time and require more complex maneuvering than Phinny's resurrection had required.

Several hours later, after Natalie's core body temperature reached ninety-six degrees, the pulmonary team started the lung machine.

Everyone watched the monitors. A blip moved across the heart screen. Then another and another. The cardiac team confirmed the heartbeat. A cheer went up.

SJ swallowed several times to moisten her parched throat. She held her breath as the pulmonary attendant worked to slide an endo tube into Natalie's mouth. Seconds later, Natalie's chest expanded ever so slightly. Then it expanded again, aided by the ventilator. The slow, hypnotic hiss of the machine fell into a rhythm, and O2 levels appeared on the monitor.

SJ exhaled and stooped to speak into Natalie's ear. "Wake up. Wake up. It's time to wake up, Natalie."

Natalie's eyelids flickered. Her heart pattern showed only slight arrhythmia, and her core body temperature had risen to 97.6 degrees. Several residents wept.

Exhilaration flooded SJ. The resurrection was a success.

"Now all we have to do is wait for Natalie's brain to regain full consciousness." After much congratulation from all the team members, SJ left the arena to deliver the good news to Natalie's parents.

Jess fell to her knees and held up her hands. "Oh God, oh God. I can't believe it. Our baby's gonna live. I can't ..." She slumped over and began to sob. Steven put his hands on her shaking shoulders and gently helped her up and into a chair.

SJ sat beside her and patted her hand. "Natalie's not yet conscious, but everything looks promising. It's just a matter of time."

Jess dabbed at the tears coming down her face and then gripped SJ's hand. "I know things will be different when she comes back, but I don't care. I'll take my chances."

Steven took a seat on the other side of Jess. "We've had our clashes with Natalie. I'm sure you saw her tattoo, Doc. She got involved with some religious group. Brought home their propaganda. The Book of Wisdom, she called it. She said it had everything in it that anyone needed to live a wonderful life, but I told her such talk was all just fairy tales and lies."

He frowned. "Have you ever heard of it? The Book of Wisdom? It's something that was written ages ago, and not just one book but a bunch of little books put together. Crazy stuff."

SJ's heart flopped in her chest.

Jess let go of her hand and patted her husband on the shoulder. "But we don't care anymore what she believes, right, dear? We just want her back."

"Do you know where she got it? The book?"

Jess's brow furrowed. "I'm not sure."

"My interest comes from my research." SJ smiled at Jess. "I'm conducting a study of people's end-of-life messages and the compulsions they cling to—like believing in an afterlife. I've heard quotes from the book, but I've never seen one."

"We'd be glad to bring you Natalie's copy if it would help you out." Steven sat on the other side of Jess and continued to hand her tissues.

"We can talk about that another day, but it's not a topic for today. The only thing that matters now is Natalie waking up and getting better." SJ spoke in soothing tones.

"Jess and I tried to teach our Natalie the benefit of contingency strategy—how everything can be conquered through logic and reason. Didn't we, hon?" Steven gave Jess a side hug. "Just think of it. When Natalie becomes conscious, she'll realize she's the first person to be resurrected and have even more reason to see that our words are true."

SJ extended her hand. "Congratulations. I'm going to get back to the arena. I'll be back with more news about Natalie as soon as I can."

SJ left the room. The puzzle of the book would have to wait. Natalie was alive!

The ensuing schedule throughout the next few days kept SJ busy. She and the team completed resurrection procedures on several more candidates. Except for Natalie, all the candidate's life function stats continued to rise. Natalie's oxygen uptake level remained low and then slid backward into complete failure at seventy-two hours. SJ officially recorded Natalie's second time of death and declared the resurrection a failure. Rejuvacatin would not be administered again per Jess and Steven's prior request. There was nothing else to do but document findings and tell them the news.

SJ lingered in the procedure room while staff completed their final tasks. When everyone was gone, she whispered her apologies to the draped body on the table. Then she marched to the conference room—the same room she'd stood in three days prior, announcing success—and opened the door.

Steven and Jess rushed to greet her.

"I'm so sorry," she whispered. She swallowed back the nausea of her next set of words. "Natalie didn't make it."

Jess put her hands over her mouth and shook her head. Then she gave a little moan, "No. No. Please, no." She buried her face in Steven's shoulder.

Steven put his arms around her. "Her worst fears have come true. But I try not to think of it that way. Her trial is not in vain. Someday a parent or spouse will be hearing the good news permanently, and Natalie's trial will have been a step that led to that day."

SJ nodded. "But I wish with all my heart that it had come out differently."

Steven wiped away tears and let go of Jess. He pulled something wrapped in a brown cloth out of his satchel and held it out to SJ. "Take this. In exchange. We want her body back. Preliminary studies are okay, but we've changed our minds about any future experiments and wish to cremate her."

Horrified at his insistence of giving something to persuade her, SJ pushed the object back into his hands. "Oh no. Goodness, no. You don't have to give me anything to get me to agree to your request. Please. You are her designated kin, and you have authority to decide."

Steven thrust the bundle back into her hand. "It's the book. We want you to have it. It's not something we want hanging around. It reminds us of less happy times, and we would rather focus on the good memories we had with Natalie."

SJ grasped the bundle. It was the least she could do. "I understand. And again, I'm so sorry about this outcome."

Steven nodded and took Jess's hand.

SJ cleared her throat. "If you don't mind waiting here a minute, I'll have a clerk bring the legal documents you need to sign to reverse the donor choice. But I'm putting a call in now so the paperwork will only be a formality. It's already done." Then she tucked the bundle into her bag and stumbled away before her heart tore completely apart.

Resurrection did not buy life. It only bought time, and in Natalie's case, it bought nothing but pain.

CHAPTER 32

EVIE GRIPPED THE rosy Bartlett. With a small twist, the pear released into her hand. The perfectly ripe fruit would be the crown of her arrangement.

She climbed down the ladder and placed the pear inside the picking basket with the rest. On top of them, she layered lily of the valley stems, the flowers she'd use to fill the gaps between the pears. The entire pear pyramid would rest on a gold platter with ivy garland adorning the edges.

Her favorite festival on Five was Substitution Day, the day everyone brought their best gift in honor of The Great Exchange, the greatest gift ever given. The procession would start in an hour, and she had just enough time if she took the shortcut that ran by the sea.

Leaving the orchard, she raced across the grass field, keeping her basket as level as possible so as not to spill her offering. When she reached the dunes, she zigzagged through clearings of beach vegetation to get to the ruby shore. Since the day she wrote her final message, she'd been on the beach several times without fear. Instead of cringing over the power and size of the jagged whitecaps that crowned the huge waves, she now found beauty.

Today the surf's surrender to the sand produced dainty foam ruffles along the shore. She smiled, remembering the herald's words. The land forms a boundary to the sea. Although the waves roar, they cannot cross over it.

A flock of gulls banked above her. They held their position in the air, gliding on the breezy current. One broke off from the rest and headed straight out over the sea.

She followed its course. Something bobbed in the water in the first crest of surf, a definite patch of golden orange rolling along the turquoise swells. Shading her eyes, she stood at the water's edge and squinted. The thing disappeared into the froth, but soon popped up until the surf rolled it under again. Little by little, the waves brought the thing closer. At first glance it looked like an animal with a pale body and attached amber tentacles. But then, the golden tentacles seemed more like hair.

It was the size of a person.

Was it a person?

Her heart pounded.

Looking down the beach, she searched for signs of anyone else. Maybe the thing was a strange sea creature. Wildlife on Five constantly amazed her. She didn't want to be late for the festival on account of a creature, but if was a person …

She placed her picking basket on the sand.

It was definitely a person.

She could see limbs but no movement. She waded out waist deep and called a greeting. Only gulls responded, screeching above the sound of the water.

Should she run and get help? She pushed forward in the water until it reached her chest. A mountainous wave heaved and lifted the person closer. Uncertain about what she saw, she dove under and swam nearer. When she came up for air, a gull hovered just above her and kept pace with her until she reached the person. A woman floated on her back. Chestnut hair fanned out from her head.

Evie grabbed the lifeless arm and struggled to the shore. She stumbled in the shallow swells and dragged the body as far as she could. Then she flopped onto the sand, gulping in air to ease the pain in her lungs. Her thoughts centered on two things. The woman had no life, and she'd need a herald's miracle to get it back.

Evie stood and whispered, "Help me." Then she took off running—speed running—skimming large stretches of beach between paces to reach the closest herald outpost over ten miles away.

When she arrived at the front of the banana leaf doors of the Ruby Sand Beach Quarter, she bent over to catch her breath. Two heralds playing a game of shuffleboard paused their play, and a third one, resting on the sideline, jumped up and rushed to her.

Between breaths, she gasped, "There's a woman. No life. On the beach."

The curly-haired herald from the sideline tilted his massive head and rubbed his chin. "On our beach? No one ever arrives on our shoreline."

"Well, she did. I mean, I pulled her out of the water." Evie's teeth began to chatter as involuntary trembling swept over her. The effect always came after a speed running effort. "I—I—I think sh-she's a resident already, b-because she had on F-first Clothing, but she's not breathing, or t-talking, or anything."

The two game-playing heralds set aside their cues. The smallest one pulled a knife out of the sand and sheathed it in his belt. His heavy, dark-haired companion slid on a pair of sandals. The russet curly-haired one with hands as big as fan palms scooped her up. "Tell us which direction."

She pointed, and her herald took off. The world blurred as they flew to the body on the beach in seconds.

The curly-haired herald set her down gently on the sand. Then he knelt and cradled the woman's upper body, and the open neck of her gown, a muslin affair with blue embroidery, revealed a small tattoo of a church window featuring a dove in front of a cross with the bannered words "Book of Wisdom" written across the base.

"It's true. Author Perfector spoke it, but I cannot believe it." He laid the woman back on the sand and stood.

"What's true?" Evie asked.

"Resurrection. They've reached the power, but without the protection of faith, it only hastens their disaster."

"But she's not alive." It seemed odd to point out the obvious.

"Her name is Natalie, and she most certainly is alive." The wiry smaller herald, whose features reminded Evie of the baboons that played near her tropical home, seemed insulted.

"Gently, Cyril. Soul Evie does not know the three deaths."

"Three deaths?" Evie puzzled over the idea.

"Yes. The body, the soul, and the most serious one of all, when the spirit departs and eternal death comes. It happens to those who refuse to recognize wrong and do not accept The Substitute as the exchange for their life. Thankfully, although Natalie is dead in her body, because she agreed to The Substitute, then her soul and spirit are merely at rest. She's only sleep dead."

Evie's transport herald picked up Natalie and carried her to the soft dune sand and laid her down. When he stood, he pointed to Evie. "Would you like to waken her?"

"Me? Oh, my goodness, I've never done such a thing." *Only heralds are capable.*

"Well, it's time you learn. It was commanded of the first followers, but few understood the timing and source of power for resurrection." He gestured to the dark-haired herald beside her. "Take Humor's hand."

Evie braced for the grip that caused heat to creep up her hand and arm.

Then Cyril dropped down on the sand and propped Natalie up in a sitting position. After this, he joined the woman's slack hand to Evie's free hand. "We are ready, Spero."

Her curly haired transport nodded. "Proceed."

Cyril tilted back his head and held up one hand. "Author Perfector, giver of life. We ask for your power to revive Natalie's soul and spirit. We ask this by the power of The Substitute's great name. Amen."

Evie looked down on the motionless woman and saw no change. Then, a gust of wind swept across the sand. It grew into a powerful gale that parted the beach grass and split the dune sand, eroding a gully which advanced directly toward them. The heralds stepped back and bowed as it passed in front of them. A pressure pushed Evie to the ground. She bowed too, imitating the heralds, but in doing so, she lost her grip on Natalie's hand, and Natalie's body fell back.

A voice spoke in her ear. "Take her hand. Do not let go. Use her name and say, *Arise.*"

She opened her mouth, but no words came.

"Do this, I say." The voice whispered, urgent and clear.

Evie reached again for Natalie's hand, pulled her firmly and said, "Natalie, arise!" The cool skin of the sleep-dead woman turned hot and ignited Evie's fingertips, but she did not let go.

A rush of color flooded Natalie's ashen cheeks, and her limbs twitched. She opened her eyes and pulled against Evie's grip. "Where am I?"

"You're on Five," Evie whispered.

Behind her, Evie heard a chorus, low and sweet. The melody came from the heralds. "Praise to the one whose death makes all things new. Your word and promise are always true. When skies are fallen and mountains broken, what you have spoken shall not fail."

The chorus resounded in one acclaim with the sea and the gulls and the wind. All gave praise for the Life Giver—The Substitute—the Perfect Exchange. Evie closed her eyes and listened to the last strains of the song, wondering if a more beautiful arrangement had ever been heard.

"Soul Evie?" Spero tapped her on the shoulder. "There's still time." He held out her picking basket.

Evie took it and slipped the handle over her arm. "Thanks. But I'm not certain that I'll still go. My flowers look a bit droopy." Her goal no longer seemed important compared to the wonder of the miracle she'd just witnessed.

"Please don't miss the festival because of me." Natalie smiled up at her. "I'm fine now, although I can't explain what happened. I only know that I'm safe, and it's all because of you."

"Him," Spero corrected. "It's because of Him. Evie acted in faith. Author Perfector's power worked through her to bring back life."

"That's right. I simply did as I was told." Relief came from speaking the truth. If the only skill needed to accomplish wondrous things was doing what Author Perfector asked, then Evie felt full of potential. In the past, fear had stopped her from acting. Now, because of her healing, fear withered away.

"Doing what He wills us to do is the most important thing." Cyril pulled Natalie to her feet, and Humor provided his outer cloak to wrap around her shivering, wet body.

"It's a wonderful feeling to participate in a life's return. And the Substitution festival is all about the one who made such powers possible. I know the Son will be pleased with your offering. Let's go together." Spero patted her shoulder.

Humor poked at the blossoms in Evie's basket with chubby fingers, and his face broke into a grin. "I dare say the flowers will know their master and be on their best behavior when we arrive."

"I will take the lead, and Cyril will follow with Natalie and Evie." Spero cleared his throat and then added, "Humor can bring up the rear."

"The rear again? Is that all I'm good for?" Humor pouted but seemed unable to maintain his sour look. His radiant smile made Evie grin.

"Dear, dear brother. He put you last for other reasons." Cyril stood on tiptoe to pat Humor on his broad shoulder. "Mainly strength. We've got to take the shortcut over the bluffs to make up time. You're last only because you can scale the cliffs single-handedly without needing a push from behind."

Humor lunged playfully at Cyril and then scooped him up and carried him dangling upside-down over his shoulder. Cyril hollered and thrashed about until Humor finally set him down and adjusted his rumpled clothing.

Evie giggled at the antics, and Natalie joined in. Even Spero gave one or two guffaws. Evie had never seen heralds play. Although always kind, they tended to matters on Five with resolute dignity.

The party soon fell into formation along the path. Ruby sand disappeared under wide patches of gold beach grass. Ahead of them, the strands merged into one vast undulating wave along the base of the cliffs, dipping and swaying as if alive.

Alive. She'd seen life return.

A puff of wind buffeted her skirt, and the fabric caught on her basket. Flowers spilled when she tugged it free. The reason became obvious. The basket now overflowed with at least double the amount of flowers that she'd picked. She giggled and held one up to the wind. The perky stalk of dainty bells bowed and bounced in perfect form, celebrating the miracle of life all over again.

CHAPTER 33

SJ QUICKENED HER pace. The maze of Kerioth resembled that of the Abide, a medical institution connected by a jumble of halls, ramps, and stairs. The only difference was that no amount of walking in Kerioth would lead her to the outdoors and sunshine. She knew one thing for sure. Underground life was not for her.

She also knew something else with absolute certainty. The trials should stop. They were not ready. Leaping ahead for the gain of public glory did nothing to fill the void of personal loss. Steven and Jess had lost their beloved child. Again. She had nothing to compare except Kate. She'd not wanted to believe Kate was gone. With no proof, because she had no body, she still hoped it was all a mistake, but it would be worse if Kate returned only to suffer through death again.

How could she stop it? Cole was the key, but she had no leverage.

Her path ended at an elevator alcove with a sign indicating a meditation room off to the side. Should she take the elevator up or down?

Neither. She pushed a button beside the sign, and a panel in the wall moved sideways, revealing a dimly lit room. SJ squinted. One lone figure in a wheelchair sat facing a gray-lit window.

Picking a bench on the opposite side of the room, she sat and closed her eyes. Her bag slid from her arm, and she clutched instinctively. The Book of Wisdom. Would it make her wise?

Glancing at the window, she wondered if it was a safe place to read. Surely, the person sitting offered no threat. She took out the book and loosened the cloth. Holding her scanner light to the back of the crumbling leather cover, she found the stamped 2085 print date, which indicated that the book was an eighty-year-old black market copy. The Religious Sanction Code, passed in 2065 by Universe sector leaders, called for severe penalties against any new printing or producing of religious materials. The majority believed that devotion to religion only bore the fruit of rebellion, conflict, and war.

She traced her finger over the faded gold imprint on the cover and wondered if the title was a bogus name. Religious history studies from her child development school days suggested that illegal reprints of sacred books were intentionally composed to be discreet. The generic title, Book of Wisdom, could possibly be a substitute for the original name.

Sifting through fragile pages, she came to a table of contents. Jess was right. The book contained sixty-six small books, all printed and bound as one.

"Who's in here?" A deep voice electrified the room.

SJ shoved the book under the bench, leapt to her feet, and moved away from her contraband. The person by the window no longer sat but stood, or more specifically, glided across the room. In a bot chair? Backlit by the window, the face remained shadowed until she held her wrist light high. "Ben? Is that you? What are you doing here? Why in …?" Her questions dissolved as he navigated to her and stopped just a few feet away.

Ben stuck out his hand. "Dr. S. Good to see you—ahem—sense you." The corners of his mouth twitched as if holding back amusement.

Wondering if he could be trusted, she hesitated.

"It seems I'm here for the big one." He dropped his hand.

"Big one?"

"The first official resurrection. Permission granted because of my hard work, I suppose."

"Well, congratulations." She exhaled. Somebody thought he was trustworthy.

"And a hearty congratulations to you too. I hear the trials have been a success."

"Mostly." She swallowed hard. "But it was a team effort."

He turned the bot chair and rolled slightly closer toward the bench. "May I see it?"

She gulped. How did he know?

"It's okay. I'm actually a fan of print books, but I've only seen them in museums." He chuckled. "Well, actually—I did not see them."

"How did you know I had one?"

"You don't remember well, do you, Dr. S?" His voice held warmth. "When we met, I told you my audio skills describe what I cannot see. I heard you and your book."

She nodded. "Right. Okay, then." She returned to the bench and pulled out the forbidden publication.

Ben converted the bot chair to a sitting position and allowed her to guide his hand to touch the cover. Heat shot up her arm and into her neck from the contact. The same heat sensation had occurred at their first meeting—the day he helped pick the lock on Kate's cylinder.

She pulled back her hand.

A wide grin came over his face. "It's contraband. I'm guessing a copy of the Book of Wisdom. Very rare since RSC placed a ban to put an end to their mass production."

How did he know such specifics?

"I can smell it."

Could he hear her thinking?

"May I hold it?"

She placed the book in his hand.

He lifted it to his nose and sniffed. "A very specific paper and ink. The Book of Wisdom was headed for extinction even without the ban."

"Why do you say that?"

"Advanced technology and the human habit of posting knowledge onto data screens instead of paper affected all information. Religious beliefs are only one example." He cocked his head. "Would you agree, Doc?"

"Possibly." Trying not to think about his unsettling ability, she realigned pages and smoothed the paper until she gathered her thoughts. "My genealogy communications research on end messages suggests that very little substance on any topic is deliberately being passed along from one generation to another. Why should it? Everything is available in databanks. It's a help-yourself scenario."

Ben furrowed his brow. "That troubles me."

"Why?"

"What if one generation's decision about useful knowledge in the databank is terribly misguided, and their mistake contributes to the disappearance of available knowledge for future generations?"

"With all the experts weighing in, that seems unlikely."

"Maybe not." He fidgeted with something on his chair then shifted his posture. "Here's how it happens. Sector leaders determine what knowledge is valuable to teach in our Child Development schools. All other information comes to us through our fingertips, through technology, but again, only the knowledge that is made available. Truth becomes elusive if knowledge is selective."

"Sure. Correct conclusions are impossible if they are made in response to incomplete and inaccurate facts. Basic science formula." The all-too-familiar discussion about truth made her skin itch.

Ben nodded. "So it is."

She closed the book and wrapped it in the cloth.

"Time to go?"

"I've got to check the next trial assessments." She stood and headed for the door. When she paused to drop the book in her bag, Ben whirred around her and stopped in front of the door.

"Hear me out. I know this will sound contradictory coming from a blind person, but getting to the root truth of a matter is as vitally necessary to me as being able to live in the light." He chuckled and added, "Which is why I've no use for this underground den. No offense to your boyfriend builder, but if it weren't for the sabotage attempt and need for relocation of the resurrection trials, SHEOL would be the last place I'd choose for the dead to come back to life."

"Where would you rather have the trials take place?"

"Home." Ben's vacant eyes closed. His face became almost radiant.

"Where is that? Sector Seven?" The look of pleasure on his face made her wonder if he'd always been blind.

"Nope. A place more beautiful than most have ever seen."

Voices in the adjoining hall interrupted them. Ben came out of his trance. "Check on the trials and then call me. There's a quiet place where we can examine the book without risking discovery. I'll take you there."

An hour later, SJ trailed through the medical center behind Ben. Somehow she trusted him. From their few conversations, it seemed he followed the same purist approach to research as she did. No matter what others did or said, she looked for her own answers.

They arrived at the doctors' annex. Located in the medical main tower, the elaborate wing offered rooms for rest and diversion to team members who worked long hours.

Ben asked her to wait there while he retrieved his spare power pack. She sat on a couch in the lounge area and checked her missed calls. One came from Cole. She selected "deferred callback" and added a message about final assessments and paperwork. Cole would not be happy with her book diversion if she told him outright.

Ben reappeared, and she followed him through an exit door in the empty dining area. Once outside, the endless expanse of the cavern that housed SHEOL dominated the background. Rough rock walls stretched into obscurity where sky and sunlight would normally be. Although artificial light metered out a valiant glow in every likely spot, the effect was no match for the darkness.

Ben rolled onto a ramp that climbed, zigzagging ever higher up a slope, until it reached the final excavated ridge, where exercise paths trailed off to make various loops and connections.

"Wow. I had no idea all this existed." She marveled over the sight.

"Well, as far as I'm concerned, it doesn't." Ben laughed. "But if I'm not mistaken, there's a bench somewhere nearby with my DNA on it. A fact I know because of the birds."

"Birds?" She glanced around for signs of life on the rock surfaces. "What kind live in here?"

"They're called DARTS, which is short for Dynamic Aviator Robotic Transducers. They're designed to react to environmental changes in tremors, temperature, gas presence, or pressure. They transmit the changes through sensors. When data cycles fall outside normal parameters, it triggers a warning to SHEOL dwellers that their world is about to turn upside down."

"Well, that's a relief. It's good to be forewarned." She took a seat on a bench several yards away.

"A sentiment which makes my first experience out on the ridge kind of ironic. I've been to SHEOL one other time. On the first day of that visit, my friend and I came to explore the trails, and some DARTS took off from the ridge just as we approached. The noise threw off my perception, and my chair made a sandwich of me and the bench before I realized what was happening."

"Was it a bad injury?"

"Just my pride, mostly." Ben grinned. "But enough about DARTS and danger. Get out the book. We won't see people on the ridge during the workday. It's too much trouble to get here."

He adjusted his chair and came to a sitting position.

She took out the book and flipped to the end of it and pointed to the page number. "One thousand eight hundred seventy-six. That's a lot of pages for one book."

"It's actually made up of sixty-six books divided into two portions. The first half has thirty-nine books."

She released the book into his hands, and his face held a faint smile as he sifted through the pages. Then he closed the book and handed it back. "The second half is more like a quarter of the total book, but it contains twenty-seven distinct sub-books. Some of the books are more like letters written from one person to a group of people." He delivered the information methodically, with his eyes closed.

"How… how do you know so much?" She stared at him, her mouth agape. "I thought you'd never seen a book, let alone a Book of Wisdom." She spoke with more sharpness than she intended and immediately regretted it. "I'm sorry. I guess I assumed that part."

"Don't be upset." He put his hand on her arm. "I didn't want you to know at first. Yes. I've had some experience with the Book of Wisdom, but not in the way you think. I wasn't trying to deceive you. I wanted you to choose your actions about the book without my influence."

"I suppose that's fair. A relief actually, given the size of it. Now you can tell me all I need to know in much less time than I have leisure to read."

"But that's exactly what I can't do. You must read it for yourself in order to discover what it is you need to know. Approach it the same way you approach your research as a scientist. Don't take my word about any of it. Know the Book of Wisdom for yourself."

"The messages I received all contained the number forty-three." She thumbed through the pages. "Maybe that's the forty-third book. Perhaps that's where I should start."

"I always think it's best to read a bit of the beginning to get a feel for where it's going."

"Fine. I'll do what I do with most books. I'll start at the beginning and skip to the end." She declared her intentions with a half-smile.

"Read it aloud, if you don't mind. I'll be your only audience in this desolate place." Ben tilted his headrest and leaned a little to his right side and closed his eyes again.

Over the next hour, the words of the ancient text came alive as she read. Her voice spoke the description of the beginning and the one who breathed life into a dust man. Then came contrary times, the decision of the first man and woman, the consequence of the decision, and a brother's murder. A list of ten generations of families followed the murder. She marveled over the lifespan of the people listed. Some lived more than seven hundred years.

The next section contained stories of a boat builder, a zoo on water, a catastrophic flood, a mercy, a rescue, the birth of nations, and a scattering of the people. Then came another ten-generation genealogy list.

SJ paused her reading. She'd discovered a pattern. It existed in the form of a relationship, a continuous cycle of connection, either broken or regained, between the one who breathed life and the people who received the breath.

What did it mean? If she considered it a fairy tale, then it meant nothing.

She looked over at Ben to get his opinion, but he seemed to have fallen asleep. She began reading again but this time silently.

The next few passages revealed the travels and trials of a childless septuagenarian who received a generational promise from the one who breathed life.

She did the math. The stories and genealogy accounts she'd read about in the first fifteen pages of the book amounted to a relationship spanning over two thousand years and twenty generations. That was a long relationship. If any of it were true, then the breath giver had an order to life that brought good to his dust people.

Was the breath giver still alive in book forty-three?

She thumbed through dog-eared pages and found the text tied to the first set of numbers, 43.10.10.

"The thief comes to steal, kill, and destroy. I come that you may have life to the full."

It was there. A description of two beings. A life giver and a thief.

An alert came from her wrist scanner.

It was the psych-social team. They demanded a briefing.

She stowed the book in her bag and patted Ben on the shoulder. "Wake up. There's a meeting. I've got to go."

He put his chair in gear, and they headed down the ramp. Inside the medical complex, they parted ways. Ben had assessments to complete.

SJ located the briefing room and stepped inside a buzz of excitement. Team leaders gave reports. Most of them were good. The post-resurrection trial candidates' physical parameters were within acceptable ranges. Post-resurrection mental acuity measured consistent with the pre-life knowledge and memory of the candidates.

There were two areas of concern, however. The lesser one centered on the unexplainable sensation of intense heat felt by anyone who touched the skin of the resurrected.

The other more worrisome concern, brought to light by the psych-social team, showed that the M&E scan (mood and emotion) continued to register dangerous lows or even absent amounts altogether. This type of result usually indicated the presence of extreme sociopathic impulses.

The nervous woman who delivered the stats concluded her remarks with the team's cautious recommendation. "We believe that the resurrection candidate's medical release should be contingent only with a direct admission to a Level Four institution that provides psychiatric care within his home sector."

Outbursts filled the room. Scoffers rejected the concern as too soon to warrant such action.

Above the fray, SJ heard the woman's voice grow loud and warning. "Besides the scan readings, there are detached and unemotional reactions to known family members. Multiple times a mother approached the staff to ask if her usually considerate son had been drugged because of his indifference. When we asked her to describe what she observed, the mother declared, 'It's him, but it's not him. He's alive, but he says and does things he never would. It's as if he has no conscience—no soul.'"

The room erupted again. Much of the staff rejected the psychology team's concerns. Many did not believe in the notion of a "soul" as the mother used it.

SJ called for order. "The essence of being alive has been established for ages and is explainable in terms of biological and cognitive matters and physical laws. Still, as the team leader, I'm responsible. If resurrection alters in a negative way the protein and carbon dust pile that makes us human, then I must insist we cease the process until we can determine the impact. The news is disturbing. I will personally observe what has been described and make my decision."

She'd never imagined a renewed "breath of life" would blow out a man's soul, but now she had a chance to stop the trials.

CHAPTER 34

SOUNDS OF SLURPING filled the boardroom. Four heads bobbed over four bowls of pho soup from Charlie's Lunch Cart. Cole knew his next words would astound, so he chose to overlook his cronies' inattention and ill-mannered ingestion.

"Gentlemen and Rumi." Cole cleared his throat. No eyes looked his way, except for Rumi, who sat motionless in front of a fifth bowl and appeared to be studying him like a cat.

"It's happening." Still nothing from the others. Cole began circling the room, an activity which usually made his subordinates anxious. "Resurrection trials have begun, which means our own little experiment is now in motion."

Heads remained bowed over the elixir before them.

He refused to give in to his mounting anger. He, too, could be patient and kind. He would entice them with glorious words. His day—the day when all the universe would worship his leadership—drew close. Mortar was not the only one who could bestow grace and inspire wonder.

He attempted a Zen-like composure and pushed a vacant chair back into position ever so slowly. Then he started again, speaking softly through clenched teeth. "My friends, don't let me interrupt your lunch. Please continue while I give you the good news. News that will forever anchor our corporation as the world's top shipping company. As I said, *Resurrection Trials* have begun."

He waited for the effect of his words to hit them. Nothing happened. How could they be so uninterested? Outrage poured over him as hot lava. He elevated his voice to counter his fury. "*This* accomplishment comes only because of our support. As we supply men with life, the most basic need of all, our age-old slogan, Delivery Conquers Need, becomes even more potent. DCN will bring new increments of existence to every man, woman, and child who needs it. For all contingencies, we are truly a one-stop shop—the source of everything, the bonanza of bazaars, the supreme of superstores, the most majestic of monopolies."

He searched the room. Only Rumi made eye contact, and her mouth twitched ever so slightly in a way that he could not discern. Why was manipulation so difficult? If the world were up to him, he would never give free will to anyone, human or heavenly. Robots would choose his will without question, but Mortar placed some kind of glory in being freely chosen.

He turned up his lips at the top of their hideous heads. His power could crack their skulls wide open, but then he would have to start all over again to find a new body for them to indwell. The best he had available would sell their birthright for pho soup.

"Gentlemen. You must comprehend the irony of it all. Don't you see how resurrection greatly increases our power and control over men? It turns Mortar's influence over his images to dust—not unlike the dust from which they are made. Such a wonderful mockery."

Morbid looked up and gestured with his spoon. "How is resurrection a DCN advantage when it's not a product we can transport?" The ancient gave a sly grin and then dove back into his apparent quest of trying to shovel as many rice noodles as possible into his mouth before they could fall off his spoon.

Cole winced. He strode to Morbid's chair, snatched the spoon from his hand, and spun the old maggoty man around. He squelched a gag as Morbid's peculiar overpowering stench filled the air.

"Such a literal you are, Morbid. Always pretending you can't follow my spin. Of course, resurrection is not a product, but the needs arising from the prospect are deliverable. There will be bodies to transport, and all sorts of necessary tangibles related to the process. In addition, DCN's donations to the Resurrection Project far exceed any other source. We will be credited with the success and gain another notch in our belt to keep mankind fused to our power and dominion."

"What about Five? The messages? Won't people figure out there's more than one world and that the door opens to the next one through death?" Lucas predictably tossed him another challenge.

"But they *don't* know that now, do they, Lucas? We've been countering their belief systems for years. DCN's faithful work to decrease access to the Book of Wisdom has allowed Mortar's recent little instigation to fall on ignorant ears. Interest will die down. Messages from Five will seem insignificant when broadcasts of Beast's live resurrection permeate every sector. Humans have always hated death. Now we can reverse it. That's the bigger news."

Excited over their attention, Cole couldn't resist a little show. Getting the group to perch on the same roost with him conquered important necessary groundwork before his next revelation. He waved his hand to send a hologram into motion in the center of the board room.

The soup slurping subsided, and the gang watched a newscast where a journalist discussed the benefit of successful resurrection with Cole.

The hologram journalist commented, "People want to know what prompted your vision of helping the science community reach successful resurrection."

In the hologram, Cole responded, "Many have grieved a loved one's life being cut short. Death is as the unseen snake in the grass that strikes and kills without warning. Consider all the great minds we have lost. Having the ability to resurrect the best of humanity will make us strong again. By partnering with the resurrection team, our company hopes to become a beacon of hope and promise for that greater good."

Lucas snorted and the others broke out in gales of laughter. It seemed his show of concern for human life and goodness delighted them.

When the hologram disappeared, Cole patted the shoulders of a dark, glowering willow of a man hunched over his steaming bowl. "Apologies, Snake. No offense intended."

Across the table, Abaddon dipped his spoon up and down in the clear broth and grunted, "Why does it always have to be so hot?"

Cole pounded the table. A crack spiderwebbed across the marble surface. Soup splashed out of each bowl. "Soup is supposed to be hot."

Everyone put down their spoons. Abaddon swept back rivulets of soggy hair that had landed in his bowl. He accepted Lucas's offer of a napkin and dabbed at his locks.

Cole clapped his hands, and the soup broth left the bowls and pooled on the table, making a pond in the center of the assembly. Then Cole made a circle in the air with his finger, and the soup puddle became airborne and swirled off to the corner to hover obediently over the trash can. Cole pointed down and heard the collective sigh from the sorrowful soup eaters as they watched their lunch disappear into the receptacle.

Lack of attention was no longer a problem.

The heated gaze of disgruntled eyes settled on Cole. Too bad about the soup, but he had a kingdom to run.

He returned to the head of the table. "My next point of discussion will be our expansion strategy. Enlarging our territory will be much simpler now that resurrection is achieved. When my father, Beast, becomes the first official and televised resurrection, we will gain the benefit of his reputation to aid us in the promotion of our Carbon Code Contract and the roll out of our fusion generators. All who agree to the contract will have exclusive access to purchase them. None will resist the opportunity for complete fulfillment of all their needs on their own terms."

Snake raised his glass. "A toast to the rising of the Beast."

All held up various beverages. "Hear, hear."

Cole inhaled their praise. He sat and lifted his glass of cider to his mouth. Light effervescence tickled his nose. He gulped instead of sipping, causing his throat to spasm. The others stood and gathered their belongings even as he sputtered and coughed violently. He gestured for them to remain and finally managed to bark, "Sit!"

Snake and Abaddon obeyed, but Lucas and Morbid remained standing.

He motioned to them. "Would you leave before you've heard the most important thing?"

Morbid flopped into a chair. "Of course not, our liege. What is it?"

Lucas did not budge.

Cole laced his fingers together, closed his eyes, and summoned every ounce of restraint. When he opened his eyes, he sensed the room and smelled fear. Not all, but some reeked of it, and that was good enough for now.

"Hear my words. Resurrection amplifies our opportunities. With it, instant possession will become our *soup du jour*." He waited for encouraging chuckles, but no one seemed to get his joke. He sighed. "Think of it. If we are present to possess a human the moment they come back to life, then we bypass the hard work of manipulation and persuasion altogether. If Mortar's returning spirit puts up resistance, I'm convinced we can ambush. Knowing in advance the likely moment the Breath of Life returns will give our readied spirits an advantage to indwell."

"Really, Cole? An ambush? How will that work? We're not on the medical team. We'll never be allowed in the arena." Lucas's scoffing dangled temptation in front of the others.

Cole expected the challenge but not the sneaky looks exchanged around the table and especially the one Lucas gave Rumi. The two had recently communicated. He was certain of it. Rumi offered no threat, but Lucas lapped at every opportunity to disrupt. Lucas wanted Cole's position in the kingdom.

"This is the plan. We will be present during the resurrections, but invisible. I'll know the timing of the procedures through SJ. At the moment life returns, we will have a pre-selected and expertly trained spirit indweller slip inside the body and assume control."

"What if one of Mortar's souls comes back to claim the body?"

"Always looking for a fight, eh Lucas?" Cole locked eyes with his opponent until Lucas turned away. "It's my opinion it's whoever gets there first gets the territory. But no matter what happens, any display of spirit conflict must stay masked. Rumi will help with that. We don't want humans to become aware of the spirit world, because that's when things get out of control."

Chatter ensued but then ceased when Cole's wrist alert sounded. SJ wanted to talk.

"Meeting adjourned." He waved everyone off. All hurried away, probably to find the lunch cart, he imagined.

Only Rumi remained seated.

He nodded at his sibling and then focused on his call with SJ. "Yes, I heard. Congratulations. What an achievement. You must be proud. What? No, I did not hear that. We'll discuss whether that's necessary. No. I realize you're the one in charge, but I think you might be making a hasty decision. Give it more time … right … love … I'm only saying …"

He squirmed under Rumi's inquisitive gaze. "Let me call you back in a bit. The board meeting just ended. I do want to talk to you. I'll call you right back." Cole disconnected.

The two sat in silence. Then Rumi spoke. "Let me guess. There's been a complication, and she wants to put on the brakes. What is it? Physical incapacity? Mental amnesia? Something worse?"

He smiled. Rumi could never imagine this one. Then he laughed boisterously. "Actually, it's none of that. And I for one would categorize the development as a great advantage and not a potential disaster as she would. Something rather good has happened, for us at least."

Rumi cocked her head. "Stop dancing and deliver."

"She says the trial candidate's family believe the man they knew has returned through resurrection, but he acts as if he has no soul."

"How can that be? What do they know of souls and spirits? They don't believe in them. Besides, Mortar would never allow it."

"I don't know, but they observe something different and call it a soul. It sounds to me as if Mortar does not return to claim these resurrected. If this is true, then our plan to possess resurrected human life without contest is guaranteed. All we must do is convince SJ to keep moving forward. Resurrection will provide a population of the best of both worlds. Our unified kingdom will reach even greater heights and achievements. It won't be like Mortar's kingdom. It will be greater than Mortar's kingdom."

He sat back in his chair relishing the thought. "Think of it, Rumi. This strategy, to take over resurrected life, allows us to become the deadliest of snakes to ever lurk in Mortar's grass."

CHAPTER 35

SJ REVIEWED THE Pysch-Eval reports of the newly revived resurrection candidates in an empty conference room. Technicians conducting the tests used virtual reality scenarios. Multiple examples of deceptive, impulsive, cruel, and uncharacteristic behavior were logged.

After viewing the last candidate, a woman remembered by her family as an animal lover and doting mother, SJ shut off the wall screen and massaged her throbbing temples. The results were chilling. The woman had chosen to beat a puppy to death with a bat after being subjected to its incessant barking.

She had to call a halt to the trials. It was her duty. With Cole's help, she'd sidestep Birch and go directly to the council. Her hesitation over the timeline of the trials now had shape and form. If resurrection candidates revived to roam the world with newfound psychotic impulses, then science had created more problems than it solved.

That night, between appearances of house staff carrying endless gold plates of Bosma's culinary offerings, she pleaded with Cole to help steer the council. "To continue would be reckless. We need time to study these behavior shifts."

"You've spent your entire life for this moment, and now you would throw it away because of what? Family members who claim their relatives acted differently in their prior life? Maybe they forgot the bad parts. People tend to do that after someone dies. They make them into saints and angels."

He pushed a pile of little bones onto a saucer after removing them from his duck breast. "You aren't thinking straight. That's why you need my help. You've accomplished the grandest of victories—the reversal of death. It's celebration time." He poured a glass of champagne and held it up. To us and the glory of conquering death."

She sighed. "You're not listening. Resurrection holds no glory if the outcome brings fear and cruelty."

"Ah, there it is. Your fear." He set down his glass. "Time's running out. You know the population stats as well as anyone. Your foolishness stands in the way of benefit for the entire world."

"But that's the point. There's a risk that outweighs the benefit. What wisdom is there in proceeding? Beast could be affected by the same disturbing outcome. Doesn't that possibility alarm you?"

"No. My father will be fine." Cole pushed his plate away. "You, on the other hand, concern me. You refuse to see the great advantage this accomplishment brings. You lack consideration for the wonderful tonic of optimism that many indulge in without harm."

Frustrated by his familiar goading, she stabbed at the perfectly sautéed vegetables with her fork. She held back for several silent seconds, but then her compulsion took over. "Waiting for the truth to unfold is neither pessimistic or optimistic. It's just waiting. We need more studies before we continue with new trials."

"And there it is. Your other treasure. Truth." He slammed his hand on the table. "The god to which you will sacrifice all else. An undeniable obsession—the constant quest of looking for truth."

Heat flooded her face.

"I knew we'd get to it. Our peculiar stomping ground." He wiped his mouth and pushed back his chair. "It's sad, you know. You of all people should be more aware that truth is a variable and not a constant."

"What do you mean?"

"Truth changes depending on the situation. This recent development is a perfect example. As a scientist who takes pride in operating with facts, you should see that the supposed personality changes in a few cannot possibly outweigh the need for continued resurrection efforts to benefit the masses. The rapid decline of human species in this last decade is our most serious threat. That's a true fact."

"And my simple statement of wanting to wait for more facts to unfold is not heresy."

"No, heresy is something else." Cole left the dinner table and walked to the sideboard and appeared to be studying the painting of fruit hanging above it.

She tried to keep eating, but her stomach remained in knots. Maybe his anger and pushback came from reasons other than his will to control. Perhaps he genuinely grieved the additional time that would pass before his father could be resurrected.

Taking a deep breath, she pushed back her chair, walked behind him, and placed a hand on his shoulder. "I'm so sorry. I know you wanted your father—"

He whirled around. His eyes brimmed with fire. "You know nothing! And what is most profane to me is your acclaimed position of truth detector that you cling to ever so dearly."

"What do you mean?"

"Your quest for honesty and truth is just so ridiculous."

"Why do you say that?"

His face contorted, twisting and grimacing as if manipulated by an unseen foe. He finally spat out senseless words. "Because you're immersed in a great lie."

Her gut twisted on the pointed end of her resolve. *Don't retreat.* "What exactly is the lie I'm immersed in?"

He moved away from her, reached for a carving knife from the table and slashed through the air, as if sword fighting an opponent.

Before she could react, he laughed hysterically and then rushed to grab her at the waist. Holding the knife high with his free hand, he twirled her about in an uncomfortable dance. "Let's make a deal. I'll ask you some questions, and if you can give a true answer to any one of them, I'll immediately back your request for delay at the council. But if you can't give even one answer, then you'll complete my father's resurrection. No delays."

Her heart pounded and her mouth went dry. He was a madman.

He stopped spinning her and asked, "Is Kate alive or dead?"

"I'm not sure … I think … well … just not sure." Why was he asking this?

"Are the messages from Five true or a hoax?" He let go of her waist.

"No one knows that. It's being studied."

"Were you the target of the relocation protesters' sabotage or could it be something else?" He winked at her.

"I'm not …" She gulped and tried to recall details of her drugging.

"Can you answer any one of the three?" He moved to tap the flat edge of the carving knife three times on the back of the closest dining chair as if knighting it.

"Of course not. They're impossible questions. All the facts are not available. No one can answer them."

"Actually, that's where you're wrong." He placed the knife back on the table. Then he yanked her by the hands to pull her close. His lips curled in a sneer. "There's someone who knows the truth about all of it, but since it's not you, then our agreement stands."

"Who could possibly know the answer to those questions?"

He smoothed a stray lock of hair back behind her ear and whispered, "You'll honor our deal. Raise my father from the dead and leave the souls to me."

SJ stared at the ceiling. Thoughts swirled through her mind. Past midnight, Cole's breath sounds came from across the room in a regular pattern. Scooting to the edge of her mattress, she slipped one foot to the floor, paused a few seconds, then swiveled her other leg around. Then with both feet on the floor, she slowly stood and padded toward the door.

As she made her way out, Cole turned over. She became a statue until snoring filled the room again.

Moving through the house, she used only her wrist light.

Somehow, she'd let Cole dazzle her into allowing him to think for her, and she'd become blinded to important details. Even tonight, when he claimed that if she resurrected his father, he'd worry about the souls. This was nonsense. His catchall formula, that if she relied on him then all her troubles would be remedied, had become an all too familiar anthem. Worse, she'd let it happen. She must remedy this.

The weight of his mockery carried a bit of stinging truth. His transport business could not exist without worldwide connections. Perhaps one of those contacts knew something about Kate, the messages, or the attempt on her life. But who? What did they know? How could she lack explanations to so many pieces?

Her life had been hijacked. She didn't have answers to personal matters, and now with resurrection, an achievement she'd spent her whole life's work to gain, there seemed to be a significant flaw. Repopulating a declining species with ruthless nihilists was not an option.

She needed a new plan.

When she reached the study, she sat at the desk. On the top of it sat the Elle Cam, an elephant statue security camera, one of the many gifts from Cole in her lushly decorated environment. She picked it up and inspected the date engraved on the crystal tusks, a reminder of the day they'd met. She placed it back on the desk but facing away from her.

Years ago, Kate showed her a way of diagramming when something significant was at stake. She'd called it "scribbles."

SJ studied the desktop. She tapped the top left corner. A list of apps appeared, confirming the surface was a touch screen. She selected the drawing app, and a giant sketch pad filled the space and flipped to a blank page. She chose unaltered magenta from the corner color pallet and used her fingertip to write the word "Resurrection." Magenta script flowed across the page. She pushed the word to the top and then split the space underneath using a single wide band of ultimate orange to create two columns for pros and cons.

Halfway below that, she made a header band of crimson. On it, she centered "Cole's claims" as an overlay title using the color stone for the font.

Next, she picked up lemongrass and wrote "Five" on the left side under the crimson header and "Kate," on the right side, and underneath that, she wrote "Sabotage."

Colors swept across the touchscreen. Scripted loops and lines gushed outward like a living thing. The ordered outline of matters she could address vanquished the tangle of hopeless detail thrumming in her brain.

Re-energized, she turned on the wall screen and searched for news updates. Nothing about Five or the messages. She wrote the words, "the same" across from the word "Five."

Confirmation through George that Kate's body was missing provided no answers, so she put a big question mark across from "Kate." She'd have to wait on the authorities for more information.

The sabotage attempt on her life remained another puzzle. Who drugged her? Cole wanted her to focus on her work. What reason would he have to drug her? Except of course, it fit with his need for control—to have SHEOL named as the new location for the trials. She wrote the words "not Cole" across from "sabotage" but then added the word "SHEOL" and a question mark.

One question still dominated. Should she continue to perform resurrections, and specifically the one on Cole's father? Birch stood ready to take control if she faltered on the matter. Her power over the process was a sham. Replacements waited in the wings.

She groaned. Finding direction on that matter would take more than a few scribbles.

Should she try it? Call to the empty air for help?

She'd done it twice. The first time she pleaded for Kate's return to life, a request now complicated by Kate's missing body and the resurrection of degenerates. The second attempt happened before the trials began. The answer that came, to seek consensus with Birch, did not turn out well. Would a "third time's the charm" mantra apply in this case?

She would try again. "I need truth and solutions," she whispered.

The air offered nothing but emptiness and the weight of her burden.

The clock showed 3:16 a.m.

She selected the video function and programmed the wall screen to pull up her end message research. The monthly summary contained some new recordings of test subjects in the moments just before their deaths. The database resumed with number seventy-eight, the last case she'd viewed since Kate's death.

She dimmed the light and settled into the chair.

When a pain in her neck woke her up, she realized she'd dozed off. The number eighty-four on the screen image confirmed it. The test subject, a larger than life, prickly haired ancient, wheezed and sucked air like a fish out of water. He coughed, cleared his throat a multitude of times, and then in gravelly tones, he spoke to his off-camera audience.

"It's up to you now, Billy. I've done my part. You have to carry the torch. Each generation passes the best they can to the next. It's as simple as that. There's no going back. It's forward all the way. Don't let no one tell you otherwise. That's how it's played. Until generations ain't no more." The ancient sage spasmed and sputtered and a hand loomed to adjust his airflow tube, but then the camera cut off.

SJ paused the case profile and replayed the footage. She watched the message several more times. Something in the words called to her.

Until generations ain't no more.

She shut off the program and turned her attention back to her desktop diagram and found the words and colors were no longer distinct. She must have hit "meld."

"Aw come on, for gosh sakes. Now I've got to redo everything."

The word "resurrection," was the only text that had stayed intact. It now floated atop a newly meshed shape. The image, a red-orange cross structure, had most likely formed by the blending of all her question marks and the horizontal band of crimson.

Her attempt to retrieve her original diagram by tapping on the bottom to bring up her choices failed. Only the forward screen arrow appeared. She touched the arrow, and everything disappeared except for a small elephant, perhaps the Elle Cam icon.

"No. No. No." The sketch was gone.

After tapping on the icon, the options "record" or "dismiss" appeared. She chose "record." The screen began a live feed view of the shelves across from where the camera sat on the desk. The small head swiveled along the shelf capturing a systematic scan as it moved. The magnified view revealed an assortment of items. Grotesque miniatures, the kind that Cole liked to collect, several framed inspirational quotes, and a row of rare gems and minerals paraded across the screen. The camera signaled "scan end" when it came to the far end of the shelf.

She adjusted the angle to capture the next wall. When it began to scan again, a cream binding and the words "thermoscan" jumped into view but then disappeared. *Thermoscan?* Her heart thumped loudly in her chest as she tried to re-scan the view but couldn't make it work.

Pushing aside her chair, she walked to the shelf and hunted for a cream-colored binding. She found a book and pulled it off the shelf. Inside the blank cover, she read the gold script title, "Book of Wisdom." The lettering had fared much better than the imprint on Natalie's copy.

Something slipped from the pages and fell to the floor. She stooped to pick up the item and discovered it was a folded thermoscan printout. Dumbfounded, she set the book aside and unfolded the paper. It contained the familiar words of the first message, the letter supposedly written by a woman named Evie. The last place she'd seen the printout was in the lab the day Kate brought it to her attention.

"Sleepless night?" A voice spoke behind her.

She whirled around and found Rumi standing in the doorway. "What? How is this … possible?" She stammered and waved the thermoscan printout.

Rumi swooped in and picked up the book. "It's Father's. It went missing for a while."

"No. I mean, yes. Of course, there's that question too. But how did my message get inside?"

Rumi pointed to the chair. "You might want to sit. There's a lot to tell."

CHAPTER 36

SJ SHUT THE study door. "I should warn you, I hate being deceived."

Rumi's face contorted. "Please understand. I took it because I needed your help." She dabbed at her eyes.

"That makes no sense. Why would you do that?"

Rumi unwrapped her neck scarf. The revealed skin showed unmistakable signs.

SJ held on to her suspicion but decided to play nice. "How long have you been ill?" She already knew the answer. The location and extent of the bruising indicated a lengthy case.

"Four years and two days." Rumi dropped the scarf on a chair. "I've passed the corpound stage. Diagnostics show I've moved into elwinde."

SJ sighed. Rumi's jaundiced eyes screamed pain. No masking imitation could produce this effect.

"Death. Maybe weeks. Maybe days. I don't care anymore." Rumi placed the book on the desk and moved across the room to the shelves where she picked up a figurine. "All I want is to be resurrected and live again without the noose of my disease, but Cole says no."

SJ shook her head. "He has no say in the matter. Everyone gets their dose of Rejuvacatin."

Rumi returned to the chair, picked up the scarf and twisted it between her fingers. "It's all true you know. Five. The messages. But Cole doesn't want you to believe it. He took the message from Kate's apartment. I found it later and placed it in the book so I could someday prove his intent. Cole's been banned from Five, which is why he wants lives renewed elsewhere. You've got to help me."

The claims about Cole and Five sounded like lunacy, but delusional states only came at the very end of a Biomalism condition. "Listen to me." SJ took a deep breath. "You'll get your dose of Rejuvacatin and be processed for resurrection just like everyone else. I promise."

"Now who's deceiving who? It's no secret you want to halt the trials. Psychotic rebirths aren't welcome, and for that matter, neither are eligerens."

"What are you talking about? Resurrection science will continue. We just need more time." SJ spread out the message on the desk in front of her.

"It won't matter." Rumi flopped into the chair. "Cole plans to have only male and female resurrections. Those with the physical capacity to contribute to human reproduction. Since I never followed through with gender selection and surgery, I don't fit the criteria. It's all part of the new access agreement."

"But Cole wants resurrection to be available for everyone. That's what he's told me." Heaviness came over her as she considered the probability of whether Cole was ever truthful to her.

"I figured you knew by now that Cole says whatever helps him accomplish his purpose. That's his nature."

SJ shook her head. "This is crazy. How could he do this to you?" Her mind wrestled with the even bigger problem. How could she have let such a deceiver into her life? She moved to the chair behind the desk and sat. "Does he even care about anyone?"

"In his own way, I think he does. He tries to comfort me and claims he plans to have my spirit return and enter another resurrected body. He believes it can be done this way, but I don't think it can." Rumi leaned forward across the desk. "And if it does, I don't want to come back as anyone but myself."

"First of all, Cole's not in charge. I am." The waterfall of fantasies spilling out of Rumi's mouth was nonsense. Perhaps the fairy-tale perspective was Rumi's way of coping.

Rumi laid her hand over the message. "No. In appearances, you're the leader, but if you cross Cole, you'll lose your position, and Birch will take over. If Birch doesn't do Cole's bidding, then my brother will put someone else in his place. It doesn't matter. Cole controls everything. He's been using me to mask as any power player he needs to cement the deals necessary to put his plans in place. Anyone who discovers the ruse or tries to block him is eliminated. Once I die, he'll find someone else." She sniffled and averted her gaze. "The masking and manipulation will continue." The last words came out in a sorrowful whisper.

Gently sliding the message out from under Rumi's hand, SJ folded it and put it aside. "Look at me."

Rumi turned her head.

"What you say is impossible. Cole is very mistaken. Even if there were such a thing as souls, I'm certain they can't pick and choose what body they go with. I was about to ask for a pause in the trials. Now I will insist on a full stop. None of what you say makes sense, but I know that something about psychosocial integrity is being affected by the resurrection process."

Rumi nodded. "It's true. Cole thinks Mortar won't allow souls to return, but he has a solution. It starts when you raise Father."

"Who is Mortar?"

Rumi tapped on the book. "He who holds all things together. It's all in here. His book. Find the messages. Then you'll see."

SJ pulled the book to her. It seemed small, but she could not compare it, since she'd accidentally left Natalie's copy in the conference room where she reviewed the reports. Her fingers traced the name embossed on the cover, "Evelyn Dittmar." The name "Evie" appeared on the dedication page beneath the message, "Our Baby Girl, May 5, 1958." *Evelyn? Evie?* She slammed the book shut. "You're lying, and I'm such a fool to believe otherwise. This isn't your father's book. It belongs to someone else."

"Believe me. It's his."

"How can it be? The owner's birth date was over two hundred years ago. Cole told me your father's life ended just a few short years ago, and he was only seventy-two when he died."

"There's more to that." Rumi leaned over the desk and traced her finger across the surface as if writing something. "You see, the body my father inhabited died, but did Cole tell you that our father is an ageless spirit?"

The word "Beast" appeared in vermillion red.

SJ slapped the book down on top of the inscription. "Listen, Rumi. I feel sorry for you, but I'm not a fool. I don't believe in souls or spirits or gods or whatever else is part of your convoluted made-up world." She tapped on the desktop and the word disappeared.

Then she scooted her chair back and rose to her feet. "You've painted me a striking picture, but unless you give me real proof, I won't consider any of it true. I can't begin to understand the dynamic unholy mix between you, your brother, and now, your father. What I do understand is this. I won't compromise the integrity of the resurrection trials."

Rumi sighed and then spoke in an expressionless voice. "Very well. You leave me no choice. What I'm about to show you must stay between us. Cole must never know." She picked up the book and held it out to SJ. "Hold on to it. Whatever happens next do not make a sound or move an inch."

SJ took the book. A prickling sensation poured over her.

Rumi pointed to the corner of the room. "You must hide. He can't know you're here."

He?

Rumi stood and led her to the window and arranged clustered folds of heavy drapes over her.

"What are we doing?"

Rumi put a finger to her lips. "Just trust me. You asked for proof." Then she turned off the lights. The only light came from the fake moon glow outside the window. It cast shimmering ripples across a pool and highlighted trembling tropical plant leaves made restless by a manufactured breeze.

Rumi walked to the collection of grotesque miniatures on the shelf and toppled one to the floor. Instead of breaking, the statue exploded into a ball of light. It sputtered and rolled about and then assumed the eclipsed shadowy form of a man. The man's shape continued to grow until it reached ceiling height. The outer edges of the man exuded sunlight brilliance.

SJ squinted for self-protection from the dazzling effect.

"Why have you summoned me, worshipful one? Is it time? The soul I oppress is one whisper away from choosing death. Speak the word and his Rejuvacatin injector will be yours. I'll see to it." His voice rumbled like thunder.

"Shh. Please, Lucas." Rumi signaled to the door. "Cole's asleep."

The being shrank into a light-pierced outline of a normal-size man, but his features remained shadowed.

SJ's eyes widened. Surely the effect was some form of hologram.

Rumi moved along the wall, pausing every now and then to pick up an item from the shelves. "It's all good news, really. Cole's gotten SJ to agree to raise Father. Soon we'll plead our strategy before Beast in person. I know he'll choose our way over Cole's, because Cole's is too risky. Simple resurrection will become the operation of the day. But I'm wondering what Mortar will do about it—humans recycling human bodies—since no new souls will be added. Perhaps he will call for the end of time."

The being laughed. The reverberation of the sound caused the room to shake. "Really?" The being snorted. "Simple resurrection? If it's done to completeness, then there's nothing simple about it."

"The label is one I use, but it fits how they approach it." Rumi stood close to where SJ hid and appeared to be taking in the moonlit view.

The being moved nearby.

SJ shrank back.

The creature's heavy, ragged breath fogged the window. "They acknowledge no place of life and no power other than their own. They see resurrection as a simple process to aid in the cure for their declining species." The creature touched the windowpane with a black gloved finger, and the window glass cleared. "They falsely believe life is theirs to give and take by their will. They play at life's surface and make no attempt to account for what is unseen."

Rumi turned and gave a slight bow to the being. "That's why I choose you to lead over them and not Cole. I believe as you have said. Kingdom expansion has always relied on our influence over humans. It's a time-proven strategy. Attempting to inhabit newly resurrected humans at the time of revival with spirits loyal to us is a needlessly risky endeavor. We need to move en masse. Mortar's clock is ticking. Cole is unfocused and out of touch with the goals of the Conquering."

Rumi moved out of SJ's sight range, and the air around SJ became cool.

The bulk of Lucas's form fluctuated, increasing or decreasing with inhaled or expelled breaths. The constant shifting of his shape kept his features indistinct.

Unbearable cold stung SJ's skin. She gulped in shallow breaths and reached to pinch her nose as a sneeze tickled.

The hooded head turned her way.

She clutched the book. Did he see her?

"So, your loyalty is to us and not humans?" Lucas's voice shook the room.

SJ held her breath.

"Of course, Lucas. You know that. Please keep your voice down." Rumi sounded sincere.

Lucas moved away from the window.

SJ exhaled, marveling at how well Rumi played both sides.

"I'm human, yes, but neither male nor female because of human thoughtlessness. Loyalty needs a place to belong, and I don't have one with them. My choice is with the spirits and to their kingdom … soon to be yours, if Cole loses favor." Rumi paused and her face held a conspiratorial look.

A chuckling snort came from the hooded figure.

"Spirits loyal to my father will triumph over the humans, and mankind will depend on us to supply their every need." Her voice rose with her declaration. "I'll commit to this framework and do whatever action is necessary. Is this good enough for you?"

The hooded figure nodded. "And … to that end, you'll live again, at least another span. I'll bring the injector to you. You'll return as Rumi, an eligeren, and not as someone else. Cole is ludicrous to think he can control this."

Lucas grew ceiling-tall again. The mountain of murky deep outlined in dazzling light growled, "This place is too warm. I must leave."

Rumi stooped to retrieve the small statue that had fallen to the floor and placed it back on the shelf. After she did this, it seemed as if Lucas folded in on himself, and the action produced an explosion of white and prism-colored light that faded into inky darkness. The dark cloud drifted to the statue and dissipated into it.

Struggling to keep her teeth from chattering, SJ waited.

"He's gone. You can come out now."

SJ emerged and tugged at the drapes to cover the window.

Rumi laughed. "He's not outside."

"Where is he?" Involuntary trembling took over SJ's body. "For that matter, who is he?"

"He's a herald. Not Mortar's but one of ours." Rumi pulled a blanket from a shelf and held it out.

Grateful, SJ wrapped herself in warmth. "What's a herald?"

"You should know. You've been around several."

"I have never been around anyone like that." SJ's words came sandwiched between deep breaths of air. Her body seemed to think she'd run a marathon. Maybe it was self-preservation, a demand for more oxygen to wipe her head clear of the peculiar things she'd just seen.

"You've been in the company of heralds. Cole and Frank are two, of course."

SJ's spine tingled. "Frank is just an ordinary Ancient. A man I met who does transports. And Cole …" She broke off in a whisper and then swallowed hard.

"There's no time to discuss. We have to leave now. I'm taking you to see Kate's body."

SJ froze. *Kate.* "Where is she?"

Rumi yanked on her arm. "We have to go. Grab the book if you want."

SJ hesitated. "I had a copy but left ..."

"There's no time. I'll show you where Kate is and then disappear. Cole mustn't know how you found her."

Heat poured over SJ. She threw off the blanket and seized the book.

Rumi cocked her head. "Well?"

SJ swallowed several times to moisten her parched mouth. "Let's go."

Out in the hall, Rumi pointed to the darkened dining room. "We'll go through this way."

SJ's quick steps behind Rumi matched the racing of her heart. Everything she'd just seen and heard seemed impossible. It was as if someone had taken a postage stamp-size picture of a flower off the wall, removed the frame, and unfolded the picture multiple times until it revealed an entire field of flowers, hills, sky, and all of life. All she could think about was how she needed a bigger frame.

CHAPTER 37

BY THE TIME they reached the car, reason returned. What she'd just witnessed could be easily explained. Lucas's appearance must be some sort of masking mirage. If Mortar authored the Book of Wisdom, then he'd been dead a long time. Maybe his followers still carried a torch for him, and somehow their loyalty conflicted with Cole's agenda. She knew one thing for sure. She had no use for Cole's political futures. The cost to help build his empire had become too convoluted to pay. She would retrieve Kate's body and get out. When she got back to Sector Seven, she'd find a way to end the partnership.

Rumi unlocked the parked Morenci, and they climbed inside.

"You're disappointed. I can see it in your face."

Who wouldn't be? She'd been such a fool.

"Like you said. It's just a matter of time." Rumi fiddled with the controls. "One day, Kate will be resurrected."

SJ's jaw tightened. "It's not likely to be soon. I refuse to revive bodies to become sociopathic shells."

"Wait until Beast's resurrection is complete before you decide. It won't be the same. You'll see. And his influence will keep Cole in check."

SJ groaned. "Why aren't you hearing me? You need to understand what I'm saying. Yes. The candidates came back to life. They resurrected. But they score off the charts for deviant psychosocial behavior. That's a big risk. Why would your father's recovery be any different?"

"Because … he's … not … like … any other candidate." Rumi spoke as if talking to a child.

SJ sighed and shook her head. It was no use. She yanked on her safety strap as the engine ignited with six-hundred horsepower.

A red whirlwind icon appeared on the dash screen, indicating a geothermal storm forecast. Gusts pushed back on them as they sped through cross tunnels that led away from Mi Manera and the SHEOL dwellings and on into the business park of the lower valley. Once they reached Kerioth Medical, the Morenci self-parked, and Rumi silenced the engine.

Raking fingers through her tufted hair, Rumi turned to SJ. "Now it's your time to listen. My days are running out. I can feel Cole's eagerness about his grand experiment. He doesn't want my body. Just my spirit. To indwell another person's body. Promise me this one thing. When it's time for me to die, then let me die, but be sure I get the Rejuvacatin, so I have a chance to live again. Promise it. On the book." Rumi reached over and patted the Book of Wisdom resting in SJ's lap.

"I promise. But I don't need the book to make it sincere. I'll do everything I can to carry out your wishes." The words flowed smoothly, despite the nausea building in her gut. What kind of man believed he could manipulate the world with such focus? "Rumi, I need you to tell me something."

"What?"

"It's about Cole. I mean, I know he's your brother and my life partner and a powerful businessman …" SJ paused, stumbling over the next idea. "And you say he's a herald. But my question is about him. Now. In real life. She pulled the thermoscan message free from the book pages. "This message says he's a thief. I know you've read it."

Rumi turned her head away.

SJ scanned the message again as she spoke. "The writer, Evie, claims to be my relative. She says Cole controls a band of delivery thieves that must be stopped. I think she must have some sort of mental disorder because she claims to have been alive for five generations, but perhaps some part of her warning is true. Cole does manipulate. He does mislead and withhold information, and he has taken advantage of situations to further his agenda. So, is the message right? Is Cole a thief?"

Rumi pressed her lips together.

"I'm not afraid of the truth, you know. It's one of the things I value most in life."

Rumi shifted in her seat and gave a half smile. "He said that about you. You want truth as much as he wants to rule the world by supplying everything that the world wants. That's the empire he's trying to build. Does that sound like stealing?"

"I don't know. It's his method that bothers me. He tramples anyone or anything that gets in his way."

"You criticize, yet you, too, want to rule. By your hand, you decide a man's life."

"Touché. And you aren't immune either. You haven't hesitated to plead for your father's resurrection as a means to tame Cole. It seems every need has its day. The real question is which need is greatest and most worthy?"

"For me, it's gotten quite simple." Rumi re-wrapped her scarf around her neck as she spoke. "I can't keep my life in order on my own. My illness is only one evidence of that fact. I no longer want to be Cole's pawn. A long time ago, someone stronger than death came to earth. Mortar's son. He came to show people how to live, but he was murdered for his efforts. Mortar brought him back to life again. Mortar said that if anyone believed in his son and his words, then they would live free and eternally. That's the kind of life I want."

"Well, okay. But what if that's not true or possible? Then what?"

"Then I've lost. But it's not like I'm winning, anyway. I've run out of choices."

Rumi's frank resolve stirred SJ's heart.

"There's something else." Rumi turned off the console. "Promise you'll complete Father's resurrection. Then he'll—"

"Keep Cole in check." SJ finished the sentence. "I know. I get it." But she didn't. Rumi wanted the help of both Mortar and Beast, and they were on opposite sides. How was that supposed to work?

"Are you ready? This storm is a strong one." Rumi opened the car door, and a blast of warm air shot through the interior.

SJ wrapped the fragile book with her jacket, slipped it into her bag, and ventured out.

She followed Rumi across the parking lot. Her hair whipped, and grit blasted her face. A brief gap in the warm wind came, and a flock of DARTS on a nearby ridge took to the air and passed in formation over her head. Then the robot birds banked to the west, circled around, and sped into the mouth of the high west tunnel, the source of the turbulence.

She caught up with Rumi and took her by the arm. "Incredible force, isn't it?"

Rumi nodded.

They pressed forward together, moving with heads down through the snarling wind to reach the hospital entrance.

The door opened. A figure shouted. "Good morning, early birds."

Rumi stopped and resisted SJ's pull forward.

SJ stopped tugging when the hood fell back and revealed the doorman's features. "It's Cole. How in the world?"

Rumi gave no answer. It was as if the wind had swallowed the question.

In three strides he reached them. He grabbed Rumi and pushed her ahead of him and waited for SJ to follow. Once inside the building, he took hold of Rumi's arm while his eyes sought out SJ. "Where are you two going?"

"I'm sorry. Couldn't sleep. Rumi offered to …" SJ's words drifted.

Cole smirked. "It appears that a sleepless night has challenged us all. Too bad. Today is such a big day. Tomorrow will be grand as well, because it's Father's resurrection day. But today we have a party."

"What party?" SJ looked at Rumi.

She shrugged.

"Rumi's farewell party, of course. Since tomorrow all eyes will be on Father's resurrection, I want her to have her own day. A sendoff party. She'll soon be taking a much-needed trip, and we won't be seeing her for a while. She's in desperate need of some rest and relaxation, aren't you, my dear?"

The chilling look exchanged between the siblings left SJ paralyzed. *Rumi. Stay strong.* He had no right. She wanted to puke when Cole released Rumi and she gave no protest against her brother, but the eligeren simply nodded and passed through the door.

Cole sneered. "She knows what's best."

SJ followed after her.

"It's a triple celebration, really." Cole's voice came close behind. "Ask me what's the third reason to celebrate."

"What else are we celebrating?" SJ gulped in air and walked faster.

"The discovery of Kate. I assumed that's why you're here. Isn't it wonderful?" His breath fell on her neck.

SJ spun around and pushed him away. "I don't call anything about the death of my dearest friend wonderful." Heat rose in her face.

"Ah, but it is. Because you have the power to bring her life back. And I intend to help you keep that power. That's my gift to you." Cole smirked and practically danced a jig in front of her and then rushed off after Rumi.

SJ followed a few steps behind, racking her brain for ways to thwart his insanity.

Rows of microtherm cylinders stretched out across the preservation room. DCN agents maneuvered one of them into a vacant slot nearby.

"Isn't it marvelous? They've been arriving daily since the sabotage." Cole nodded to the workers, and they stepped aside. He beckoned SJ over and pointed to the cylinder monitor. "See how well we're doing in our new storage business."

She worked slowly, checking through all the monitor functions. Stalling Cole might buy some time for Rumi to get away.

Cole tapped his foot. "Well?"

"It's within range for viability, but why are they stored upright? In the Abide, our resurrection candidates are placed horizontally in module banks."

"I ordered it. It's an improvement, and more convenient for priority selection. Not all life restorations are equally urgent." He winked at Rumi.

Rumi scowled. "My brother's talent for efficiency. Good old DCN." Her voice dripped with sarcasm.

"In the end, our competence makes life better for everyone." Cole crossed his arms. "Including you, dear Rumi."

"Who's qualified next after Father, dear brother?" Rumi mimicked his tone.

SJ jumped in. "There won't be another resurrection, your father or otherwise. I'm calling for a halt."

Cole's eyes narrowed. "Really? I thought you'd want your beloved Kate back as soon as possible."

"Not as a psychosocial deviant. No one will be resurrected again until the setback is corrected." She glanced toward Rumi, who seemed to be in a trance.

"So you've proven it, my darling?"

Cole's sly challenge and use of endearment prickled SJ's skin. "We need time to establish connections to the poor behavior outcomes. Then we can alter the process to prevent these results. Until this is done, there's too much risk to proceed."

"Your caution is admirable. But I'm not sure Birch will agree. Besides, I asked special permission for Kate's resurrection to be scheduled. Council agreed. She is, after all, your family." His words, silky smooth, carried both intended charm and threat.

SJ kept her eyes on Rumi. It was better to let Cole have the last word.

Cole beckoned to a worker. "Show us to the data room."

Keeping Rumi's arm in his grip, Cole fell in step behind the man, and SJ trailed behind. She was certain Cole's request for Kate's resurrection had nothing to do with compassion. It served his purpose. Either he was priming for an audience trick or making a show about his power. She bit her lip and quickened her pace. Protecting Rumi's life and Kate's body from Cole's manipulative ideas was all that mattered.

When they reached the data bay, the DCN worker swiped the door's lock panel, and it opened. The man left, and they entered the bay.

Inside, they found a microtherm cylinder locked into position on the scan threshold.

SJ came close to it and read the name. Kate Auburn Rigsby. Moisture flooded her eyes. Disbelief all over again. How could Kate be dead? They'd been through so much together. Kate's wisdom always kept her from harm. If she'd listened to Kate, she'd have avoided her troubles with Cole. Kate was right about so many things.

"The codes synchronize, so the verification is positive, but I know you'll want to re-confirm and run the ectogram yourself." Cole's eagerness tasted like treachery.

SJ blinked back tears and moved quickly to the console screen. Cole mustn't see her sadness. She found the illuminated cylinder icon on the screen and tapped it and then selected *scan*. While the images molded together, she slid off her shoulder bag, heavy with the weight of the book, and tucked the satchel under her chair.

The ectogram initiated. Beginning with Kate's name, a mechanical voice delivered identification stats. Hearing the data drove away the crazy hope that Kate might still be alive. The need for revenge against whoever impersonated Kate filled SJ's thoughts.

"Isn't it exciting? Kate's life is yours to deliver. Soon you'll speak with her again. Think of this great gift you've been given. Bringing others back to life restores their relationships. It restores all contingencies. Life's greatest losses are caused by death, and these voids are now vanquished by your power."

Cole's flattery burned in SJ's ear. She turned to answer him and became caught by his gaze. His eyes had changed color.

A siren wail punctuated the air. Two more came, followed by an announcement. "SHEOL alert, level four. Responders must return to Command Center."

A shock wave rolled under her feet and SJ grabbed the console. Something struck against her foot, and she looked down and found the book lying at her feet. It must have shaken loose from the bag. She reached to push it back under her chair, but the floor heaved again and sent it sliding across the room. She scrambled after it but found it pinned underneath Cole's boot.

Rumi joined in the effort, but Cole kicked it out of reach.

A third tremor shook the room, throwing SJ to the ground. A crack expanded across the granite floor. She pulled herself up by the console and braced for the next eruption.

"Imagine it. Stone on bone. You'll be crushed and buried alive if a big one hits." Cole's voice, cold with threat, came from behind her.

She turned and faced him. Inches away, his features twisted in a snarl, and his eyes scanned hers relentlessly.

The room temperature dropped.

"Truth be told, and I know you dearly love truth, my dear, I've no concern of being crushed alive, because I'm not human. I'm a herald." He sneered at her. "You two, on the other hand, are as human and weak as can be." His feet crunched on loose stone as he strode to where the book lay and pointed. "Pick it up, Rumi."

With staggered gait, Rumi moved and picked up the book.

Cole seized his sibling by the arm. "So, here's what I think. I think the two of you have been conspiring. I'll soon find out. On my way to Command, Rumi can tell me her side of things. When I return, SJ will tell me her version, and we'll see who's the best at telling the truth."

"Really, Cole, there's no need to be—" SJ stopped speaking when Rumi shook her head.

Cole yanked Rumi along with him to the doorway. Then he turned and gave a wicked grin. "There's no need to what? Be suspicious of you? It doesn't matter. I track every move you make, thanks to your little arm chip. At herald speed I can reach you in minutes. I'm the king over all contingencies. You're stuck with me." Cole blew SJ a kiss.

SJ's stomach roiled, and her mouth went dry.

Cole turned back to Rumi. "Have you confessed your deceit?"

Rumi jerked her head away. "I don't know what you are talking about."

"Oh, I'm sure you do, since the two of you are now soulmates. Did you tell SJ you were the one who masked as Kate at her meeting?" His lips curled and he shot a fiery glance in SJ's direction. "Remember, love, truth is only an illusion." He twisted Rumi's arm. "This harlot, too, plays with facts when it suits her purposes."

Rumi came alive. "No. Please, SJ. It's not like it sounds. And there's something you should know. Cole wants to put my spirit in Kate's body so—"

Cole reached to muffle Rumi's mouth with his hand, and she swung at him with the book, but he ducked, sending the book spinning into the air. She struggled and broke free for an instant, but then Cole shoved her against the doorframe, and she stumbled and fell.

SJ rushed forward to help. Her body lifted and slammed against the console base. Pain shot through her neck.

Rumi? She rolled to one side and pulled herself to a standing position. Rumi and Cole were gone. She limped out of the data bay and into the preservation room. There was no sign of workers, but several cylinders lay topsy-turvy in an aisle.

She trembled. Any moment, the ground could swallow her alive. She staggered back to the bay. Dizziness came over her. She slumped to the floor. Her dry lips formed words, "Help me."

Choose.

She looked for the source. The book? It lay on a heap of debris nearby. She strained to reach it. Her fingertips touched the cover. Courage returned. She grabbed it and sat, breathing heavily. Then she stood and surveyed the wreckage.

A large piece of panel from the console rested against Kate's cylinder. She set the book aside and shoved against the fractured piece. It crashed sideways to the floor.

Now what?

Choose. The word came again, a voice but not a voice.

What should I choose?

She knew what she would not choose. To help Cole. His despicable actions were not done out of ignorance or by accident. They were calculated and all about his gain. He chose to act in ways that stole from others. If she continued as his pawn, then she would become like him—a thief.

She saw it very clearly now. Evil's truest colors had gleamed in his eyes—black for the color of deceit and red for the color of blood.

Her blood.

CHAPTER 38

THE FLOOR SHUDDERED under her feet. SJ staggered and caught herself.

Choose.

"Who are you? What should I choose?"

Whatever is not Cole. The opposite of evil. My goodness.

That was easy. She'd rather die than be afraid and controlled by Cole.

"Okay. I choose." She spoke aloud and then added a whisper. "Your goodness."

It made sense. If evil purpose existed—not just mistakes or ignorance, but real evil—then the opposite of evil, pure good purpose, likely also existed.

She waited for her rescue to unfold but nothing happened.

"What's next?"

Get out.

Spinning into action, she found a map tile near the door frame. It displayed the evacuation route between Kerioth and Remit, the main exit out of SHEOL. Her finger traced the path while her mind formed a plan. She would blend in with all the other workers leaving Kerioth and pick up a shuttle at Remit, one headed to the Upper East, the same underground speedrail Frank would have taken to get her back to Sector Seven.

Tapping on her wrist screen illuminated it. The last tremor alert. Twenty minutes had passed. Speedrail transit might be compromised, but she had no time to second-guess. She snapped a picture of the map, in case GPS glitched.

Then, hoping comms were still working, she recorded a message for George about Cole's threats and that she refused to rob the future to pay the present. She pressed send. When she reached Sector Seven, she planned to cash in on every favor owed her and persuade the council. A majority vote could stop the trials.

The lights dimmed. Electrified humming filled the air, and sparks popped from the torn wire ends of the broken console.

An evacuation alert jarred the room.

She gulped air. "Please, help me," she whispered. She needed all that good had to offer so she could move Kate's body, escape SHEOL, and stop the trials.

A second alert sounded. Tremors followed. Wall panels separated and fell crashing to the floor, missing her by inches. Shaking, she turned her effort to the microtherm cylinder housing Kate's body. Moving it would take at least four people or a transfer bot.

Unlocking the cylinder released it from the ectogram machine. Now all she needed to move it was a bot. After a fruitless search of the fractured data bay, she shoved against the cylinder with all her might, but it did not budge. Perhaps something in the room could be used as a pry bar, and she could carefully tip the whole thing on one edge and roll it. It wasn't ideal but it might work. She could not leave Kate behind.

Locating a hanging panel cover, she tugged on it, and the unwieldy piece came loose and smacked against the cylinder base. The container moved sideways.

How was that possible? The impact alone could not have budged the weighty vessel. Dropping to her knees, she discovered a telltale rim encircling the cylinder about six inches up from the bottom. Pressing on the rim set the cylinder in motion again. The design was part of a seamlessly fitting transfer bot. The DCN logo on the side gave tribute to the maker. She almost smiled. Cole's tweaking would aid her escape.

Transfer bots moved directionally by a sensor and were usually pre-programmed to return to a designated spot. Somewhere on the cylinder base was a manual override option, but functions were difficult to discern in the dimness of the emergency lighting.

She gave up the quest and focused on clearing debris to make a path to the door. Grabbing the book, she placed it in her bag and then began kicking the bot rim with her foot, moving the cylinder forward through the door.

Once outside the data bay, the bot glided in longer stretches but did not seem to be programmed for a specific return path.

Her prompting came to a halt near the end of a row when she spotted shadowy shapes maneuvering along a border aisle. Guards? Straining to see through the dusty haze of the preservation room, she discovered there were two of them, one tall and slightly hunched and the other gliding smoothly as if on wheels.

"Who are you? Give me your name." She demanded the identity as if she was in charge and waited with bated breath.

A familiar voice growled. "If you're still kickin' around in this underground noodle bowl, then you'd best take your butter and fly. This snake hole acts like it's gonna blow."

"Frank?"

"In full person."

Her shoulders relaxed. "What are the odds?" Her mouth gaped when Frank emerged, and the second figure rolled up beside him.

"Ben?"

Frank snickered. "What do you think?" He gave her a knowing look.

"I have no idea." She shook her head. "But there's no time for speculation. Cole's headed back here. I need to be gone. With this." She tapped the cylinder. "With Kate. I'm returning to the Abide. Can you help me?"

Frank placed his hands on both sides of the cylinder. "Are you sure you want to travel so heavy?"

She nodded.

"Okay." He turned and patted Ben on the shoulder. "Her plan's a go. You do the bot, and I'll do the tarp."

Frank left and returned shortly with a lime green bundle. He cut through the tie wrap and shook out the material. "Level three priority wrap. Ordinary delivery. No one will question."

While Ben gave commands to his wrist scanner to program the bot, Frank secured the vividly colored tarp over the cylinder.

SJ studied every move Frank made. His DCN garb and demeanor suggested an ordinary deliveryman. He displayed no magical powers. She contented herself with the idea that it was just as well. A herald with Frank's personality and aversion to convention seemed unfitting, but she really did not know how heralds were supposed to act. Cole and Lucas were her only other references.

Ben clapped his hands. "I'm done. What about you? Are we going yet?"

Frank grinned. "You betcha, buddy." He took the lead, steadying Kate's cocoon with his hands as the bot maneuvered through the room.

When they left the storage area, they were swept up in the exiting crowd of Kerioth workers. The blaring noise of the alerts became more frequent. Minutes later, they stepped outside the building and found people standing and pointing to the cavern wall where a large portion of rock had broken off along the upper ledge. Below it, the auto park was littered with stones. Tiny flames fed by seeping lava leapt from a thin, lengthy crack across the west wall of the cavernous space. The flow funneled into channels carved along the perimeter.

Emergency workers cleared stones off the evacuation route.

Frank rambled further ahead of SJ and Ben, creating the appearance of separate travelers. People moved toward Remit, the covered travellator that carried pedestrians to both the Upper and Lower East.

When SJ arrived at the entrance, she took her place in the crowded line. She hoped that having Kate's body would keep Rumi safe. If Cole wanted Rumi's spirit in Kate's body, then he'd need to have both present at one time to complete his plan.

She exhaled. She'd chosen goodness, and help had come.

She kept a hand on Ben's bot chair and clutched her bag with the book in her other hand. All the messages, Bow's story, Natalie's belief, Franks' questions, and Rumi's revelation spoke of something greater. They reminded her of her father's protest a long time ago. He said he'd found something bigger than death and would not agree to become a trial candidate for resurrection because of it. She couldn't ignore the uncanny echo. Possibilities thrived if she chose to accept the book's words as truth and watched to be proven wrong. And if Mortar still existed, then perhaps she could find his son and ask him to explain how he resurrected. Then she could apply it to the trials.

She stepped onto the travellator.

A voice boomed, "It is finished."

She turned to find the source. Her heart jolted in her chest. Cole pushed toward her through the throng. The words could not have been his, as he uttered none. Instead, he roared, snapped, and growled like an animal. Her breath stopped as he drew close, and his face transformed into that of a lion.

Something pinched her shoulders, and a heavy weight pushed her down. The crush of people around her opened, and several gasped. She looked up. Scaly legs and the belly of a giant eagle-like creature blocked her view. Knobby talons held her fast. A second, similar creature swooped low in front of her, snatched Kate's cylinder, and flapped upward to the top of the cavern. It dove sharply to enter the yawning crevice above the Remit passageway. People screamed and pointed at her.

Thrashing and twisting to free herself from the bird's grip, SJ yelled for Frank, whom she could no longer see. She grabbed Ben's bot chair to anchor herself, but the chair was empty. Unrelenting, the behemoth bird pulled her up just as Cole arrived, snarling.

The upward motion continued. Colossal wings, with feathers three times the length of a school child, flapped in steady motion. Cavern walls grew large even as the people in line below her became tiny screaming specks.

Dizzy, she closed her eyes. A sudden turn and the sensation of being hurtled downward forced her to look again. Her creature seemed intent on diving into the same crevice as its mate.

When she grabbed the leg above the talon, her bag slipped from her shoulder. It flipped upside down, and the book fell from the opening. It floated just beneath her and then beside her as they plunged. Reaching out her hand as it passed her, she almost touched it, but a current swept it away, tumbling it into the vast cavern below.

She wished, among many things, she'd learned more of what the book said.

But it was all too late.

CHAPTER 39

"IT IS FINISHED!" A thunderous voice split the air.

Light blinded Cole. He tilted his head back and roared.

In the white silence that followed, an acrid scent seeped into his nostrils. When his eyes adjusted, he confirmed his punishment—paws for hands and feet.

What was his crime? Manifesting a rage that would kill. Why shouldn't he be angry? SJ had been his conquest. Now Mortar claimed her and kept him from her.

His banishment wouldn't last long. It never did. As long as Earthland still spun, he had time to tempt her.

The noxious smell of cat urine pervaded everything. Dried scat piles punctuated red dirt.

How disgusting.

Cole used his giant cat paws to climb the ridge. The heat of the savanna left him panting. His breaths beat out a pattern—a numbered count of souls he'd win for his cause. The tally would be far greater than Mortar's score. Then, when the Day of Reckoning came, glory would come to him and not Mortar.

Vultures circled in a lazy pattern, gliding lower and lower until they disappeared in the tall grass. When a marabou arrived and targeted the same location, Cole knew a carrion feast awaited him.

He paced around the boulder's crest searching for his human trappings. Finding his wrist scanner would be nice, even though he'd have to paw at it until he hit the right command.

The dry grassland and sparse trees around him spoke of little water, but if his officers responded quickly, he'd be spared an encounter with the pride males.

Mortar promised his grace would always allow Cole's punishment to bring him somewhere near a lion pride where food abounded. Cole couldn't care less. He hated the receiving end of Mortar's grace. The unnecessary promise proved humiliating. Once the greatest of all heavenly heralds, he'd been cast out. The trappings of earth, Earthland, and even now, Meritus, where humans sought to rebuild, had become his consolation prize. In the scheme of this fact, how did animal transformation reflect any portion of Mortar's grace?

He shook his hairy halo and tried to spit his contempt, but a lion couldn't spit. The curse of his rage rose to full transformation. A gathering of bush crows became his next target. With one lunge, he sent them shrieking into the air.

He roared again. A lion's appetite gnawed away inside him, the kind of craving that only flesh and blood would satisfy. If his legion did not show up soon, he'd have to fight a resident male to gain the food gifts of the pride's lionesses.

How tiresome. When Mortar's silly game of souls came to an end, he'd retaliate for this disgust. But his revenge pièce de résistance still lay cloaked in resurrection. Soon all would see it, too. Newly resurrected, Beast's compelling form would be a sight so singular and unmatched that nothing in Mortar's realm would ever compare. Father Beast and son Cole reigning as one.

He salivated. How many centuries had he hungered to appear as his true self? Centuries? No. Eons. Mortar's game to hold his magnificence hostage was criminal.

Descending the rock steps, he searched for a kill site. When he found it, the place held a bonus. A still warm gazelle lay beside an older carcass.

Birds pecking at the stale meat flew off as he circled the feast. He clamped his jaws on the head of the gazelle and tore away the eye socket. Brains had always been his favorite. The custard-like texture reflected perfectly their usage by men. Human reason was always so soft and pliable.

Eating dessert first merely whetted his appetite for more. Groveling repulsed him, but captive in lion form, uncontrollable natural instincts superseded his will power. Irresistibly drawn, he flattened onto the ground on his stomach and lapped at the liver.

A snarl from the nearby brush summoned his attention. Two male lions emerged. He allowed them to circle close before he lunged at the oldest and largest of the two. Pinning him on his back, he slashed with razor claws across the tender underbelly. The satisfying tear of his nails along the slack skin caused enough injury to send his victim moaning into the bush.

Then the younger lion sprung at him, wrapped paws around his head, and tried to bite his shoulder.

Cole closed his eyes and became one with the animal form he was forced to wear. Snarling, he thrashed against the youth with such complete effect that when he opened his eyes again, only a heap of blood-soaked fur with the side of a muzzle torn off, remained. Inside the separated chest cavity, a heart contracted one last time before it stilled.

Sometime later, he left the kill licking his lips. He climbed back to the top of the crest and flopped down in the warm sun and began to purr. *So what if it's unnatural to eat one's own species?* The salty sweet taste of young lion soaked with blood quenched both thirst and hunger. Almost.

He remained hungry for something else. *Something more.* He closed his eyes and fantasized about how irresistible he would be when he reached his shining moment, when he had the supreme admiration of all the world, and everyone bowed to his brilliance and provision.

"Wakey, wakey." A voice broke through his tummy-full slumber.

The old coot, Morbid, waved a flask at his face. Anise scent filled the air.

Cole yawned and showed off his teeth.

True to form, his hunched crony jumped back.

Cole laughed, but it came out a growl. He tilted his head back and opened his mouth.

Morbid's hands shook as he poured the nasty liquid down Cole's throat. "The good news is, you're getting easier to find, because there are so few lions left anymore. And the bad news? You've got to stop letting your anger get the best of you, or the savannah might end up being your regular home away from home."

Cole snarled, and the liquid went up his nose. He sputtered and slurped and then closed his mouth. It would be foolhardy to waste the precious liquid.

Morbid stood out of striking distance, wringing his hands.

Cole grumbled a sigh and then rolled onto his side as dullness settled in. The first few minutes after the tonic always subverted his senses and abilities, but it was worth it. He couldn't risk being taken out of operation by a prolonged punishment. Time ticked on.

Twenty minutes later, the sour taste came across his tongue. A sure sign that his voice would soon follow.

Morbid waved a honey bottle. "Are we ready for this?"

Cole sat and gulped the remedy. Then he swirled his tongue to get the stickiness off his chin. "Roar—whererrrthey? Rrrr—what's taking them so longrrr?"

"There, you see? It's working already, and you have plenty of time. Remember. The time conversion works in our favor here."

Cole sprang to the top of the ridge and tilted his head to the sky. "Theyyrrr should be here by nowrr."

"Of course, my liege," Morbid soothed. "But you sent them all over the kingdom. They'll be here shortly."

Cole circled the withered wisp of a man. "RrrrWhat could possibly be morrrr important than attending to me and getting to Beast's rrrrrresurrection?"

Morbid coughed and spoke in hesitant tones. "Well … of course … the resurrection of your father is so very important … still … Snake and Abaddon are up to their necks tracking the messages. So many are appearing now. And Lucas prepares for the invasion of Five." He coughed again. "Excuse me, my liege. And I … I attest most humbly that I've been engrossed in lining the pockets of our allies."

Cole stopped his circling and sniffed the air. "Whoo-ee, Beed. You stink. You're definitely still our stenchman, aren't you?"

The old man straightened and brushed off a cluster of worms emerging from the pock holes of his cane. "Rotting the minds of leaders is an uncomfortable but noble effort. I'm not ashamed of my calling. Our kingdom will be stronger because of my diligence."

Cole laughed. "True, true. It will be the best. Much better than Mortar's sappy conquest."

A familiar tingling came into his feet. Cole looked down and saw toes. "It's beginning to work. Oh, Beed!" A bit of joy slipped into the darkness of his heart. "You are the consummate physician, as well as loyal to your king. Your faithfulness will not go unnoticed by me in the days ahead."

Morbid bowed and smiled. "I'm glad it pleases you, sire."

"It does, and what pleases me pleases Beast. We are truly one power, you know. I'm certain in due time, he'll … *we'll* give you your own region to rule as well."

"Yes, well … let's not count those—" Morbid stopped speaking, stepped to the edge of the precipice and shielded his eyes. After a moment of silence, he continued. "Chickens, and in our case, hawks … the others are here, sire."

Three hawks dove from the sky and landed on the rocks, and each promptly grew to twice the size of a man.

Morbid spread out a net, and Cole climbed into the middle of it. Then Morbid transformed into a fourth hawk, and the giant birds took off with Cole-the-lion-man as their cargo.

Above the savannah, Cole called to the pride lions below him. "To a king's arrival I must go. *Au revoir*, my pets."

His tone was light, but Mortar's interference and SJ and Rumi's rebellion filled his heart with revenge.

CHAPTER 40

EVIE MANEUVERED AROUND smooth gray boulders. When the grass and sand patches between them disappeared, she climbed on top of them and stepped from one to the next until she reached the cliff face. From there, the ascent became steep.

She imitated Spero, reaching for the same cracks and crevices he used as steps and handholds. Cyril kept up with her basket and at times offered his free hand to pull her up, while Humor remained a steadfast support from below.

Soon the party reached the summit. After a brief rest, they walked to the smoother side of the peak and gazed down at the festival in progress. Confetti kites danced in the wind, providing a joyous array of color in the lush green valley.

The descent proved much easier. Evie thrilled over the discovery of more of her favorite flower—lily of the valley—and added stalks to her basket. The blossoms thrived in clusters between the stones and released a divine scent as they brushed through them.

At the bottom, five donkeys stood tethered to a nearby laurel tree.

Natalie smiled. "Five, of course. Very convenient and not surprising. So many things are grouped together in fives. Is it because of the name, Five? Why is the island called that?"

Evie shook her head. She'd heard rumors about the significance, but never a complete clarification.

The three heralds kept silent, too, as if something should not be said.

Then, Spero nodded at Humor and Cyril, and the two of them began untying the donkeys.

Natalie chuckled. "I guess I've asked a forbidden question."

"Not as much forbidden as difficult to explain. More understanding becomes available when the permanent is complete, but for now, I can say that Five reflects the significance of community." Spero reached for the largest donkey's bridle and patted its head. "On Five, you live in the constant company of five. Author Perfector, who is the three in one, Author, Son, and Counselor, and then you and your fellow resident become the other two—all added together to make a community—Five."

"Of course," Natalie pointed to Evie. "You and me. How perfect."

"What about heralds? Why not six?" Evie asked.

"Heralds do as Author Perfector directs. We carry out his instructions in all realms. That's all I can say for now." Spero's eyes twinkled and he turned and mounted his donkey.

Humor and Natalie picked two of the others and mounted while Cyril held the reins.

When Evie's turn came, the young jenny shied away from her.

"It's the basket. Give it back to me and then try." Cyril's donkey skills proved true, and she mounted securely without the basket. Cyril strapped it in place behind her instead.

The group set off. Midway across the valley, they reached the outer booths, where herald organizers distributed kites.

Evie caught sight of two women sitting on the grass helping a boy untangle a kite string. She called their names. "Martha. Kate."

Martha stood and waved, and the boy took off with his kite.

Evie dismounted, turned the reins over to Cyril, and rushed to hug her friend. "I've so much to tell you—a resurrection and a new resident on the beach and—" She stopped when she felt a strong tug on her hem. She looked down to see Kate, who held a finger to her lips and then lifted a corner of a blanket draped across her lap to reveal a tiny baby—a Pre-born. The child would be brought to the Son to be named.

With every festival, new infant arrivals were brought and dedicated back to the glory from which they came. Heralds called them Pre-born, because for various reasons, the babies never grew to live outside their mother in their first world. After their dedication day on Five, the children were part of the procession every fifth year of life until they reached the age of thirty. After that, they came every year for three years until the age of thirty-three—the Son's age at perfect substitute. They remained this age forever.

Her eyes sparkling with excitement, Kate told them that childcare was her favorite activity, and she'd eagerly volunteered when a herald requested help caring for the baby until it was time to present the child to the Son.

Martha met Natalie, and the two women helped Evie with her arrangement. Red and green pears formed the tower on the gold platter. White lily of the valley filled the crevices. Humor's words held true. The flower blossoms revived to perfect form.

Satisfied with the overall result, they joined Kate in the final stretch of the procession line, the part which contained mostly heralds, each holding a baby to be presented and named by the Son.

When they got close to the throne, Evie's heart beat faster. Every time Substitution Day came, she both hungered and feared the sound of Author Perfector's voice. Sneaky doubts competed with her anticipation. She wanted to bring her best and please him, but heralds warned against such expectations. The exercise of bringing offerings existed as a symbol of the sacrifice he'd already made—the gift that set the standard of perfection.

Between the figures of heralds in front of her, she caught glimpses of his presence.

His hair cascaded down, brilliant white as the snow, and his feet glowed as burnished bronze. The sound of rushing water filled the air. She had to shield her eyes because of the glow coming from his face.

Soon, only the herald carrying Kate's Pre-born stood between Evie and the throne. Blinded by the light, she closed her eyes and listened, letting his gentle words bathe her soul.

"This one will be called Samuel. His mother and father love me very much." A herald chorus rose and incorporated the baby's name in a song that echoed around the throne.

Then her turn came. Blindly, she stepped forward and felt the weight of her offering lifted from her hands.

Welcome words came.

"Well done, Evie. Do not be afraid. I am The First and The Last. The Ever-living One, and in you, I am pleased."

She knelt. Beloved hands brushed away her tears. She waited to be led away as was the custom, but instead, something different happened. A hand lifted her up, and all became quiet. Usually a chorus swelled at the end of each turn. This time the sound of trickling, gurgling, and rushing water returned, and the light diminished to a bearable glow.

She opened her eyes and discovered she was alone, except he was there, too.

Her offering rested on his lap. He picked up the top pear and handed it to her and said, "Eat. You will share in my knowledge about a name. Your three-times-great-granddaughter has chosen. Soon, I will write her name in the Book of Life, but it will not be the name she knows. She believes her name is SJ, but I tell you that it is not. You will share this knowledge when the time comes and give her the name I've chosen for her."

Then the Son bent close and whispered the name in Evie's ear. When he lifted his glorious head, she caught sight of the color of his eyes. The unexplainable hue reflected every shade of perfect, good, and true that ever existed, or ever would be.

CHAPTER 41

HER CHEEK PRICKLED. SJ opened her eyes and batted away a veil of coarse grass. The sound of rushing water and a soft pinging noise came from nearby. Pushing against the ground to stand, she almost fainted as pain shot through her shoulders and left her gasping. She explored the torn holes where her sleeve top used to be, and her fingers came away sticky with blood. The birds. Where were they?

The grass sea in front of her and blue sky above offered no evidence of the giant raptors. Bordered by trees on all sides, it parted only for the occasional boulder and yellow patch of bellflowers.

With careful steps she moved toward the sound of the pinging noise and discovered Kate's microtherm cylinder resting on its side. "Oh no. Please, no." She brushed debris off the screen. A power alert scrolled across the bottom.

The empty space where the chronometer had been attached spelled trouble. Without the timer, she had no idea how much time was left. It could be hours or only seconds until complete power failure occurred and Kate's chance for resurrection would be over.

She searched the grass for the timer and her wrist scanner, which was also missing. Although the midday sun radiated warmth, her mind stayed frozen. All she could think about was how long Kate had left and the fact that the last time she'd awakened from an unconscious state, Cole had been near.

Was he here? Her chest tightened. She pressed a hand against her heart and leaned against a boulder, catching her breath. Perhaps the birds, like the DARTS, were Cole's invention, and he'd sent them to toy with her.

She shuddered and scanned the terrain for hiding places. Gentle rounded peaks of green rose up behind the tree bands at the edge of the field. The summits held no similarity to the jagged snow caps above SHEOL.

The rushing water sound came from the direction of a stand of willow trees about two hundred yards away. If she followed the water flow downward, then perhaps she'd find a road and civilization.

She willed her legs to move. One step. Then another. She approached the trees, watching for movement. Peeking through some branches, she spied a waterfall.

Her plan was good, except for one thing. If she followed the stream, then she'd have to leave Kate.

No choice. The cylinder alarm told her to hurry. She tore the rest of one sleeve off entirely, found a stick, and attached the cloth to it. Then she pounded the handmade pennant into the ground by Kate's cylinder, marking the spot for her return.

She stepped back to see the effect. It looked as if she'd volunteered to surrender. *I'm not. I'm coming back. Wait for me, Kate.*

She set off for the waterfall, but the sound of a high-pitched squeal stopped her in her tracks. She ran back to the cylinder. "No. No. No!" The message on the screen indicated the auxiliary power supply had come to an end. She ran her hands around the entire unit hoping for an alternate solution. When the squealing stopped altogether, she beat against the side of it. Tears wet her face and blinded her eyes. A final strike jarred her injured shoulder.

She slid to the ground, curled into a ball, and sobbed. Death won. All the years of work, but she still couldn't stop it. Like children at play, it simply reached out, tagged her triumphantly on the back and yelled, "Gotcha."

A loud snap interrupted her grieving. She flattened onto her stomach.

Was it Cole? An animal?

Moisture tickled her nose. She pressed her face into her arm.

After a long time, she picked up a stone and tossed it in the direction of the sound. She waited a few more seconds, then selected a heftier stone and stood, ready to attack.

"That's one way to do it, but I dare say my skills will prove more effective than your brute force." A man's voice mocked her.

She whirled around.

A figure slipped out from behind a tree several yards away.

She took a step back. "Who are you? How did you get here? Was it the birds?"

"Which answer do you want first?" The figure moved out of the shadows. His TRIUMP blues attire clashed with his hair, which gleamed shockingly red in the sunlight.

"Ben? Is that you? How are you standing without your chair?"

Ben smiled. "Now, that's the question I'd bet you'd want me to answer first. The one about me standing, and I'll raise you one more. How can I see?" He reached down, picked up something from the ground, tossed it in the air, and caught it. Then he handed SJ the object—her wrist scanner.

"Thanks. How did you do that? Some new technology?"

"Nope. And I wouldn't turn that on if I were you. Cole can track you with it."

She nodded and placed it on her wrist.

"As for my ability to stand, I have a rare genetic disease known as atmospheric primal myopathy. My blindness and paralysis happen only when I'm inside. It's my body's response to exposure from an unknown antigen."

"But you're walking. You're cured."

"Only if I stay outside."

"Then why don't you work—"

"Outside? I like medicine. My illness plants me square in the middle of it. Maybe I'll invent a cure, and I find the side benefit of elevated hearing addictive." He winked at her. "It helps me rescue hapless people from uncooperative locks."

"Don't go feeling too sorry for him. He's failed to mention his primary occupation." A man dressed in a navy blue uniform and jacket slipped out from behind a clump of tall grass.

Her back stiffened. A DCN guard? Had he followed Ben?

The men stepped closer. "I might not fix locks, but I'm good with other remedies." Deep blue eyes twinkled from underneath white bushy brows. "Your hand, please."

"Frank?" She exhaled and then looked down at her hand as if it were an alien. She held it out.

He gripped it, and fiery warmth tingled in her fingers. Lightning quick, the sensation traveled up her arm and into her wounded shoulders. She jerked back. "Ow. What—that hurts!" She rubbed one shoulder first and then the other and found smooth skin. Her pain diminished to almost nothing at all.

Frank smiled at her. "Better?"

She nodded. "That's impossible. How did you …?"

The two men exchanged a silent communication.

"Come on. I mean it. Please explain. What's happening?"

The men moved away from her and exchanged indistinguishable words. Somebody said something about her being chosen. When they returned, Frank cleared his throat. "Here's the thing. I think you know I'm a herald. Right?"

"Maybe?" *How does he know what I know?*

Frank gave her a studied look.

"Yes. Okay. I know. But I'm not sure I understand what that is."

"There's a lot to it, but at the moment, here's all you need to know. Ben is also a herald, but he's what we call a Lifer, part of Mortar's secret Elite. Lifers accept an assignment to live from birth to death as a human would live, and oftentimes with a physical impediment."

"Why would Mortar ask such a thing?"

"Because, although all human lives are precious to Mortar, not all live in the same amount of danger. Lifers are assigned to watch over specific people in precarious situations."

Warmth trickled over SJ, and a smile tugged at her mouth. "Is that supposed to be me? Am I your assignment?"

Frank shrugged and nudged Ben, who grinned from ear to ear. "If the shoe fits …."

Then a cloud came into her thoughts. "Does Rumi or Cole know that Ben is a herald and a Lifer?"

"Rumi and Ben have never met, but Cole has seen Ben in the Abide. Cole knows who I am, but he does not know about Ben. He sees Ben as only a blind paraplegic TRIUMP intern. Ben is cloaked by Mortar's supernatural, and Ben's illness condition is a real physical boundary and protection if he stays on duty."

Frank's summary zoomed over SJ's head like a flock of starlings. If it was true, it sounded nice to have an elite bodyguard, but the reason behind the special treatment made her shiver. She took a deep breath. "I don't know what to say. It's a lot."

Frank nodded. "It is."

She walked past him and stood several yards away. Wind touched her face. The scent of grass and earth rose from the solid ground under her feet. All her senses were tied to what she knew was real. But nothing of what she had just heard, seen, or felt regarding Ben or Frank seemed to be in the same category. Yes. She'd made a choice to believe in the greater-and-more-good-than-she-could-understand entity and see where it led, but there was no law against asking for proof.

She walked back to the two of them. "If what you say is true, and you serve the side that's good, then make Kate alive, or at least restore power to the cylinder."

The look on their faces changed to something indescribable.

Frank snorted. "By Mortar's name, miracles like that are seldom granted."

"But isn't Mortar good?"

"He is only good."

"Then why can't you or he do it? You healed my arms. Why not help with Kate?"

"Mortar's miracles are seldom solely performed to provide proof. And as heralds, we can never interfere with human life without permission." Frank's tone softened. "Don't you yet realize where Kate is? She's safe and well and happy. She's on Five. All this is …" Frank patted the cylinder. "This contains only her shell."

SJ shook her head. "No. No. I want to see her and talk to her. Here." Tears flooded her eyes. "I didn't think—I just want her back." She turned away. Huge sobs gathered in her chest.

"There is one thing we can do," Frank said. "We can help you bury her. This field is a beautiful spot."

"I don't even know where we are." Her voice cracked. How could she leave Kate in the middle of nowhere?

"You're almost home. We're not far from the Upper East."

She turned around. "Where is it?"

Ben pointed. "You can't see it. It's past that grove of trees. There's a way station on the other side of the river. We'll cross over and enter the speedrail there and resume our route to the Abide. If that's still where you want to go."

She sniffed and wiped tears off her cheeks. "Yes." She cleared her throat. "I have to stop the trials."

The men nodded.

"It's what Kate would have wanted too." She knelt beside the cylinder and spread her arms around it. "I'm so sorry. I didn't want it this way." She pressed her cheek against the cold metal. "Goodbye, sweet friend. I'll always love you." Her breath caught, and tears threatened again. She bit her lip until she tasted blood. Pain to shut out pain. She stood and brushed herself off.

The men had moved several yards away, their backs toward her.

She coughed. "Tell me, if it's not forbidden or anything, do you know where Cole is right now?"

They turned around, and Ben tilted his head back and seemed to be studying the sky. "Almost five hours away. And tunnelway travel is crawling, thanks to my fellow Elite."

"Is that how you got here? I dreamed a giant bird carried me. Tell me that's impossible."

Ben nodded. "No and yes." He gave a little shrug, and then his shoulders twitched and shook alternately. Frank said nothing but seemed affected by the same spasm. Soon, both men fell into a kind of chicken-step dance and stroked their throats as ruffled collars of brown and white feathers erupted from their necks.

Her skin itched at the sight. "Stop. I get it. You two were the birds. But I don't think I can stand an entire transformation. I have to pace myself."

The dancing ended and the feathers receded.

She pointed. "I want to bury Kate. Over there. Under the willows."

The men agreed, and the project began. Ben helped her gather stones to mark the grave, while Frank determined the place and dimensions to hold the cylinder.

They stood under the willows, and Frank blew on an outline in the dirt. An orderly rectangular cloud of dirt lifted from within the outlined space and settled in a tidy heap alongside it. The men maneuvered the cylinder into the grave. Then Frank blew again, and a dirt cloud rose and fell, blanketing the last remnant of Kate.

Her heart broke afresh. *Oh Kate.* She took the bouquet of gold field flowers Ben had picked and placed them on the stacked stone marker.

When all was complete, Frank spoke a prayer.

She chose a stone to take home with her as a reminder, not that she needed prompting to recall the disappointment and limitations of death. None of her planning and training had saved Kate, but if she believed Rumi, and now Frank and Ben, then life had little to do with her control and contingencies. Something better existed.

Something greater.

As she followed her guides across the field, the new idea beckoned for her attention. It called to her from the natural world and from one source in particular. The flowers. Patches of them grew denser as they walked. Ben called them gold stars. The expanse of them changed the grass field from green to gold and filled the air with sweetness.

Something greater.

She stooped to pick one and held it to her nose.

Ben called to her, "Smell them while you can."

She hurried to catch up with him. "What do you mean?"

"They're here today and gone by tomorrow's sunset. Like all of life, they thrive only in the time span Mortar gives. But there's another place where life continues on in eternal form."

"I guess you're talking about Five?"

Ben slowed his pace. "Five is part of it."

His explanation made her wonder. If Five existed, then grasping for resurrection seemed less and less important.

The idea hounded her all the way to the grove.

CHAPTER 42

THE GRASSY FIELD changed into patches between clusters of trees. The tree clumps were spread out at first, but soon the vegetation grew closer together and the canopy filled in. SJ stumbled over something in a drift of decaying leaves. The impact knocked her shoe loose, and she sat on the ground to adjust it.

Frank kicked away some leaves and unearthed the end of a huge squared off log half submerged in the dirt. "Rail timber."

"That explains it," said Ben, pointing. "Fewer trees in this gully. I'm guessing we've walked onto the old movie set of *Murder Track*. It was filmed in this area and very popular some fifty years ago. People wanted nostalgia movies depicting prior life on Earth." He smiled. "Just think. If we had lived two hundred fifty years ago on Earth, then we would be riding a railcar to the city today."

"Highspeed tunnel travel suits me just fine," SJ said.

Ben gave her a bemused look and held out his hand.

She grabbed it and stood. "I guess if Cole had lived in those days, then he would have been a rail tycoon."

"He did live then. He's ageless. Same as we are." Ben rushed after Frank before SJ could ask her next question.

Did ageless mean that heralds never died?

She brushed off her pants and followed after the two men.

What other powers did heralds have? And more importantly, how could she stop a herald from doing whatever they wanted to do? Like Cole. "Wait up, guys. I've got questions."

The two heralds did not stop.

She yelled. "Hey, slow down. I've got to talk to you." It was no use. The wind drowned out the sound of her voice.

She hurried after them, kicking through leaves as she went. When she caught up to them, panting and out of breath, they stopped and turned around.

"What do you want to know?" Ben said.

"So you did hear me. Why didn't you wait?"

"We were working out our plan."

"To stop Cole?"

"No. To get you to the Abide." Ben nodded at Frank. "It involves some smooth talking from him and a little hacking from me. My specialty."

"It seems to me it would be quicker to change into birds and fly me in. Not that I want any new shoulder injuries. Perhaps I could ride on your back."

"Birds were an emergency maneuver. Wasn't supposed to happen that way." Frank chuckled. "For the most part."

Ben cleared his throat. "When operating in the realm of men, heralds are first obligated to use human methods. We wouldn't airdrop you in the city, because someone might notice. If that happened, then helping you would become more work than necessary. Witnesses would hunt you down and try to get explanations."

"Wow. There's a lot to learn about this herald stuff."

"What did you want to know about Cole?"

"I think you've answered it. I wanted to know that if I don't have my wrist scanner activated, then can Cole still find me anyway because of some kind of herald GPS superpower?"

"No. Since he's operating as a human, he's limited. He can only use methods of human discovery, like detecting your location by searching for your activated wrist scanner, or following you, or asking others if they have seen you."

This put a huge dent in her plan. How could she make contact with her team or the council and not alert Cole? And how did Frank find her? At SHEOL and in the tunnel. These could not be coincidences. "What about me? Your delivery route in the tunnel. Was that a coincidence? I didn't even have my own wrist scanner. It was Rumi's."

Frank grinned. "Caught me. Here's how. If heralds are assigned to someone by Mortar, then the herald receives intel that helps them locate their assignment."

"If I'm your assignment, then why don't you two just stop Cole and leave me out of it?"

"We can help you, but you have to make the decisions and lead the way. You said you wanted to return to the Abide and your team, and that's what we're helping you do."

Ben nudged Frank and pointed to the sky. "We've got to move."

They took off, and for the next hour, SJ pummeled them with questions about the capability of heralds. Her scientific curiosity ran rampant, and Ben and Frank patiently gave answers.

Yes. A herald could assume the identity of another species—human or animal. Capable of superhuman speed and strength, they could also sometimes heal. They could alter the natural environment, emit light under specific conditions, and when they touched a human, they generated heat.

No. A herald could not read her mind, but they had superior intuition and had studied human behavior for eons.

SJ's questions about heralds came to a halt when they arrived at a dilapidated trestle bridge. "We're not crossing on this, are we?"

The two columns of eroded timber pilings seemed incapable of supporting the wavy bridge deck, which gapped in several places.

"We are," Frank said. "Nothing to be concerned about."

Worrying about Cole took a back seat as SJ followed Frank and Ben onto the crumbling bridge.

She exhaled when they stepped onto the other side. There, they swapped the rail trail for a narrow but well-worn path through viny undergrowth.

After they walked a ways, they came to a spot where the footpath widened out. Frank stopped and took off his jacket. He handed it to SJ. "Wear it to cover your shirt. We'll soon be at the Fairway. There will be a lot of eyes and ears there since it also connects to the IT81 tie-in tunnel running down from the North."

Ben grinned. "It's his special incognito jacket too."

"What does that mean?" She slipped her arms through the sleeves of the plain navy jacket.

Frank frowned. "Not now. We've got to go."

Minutes later, the trio emerged from the hiking path and mingled with other travelers congregated at the hub. People stretched their legs and captured scenic views on their data screens.

"I'll find the station manager and request use of a stock van." Frank pulled out a cap from his pocket and tugged it over his head. The DCN transport logo matched the one on his shirt.

"You look official," SJ said.

"I am." Frank tapped his data screen. "Thanks to brainiac." He pointed to Ben. "I have a legitimate pick-up code for TRIUMP cargo at the Abide. Top priority."

"Do you think this will work?"

"I do. Keep the jacket on. The inside liner blocks your bio chip transmissions, and the right sleeve top layer has a Spartacus chip in the shoulder that will produce any number of generic identities when skimmed. It will present the same ID at any hub and checkpoint scanners we pass through until I reset it."

"What if I'm questioned, and what about the Abide? They won't let just anyone inside. At least not in the lab areas."

"We will pray for miracles, and I have another cover for you when we get there."

"What about you?"

"That's the beauty of the plan. I'm on assignment, so my alert is expected." Frank nodded at Ben. "Are we good to go?"

"Ready if you are."

Frank took off, and Ben led SJ away from the hub to a trailhead sign about a half mile away. They waited there for Frank near the sightseeing turnaround. When Frank pulled up, they climbed into the back of the van. Inside, they hunkered down, bracing themselves on the turns as Frank looped back to enter the tunnel.

Frank turned his head away from the camera at the entrance, a trick that prevented DCN's security system from making an identity match.

"Guess what?" Frank's grin reflected in the cargo mirror.

"Not guessing. Just tell us," SJ said.

"I heard from the hub manager that tunnel congestion out of SHEOL has transport backed up and diverted to IT25 southbound. From there, travelers will have to connect to IT40 for any east or westward travel. We'll beat Cole into the city by at least a couple of hours. In case you wondered, that's really good news."

"That's great." She mouthed the words with little enthusiasm. Their advantage should thrill her, but instead, all she felt was dread. Heralds might be used to high stakes and chase antics, but her typical life involved repetition of methodic rituals, some might say a cycle of scientific boredom. Although resurrection research had elevated her pace and the trials brought a giddy excitement, all the positives dwindled away, consumed by the constant gnawing in her stomach since partnering with Cole.

Her stomach flip-flopped as the van sped through the tunnel. Seeing truth meant accepting the fact that she'd been on the run from Cole since the day she'd left her office to hunt for Kate's body in the Abide. Her world had become a frantic digression of events triggered by Cole's foils, a cycle she was ill equipped to end.

In the cover of dark, she whispered her new ritual words, "Help me!" She directed her plea specifically to Mortar, Cole's faceless nemesis. She would continue to test her decision. Although she'd crossed the river of skepticism and stood on the banks of belief, her mind dripped with doubt. It would be so much easier if she could meet Mortar, or his son, or if she still had the book.

As they traveled, the two heralds chatted of fantastic adventures. The glow of their conquests left her feeling both hopeful and powerless. Mostly the latter because of Mortar's restrictions on their ability to help bring Kate back to life. What other restrictions would she encounter?

"Any thoughts from our conquering doctor?" Frank's voice drifted into her fog.

She took a deep breath. "Nothing to brag about. I need a face-to-face with George. He's not likely to be at the Abide. He spent precious little time there. Mostly, he stayed on the move as he supervised three division locations. It'll be hard to find him without activating my wrist scanner for the contact, but if I do that, then Cole will know exactly where I am."

"George might not be as hard to find as you think," Ben said.

"What do you mean?"

"It's Laura's day today."

Of course. Why didn't she think of that? "How did you know?" She strained to figure out the connection.

"Herald privilege." Ben sounded amused. "Heralds are given pertinent knowledge related to the situation at hand at the time it's needed."

Possibilities churned. Ben's suggestion was right. George would be taking the week off. He grieved Laura's death every year at this time.

"Any idea where he'll be?" Ben asked.

"Don't you know?" She assumed Ben's knowledge included this detail.

"Nope. Not that."

How odd.

"Well, I guess it won't be too hard. We'll just drive up and down all two hundred ninety-eight streets of the Human Science quarter and holler his name in front of every townhouse until someone comes out." Frank laughed.

"Actually, he lives on the divide between Literary and Construction. I know exactly where that is. I've been there. Brought George some supplies when he was helping his daughter, Laura, remodel it shortly after she bought it. George requested her home as his residence after she died and used his option to relocate from Health Science to her subdivision. He wanted to keep her memory close."

George's words about his daughter at her funeral still echoed in SJ's mind. "She was the good of me that was supposed to carry on, but now it's all back on my shoulders to keep doing what is right."

She planned to remind him of the sentiment when she saw him.

CHAPTER 43

THE VAN ENTERED the city on the speedrail bypass and took the exit leading to the divide between Literary and Construction.

After several miles of travel along the boundary, SJ pointed to a blue clapboard home with a wisteria arbor in front. It was just as she remembered.

She directed Frank to park around the corner. "Wait for me."

She got out of the van and walked back to the house. Sweeping fronds of lacy green brushed her shoulders as she passed under the arbor. She climbed the porch steps and knocked on the door. After several more attempts, she turned to leave but then heard a loud thud from inside. She banged on a window and yelled. "George. Open up. I know you're in there."

The door flung open, and after a quick glance up and down the street, George pulled her inside. He pointed to her wrist scanner. "Turn it off."

"It's not on." She didn't expect the gruffness of his tone.

"My ticker's gonna croak. You know they'll find you if you turn that thing on, and I don't want it to show we were together. Please leave it off!"

"Okay. Okay. I've got it."

He rushed to a nearby table as if ghosts were after him, grabbed a couple pills from his Med Pod dispenser and gulped them down. Then, pressing his hand to his chest, he breathed heavily and slumped into a chair, his color ashen.

She sat beside him, waiting for his wheezing to end.

Finally, he managed a whisper. "You shouldn't have come. Cole contacted me. Wanted to know if you stopped by."

"Please don't tell him. I need time. You know why I'm here." She waited for his acknowledgement, but he sat frozen and glassy eyed, his hand rigid on his drinking cup.

She pried the cup away, and he made eye contact. She spoke to him in measured pauses as if explaining bad behavior to a child. "George … the resurrections … are … a mistake. We need to call off the trials."

He reached out and clapped her on the shoulder. She yelped from the pain.

He jerked his hand back. "Are you hurt? Who did it? Was it him?"

"No. I'm fine. Just a tender spot."

He scratched vigorously at the skin on the top of his hand and then wiped his sweaty face. "You must know that SHEOL is shut down. The tremors have done considerable damage. All medical teams and patients are being routed back to the Abide. Resurrection candidates too. Sabotage and resistance sympathizers are being monitored. I guess you know you've been labeled as one."

"Well, that's crazy. I'm not, and you know it. I'm dedicated to delivering responsible resurrection. So far, the trials show we're propagating sociopathic beings who can't tell right from wrong. I need you to call for a council vote."

George removed his glasses and rubbed his eyes. He raked a hand through tufts of wispy gray hair and then replaced his eyewear. "Don't you see, S? I can't. I'm done. I'm retiring."

He staggered to stand. "In fact, I was just heading out the door. I'm off on a scout trip to Sector Thirty-One to find new living quarters. They say once transports are done, anyone left will be on their own. That's all I want. To be left alone to live as I please." His voice had a singsong manic tone she did not like.

She watched him pack belongings in his suitcase. "George. I don't believe you. That's the relocation sector. It's a no-man's-land. What about Laura? This house?" She couldn't understand why he would voluntarily choose to move over seven thousand miles away, to an area of unrest.

"Laura's dead. I've got to face reality, and so do you." He rubbed his face again and then jammed his hands in his pockets. "For years, people have received Rejuvacatin in their final moments, clinging to the hope of later resurrection."

"But if we are harming people it's not—"

"No. No." Gesturing wildly, he cut her off. "Listen to me. Achieving this goal has been your focus since the day you got out of school. Before that, it was your father's ambition. The fact that there are a few hitches does not mean we should stop the entire process. The only way to perfect the procedure is to keep moving forward."

He shut the case, put it by the door, then went back to the table and unfolded a thick black cloth.

Her heart sank at the coldness of his recitation. He never talked this way. For as long as she'd known him, George had always chosen excellence over compromise.

He stopped and fidgeted with his wrist scanner and then thrust the life clock view in front of her and tapped the current stats. "See? Even today the population decline has accelerated. It's sunk lower than anyone expected. We are out of time. Universe's decision to give primary funding and support to the resurrection trials is well promoted. It's the best contingency measure to prevent humans from becoming extinct altogether. The trials give hope to the masses who are dying. You're wrong to try and change the direction of progress."

George wrapped his Med Pod in the cloth and then placed it in its hard-shell case. "Can't leave home without this baby. Latest compact pod, but it prints every pill I need. Doc Tom switched my heart meds again, and he told me I'd have to fill my new one at a Universe APM, because the Med Formulary hadn't updated."

"But guess what?" He patted the case and the latch self-sealed shut. "Doc Tom was wrong too. Little Suzie does spit out my new dope and in sixty seconds flat without a hitch."

Grinning a half smile, he placed his old flat brown cap on his head and picked up the case. "Here's the real problem, S. Not only are you labeled as a resistance sympathizer, Cole says you're having a breakdown, and when you're found, you'll be placed under lock and key until you are well again. Birch has been declared the team leader until further notice."

Fear gripped her heart. If Cole managed to have her declared mentally incompetent, she'd never work in research again. "You've gotta help me, George. Isn't there something we can do?"

"There sure is. Not we, but you." He opened the door and pointed outside. "Run. For our friendship's sake, I won't tell Cole you stopped by, but that is the last favor I can grant. Please listen to what I'm saying."

"I can't. There's so much more happening. I'm fairly certain there's another realm. I believe Five is real. It might be where our souls go after we die. I'm not sure we can bring people back from the dead with their souls intact. It's not safe. I'm no longer sure resurrection is our best chance toward a thriving population. There may be other ways."

"You're outnumbered." He shook his head. "Everyone wants resurrection. It's the contingency plan for death, and it's at our fingertips. From what I see, you don't seem to be having a breakdown as much as a change in direction, but you should know by now that when Cole declares something to be true, people believe it. Do yourself a favor and get as far away from here as possible." He pushed past her to the door.

She followed him onto the porch, and he locked the door behind them. Under the arbor, he stopped and inhaled. Then he rushed to his car and loaded his things.

The blue-sky day around her covered the hovering darkness. The murkiness of it reached inside her heart and probed with icy fingers. *George. You've got it all wrong.*

He turned and shook her hand. "I'll contact you in a couple days if you want."

"That's okay. There's no need." Holding back tears, she smiled at the man who'd been her boss and mentor for years—a second father.

He tugged the cap low over his now darkened glasses and got in his car.

She reminded herself that he was only a man. At work, his head always appeared large on her office wall screen, but in person, he stood hunched over and rose only slightly taller than her. She watched as his car turned left and disappeared. Then she followed the sidewalk to the van where Frank and Ben waited.

Frank opened the door. "How did it go?"

"He's gone." She climbed into the van. "Out of the picture. He says he's retiring, and I'm not sure it's voluntary."

"That's too bad." Ben spoke gently.

Frank shut the cargo door and got in. "Maybe he'll change his mind and come back."

"Not a chance. He took his Med Pod. It'll print anything he needs. It's just like the ones in the Abide. He took some new pills his doc ordered. If it's in the Med Formulary, then it can be printed."

Her words echoed inside her head but with a twist. If it was in the Med Formulary, then it could be printed … but if the formula was gone, then it couldn't.

She pounded the back of the driver's chair. "That's it. I've got it! Go! Go!"

Frank put the van in autodrive. "Where to?"

"The Abide. If Ben can hack into the med vault processor, then I can reset the formula for the resurrection meds. I'll change the formula to something else. Something that will physically look the same but be ineffective and harmless. When the prep team fabricates the meds for the next trial, they'll make a placebo instead." Her thoughts raced. "What time is the next resurrection scheduled?"

Frank selected the media icon on the console screen and asked the question. A woman's voice answered. "Resurrection of the Beast will broadcast live at 1:00 p.m."

SJ groaned. "How can it be? John Doe trials are incomplete." Cole must have pushed it up. "That's less than an hour until start time."

"What do you want to do?" Ben asked.

She wanted to go back in time to the days when Kate still lived and Cole seemed only a bossy boyfriend.

"The Abide? Yes or no?" Frank touched the map screen.

"Yes. Yes. The Abide. I have to at least try." Her jaw muscles tensed. Her choice was a gnat flying in the face of a giant.

CHAPTER 44

THE VAN PULLED up at the main entrance of the Abide. A bot chair rolled down a ramp to meet them.

"That's my ride," said Ben.

Frank got out and helped Ben secure himself to the chair. "We'll see you in the formulary."

"Roger that." Ben entered the destination on the arm control. The chair made a slow U-turn and then accelerated up the ramp.

The van door closed, and SJ caught a glimpse of Ben through the side window as he maneuvered around pedestrian traffic and rolled to the entrance.

Frank climbed back into the driver's seat and set coordinates for the utility entrance. He turned on the media app and tapped out a beat to the music as the van pulled away.

Her stomach twisted in knots. How could he be so calm? She raised her voice above the tempo. "How will I know it's you?"

Frank turned his head in her direction. "What did you say?" He lowered the volume.

"Our plan. How will I know it's you?"

He stopped drumming. "Easy. I'll give you a code. A secret word. If you ask for it, I'll say it back to you."

"But you'll look entirely different?"

"Yep."

The van looped around the facility, then veered off and charged down the service road.

She closed her eyes. The circumstances around her life kept changing. It was as if she lived in a monstrous book entitled *Your New Life—All Is Not What It Seems*. Her orderly life had given way to chaos. Unlike research, which dealt with getting to what lay beneath the surface of appearances to find a rational explanation, it seemed that with elements of the supernatural, no human logic flowed between discovery and understanding.

She opened her eyes and leaned forward. "Why do you appear different to me than you do to someone else? Except Rumi of course. When she saw you in the tunnel, she worried about me hitching a ride with an Ancient."

Frank snickered. "She would. It was all Author Perfector's design, or Mortar, as Rumi calls him. You were expected to respond more favorably to an Ancient. To be honest, you have daddy issues. And since Cole is the son of the Beast and the biggest liar of all time, special care was necessary. For Rumi it was for other reasons."

"Can't you do it now? Change into this new other person, so I can get used to it before we get inside the Abide?"

"It will happen soon enough. Let's just keep things how they are for the moment."

"I guess it's the same thing as Rumi or Kate when they mask as another person."

"Not entirely. I'll be completely 'in person' and not just masked. It won't be makeup or a wall screen trick. But just remember, it will still be me. Underneath it all."

Frank parked a short distance from the crowded loading zone. He turned to SJ and held out his hand. "Let me introduce myself properly."

She grabbed his hand, and familiar warmth crept up her arm. "This feels so odd. I've known you as Frank. Aren't you still him?"

"I'm Michael. That's my herald name. But I'm still Frank. You can't understand this, but it's important to trust that, no matter what you see." He let go of her hand and donned his DCN cap, positioning it low on his head. "I'm still Frank."

She stared at his familiar leathery features.

"Think … hermit crab." Frank shut down the engine and pulled on his cargo pack.

"Okay. Why that?"

"The names I bear are merely titles to the shells I wear. I appear different to different people. You've only seen me as Frank. But underneath it all, I'm still the same old crab."

She laughed. "Okay. Got it. But I need that code word. One that few would guess."

"How about 'namesake'? A thoughtful expression crossed Frank's face as he scratched his jaw. "Yes. That seems appropriate in a reverse kinda way."

"What do you mean?"

"Well, instead of a person or thing named having the same name as another, I have multiple names that all add up to one thing—me, Michael. Heralds only see Michael, but in the case of humans, I can appear however Mortar, aka Author Perfector, requires."

"Okay. Namesake it is."

"And one more tiny detail. For the sake of your mission, I need to appear in a form the workers know. So, I'm gonna be Jack." He smiled, and his aged skin became even more crinkled.

"Jack?"

"Yes."

She waited, but nothing happened. "You look the same."

"I know. I haven't changed into Jack yet. I'll look different when I return. Remember, our code word is namesake." Then Frank, Michael, or Jack slammed the van door and hurried off in search of a cadaver trolley.

SJ moved to the front seat of the van and positioned the screen to reflect a live feed of the receiving bay hub, the place where the waiting dead were processed and shuttled on to Containment, a collection of rooms where bodies were catalogued and then placed in microtherm cylinders.

She groaned. If she succeeded in altering the resurrection drug formulas, then candidates would be waiting even longer. Continued resurrection trials would fail. Her heart hurt over what would happen. And what about Rumi? Cole believed Kate's body was still viable and a suitable body for Rumi's spirit.

Now that Kate was gone … she shuddered at the thought of what Cole would do when he discovered the sabotage.

Would her plan work? If discovered, it was a suicide mission for her and the lab.

She exhaled, and the van window fogged. She had more questions than answers.

Minutes later, a man walking beside a cadaver trolley approached the van. As he got close, her heart ricocheted inside her chest. It was Cole. She slouched down out of sight and closed her eyes. No … no… it couldn't be …

Footsteps crunched outside the door. She kept her hand on the manual lock.

Pounding shuddered the thin van wall. "Namesake, Doc. It's namesake. No worries. Open up."

Trust no matter what you see. She willed herself to respond. Pressing release, she watched as the door slid open to reveal Cole or his identical twin.

"It's me. Michael. But this is my Jack suit." He turned around in a circle as if posing for a fashion shoot. "Sorry it has to be this way. I didn't want to tell you, but I've been running around this bay in my Jack suit for a long time."

"I'm not sure …" Her tongue stuck to the roof of her mouth.

"Now I know I look like him, but remember, I'm not him. Workers think I'm his relative. The disguise means I do mostly as I please without questions. Cole hates slumming with underlings, so he seldom appears in the bay."

"But I still don't see why you can't just go as Frank?"

"Because security will be looking for you and Frank, so I had to go with Jack." Frank, Jack, Michael, or Cole smiled at her.

Her dry mouth and racing heart still had hold of her brain. *Think of his voice. It's entirely different. His voice.* She closed her eyes and tried to steady her breathing.

"Knock, knock."

"Who's there?" Weak comfort came. Frank told the stupidest jokes.

"No one but me. Doc, we gotta go. I know you can do this. Just think of the hermit crab."

She climbed out of the van. "You're right. But I'm gonna have to call you Frank. Or maybe Jack Frank. I can't deal with all your identity issues. I have to stay calm." She examined the rig. "How's this going to work?"

Jack Frank patted the setup. "You'll be transported comfortably in this three-unit stack."

"You sound like a car dealer."

"Glad you're amused. The bottom suite is yours. Having the rig outside is cause for a protocol violation, but we have the advantage. TRIUMP workers are swamped with extra duties because of Beast's pending resurrection and live broadcast. Their only goal is to get through their shift. They'll ignore the infraction to avoid having to fill out any tedious irregularity reports." He grinned and placed his hand over his heart. "Besides that, they trust good old Jack here."

She breathed easier. Cole seldom smiled, and if he did, it appeared more like a mocking smirk than a genuine facial expression of goodwill. Unlike Frank, whose every smile radiated honest concern and affection.

He opened the bottom slot.

Passing her hand along the upper unit, she examined the space. "Are there bodies?"

"You've got two suitemates. But nothing but you in the bottom space." He chuckled.

"I'm not squeamish about dead bodies bunking above me. It's the ratio of air to me that worries me."

"I loosened the hinge, so the lid sits slightly off. You'll be fine."

Her brow furrowed and she bit her lip.

"Second thoughts, Doc?"

"No. It's what I have to do. We're too close to my lab. Someone might recognize me."

She took a deep breath, got into the container, and laid back with her arms straight down on her sides but then switched them over to cross on her chest for more room. Just before he shut the lid, she grabbed his hand. "Good thing you're a herald. I know you'll come to my rescue if things go wrong."

"I'll fight to the death if necessary." His eyes flamed with fire. Then he lowered the top.

Wait. What did that mean? She banged on the cover. "Hello? What death are you talking about? I thought you were immortal." Over the rumble of the moving rig, she strained to hear his answer.

"Of course. It's just an expression. A human one. I'm immortal and so are you, but you're the lucky one. You bear his name. I gotta zip it up now, Doc. We're about to pass a gaggle of your cronies. I'm certain if they hear me talking to my rig, I'll get some attention. Especially if my rig talks back."

What did he mean? She was immortal? She bore his name? Whose name? Another riddle to solve.

Exhaling, she closed her eyes. Posing as a counterfeit corpse in a module stack of three offered little scenery anyway. Her only location clues became the sounds of workers' greetings and Frank's occasional shout of caution as he maneuvered her hiding place.

As she traveled, she fought the urge to kick her way out of the module and focused instead on Frank and his many disguises, including the masquerade of the moment, and her bigger concern. Was she doing the right thing? She could still call it off and blend into Cole's scheme for her.

Running through a mental summary of her findings, just as she did with her research, would bring clarity.

One. If resurrection of humans resulted in a body without a spirit or soul and this presented a danger, then more research was needed before continuing the trials.

Two. If the messages from Five indicated life after death already existed, then resurrected life would be counterfeit.

Three. She'd only be altering the resurrection drug formulas Corpicom and Verdegan to render them ineffective and bring a halt to the trials. The formula for the resurrection prep drug Rejuvactin would remain untouched.

Four. Her actions would cost her if the sabotage were discovered. Only credentialed pharmaceutical scientists were allowed in the Abide formulary room to make approved changes to resurrection drug designs. But then again, if George was right, her punishment was already started. Thanks to Cole's power and connections, she'd been labeled a resistance sympathizer and mentally incompetent. If the branding stuck, her future as team leader and research scientist was already ending.

She squirmed and tried to shift her body, but the streamlined space offered no room for adjustment. She tapped on the lid.

Frank whispered. "Just a few more minutes."

Ages later, he opened the cover. Although fresh air hit her face, complete and impenetrable darkness hung all around her. "Where are we? Why is it so dark?"

"We're on a landing on the emergency stairs leading to the lower level. The exit is next to the formulary."

"You went up just to come back down?"

"Yep. There's a huge influx of bodies entering from SHEOL, and containment rooms are swamped. We don't have time to wait in line for a security check there, so I found a little shortcut."

He helped her stand. "Now step sideways two steps and go forward one." He kept a hand on her back. "Good. Now wait a second while I move this rig aside."

It dawned on her. "Can heralds see in the dark?"

He chuckled. "Yes. The darkness is as light to us."

The squeak of wheels and a thump sounded beside her. "At least I can't see you in your ugly Jack suit."

"I thought you found Cole good-looking?" Metal clanking and a snapping sound occurred.

"Haven't you ever heard the expression that good-looking is as good-looking does?"

"I've not heard that."

"It's true. No matter how handsome he is, Cole's deception and manipulation make him ugly to me."

"Okay. Now …" He took her hand and placed it on a cold cylinder shape "This is the stair railing. We're going down. About fifteen steps to a half landing, then a turnabout and another fifteen steps before the door. Gotta stay dark, because camera scans pick up all stairwells."

"What about the bodies and the rig?"

"Don't worry your little head about that, Doc. I'll be back for it. Right now, we've got to get to Ben. He's already working on the database."

She gripped the stair rail and moved with care down the stairs.

At the bottom, Frank held open the door, and she stepped into the light of a familiar hallway.

"How will we get in?" She patted her shoulder. "The Spartacus chip ID has to match my facial ID. Also, the identity scanned off this chip in your jacket has to be credentialed. Authorized personnel only in the drug formulary."

"Of course. And it will. You'll be entering as Birch. I'll slide in with you after confirmation."

"Birch? Then I assume I'm masking. How will that work if his face-scan shows up somewhere else or at the formulary at the same time? It will trigger an alert."

"It's a risk we have to take. But Birch is busy with the resurrection trials and behind procedure doors. When they run the monthly formulary room log, no one scrutinizes if personnel are actually in the room and nowhere else. It's not been a concern or suspicion." Frank paused. "Your identity, on the other hand, is set to trigger a level six alert. Something we must avoid."

"I just wish there was another way."

Jack Frank slid off his cargo pack and dug out a facescreen mask and replicator wand. "It's not a perfect plan, but worth a try if you still want to carry through with the sabotage. Remember, no one will know what you have done."

"You mean no one but Cole. But if he does find me in the formulary, then he will figure it out."

"Then let's not let him find you."

CHAPTER 45

A HERDSMAN APPEARED ON the rocky ridge above them. Evie signaled to Martha, who waited near the lamb pen. The privilege of choosing a namesake lamb seldom came to residents of Five. Usually, Author Perfector's son made the selection. Every day he walked among the flocks and played with the little ones. Even though the mass of them counted into untold numbers, he knew each one by name.

When the herdsman arrived, he opened the gate. They had to push between ewe mammas bleating at their frolicking lamb babies to get inside.

After much laughter and examination, Evie decided on a stocky one with matching black spots on both shoulders, ears, and nose, and black boots on three legs.

The shepherd corralled her selection and placed it in her arms. "She's a Jacob sheep." His voice had an odd sounding rasp like quality, and Evie caught a glimpse of an ugly scar on his cheek.

Curious unease settled over her, but she shook it off and focused on the lamb, pushing her face into the soft, curly coat. The creature bleated as she whispered SJ's new name in its ear.

She'd barely finished her introduction when it wriggled out of her arms and skipped off to its waiting mother. Their reunion turned purposeful as the lamb nuzzled for milk.

"When the feeding is over, we'll say goodbye to the mother and move your little Jacobite to Namesake Field to be with the others." The shepherd averted his gaze as if shy. "You can spend the first night there with it if you'd like."

"We'd love to." Evie looked at Martha, who nodded affirmatively.

"Only one. Just you." The herald pointed to Evie with his crook. Then he whistled, and a wolf-like dog bounded out of a shed.

Evie rubbed her cold hands together and tried to ignore the increasing feeling of dread.

The shepherd's dog, a strange hybrid creature named Diablo, provided a distraction as it put on a display of canine tricks which concluded with it standing on its hind legs and putting its paws on the herdsman's chest to receive an embrace. When the shepherd pushed it away, it ran after the ewes.

The shepherd grabbed the namesake lamb. "Follow me."

A warning wind in her ear said, "Don't."

About an hour after they'd left the lamb pen, the shepherd left the road and entered an apple grove. Rows of tree trunks held twisted branch crowns to the sky. Gnarled limbs and the absence of fruit and leaves indicated disease.

Evie followed behind but stopped to touch a withered leaf cluster. "Is this blight?"

The shepherd walked on as if he did not hear.

The Wilds. Surely the grazing fields were nearby.

She tramped behind the shepherd who kept a tight grip on the wriggling lamb. The creature bleated loudly but hushed when the shepherd commanded, "Subsiste sermonem."

Evie knew the words meant "stop speaking," but the herdsman's use of the forbidden Darkonium language alarmed her.

She pulled her shawl tight around her. *Nothing here can harm me.* Maybe shepherds had special permission to use the ancient tongue.

When they got to the far side of the orchard, a choice of roads lay in front of them, a wide one that sloped down from them and a narrow foot path that twisted upward into deep woods going the other direction.

"Which way?"

"Both routes lead there."

"It's not possible." Although grateful to hear his answer in Common Tongue, she couldn't resist pointing out the obvious. "They go in opposite directions."

"So it would seem. Your doubt is admirable."

"Let's take the road." She spoke decisively and started down the slope.

The shepherd murmured, "A perfect choice."

Trying to ignore his strange praise, she focused instead on the comfort her selection provided. The thought of traveling along an isolated hiking trail with her odd companion made her nervous. The potential for encountering fellow travelers existed if they took the wide road.

She second-guessed her decision much later when the light shifted. Although complete darkness never came to Five, the bright beams of day returned to the horizon at night, sending stripes of gold and orange on cirrus clouds across the heavens.

They'd been walking for hours it seemed, traveling through shrub land with no sign of pastures.

She looked back at the lamb. Its legs dangled limply from under the shepherd's arm, and its head moved only with the rhythm of his pace. It appeared the creature had fallen asleep.

How much longer? To soothe her anxious thoughts, she imagined herself resting in a soft, grassy field curled up by the lamb.

Then pain came into her step. She stopped to dislodge a stone from inside her shoe.

The shepherd passed by her and entered the grass gully beside the road. He motioned for her to follow.

"Are we taking a shortcut?"

"Merely a refreshment detour as we're not quite halfway," he said.

Not quite halfway? She should have asked more questions at the beginning. She hated not knowing her route or location and having to rely on the herdsman.

After pushing through several yards of head-tall grass, they came into a clearing containing another orchard, only this one was lush with many kinds of trees, and the fruit looked delicious.

"Eat. Take your pick. All are good, but in fact, there is one that surpasses all the rest."

Amazed at the lush abundance, she followed him to a central tree with fruit so beautiful and unusual that she became eager to have her fill. Fruit on Five was incredibly satisfying. Having an opportunity to taste a new one with such a grand reputation was exciting.

She picked a fruit and marveled at the sweet scent it released when she rubbed the golden, pear-like skin. "What is it called? Why do you say it's better than all the rest?"

"It's been called many things. Whoever eats it will know its benefit as soon as they taste it." He took a bite of his own harvest.

Although more than eager to consume her reward, she hesitated. His words brought to mind the advice she'd heard in her earliest life on Five. "Eat fruit only until you are full, and of the healing fruits, eat only when you're ill, otherwise, detachment will take over your spirit and only with great effort will you be brought back to wholeness."

"If this fruit is for healing illness and I'm not sick, then perhaps I shouldn't." She spoke with caution, but her mouth quivered with anticipation as she watched him wipe the juice off his lips with his sleeve.

"There's always an illness to be cured. This one provides the remedy for all of them."

She heard the crisp cut his teeth made as they tore into succulent flesh and chewed.

He swallowed. "Your illness is fear. Eating from the fruit of this tree will give you all knowledge, so you can know what is coming and what to do about it. Think how life would be if you had this wisdom. This benefit will be yours once you eat the fruit."

"My fears are almost gone now." How did he know her story?

"What you say is true and untrue. You're still afraid, and you still have doubts. Doubt is the origin of wisdom, and with the help of this fruit, you will soon know all things, and then all things can be conquered by you. Isn't that wonderful?" He took another bite, and the juice ran down his chin and into the corners of his scar.

Thirst and hunger intensified at the sight of each bite he took. The logic in his words made her crazy for a bite of her own.

She closed her eyes and opened her mouth for the first sweet taste, but then, a sudden sharpness ripped across her palm. She opened her eyes. Blood dripped from her hand where the fruit had been. An arch herald with blazing hair held a gleaming sword with her fruit speared on the tip.

The lamb bleated and thrashed against the shepherd. The side of his cloak pulled apart, revealing a glint of armor.

The fruit-spearing herald roared. "You have no claim on her."

Evie's heart raced in her chest. Shame poured over her.

"Soul Evie freely chooses all that is offered." The herdsman's voice slithered over her name with ease.

I never told him my name. Humiliation shifted into fear. Her teeth chattered. A cold breeze swirled.

The fruit-spearing herald flung her fruit to the ground and then touched the tree with his sword tip. Instantly, the branches withered, and the fruit dropped rotting to the ground. Within seconds, the ripple effect swept the entire orchard. Trees writhed and twisted as if in agony. Howling wind and rain surged down from the sky and pummeled the fruit on the ground. The smell of rotting fruit mingled with the buzz of flies that swarmed out of the storm and covered the molding crop.

Then the arch herald picked up her fruit, tossed it into the air, and split it with a swipe of his sword. "Be gone!" His motion sent the flies into a frenzied funnel. The fly siphon spiraled up and away along with the wind and the rain until all became still.

"You are a thief." He pointed his sword at them. "The lamb's life is declared. By her first choosing." His voice shook the ground. "Are you so prideful to believe that you can re-create the choice? Would you turn this haven and its people to do evil as you did in the garden long ago? Your fate is sealed, thief. There's nothing you can do to change that."

Evie wanted to run but no escape route seemed safe. She stepped back into the tall grass. The garden? Thief? Then she understood. The words were for the herdsman. Not her.

The shepherd growled and raised his sword high. Still holding the lamb, he charged at the arch herald but stopped short by several yards when a great light spilled out of the sky.

The arch herald bowed his head.

A voice spoke from the light. "In the name of him who endured all death and was resurrected, be gone, nameless one! Go back to your kingdom, for the day of reckoning is not yet here."

"No. I will not leave." The herdsman faced off from the arch herald again and brandished his sword.

The elements exploded. Thunder, lightning, wind, and rain entered into a savage dance all around, as a violent clash of swords ensued.

A blow from the arch herald's sword cut through the shoulder of the herdsman, amputating his arm.

The limb landed at Evie's feet along with the traumatized lamb.

She scooped up the frightened creature but then froze as the howling shepherd swooped toward her. He stooped and gathered up his severed arm and placed it in position in the bloodied gaping socket of his shoulder. Something familiar about his manner tugged in her mind. Mesmerized at first by the sight of flesh that re-wove limb to bone of its own accord, she shifted her gaze to his face.

His eyes gleamed red, and he smirked at her. "Unlike with you, the slice of the sword has no hold on me."

Then her heart remembered. She stared into the face of her murderer thief. It was him. Fol. Father of Lies.

The voice of the arch herald filled her ears. "Soul Evie. Take the lamb and run. Don't stop until you reach the narrow road!"

She clutched the lamb tight and ran.

CHAPTER 46

SJ PUT ON the facescreen mask while Frank punched in a request on the replicator wand. When all four lights on the wand illuminated, Frank swept the device across her face. Then at his signal, she stepped into the camera view of the formulary door.

Her shoulders tensed as the scan triggered twice.

"Steady. We're almost there," Frank said.

Seconds later, the auto reader confirmed Birch's name. The door lock glowed green and then opened. Inside, they found a sole occupant sitting in front of the wall screen, his hands poised in frozen gesture over the tabletop keyboard. A log-in command box flashed empty in the center of the wall screen. A timer in the side margin counted down the remaining seconds.

Ben. He'd made it. But why was he so still?

She shook him. His ashy cool skin meant only one thing. She turned to Frank. "Is he …?"

Frank placed two fingers on Ben's temple. "Nope. Not this time. He'll be with us shortly." He wore a sly smile.

"What's going on?" Heat poured over her. This was no time for herald shenanigans or humor.

Taking a seat beside Ben, Frank motioned for her to sit too.

She remained standing.

Frank picked up each of Ben's flaccid hands one at a time and then let them fall.

"What's wrong with him?" She checked her wrist screen. "There's no time to stall. If we want to stop Beast's resurrection we have to act now."

Ben came alive. "Sorry about that. I'm in lessons. Learning Sofit code. Just a few more minutes and then I'll be able to break in without …"

"We don't have time! Please. Use my password." She reached to put in her password, but Frank pushed her hand away.

"He'll do it. Trust me."

Trust? Nothing around her proved trustworthy, including, at the moment, Frank in his Cole clone suit. But she'd made a choice. Right? To stop Cole's corruption of the uncertain trials. To keep trying to abort no matter what. For the good of all.

Log-in data began rolling down the screen. Ben tapped rapidly through the many options.

"See? He's a genius." Frank flashed a toothy grin.

But then a second verification screen demanded confirmation. Without it, the lockout screen would appear next.

The thought of failing or being found out seized her by the throat and cut off her breath. "What can we do?"

"A lot, if I had more lesson time." Ben shifted in his bot chair and rubbed his temples.

Frank pointed to the screen timer. "She's right. There's no time. They're already in prep. We'll be lucky if they haven't printed the meds."

"It would show in the delivery block." She traced her finger to the faded bottle icon at the bottom of the pharm screen, but since she wasn't officially inside the program, the option remained obscure.

A snarky computer voice repeated the request for verification. "Thirty seconds until reset," the mechanical voice pronounced cheerfully.

"No. No." She bit her lip. "My password. My chip to confirm. We've gotta do it." She took off Frank's jacket and grabbed a chip scanner from the wall and handed it to him. "I'll take my chances."

"You sure?"

She nodded. "It might not even work. Cole may have locked out my access."

Frank swiped her shoulder.

Seconds later, her identity details flowed onto the screen.

"Well, he didn't, and we're in." Ben grinned, and his hands swept across the keys as he navigated the cookbook database.

Herald ability alternately perplexed and amazed SJ. The effects of Ben's blindness had returned since entering the Abide, yet he grappled with unfamiliar software and deftly navigated data he knew nothing about. "How come heralds sometimes seem to know everything, and then other times they don't?"

"It's not up to us. Our wisdom comes when Author Perfector decides." Frank spoke from the corner of the room as he worked to interrupt the camera feed. "It mostly happens when we are in motion doing what he asks. It's then that he gives us what's next. The process is no different for you."

"But I've always had to study and learn what I know. Nothing just comes to me."

"Studying is good. Hard work is good. He gives minds and hands to do those things, but sometimes those things fail. He is the constant that never fails."

"Okay. Guys ..." Ben pointed in the direction of the wall screen, where the resurrection drug formulas appeared. "This is it. Second thoughts?" He cocked his head. "The choice is entirely yours. We're only here to help."

Uncertainty washed over her. Again. It seemed as if the whole sorry mess was a test or a trick. A bad dream. Something she'd wake up from and be happy with relief that it wasn't true.

"Doc?"

"I know I should be grateful. You heralds are very diplomatic." She swallowed hard to moisten her dry mouth. "Why give me the choice? It seems heralds have close contact with Mortar or Author or whatever you call him, and you have wisdom from him. Why don't you two decide? I just keep thinking maybe there's another way."

"Nope. Ben is right." Frank moved back to her side. "Heralds don't make choices for humans. We give help to those who follow Mortar, which is the clunky name Cole and his band gave him, because he binds together all things they seek to destroy. To us, he's Author Perfector."

"I don't care about his name—just if I'm making the right choice." A heaviness came over her, and her temples throbbed. "People have waited a long time for resurrection. Our progress will be destroyed when the formulas are changed."

The line on the screen blinked, asking for confirmation of the formula alteration, while a computer voice requested identity verification for the changes.

Frank exhaled. "Here's the thing. What you say is all true. You can walk away and hope for another plan. But if you want to stop what Cole intends and slow the trial process down today, then this is your chance."

"I'll do my best to cover your tracks, of course," Ben said. "And I'll replace the formulas with something harmless so people will think the medication is functional."

Agreeing to tamper with the same formulas she'd devoted her life's work to develop became a monstrously impossible thought. She closed her eyes. *Remember. Something greater.*

She opened her eyes and stuck out her arm.

Frank swept the scanner over it once again. "Your ID scans will trigger alerts about your location, but Ben bought us some time. He rerouted the signal to project the alert in a parallel corridor on the other side of the Abide. We'll get you out before security untangles it. Of course, you'll go back out the way you came in. Enthroned with the dearly departed." He chuckled.

She frowned. "How fitting. I'm already declared dead to this project." Her gloom turned to alarm when a read error came on the screen and a fifteen-second countdown initiated.

The computer voice warned, "Operator error. Please repeat scan for verification."

She grabbed the wand from Frank and ran it several times over the skin surface where her chip was buried until the word *confirmed* flashed on the screen.

"Final step. Tap 'delete,' and the formulary will upload my chosen replacements." Ben pushed back from the command table.

Her hand hovered. Her entire life's work. She gulped at the air. "Maybe a quick backup copy is in order."

"As you wish." Ben rolled back to his position.

Frank pushed his hand from the keyboard. "Whoa there, partner. Author never said we couldn't reason with them."

Frank turned to her. "Sit, Doc." He pointed to a chair. "Let's talk about this."

Her wooden limbs obeyed.

Frank knelt in front of her like she was some kind of royalty. "I know this is weird, but you gotta hear and see me when I say this. Don't be fooled by what you think you see."

The irony of his words came to her as she gazed into the slightly glowing face of a herald who wore the trappings of a man who looked like Cole but acted completely opposite and spoke in the voice of Frank.

"Keeping a secret copy of the formulas would become a heavy chain for you."

She squirmed. "I know. But just in case. We've come so far. If we can revive the dead without the factor of psychotic impulses in this generation, then maybe in future generations we will have solved the problem of dying all together."

"You're assuming a problem exists simply because nobody has yet found a solution. Is that right?" His brow furrowed slightly.

"I think so." *Do I really?* It sounded odd the way he said it.

"Then you and Cole are alike in this." Shifting his position to the floor, Frank sat and propped himself up with his arms.

"I don't like you saying that." The man was getting on her nerves.

Frank held up a hand. "Wait. Hear me out. You asked us what you should do. I'm just pointing out that Cole believes the answer to life problems lies in him, his rule, and resources. The illusion requires him to always fight for control and prepare for every contingency. Doesn't that seem exhausting?"

"But this is my life's work. The work of my father and all that have gone before us. Everything I am and have done is tied to succeeding in the process of resurrection." She sat up straighter. "We are saving human life."

Frank tilted his head. "But what are you saving them from? You already asked that question. What if resurrecting human life brings people back from another place?"

SJ groaned. "Then what do I do?"

"I can't decide for you, but I will tell you that if you think life's meaning is found in knowledge and achievement, you're echoing Cole's views. Author designed you for a purpose far greater than chasing insatiable appetites. Under Author's rule, you've always been significant, and his perfect plan for you excels beyond all others."

The plea in his words touched her heart, but the phrase, "you and Cole are alike" burned as fire in her ears. She turned in her chair and hit "delete" before she could think again.

Frank scrambled to his feet and nodded at Ben, who immediately began tapping in rapid staccato, and a string of data flowed across the screen. New percentages and ingredients lined up inside the boxes where the details for Verdegan and Corpicom were displayed.

She studied the sequencing. "What's the harmless replacements? Herald mojo juice?"

Ben laughed and kept tapping. "You could call it that. They're the formulas for forgiveness and love. They already run through your veins. It's how Author made humans. I just isolated it and threw in a little stabilizer and made it soluble." He paused and then rolled his bot chair aside. A smile crinkled in the corners of his mouth. "Voila! Your new 'resurrection' drug formulas. Ready for dispensing."

"How can love and forgiveness be made into a formula?" The idea sounded crazy to her.

"The combination works best when Author Perfector is allowed into life. Of course, in a dead man, the ability to act from forgiveness and love is gone. Still, administering these two compounds will either have no effect at all, or at least, nothing harmful." Ben's hands danced once more across the command keys.

"But actions of the mind such as love and forgiveness can't possibly become a physical ingredient. Can they?" She looked to Frank hoping to get an answer that made sense.

He nodded. "But unfortunately, since the Book of Wisdom has become obsolete, humans no longer have any idea about what's possible. They just think they do."

Then she saw it. A tiny, red blinking light behind him above the doorframe. Her presence had triggered the individual room alert.

She moved to the doorway.

Frank blocked her.

"No. Please." She stepped to the side. "You said choose. I've gotta go. There's something I can do. Stay with Ben and cover my tracks in the database. I'll be back."

His eyes held hers. Then he stepped out of her way.

She raced down a familiar corridor and took the shortcut to her lab.

The unlocked door came as a surprise, but she had no time to investigate.

Flipping on a single light panel, she hunted in the drawers for a scalpel. Grabbing sterilizer, she wiped off the top of her arm. Then, clenching her jaw, she sliced into her shoulder just above the faint scar.

As blood seeped out of the wound, she rooted in her flesh until the chip end became exposed. Then, using forceps, she yanked out the bloody gold square. Moaning, she slumped into a chair and put pressure on the wound using gauze from the emergency kit stored near Phinny's cage.

She stared at the empty cage. A tag marked "terminate" dangled from its door. Protocol required cremation of lab-bred subjects once an experiment ended.

She touched the tag, and it flipped over. There was handwriting on the back of it.

Phinny's safe. Paradise Cove. Ask for Nathaniel. He'll take you to him.

Her heart swelled. Good old George. She pulled off the tag and stuck it in her pocket.

The lab door opened.

"Who's there?"

A figure stood in the shadow then bounded across the room. He looked like Cole.

"Frank? I said I'd be back. You didn't need to come get me."

Without a word, Frank lunged at her, and his hand smacked against her open wound. Her flesh sizzled under his touch.

Yelling, she kicked him in the shin.

He growled and reached for her.

She stepped out of his path and covered her shoulder with her palm to protect her wound. "What are you doing?" Her fingers touched smooth skin.

"Healing you, my love." The voice was Cole's. Unmistakable. His manic grin chilled her heart. "You can thank me later. But now it's time to leave your pauper's throne and join me. Rumi calls for you."

She grabbed the bottle of sterilizer solution and threw it as hard as she could at his head. He ducked, and it crashed against a cabinet, providing enough distraction for her to escape. Halfway down the hallway, she stopped running. *Rumi.* She'd made a promise. Turning to retrace her steps, she heard Cole's voice.

"Not that way. I'm here. In front of you." The sound came from the shadows at the end of the hall. A herald trick, most likely.

She called out to him. "What does she want?"

"To see you. Her last wish before she dies. I'm sure you'll want to grant her this last request."

With feet of lead, she came close. Cole emerged and gave a mocking bow. "There you are. Ever my queen of mismanaged intentions."

"Take me to her."

"As you wish."

His breath fell on her neck as she walked ahead of him. Being discovered by the Abide's security team would be better than being alone with him, but the chip she'd just removed from her arm made that outcome unlikely.

When they reached an empty alcove where the elevator waited, he grabbed her elbow. "Did you know that my men are closing in on Kate's cylinder this very minute?"

Steady. Stay calm. "Good. I'm glad they'll find it. I'd hoped to save it from damage." *He's bluffing.* How could he know Kate's body lay buried in the field in such a short time?

When they got inside the elevator, he took her by the chin and tilted her face toward him. "Look at me," he growled. "Why do you resist so? I am yours and you are mine. We are partners."

She pushed his hands away and pulled back. "You're taking me to Rumi. Nothing else."

"Of course." He leered at her. "As you wish."

The door opened, and he shoved her out into the Maze. "Here we are, darling. Our shortcut."

In a pretense of cooperation, she allowed him to steer her along the dimly lit passage, but her heart sank. Traveling through the Maze meant fewer security checkpoints and less of an audience to pressure his behavior.

"I'm glad that you trust me and have stopped resisting. Eluding Abide security can be quite a challenge. The key to your freedom and future work is in my hands. After you greet Rumi, we'll meet Father at his resurrection and then you'll be taken to a special place that I've prepared for your recuperation. No doubt you'll need it."

His thinly veiled threats about her future showed his intent to keep her alive. But what about Rumi? She tested the waters. "Rumi told me she wants to be resurrected."

"Sure. But you'll only make it look like she's getting Rejuvacatin. There's no reason for an eligeren to be resurrected. I only want candidates who can contribute to society by brains or bloodline. Her body has no ability to reproduce."

"Really, Cole?" Her own blood boiled at his bravado over manipulating candidates. "Are you a god who would decide who should be resurrected and who should not?" Her fury grew and replaced all fear of him. "If Rumi wants Rejuvacatin, then she will get it."

"Spoken like a true queen. You and I are alike in this game," he hissed at her. "Think of it. I am the god, and you are the goddess. You dictate outcomes all the time. Especially when you took Kate's cylinder without proper procedure."

Her heart pounded. Did he know? Even worse … were they alike?

"You see, it's true. It's *you* who are the unruly dictator." He pushed her against the wall. "*You* hid Kate's body with the help of sympathizers. It's *your* voice that calls for a halt to the resurrection trials, because *you* decided there's some mystery affect happening to the candidates and *you* need to run more research. It's all about what *you* decide."

The sting of his words seared her conscience. His idea about what happened to Kate was false, of course, but was the rest of his claim true?

Cole snickered. "You see it too. Right? Your need for perfection rules over the cries of the entire world. Populations are dying in droves from sickness and disaster. Despite all this, you would control." He grabbed her hand. "Come. You are so tiresome. Try to keep up." He yanked her along with lightning speed, his grip unrelenting as he moved.

Her mind filled with dread at the parallel he drew. Each step she matched with his pulled her down. It was as if she slogged through quicksand. Was it true? Was she more like Cole than she cared to admit? Her recent tampering to render the drug formulas ineffective could be considered the same. Unlike Cole's pretense with Rumi, she wanted to believe that her choice came from a purer instinct. Still, she secretly chose to change something that would affect everyone. Did this make her the same?

When a group of DCN workers passed through an intersecting hallway ahead of them, Cole checked his stride. "Yes. It's true." He whispered shaming affirmation in her ear. "It seems you might even be the best at playing this game of god. Which, of course, is exactly why we should work together. We are the same."

Overcome by his merciless accusations, she offered no further protest or resistance. Her heart simply broke in two.

"There now." His grip lightened. "Isn't it better when you cooperate with me? Father's resurrection will be a great success. It's not too late to claim the fame. After all, it's your work that will make history today."

Suddenly, something else broke through. She was not the same as Cole.

A tremendous desire to put distance between them came over her. The rhythm of the thought came with each stride.

I am not the same.

I am not the same.

Her pace quickened, which seemed to please Cole, and when they overtook a group of interns filling the passageway, he released her hand. In the timing of the opportunity, she moved away from him and entered her passcode to activate her wrist scanner. Perhaps security would find her.

When they cleared the congested area, Cole caught her hand again and spun her around. He yanked on her wrist strap. It broke loose, fell to the floor, and he stomped on it. "There." He picked it up and dangled it in front of her face. "It's quite useless now, my darling. Don't worry. Just accept it. Do what I ask, and your life will be safe." He tossed the device aside and resumed his bone-breaking grip on her arm.

She remained silent. Showing fear or resistance only increased his bullying.

"Ah … there it is. Your silence. Such familiar territory. But you see, I can't help you if you won't talk to me. You risked your capture to come here, so I know there's something important you're not telling me. Whatever it is, I'll find out. Good partners tell each other everything, and you are more than good to me. You are my perfect match."

CHAPTER 47

COLE STOPPED IN front of a familiar set of doors and silenced an alert on his wrist scanner.

Why were they at the morgue?

A frown came over his face. "It seems a regrettable choice has been made."

SJ's breath quickened.

He placed his palms on the sides of her face and tugged her to him. "Innocent or guilty, my queen?"

"I don't know what you're talking about." She pulled away and tried to remain calm as he passed his hand over the lock and the doors opened. Prodding her along past a row of mortuary cabinets and gleaming cadaver tables, he directed her into an adjoining room where a covered form lay resting on a table under a single dome light. Black-tipped silver-gray hair jutted out on the pillow.

It was Rumi.

Four shadow figures stood around the table, but when Cole arrived, the figures moved back and bowed in his direction.

SJ struggled to free herself, but Cole's grip tightened, and heat shot into her arm.

"Look at me." His face displayed a dim radiance that grew more intense, as did the heat coming into her hand.

"Ow. You're hurting me. Let go, you beast."

He released her. "See how I've kept you safe? Except for my will, your life has no consequence to me. Now, it's time you accept me for who I am." His head melded into a chilling fluctuation of features alternating between the head of Cole and the head of a lion. "Ask me. Who am I?"

Her heart trembled, but she refused to play along.

"I am Fol. Ruler of this world and things you know nothing about." He snarled at her and then roared, "Abaddon!"

A figure stepped forward and gave a tribute bow. "My liege." The stocky brute of a man resembled a cross between a country farmer and a thug. Cascading rivulets of black, unkempt hair partially hid his snarling features, and too-tight clothing restrained his bulging chest and arms.

"Snake." Cole simpered at a willowy, dark-skinned man dressed in black and white athletic wear, who acknowledged him with a slight head duck and then slipped off into a corner. The thin man's form shifted back and forth between a man and an upright coiling and uncoiling serpent.

Two others approached, and they seemed familiar.

The first, a young blond executive wearing a designer suit, transformed into the decrepit smelly old doctor that Cole had addressed as "Dr. Morbeed" when she recuperated in SHEOL after her drugging.

The fourth figure she knew best. Reflecting a greater brilliance than Cole's glow, the tall form with hooded features fluctuated between light and dark. *Lucas.*

Weakness settled over her. The sight of the figures shifting in an ebb and flow of details unlike any life she'd ever seen, combined with Cole's threats, overwhelmed her mind. *Find it. Something greater.* The call of goodness boomed loud in her ear. No one else seemed to notice. She scanned the room but saw no advantage.

Rumi!

Rumi? She was dying. SJ couldn't save her.

She is worthy of life.

Yes. That part made sense. Someday, somehow, despite setbacks and Cole's disdain, Rumi deserved a chance at life again, just like everyone else. But without an injector of Rejuvacatin, the option did not exist.

She stepped close to the makeshift bed. Bruising from the advanced disease made Rumi's gaunt face hardly recognizable. "I'm so sorry, Rumi. I wish …" Words seemed senseless.

Rumi raised a finger to her lips. "Shhh. It's for the best. No, I'm not beautiful anymore. Old things must die, but you will make me new again. Right?"

"Is that what you want?"

"Yes. I do. Father spoke to me in a dream. Can you believe it? He—Beast will live again. He will be a great and good leader and help many people. It's so wonderful. You will see it happen. Cole says his tests will all be normal." Rumi turned her head to Cole, who stood nearby with feet apart and arms crossed.

Rumi appeared unaware of anything but her moment of death. She stroked the blanket and spoke like a child who recounted a glorious promise. "When I'm resurrected, I'll be in charge of beauty. All things must be beautiful. I've worked for this all my life, and my work isn't finished. I must return and oversee the transformation. Father, Cole, you, and I will be family." Her eyes gleamed fiercely, and she grabbed SJ's hand. "Together, we'll lead the world to a better life."

Guilt washed over SJ. She had to speak the truth. "Rumi, there's so much we can't control … in so many things, including resurrection. I'm not sure …" She remembered her training concerning end messages and stopped speaking.

Dying people clung to beliefs to help them through such a time. True or false, they clung to what they believed they knew. When present in someone's last moments, she'd vowed to only ask questions to help them see their choice. "What do you want to happen, Rumi?"

"I want to live again. Here. On Meritus. I want a dose of Rejuvacatin. I don't trust Cole to give it to me." She gave a slight smile to her lion-faced sibling and then gripped SJ's hand, using it to pull herself up in the bed. "I know I can trust you. You'll give it to me. Yes?"

The truth screamed to be heard, but SJ could not reveal the lost hope for resurrection. She merely nodded and watched as Rumi sank back onto the bed.

Panting for breath, Rumi wheezed, "You must say it."

"I promise." SJ knew Cole had heard the exchange. The weight of her deceit and choices crushed in on her.

Then Rumi waved a feeble hand in the air as if conducting a tune. "Sing to me, brother."

"What?" Cole's voice sounded small.

Closing her eyes, Rumi whispered, "There must be music. A song. A beautiful melody to lead me away."

Cole turned to his cronies. Morbid shrugged. Snake, Abaddon, and Lucas shook their heads.

"Rumi, dear one. If I had known, I could have ordered a …" Cole's voice trailed off.

Rumi opened her eyes. "I must have music. I must have it." Her voice held a tremor.

Cole bowed his head. "It's impossible. You know I'm banned. Only a voice or a roar. Never a song. I'm so sorry Rumi. Mortar—"

Rumi put a hand to her lips as if to shush him. "Never mind, then." She pointed to SJ. "She will sing. Beauty for healing … sing … sing for me, SJ."

A spell seemed cast upon the room. SJ sat and patted the child-sized hand. She hummed a little stretch of a forbidden hymn tune she'd learned with Kate in their school days. Words she'd not thought of in years came to mind. Full phrases of redeeming grace flowed from her mouth.

As she sang, the heralds became restless. They writhed and turned about, and then, one by one, disappeared from sight. Only Cole remained, and his eyes glowed with something she could not comprehend.

She turned her focus back to Rumi who had become still. She checked Rumi's pulse and listened to her chest. No breath sounds. "She's gone."

She stood and spoke in firm tones. "Give me the Rejuvacatin. Where is it?"

Cole gave her a sly grin and dropped an injector into her hand. "The two of you make quite a picture of beauty. Your presence and her spirit. The perfect blend of life."

She held the injector up and saw that it was empty. "Really, Cole? Nothing to give her? You heard her request." She slapped the injector back into his hand.

He grabbed her. She twisted out of his hold, but he caught her again and stabbed something into her neck and kept his hand there. "It's all in you now," he whispered into her ear. Then he let her go, and she sank to the ground struggling for breath.

He circled the room speaking nonsense. "Rumi's spirit and cooperation and your body and position will help me go far to build our kingdom. When you resurrect, you will be the perfect partner."

He completed one circle as she struggled to stand. Her attempt turned into a sideways slump, and she tumbled over completely when he pushed her.

Flat on her back, her limbs of stone no longer obeyed her. She spoke with great effort. "Reju … va … c ... atin is not deadly."

"No, it's not, but the drug in your neck is Propofylozine. I've doubled what I gave you before. This time, there'll be no recovery." He shoved an empty vial in her face and pointed to the label. "In minutes you'll be dead." His mouth twitched, and he leaned over her, his dark eyes close to her own. "Don't worry. After you die, I'll give you Rejuvacatin.

"See? I have it right here." He waved an injector at her. "This one is yours, and it's full. Isn't that wonderful? Of course, as my partner, you will be given top priority for resurrection. But until then, your shell will be safe here with me."

He disappeared for a few seconds and then returned and pushed a pillow under her head. "Be comfortable, my dear. Paralysis comes first to the limbs, as you know." He leaned in close. "It was, of course, to be Rumi's spirit in Kate's body at first, but you changed all that."

The room turned in a slow circle as if it was a giant merry-go-round. Cole's head and then a lion's head kept disappearing and reappearing in a dizzying array.

She closed her eyes, blocking out the spinning.

"It was your choice. If you had not been so stubborn and hard to influence, you would still be alive." The voice growled in her ear. "Rumi showed me the opportunity to control you by your loyalty to Kate, but your continual obsession to uncover truth, and your curiosity over the messages, brought that tactic to an end."

She willed her eyes open.

A lion's head with Cole's eyes floated above her. "My men found Kate's body. When her microtherm cylinder arrived at SHEOL, we put a tracker on it. Because of your foolish actions, I had to come up with a new plan. But I'm convinced it's more brilliant than the first. Wouldn't you agree? In truth?"

She fought the only way she could. With words. "It's unproven. You believe you can force souls to enter bodies at your bidding? Mortar will not allow …"

The lion cut her off with a roar. "I am prince of this world."

Inky cold blackness swept over her. Her stone limbs became less heavy. Knowing he would hear it, she willed herself to whisper the worst of truths.

It would be her last punch. “You are not a prince. You are a thief. You steal what is not yours and call it your own.”

A terrible snarl, the snapping of jaws, and a rush of wind filled the room. Then, a ball of light blistered the air, contracting and sputtering. Lucas. By his glow, SJ discovered she was rising. Below her, in a shadow world, a miniature lion was thrown backward against the wall like a rag doll, and the sparkling light and the lion fought.

A tiny oblong came soaring out of the fray. It crackled onto the floor. A foil packet of Rejuvacatin glinted beneath her.

“Help me,” she whispered. Instantly, her rising motion ceased, and her weightlessness turned back to stone. She tumbled to the ground and with great effort managed to locate the injector. Pulling out the now empty syringe from her neck she drew out the Rejuvacatin from the injector. There was no time to wait for the injector to dispense the drug over the next five minutes.

Gasping for air, she army-crawled toward Rumi. The lion sprung at her, but the light held him back. With her last ounce of strength, she injected the solution into Rumi’s wrist.

Instantly, thunder, louder than the lion’s roar, rocked the air, and a brilliance, much greater than that of Lucas or Cole, split the shadow world around her. As the greater light continued to fracture the darkness into bits, the morgue floor turned into a mirror. Sounds of rushing water came between rolls of thunder.

“Run!” The command echoed all around her.

She staggered to her feet and took off running across the mirror surface, away from the lion’s snarl. This must be an out-of-body experience. It made sense, except for the fact that she still controlled her limbs.

Sections of the floor broke off and floated away. Darkness filled in where the floor disappeared. Like ice floes from a glacier, the cracked mirror pieces continued to drift away until only a single span remained. It stretched out from under her feet into a bank of dense fog ahead of her. Mist boiled up on both sides below her, and her suspension bridge made of mirror swayed in the air currents. She reached and discovered rope siderails. Rushing water whooshed below her.

Plaguing thoughts of Cole creeping behind her and the unlikely durability of a glass catwalk filled her mind.

"Keep going."

When she reached the lowest part of the dipping bridge, she could not make out the end, only distant fog-shrouded darkness. This will all be over soon.

A vague scent filled her nose. Bergamot. Kate grew it in a pot and brewed it for tea.

The memory carried her onward. She focused on her steps, placing one foot in front of the other and then repeating the sequence.

After a while, glints of light bounced off the surface of the bridge.

She looked up and discovered her bridge connected to an archway on the side of a fog-shrouded mountain. Light poured through it toward her, and the glow radiated from inside the dark mountain.

Darkness or fog concealed everything else except the brilliance of the light coming through the arch and the glass under her feet. The intensity of the light burned her eyes.

She finished the journey, squinting and eyes half-shut. Just short of her goal, her legs gave way and became stone. Unable to see, she slipped and grappled for the rope railing alongside her. Something else met her grip. Hands.

Obscure forms with strong grips pulled her along and then released her. Squinting and gasping, she fell back onto something solid. Patting around she felt small, hard objects, perhaps stones, dirt, and occasional strand material, possibly grass.

Unable to rely on her vision, she listened for clues and heard voices.

"She's incredibly lucky."

"Or maybe not, depending how you look at it. She didn't come through the water, so she'll likely have to go back."

"But she's here, and not on Abyss. That means she's one of his."

She tried to speak but coughed violently instead. Hands patted her on the back until she managed to squawk a protest. "Enough. I'm okay, but where am I? Why can't I see?"

"You're on Five," a soft voice answered. "It's best to take it easy."

Hands slipped underneath her shoulders and helped her sit.

"Drink this. Soon you'll be able to see again."

A water-like substance, which tasted like many kinds of fruit, filled her mouth. Even as the drink soothed, the words she heard brought shock. *If I'm on Five, then I must be dead.*

She patted the surface she rested on. She didn't feel dead. Although her vision seemed to be in some sort of demise. Things became almost distinct for a short time but then reverted to hazy shapes in motion.

In front of her, although fuzzy in focus, there appeared to be a path that curved upward until it disappeared into a dark patch—perhaps trees. Blobs of white moved on either side of the path and bleated like sheep.

She squinted at her rescuers to gather details, but their faces and forms were impossible to decipher because a prismatic glow around them kept shifting and flowing. "Who are you? How did I get here?"

One of the forms came close and seemed to squat beside her. "We're heralds. The shepherd kind. You arrived on a bridge. As soon as you're strong enough, we'll take you to him to find out more."

"Who's him?"

"Author Perfector."

The sound of barking came from nearby.

She followed the barking sound to a dark four-legged oblong which moved beside an indistinct purple figure. With a great amount of squinting and blinking, she made out details of a woman, her hair wrapped on top of her head like a crown. The white blob in her arms appeared to be a sheep.

Several figures came up to the purple-gowned woman and launched into indistinct conversation with her. Then they all moved toward SJ.

"Can you stand?" The question came from the purple-gowned woman.

"I'm not sure."

Arms hoisted her upright. Her legs felt solid again. "Maybe."

"Then you must run." A hand grabbed and tugged.

"But I can't see well enough. I'll fall."

"We will guide you. Come on."

What was it with all the running? She allowed herself to be pulled along. Her gait improved as she moved. Things could be worse. At least she was alive.

CHAPTER 48

COLE PROPPED HIS herdsman disguise against a tree trunk, but before he could reenter the body, it toppled over and startled a squirrel. The animal scrambled to a nearby branch and began chattering.

"Silence, nutcracker. Only an imbecile scolds the hand that will someday rule above all others."

The squirrel hushed.

"That's better. If you speak again, you will tell only of my great success. Cloaked in a dead man's body, I've walked the forbidden ground of Five and fooled Evie. Now I'll walk again and steal back SJ."

When the squirrel ventured down the branch, Cole lunged and caught the writhing creature and flung it into the orchard grove. Light glimmered on the far side of a tree stand. The guardian arch herald still lurked. How much longer?

He shifted his position to be upwind from the body. The stench of it sickened him. But it was better than the stench of lion scat, although the effect of his lion persona did wonders in terrifying SJ.

Using the herdsman's body to tread the forbidden land held a certain irony. Not unlike the shepherds of long ago, messengers of the biggest news to ever make history, his poor sot of a shepherd, even in his death, would convey even bigger news—the fact that Mortar lied. Five was not exclusive to Mortar's children. Heralds like him, loyal to Beast, could also roam the land with a little clever ingenuity. His foray in the shepherd's hide proved it.

Enticing the convert to end his life had been easy. The shepherd had developed a habit of believing anything Cole whispered. One final shaming whisper was all it took. The ill-speak brought the man to tears just before he slipped on the noose. It served no purpose to delay the shepherd's life with pain since the man had so pleasingly worshiped him.

He had taken the man's body without concern for where his soul might go. But the gamble paid off. The man ended his life with no change in his choice of loyalty. Mortar would not have him. That was all that mattered.

Cole no longer fretted over deciphering where a soul's destiny lay. The unsolvable mystery wasted precious time, because only Mortar knew which eternal home became the lodging for each soul. Until a man breathed his last breath, he could choose Mortar. A dying thief on a cross revealed this abominable outcome.

What a tragedy. He sighed. One of his best projects turned bad. Breathing his last breaths, the guilty man chose to switch camps and believe. Impossibly unfair, but true. The cross thief served as the poster child for last-minute decisions. Years of work turned to dust.

But a new day had come. He would turn the tables on Mortar. SJ's crossing on the bridge confirmed his suspicions. It seemed there was more than one way to enter Five. Although SJ must have chosen, because only purified souls could enter Five, her route wasn't through the Port of Souls by boat from the water, so maybe she wasn't here to stay.

All of it was a mystery he intended to unravel. By Mortar's decree, he couldn't hurt her while she was on Five, but maybe he still had the power to influence her decision.

It was time.

Rays of prismatic light still ricocheted in the orchard, a sign that his opponent still lurked.

No matter. As always, he still had the air, a space Mortar ruled held no harm for him. It was true for Meritus, and now it proved true for Five, a fact he'd confirmed in his previous explorations. Moreover, to his delight, since the atmosphere of Five was not forbidden, then Five must not be the final destination, as was the Abyss, but rather a fortress for what was to come.

Ripples of joy passed through his being. It was all so thrilling. He'd found holes in Mortar's paradise fortress, and he intended to root out every one of them.

He stowed the body in the trees for later use and prepared himself for the air. When the transformation completed, he moved quickly to an open space and flapped each spectacular wing in alternate rhythm and then together with greater force. His body lifted from his leafy resting place. He soared upward. Might as well start by stirring up fear, using his dragon suit, his favorite disguise.

Even if his temptation of Evie as a herdsman had failed in the end, his curiosity remained piqued over the fear and shame she exhibited. Her reaction bolstered his theory that souls on Five no longer remained impenetrable to him. There was room for well-crafted lies and deceit, the same potent weapons Beast had used since the beginning of time on earth.

His sluggish flight became positively buoyant when he spied her. He chuckled and burped a gurgling snort at the sight of her tiny figure still running along the narrow road with the lamb. It seemed most likely she still feared him. There was a certain comedy to it. He'd been so busy with Rumi and SJ that he'd not moved an inch to follow Evie, but she showed great determination to get away. It appeared that even on Five, his father's axiom, "a human will run far on fear and shame," remained undeniable.

How could he maximize such weakness to his advantage? With Beast's resurrection, he would soon be just a prince again. Being a prince had its merits, but he'd tasted the feast of being king, and his mouth soured over the lesser role.

He rolled his great head from side to side, alternating the motion with each wing flap. The practice helped him think.

Seconds later, the ingenious answer came. He'd steal more from Five. Why stop with SJ and Evie? His ambition would greatly please his father. Surely then, his pleas to receive new authority to rule over more than a dismal shipping company would be heard.

There was only one thing worth stealing on Five. Souls. An endless supply of them, and they all belonged to Mortar.

Cole swooped down to get close to Evie. She would expect him on foot and would not suspect his presence in the air, let alone a dragon suit.

His plan gleamed brighter than the morning star.

Who would be his first steal?

Evie or SJ?

Such a difficult choice. Evie was the most exquisite combination of fear and faith to die by his influence. Retraining her soul to serve him would be a true feat of great manipulation.

But SJ had barely chosen. Turning her choice back to him would be diabolical.

Flying high into the air, he spied Evie's destination on the slope in front of him. Namesake Field, a place well guarded by Mortar's heralds.

Circling back, he flew over the narrow road where Evie ran.

Her persistence amazed him. Those who fell easily to his temptations were weak, but the ones who endured were special.

Beast called them "runners."

He licked his lips over another chance at fearmongering. Like a moth attracted to light, Evie had shown vulnerability to it. If he spun the lie just right, then she'd believe herself to be trapped in a net woven from her own forgiven mistakes. She'd believe she still stood accused. Fear and shame woven together in seamless perfection proved his best and most irresistible deception. If she fell for it, then her resistance to him would end, and she'd be drawn back to his domain.

Grinning with anticipation, he licked his lips and tasted his certain victory. Turning the will of Mortar's creation to mesh with his will offered the most sublime reward he knew.

Power and pride surged, inflating his dragon disguise. He became invisible and swooped low, whispering insults in Evie's ear. "You will lose. I'm stronger, faster, better, and smarter than you. Because of your mistakes, I get everything. You are worthless."

Evie only ran faster.

Shifting tactics, he chose fear and command to regain her allegiance. Steal, even as he was stolen from. Gnashing his dragon teeth, he soared high into the sky for greater effect. From there he roared, "Run to me!"

When his blood thirsty cry emptied, he searched the ground for his target and found she no longer traveled the narrow road. She'd moved onto a path that led to the beach.

His success thrilled him. Landing on a cliff protruding over the path just ahead of her, he dug his talons into the rock. Soon, she would see him and be terrified.

Evie came into view carrying the lamb.

But there were other figures now, moving along a short distance behind her.

Curious, he flew into the air for a clearer vantage point. What he saw confused him.

SJ was there. Aided by heralds, she stumbled along. Whole companies of souls, flanked by heralds, joined her from several side paths.

"To the beach! To the beach! There's safety on the boundary of the beach." Herald voices rang out above him.

He writhed at the sound and darted upward, on guard for the warriors who gave the warning. They were in his territory. The kingdom of the air belonged to him.

What was happening?

Light forms filled the sky and then headed toward him. Below him, souls gathered on the dais above the beach.

Could it be? Was Mortar calling for the final battle?

He roared again, but this time, he issued the rally cry of a general calling to his legion. He thirsted for the salty, sweet flavor of the runners' blood—his prize and retaliation for being pushed out of heaven's perfection. He'd fight to take every soul with him at the beach—the one place Mortar agreed he could stand.

He roared a third time. Although the sound came out the same, the cause differed. Joy filled every crevice of his dragon suit. Because of Mortar's foolish challenge, the runners unknowingly ran to their eternal destruction.

CHAPTER 49

SJ LISTENED FOR cues from those around her as she navigated the path.

"There's a little curve ahead."

"Slopes down a bit here."

"Rock debris on the path. Better take it slow."

Soon the route became wider or at least smoother or perhaps she'd adjusted to her kaleidoscope vision. Either way, she bumped and stumbled less often. Still, her pace did not equate with any definition of speed and the orders had been to run to the beach.

"I hate that I'm slowing everyone down." She broadcast the apology aloud to anyone who would hear.

"It's just you and me, now." The answer came from the woman in purple, who had stayed by her side and matched her stride but seldom spoke except to soothe the lamb in her arms.

"Where did the rest go?"

"The faster ones and those who know the way have moved on ahead."

"Does that mean you are new too?

The woman laughed. "An interesting guess but a wrong one. I've been on Five one hundred sixty-two years, but for most of them, I've been asleep.

It's just the last three years that I've been awake. I suppose in view of eternal time, you could call me a newcomer."

"How did it happen?"

"What do you mean?"

"The sleeping part."

"I don't know. I was asleep." The woman giggled, and the lamb in her arms bleated an echo. "I'm Evie, by the way. And this little one was supposed to be headed to her new home in Namesake Field."

SJ stumbled. "Evie?" A hand steadied her body but had no effect on her heart, which beat in a tipsy motion above her jelly legs. "I know you."

"I doubt it. I'm certain we've never met."

"Yes. I mean no. But you sent messages to me."

"Oh, my goodness." A face with fuzzy features crowned by brunette braids moved close. "SJ? I can't believe it." Evie hugged her, lamb and all, with strength too great to be a three-times-great-grandmother.

Approaching footsteps and urgent voices interrupted their reunion. "You two better hurry or you'll miss the lesson."

"It's best to go," Evie said in her ear. "A lesson is an opportunity that we seldom refuse."

"A lesson? What's the topic? Running?" SJ's wit shifted into a wheeze, and her legs locked as if made of stone.

Evie laughed. "We'll know soon enough. Everything on Five is for our good. Nothing here can harm us."

"Why does that sound as if something bad is about to happen?" *Why can't I feel my legs?*

Evie patted her shoulder. "We need to move out of the way." She pulled her aside. Fast footsteps and jabbering voices swirled past them. "Runners." She squeezed her hand. "You'll soon change that habit."

"What do you mean? Getting in people's way?"

"No. Feeling as if something bad is going to happen. It's an old habit. On Five, we get to exchange old things for something new. Whatever we might see or feel, it can't harm us here. Author Perfector's rules." Evie guided SJ to sit on a nearby rock. "Let's rest a bit. It's only your first day here. It takes a while to recover from the boat trip."

"I didn't come by boat. I came on a bridge. It appeared in the room where Rumi died. Cole was chasing me—"

Evie jumped up. "Cole? Are you together?"

"No. Well, I mean … we were together as partners, but I'm not actually with him. He tried to kill me."

"It seems he succeeded, because you are here."

SJ swallowed hard and bit her lip. "Well, maybe he did. I'm sorry I ever met him. He manipulates things and lies. We're so different, but I needed his help." She paused her jumbled explanation wondering how it sounded to Evie, since she'd sent the warning about Cole to her in the first place.

"Never mind. Tell me later. We have company again. This time, heralds."

The ground trembled under SJ's feet, and a voice boomed out. "Soul Evie, we are here to carry your companion to the beach."

Carry? "No. Really. It's not necessary. I prefer to travel on my own two feet. And I don't even need to go. I can wait somewhere until it's over."

"It will be okay. I promise. And you'll be glad you went." Evie's quiet voice comforted. "The ruby sand is unlike anything you've ever seen."

SJ strained to see the heralds. Two indistinct figures as stout as trees stood a couple of yards to her right. Their shepherd-like robes barely covered their knees, and they had black chunks for feet. "What's with their feet," she whispered.

"Battle boots."

"Okay. No one mentioned a battle. I would have brought my sword." She joked to ease her racing heart.

"There's always a battle. But not always one you can see." The bellowed response came from the larger of the two heralds.

Heat flooded her cheeks. She'd forgotten about heralds' astute hearing abilities. Barely audible, she muttered to Evie. "Now I've annoyed them."

Evie giggled softly. "Don't fret over it. They always talk in riddles."

Despite the advice, the cryptic answer swirled in SJ's head as she waited for the shepherd warriors to rig her ride—a makeshift hammock fashioned out of their crooks and cloaks.

Evie took SJ's hand and placed it on the awakened lamb. "You'll be fine."

Comfort came as she patted its curly coat.

"This lamb is yours. Your namesake lamb. When a person chooses, a lamb is selected and given their name."

"I hope that's not true for this little one." The disgrace of her father's label seemed clouded and long ago, but SJ would not wish it on the innocent creature.

"Oh, but it is. She has the name Author Perfector gave you."

"You named her SJ?"

"Yes. S for Selah, and J for Joy. It's such a beautiful name, but of course, you already knew that."

SJ's heart leapt in her chest. She savored the news, and her eyes watered. So many questions came to mind. But the herald's eagerness to be on the move stole the opportunity. She'd ask for more details later.

Once she settled into her hammock carrier, she waved at Evie.

Evie offered a promise. "We'll meet up at the beach."

As she traveled, SJ blinked and squinted to make sense of the terrain ahead, but the light in her eyes made things worse. When she shifted in her sling to look behind her, a much clearer view unfolded. The path disappeared into a valley but then continued again, climbing the hill where the dog had barked. The crest of the hill, which she'd not been able to see when she first arrived, now appeared to be made from the light of dawn that flooded the sky.

A more beautiful sight did not exist.

CHAPTER 50

TRAVELING AT THE speed of heralds had its advantages. From her awkward position—mostly reclined in her cloak stretcher—SJ could hear the cheerful discussions of the souls they overtook. No one seemed anxious about the coming lesson on the beach.

Her porters were not nearly as chatty. Their limited conversation gave her the confidence to know that Five was not a world devised from her imagination. If she'd invented such a beautiful place, only the most sociable beings would be tour guides.

She resigned herself to her isolated perch and focused on what she could observe—the sky for instance. Pink-orange rays stretched across the whole clear expanse of it, except for one darker cloud which seemed to be traveling at high speed in their direction despite the absence of wind. The shape of the singular cloud resembled a bird-like lizard with a long neck.

Then something odd happened. The cloud dropped low and disappeared behind a hill. With her unreliable vision, she hesitated to announce her observation until she determined that her eyes weren't playing tricks on her.

When the cumulous apparition reappeared, it seemed more like a creature of flesh and blood—a flying lizard, or perhaps a fairy-tale style dragon than a product of the atmosphere. She'd test her theory. "There's a dragon above us."

Her porters just kept plodding along.

"Is that normal? Do flying lizards live here?"

"Soul Selah, you brought the dragon with you. But don't worry. He can't harm you."

"What?" She pulled the folds of cloth close around her. Her heart thudded. Cole was here? She'd seen him transform into a lion. How many forms could he take?

"The dragon can't set foot anywhere except on the boundary. The scribes are ready for him."

The herald's answer offered her little comfort. "Are you talking about scribes like the writing kind? If the dragon is who I think it is, then you're insane. Cole's not a shepherd like you. He's quite powerful." Warning them was the kindest thing she could do. Perhaps they were still studying and had not actually graduated from herald school, if there was such a thing.

"Really?" The herald on her right side chuckled.

Obviously ignorant, her two lackeys needed more information. "Where I'm from, Cole leads and rules over many things. He steals and twists truth and manipulates and terrorizes. He kills, too. He killed me. That's why I'm here." As she talked, she pulled the cloth back a little and scanned the sky but saw no sign of the dragon.

"Soul Selah, You're not here because of the dragon. You're here because of a choice you made."

"Wrong." The junior heralds needed to understand her predicament. She shifted upright on the litter and leaned her head out. "Here's the thing. If Cole hadn't killed me, then I wouldn't be here. He retaliated against me, because I stopped cooperating with his plans. It's hard to refuse him. So many people look to him to supply what they need. He has solutions for everything."

"Does he now?" The herald snorted. "You seem to know a lot about him. Is that your belief? Do you believe the dragon has an answer to everything?"

"First of all, in my world, he's not a dragon. And second of all, it doesn't matter what I believe. It's what everyone else believes. I'm here because I failed to stop him."

"No, Soul Selah, it does matter what you believe. The dragon is the one who failed. You're here because of the truth. He tells lies in hopes that you will choose him. He offers the deception that your life will be better with just the right answer, solution, supply, situation, or success—"

The voice cut off and motion ceased. She felt her body being lowered to the ground. With a bump, the sling dropped in a heap around her, and she looked up into the face of her towering carrier.

The massive head drew close. "You listened for the truth." Emerald eyes with flecks of gold reflected the light. "The world is not a *thing*-world. The world is a *who*-world. Cole knows this, but he steals from the truth. He tries to set himself up as the *who* by becoming the supplier for the desires he feeds." The herald shook his enormous head. "It's so very twisted, but you figured it out." Then he scooped her up, cloaks and all, and leapt up and landed on top of something.

She squealed at the sudden move.

"*Shh*h. It's okay. Look. The sea."

She peeked through his arms. They had landed on what seemed to be a giant rock plateau. Below her, a blanket of turquoise stretched out to the sky and turned to dark navy at the horizon. Mid-distance between the navy and the turquoise, an endless, unbroken wave rolled and boiled, building in height as if held back by an invisible hand. Other smaller waves spiraled in, erupting into foam on the ruby sand. It seemed certain that the entire beach would be swallowed whole if the unbroken wave wall crashed ashore.

Then the herald placed her on the ground, but her legs folded under her. She grabbed his cloak for support and pulled herself up. A stout wind swirled around her, and she hung on tight.

A steady stream of people arrived and flooded onto the plateau.

"Other truth finders." The herald's voice came from high above her.

All types gathered. Young and old, multiple races and profiles, they stood in apparent collective watch over the water. What were they waiting for?

From somewhere nearby, a familiar voice shouted her name. "SJ? SJ?"

The voice shot adrenaline into her heart. It couldn't be. Could it? "Kate? Is that you?" SJ strained to confirm the fuzzy form and features.

It was Kate. SJ let go of the herald and fell into the arms of a very undead Kate, laughing and crying at the same time. Unable to speak from the emotion welling inside, she allowed Kate to reintroduce her to Evie, who beamed at her knowingly. Then Evie introduced Martha, the woman beside her who now cradled SJ's namesake lamb.

A fourth woman approached. She reached to stroke the lamb, and a gust of wind swept back her golden orange hair, revealing a tattoo. SJ's eyes watered as she blinked and squinted to make out the image.

Evie whispered in her ear. "She's new. Her name is Natalie."

Giddy breathlessness stole every word from SJ's mouth. Slack-jawed, she stared in wonder at the happy group.

Then droves of people pointed to something in the sky, and all the chatter died down.

In her indistinct view, it looked as if a fuzzy V formation of dark things zigzagged toward the plateau.

Soon, two thirds of the sky became darkened by a swarm of black, winged creatures. At the point of the V, a red dragon hurtled down, haloed by radiating light.

People shouted, "What is it?"

Heralds answered. "Demon formation coming for territory. The dragon leads."

Within seconds, the black swirling cloud of screeching, hissing demons hovered several hundred feet directly above the plateau. The dragon veered off, and the demons took turns heckling and swooping past a massive herald who stood on the dais pinnacle and held out a golden sword.

"They stink!" People gagged and held their noses as a putrid, rotting smell filled the air.

The horrible cries of the demons' unintelligible chatter took shape and became a scorning chant, "Who will fight? Who will fight?"

The stoic herald holding a sword did not waiver.

"That's Michael," Kate whispered in SJ's ear. "He's the top herald and leader of the arch heralds. His presence means something huge is about to happen. This will be good."

Michael? Frank Michael? It did not look like him. Doubt sickened her stomach. "How can you say good? There're so many of them. No one seems ready to fight."

"It's not a typical lesson. It'll probably be the best we've ever seen."

"Have you gone crazy?" Normally sensitive to fearful possibilities, Kate seemed different, even buoyant, and her cheerful optimism bewildered SJ.

"Not crazy. Trained. Lessons on Five sometimes start off looking really bad. I've never seen demons come, so that's another reason something great is about to happen."

Perhaps the air on Five contained mood-altering ingredients.

"Dear Kate is right. Something great is about to happen." A hideously familiar voice growled nearby. "Your true leader is here to take control."

Cole?

The herald who had carried SJ pushed past her, pulled a knife, and assumed a fighting stance.

Leaning on Kate, SJ hunted for Cole but found only a shepherd, whose face remained hidden underneath a hood.

Could it be? Her mouth dried and her heart raced.

The hooded shepherd nodded his head ever so slightly, and instantly, a demon circle formed and spiraled above him.

"You're forbidden to touch the hallowed ground of Five." The warning came from SJ's porter herald, who pressed the tip of his knife against the hooded shepherd's neck while her other carrier herald grabbed him by the shoulders.

The hooded shepherd offered no resistance, but other shepherds in the crowd seemed to notice the skirmish and stepped forward.

"Herald? He's a shepherd. One of us." A tall red-headed man offered assurance.

The herald holding the knife slid back the hood of the mystery shepherd. The revealed face twitched and shimmered with alternating features. The transformations included one intimately familiar face. Cole.

"It's him." Evie's words tightened SJ's bonds of fear.

"Yes. It's me." Cole stepped sideways and gave a twisted grin. Then he threw back his head and laughed and hopped about in his shepherd form, revealing crusty, decaying feet. "These aren't my feet, of course. They belong to the poor Jerusalem shepherd who I took across the sea in my new boat, along with my most loyal troops. We've been planning for this day, and thanks to you, my dear …" Cole bowed in SJ's direction.

People near her gasped, and SJ felt the burn of a hundred stares.

He reached out a decaying hand. "You look well, my love."

SJ reeled.

Evie grabbed her. "He can't hurt you," she whispered.

"Maybe I can. Crossing the sea to Five is hard on a body or should I say soul. When you first arrive, you're not usually able to stand." His red eyes sparkled at her, and he seemed to be evaluating.

"I didn't come by the sea. The truth is—I came by the bridge." She blurted out the detail defiantly in an effort to cover her weakness.

Cole hissed. "Behold! The truth!" He whirled around in a circle, sending bits of rotting flesh spewing into the crowd.

Souls backed away leaving SJ, Cole, Evie, Kate, and a few shepherds and heralds standing in a cleared area on the dais.

The porter herald who held the knife and stood closest to Cole seemed uneasy.

"Here's another truth. Her soul is not official. She still belongs in my kingdom." Cole sneered at her.

"She has chosen. You know that, dragon," a voice boomed, and a herald almost the size of Michael stepped into the widening gap around SJ.

Cole spit on the ground. "She was so easy to deceive. Really not a fitting challenge for me. The resurrections will continue in spite of her, and with an endless supply of souls too."

The contempt in his voice pierced SJ's heart. Her pride spilled out. Shame rushed in.

Cole waved at the crowd. "If you have ears to hear, then hear this. My kingdom will soon outnumber Mortar's by a great many. My victory day comes quickly, since so few creatures are obsessed with finding the truth. Truth no longer stands in my way." Then he bowed to SJ. "More truth, my dear."

"Be off this land, dragon. You play games but speak nothing that is true." The huge, challenging herald stepped closer to Cole.

"Fight him. Fight him," the demons above Cole swirled and chanted.

"If you have ears, then hear this. Author will do what He says." With a sudden lunge, the challenging herald drew a sword and thrust it into Cole the shepherd, and an explosive force slammed Cole's shepherd body to the ground.

The body burst into flames, and a great red dragon flew out screeching from the fire. The creature soared into the air, and the demons received their leader. The whole howling mess of them swept upward until they became a small black V.

Then, the light of the sky returned.

Kate whispered in SJ's ear. "The one who fought the dragon was Thomas. He's an arch herald, and he's in charge of scribes."

"What's so significant about the scribes?"

Before she got an answer, Thomas sheathed his sword, pulled out a trumpet, and blew a long, howling note. "Scribes. Take your positions on the beach. Quickly now. The demons will return to take territory, but their plans have long since been thwarted. Today is the day Author will reveal their foolishness. He does this so that you will remember what is true."

Kate hugged SJ. "It's time. I've got to go. Evie and I are scribes."

"No. Don't do it. You can't fight the demons. You won't win." SJ's heart seized with fear over the unreasonable plan.

"You're right." Evie pressed the lamb into Martha's arms. "We can't fight them. But we've already won. Once, we were killed by the forces of Cole for the truth we believed. On this beach we've experienced a power that nothing can overtake. I'm certain we'll witness that power again."

What was she talking about? And why was Kate a scribe? SJ's mind reeled with possibilities. Cole's company had delivered supplies the day Kate died. Her havoc thoughts threatened to spin out of control, but the weight of the moment called her back. Kate. Evie. She pleaded with the Something More, "Help them."

Her heart pounded as she watched Kate and Evie trail off the dais behind the other scribes.

The lamb bleated. Martha quieted it. Then she and Natalie pressed in on both sides of SJ.

SJ shifted back and forth in her stance, her legs trembling in her efforts to stand.

The two women locked arms under hers for support. "Do you need to sit down?" Natalie said.

SJ shook her head. "If I sit, then I can't see at all. I have to know what's happening."

She looked for Michael. He had not moved. He still stood on the pinnacle with his gold sword pointed out over the water. Why didn't he go to the beach? The scribes needed all the help they could get.

Thomas blew his trumpet a second time.

"Look," Natalie said. "The waves on the shore have stopped traveling forward. They're going the other direction."

SJ squinted. She could see it. The water flowed backward. All of it was being sucked into the tall, endless wave, which continued to build. The exposed, ever-widening expanse of sand gleamed blood red.

A line of heralds and scribes formed along the beach and stretched as far as SJ could see in either direction.

Out in the distance, a ship rose from the water, majestic but shadowy in form.

"It must be the host ship for the demons," Martha said. "I've heard talk of it. Demons are most suited to waterless places. The distance across the sea is too long for them to fly, and if they touch water, then they become weaker."

"Why didn't they come on the bridge like I did?"

"Bridges exist only for someone who has chosen, and then, only if Author wills it. Everyone else comes through the water. Those who come by bridge must decide if they want to stay."

"I wouldn't want to go back. All that's here on Five is so wonderful." Natalie's soft voice offered comfort.

"Wonderful? What about those?" SJ pointed to the black V re-forming in the sky.

"You will understand. They can't win. The battle has already been won."

Martha and Natalie's assurance and calm tones pushed against SJ's fear. She wanted with all her heart to believe in the already proclaimed victory, but evidence seemed otherwise.

As the swarming cloud of demons returned to blacken the sky, SJ realized her sight had grown crystal clear. *Just when I'd rather not see.*

The dragon swooped down toward the ruby shore with his troops. Behind the great wave, the ship looked more like a beast with seven extended necks, each capped by a turret. More black-winged creatures streamed out of the turrets of the behemoth vessel, racing in straight line formation to the shore.

"Steady, souls. He who is with you is greater than these." Thomas's voice reverberated with confidence.

Black winged demons landed on the beach, and the swarm grew, blocking SJ's view of the battle. Agonized shrieks punctuated the air.

Pain pierced her heart, and she closed her eyes. "I can't watch it. Tell me what's happening."

"You must look for yourself." Martha squeezed her hand. "Look."

SJ opened her eyes. What she saw reversed every anticipated idea she had about the battle. The cries of pain came from the demons who kept hopping and sidestepping to avoid strange crisscrossing lines that rippled through the sand. The entire shoreline undulated as if alive. The lines flowed together to form words that remained gouged into the sand. It seemed as if an invisible hand wrote across every sliver of beach she could see. Demons hurried to get out of the path of the streaming movement, and they tumbled about. If they touched any part of the lines, their flesh sizzled. Unable to find a safe place to stand, they were forced farther and farther back and closer and closer to the raging water.

Excited shouts of the scribes drifted up to the audience on the plateau. "It's the messages! The words we wrote have returned!"

Natalie and Martha inched SJ closer to the edge of the dais. When SJ looked directly down, she found Kate and Evie. Relief brought out a giggle. "How's the battle going?"

The women grinned and waved back at her.

"It's fierce, but we're managing." Kate pointed to a scripted word in the sand. "Look. It's a message."

"I know. Read it to me."

"It's Evie's. She should do the honors."

Evie read aloud the words of her first message. The letter. SJ joined in at the end and mouthed the words from memory. "The thief comes to steal, kill, and destroy. I come that you may have life to the full. Book of Wisdom 43. 10. 10."

Evie's voice blended with the sound of other scribes reading aloud their messages and many with words from the Book of Wisdom.

Thomas blew his horn again, and the reading stopped. The flailing demons implored the dragon to save them. The dragon spread out its wings as if to fly, and the demons grabbed ahold of it in mass, perhaps to get away from the searing sand.

Then, Michael lowered his sword, and the long unbroken wave on the sea roared toward the trapped demons and frantically flapping dragon. It broke over them and sucked them under. The black shapes bobbed about in the rolling water and then disappeared along with the dragon and host ship, which had become engulfed by a second massive wave.

When the destroying wave approached the beach, it reduced to a gentle swell and then rippled in across the sand, merely flooding the ankles of the scribes and heralds standing there.

The wave receded back over the etched lines of the words. It left behind a frothy foam pattern, which looked for a moment like bride's lace.

Thomas blew his horn a fourth time, and a voice boomed from the sky. "You shall overcome. By the blood of the Son and the word of your testimony, you shall overcome."

A gold ray of light shot from the pinnacle, and a booming voice rang out. "It is finished. Well done." Michael sheathed his sword.

All the scribes and heralds on the beach shouted and cheered. SJ joined in with the exuberant shouts of the witnessing souls and heralds on the plateau. Then they echoed back the same joyous words of the voice, "By the blood of the Son and the word of our testimony, the dragon is defeated!"

CHAPTER 51

CELEBRATIONS WERE IN order. But first sleep. The women agreed to meet the next morning in the Mariposa Tea Room.

SJ hugged Kate. "It's hard to let you go."

"Then don't." Kate's eyes sparkled. "Stay the night. Decide tomorrow. I promise you'll sleep the best you've ever slept."

"Where will I sleep?"

"With any of us. We all have a place, but I'm certain Herald Hall will be assigned to you. They'll want you under their watch since you just arrived."

SJ nodded. "Okay. None of this seems real. But my senses say otherwise. I feel the ground, but I can hardly lift my feet."

Natalie patted the lamb who had fallen asleep in Evie's arms. "Someone has the right idea."

They got in line behind clusters of others who walked along a path leading away from the beach. No running this time. The pace suited SJ. She let Kate pull her along as her eyelids threatened to close.

Their travel slowed to a crawl at an intersection where several trails took off in different directions. A herald with a gold sword at his side stood beside a boulder at the juncture, his back to them. People stopped to chat with him, and he patted several lesson participants on the shoulders as they passed, laughing at something they said.

Frank's laugh. Michael.

He stood three times taller than a man, and when he turned around, the wind billowed his cloak around him like a great white cloud. "I see you made it, Doc." His face radiated light, and he bent down and stuck out his massive hand.

SJ took it, and warmth poured into her. Not a jolt of heat, but the kind that comforts and soothes tired limbs. "I'm here," she said. "Very barely."

He patted her hand and then released it. "What's it going to be? Stay here or go back?"

"Always blunt and to the point. Even now," she said, tilting her head back to take in his stature.

The women stepped away from her and stood off to one side, open-mouthed and wide-eyed, except for Kate, who stayed close and whispered in her ear, "We don't talk to heralds that way. They are very powerful."

SJ looked at Frank Michael and began to laugh. Glee poured over her like a sudden summer shower. Then tears rolled down her face, sadness and gladness all blended together into one soggy mess.

The women clustered around and hugged her.

When she surfaced from their embrace, she explained the weight of it. "I have to choose. I don't know what to do."

"It's okay." Kate patted her shoulder. "You have time. We will sleep tonight, have our celebration breakfast in the morning, and then you can decide."

"No. She cannot wait." Michael's voice boomed above them, and all became silent. He sighed and looked upward and then bowed his head.

SJ lifted a heavy hand to her chest and felt a flicker. A lump expanded in her throat. "There's something I need to know first before I make my decision."

Michael bent down to eye level. "I will tell you whatever I can, but your time is running out. If you stay here much longer, then you can't go back even if you wanted to."

She grabbed hold of Kate. "I will meet you in the morning."

Kate wiped her eyes. "And what if you don't? What If you choose to go back?"

"I will send a message."

All the women hugged again. Then one by one, Natalie, Martha, Evie, and Kate departed, leaving SJ alone with Michael.

She'd fought the collapse for the sake of the others but now could no longer stand, and she slumped to the ground.

Michael scooped her up, carried her to a grassy slope, and laid her down. Her eyes fastened on his. They were as blue as the sky behind him. "I'm dying, aren't I?"

Michael nodded. "Your body is slipping away. If it does, then you will stay here. But you have been given a choice and can go back and be revived. If you do, then someday you will return here. But only Author Perfector knows when."

She focused on breathing. In and out. Over and over. Stay here or go? Stay here or go?

"What was your question?" Michael prodded.

What was her question? She strained to remember. A puffy cloud appeared in the sky. The shadow of it rolled over them. Shadow? Cole! She struggled to form the words. "Is he— is he—is Cole really gone?"

"He's gone from here."

"But there. Is he gone from there too?" She raised her head just a little.

Michael smoothed her hair with his big hand, and water splashed down on her.

Tears. Michael was crying. Cole was there.

"Then I have to go back," she said.

She looked up. "I have to spread the truth and stop a thief …" She took a breath, in and out, and then whispered, "because … he'll be there … spreading lies."

Michael's sad smile beamed down on her. He placed his hand over her heart.

A jolt of pain shot through her. "Ow!" she gasped.

"Author Perfector's gift to you. It will stay inside your heart and help you with the truth, but every time you use it, your heart will hurt."

"Look at me," Michael said. His face began to glow. As the brilliance grew, the pain subsided. She closed her eyes to the intensity of the light, but it penetrated through her eyelids into her brain, body, and soul and carried her away.

SJ squinted at the blur of shapes and shadows. "What's the holdup?"

"Transferred workers from SHEOL to the Abide. The influx of Kerioth medical staff continues. Tomorrow, we'll pick an alternate route. It will be safer for you, anyway." Her assistant, Molly, reached for the armrest control.

SJ brushed away her help. "There's no need. This way is fine." She touched the forward control, and her bot chair resumed its motion. The two of them crossed the intersection.

She gritted her teeth and frowned. The overabundance of caution exhausted her. Since her return, she'd become a spectacle. The official report from Global Safety determined she'd survived a second near-fatal drugging attack. The amount of propofylozine found in her system should have killed her but instead rendered her legs useless and her vision clouded.

Newscasters blamed anti-relocation sympathizers for the attack, but she knew the truth. When she came out of her coma and tried to explain things to the authorities, no one listened. Everyone believed she'd mixed things up in her mind because of the drugs. Her reputation as Cole's mentally unstable widow spilled into the news. The mention of insanity increased, especially when she talked about Five.

She wished she could see Cole's body and confirm his death. But even then, she knew physical evidence wouldn't be enough. Although authorities confirmed his DNA and his body awaited resurrection in a microtherm cylinder, she suspected his spirit lived on somewhere. He'd spun his webs of deceit throughout time.

Her body jerked when the bot chair bumped over something. They'd arrived at the covered pedestrian way between the Abide and the Alcove. The turbulence came from the poorly restored gaps in the floor caused by the first colossal quake that occurred in Sector Seven over fifty years ago.

Preparing for more harsh jostling, she gripped the chair handles. Relief came when her transport rolled easily over the patched fractures.

"Not bad, eh? The all-terrain tires navigate rough transitions seamlessly. Once you get the hang of it, the chair will give you endless freedom."

What freedom? Molly's happy tones mocked SJ's mental state, which had taken a nosedive. She'd lost her ability to move her body when she wanted or see with clear focus. Instead of normal life, her days consisted of endless therapy. Physical, visual, and recall sessions. Most annoying were the recall meetings. Medical staff insisted that the purpose of these was to re-establish consistent memory patterns in preparation for her release.

Release to do what? Working in research seemed unlikely. The council said she needed time, but she couldn't just sit around thinking about Five and Kate and Evie. She had no idea how to get back to them and sometimes doubted if any of her experience was real. Heralds told her it would happen. The upside down feelings about reality. Nothing made sense.

Leaving the corridor, they passed through the Alcove breezeway, where noisy wind chimes underscored the jangling in her soul. She'd lost everything she cared about. How could she have been so foolish as to let Cole into her life?

Molly followed her into the session room and announced brightly, "Here she is. She managed the route all by herself."

Her recall therapist appeared in fuzzy detail. "That's wonderful. I'm all ready for her."

The two women chattered about their normal lives. The effect stung against the open wounds of SJ's grieving heart. She pretended to be focused on the functions of the bot chair and selected *Sit* on the arm control.

After Molly left, the therapist's questioning began.

"Is there anything you'd like to tell me today?"

She struggled to form words that made sense. No amount of talk would change anything. She'd made so many decisions to champion the cause of truth. Now her actions seemed misguided, and doubt plagued her every thought. If Five was real, she wished she had stayed there.

Her physical troubles combined with her tangled memories made everything seem impossible. Perhaps the cosmic lesson about truth could be reduced to exactly what stood in front of her. Reality involved nothing more and nothing less than one's own perception. Truth had been present in her life all along.

"Let's start with who you are."

"That's easy." Bitterness swelled in her heart. "I'm a reject paraplegic scientist with zero eyesight."

"Is that true?"

A current of air touched her cheek. She turned her face to it and caught sight of hazy white stars dancing in front of a curtain of grassy green. She'd been told the shapes were exotic lilies her therapist kept in an office planter.

"I'll repeat the question. Is what you said about yourself really true?"

"It's my reality." She wished it wasn't. She'd achieved this disaster by herself. It seemed the glory of giving up everything for truth provided little reward. Her last desperate stance against Cole had taken her to Five. But now her world had shifted into something small and indiscernible, except for the unprovable words of others. Her former way of life, discovering and proving her findings, had been reduced to dependence on others. She was a scientist, taking notes, observing, and recording details so others could have better lives. It was what comforted her.

"But is it true? Are the words you use to describe yourself the truth about who you are?"

"You're wearing wine today." She gave the best answer she could give.

"Yes, I am. Is that important?" The therapist's voice always sounded the same, polite and indifferent, even as her questions were rude and probing.

"My observation. Every day, you wear a different color. I can't see details, but I can see overall colors." She explained this phenomenon in case another person affected by similar conditions came along. Her words would save the next person the trouble.

"Let's try this again, Dr. Satan."

"Satan is not my name."

"SJ … I know this is hard for you, but we believe if you can discuss your experiences, then your sight will return, and possibly your ability to walk. Your body systems were almost completely shut down from the drugging. You and your partner were the target of those who wished to sabotage the resurrection trials. Many grieve Cole's death, and the same have held great hope for your recovery. In fact, Beast himself is eager to speak with you right after our session. According to Cole's team, you both were en route to see him when the assault occurred."

Beast? Her actions had been too late to stop Beast's resurrection after all.

"SJ?"

"My name is Selah. Selah Joy, but you can call me SJ if you prefer. Here's the thing. I don't know what happened. I remember Cole turned into a lion and Rumi was dead, and I gave her a dose of Rejuvacatin …"

"Now see, that's progress. You remembered something new." The therapist sounded almost giddy. "You gave Rumi the medicine, which makes sense as she was dying, but authorities weren't certain who received the Rejuvacatin when they found the empty injector. They gave a dose to Rumi and Cole just to be sure, because they were dead, but you were still barely alive."

"Was I?" She considered again the timing of her visit to Five. Had it been a dream?

She heard a door open. Light in the room became brighter. The wine blob figure of her therapist stood, moved across the room, and then became enmeshed with two others, a tall willowy form and a large head and torso attached to something that glided, perhaps another bot chair.

"SJ. Beast is here. He's fragile, but his resurrection recovery has advanced remarkably. Doctors agreed to let him visit with you. We'll continue the session later."

She could hear the awe in the therapist's voice. Who wouldn't be amazed to stand in the presence of a man who had been resurrected? And not just any man. The man who uncovered the feasibility specifics for fusion energy to be created and harnessed for household use now graced the therapy room.

"We'll give you some privacy." The door clicked closed, and the headed torso glided close.

She couldn't see his face details, but Beast's head and shoulders rose tall above the back of the chair.

A gravelly voice spoke. "The scent is strong on you."

"What?" Her heart raced.

"Bergamot. The stench of Mortar's heralds. You've been there, and you want to go back."

"What are you talking about?" Blood pounded in her head. It was real.

"I often wondered who Cole would choose as his partner. He always wanted an Eve to his Adam and to be like Mortar, only better. You were the ticket to his latest ambition, duplicating life as Mortar created, with spirits and bodies. I'm fine with souls without bodies, but my son … he refused to build our kingdom as we had planned so very long ago, so I had him killed."

Beast's tone became conspiratorial. "Don't worry, it's only temporary. As you may have guessed, he's actually still alive—in spirit form. He won't reappear until the body shell he inhabited is resurrected. The team has not succeeded with any other resurrections since mine." He sighed. "Such incompetence. Of course, you'll work to achieve that for me now that my body is revived, because we're family." He gave a rumbling snicker. "Or because you want your job back, and I can make it happen."

"If …" She stopped before she spilled her secret about the altered drugs. Her actions had not stopped Beast's resurrection, but no additional revivals had occurred since then, and that was good news.

"If what?"

She strained to see his eyes. *Five. Mention Five.* "If Five is real, then resurrection doesn't matter."

"Of course it matters." Beast snarled. "It's a provision. Providing for what people want. That's all that matters. You keep looking for the truth, Satan." He fell into a fit of coughing. "Here's the truth …" Gurgling sounds and more coughing came.

She waited, wondering if he had power like Cole had.

He cleared his throat. "When every man can receive what he needs, then we will live in a perfect society, and the one who delivers this perfection deserves to be ruler of all. Cole's company, DCN, steers everything toward this goal, and you have a place in it, by virtue of being Cole's choice for a partner. Don't you want that?"

For a fraction of a second, the chance of securing the life she'd lived rose up as a beguiling creature. But the price climbed higher. She formed her words carefully. "For the record, my name is Selah, and what you propose is impossible."

"No, it's not. We are alike. You want to control problems in the world with science and research, and I can help. We're cut from the same cloth."

"I've changed."

"Don't make the mistake your father did. He refused my offer, and his life ended up less than it could have been. I can give you so much more."

An excruciating pain split her heart, and her mouth flew open. "That which is born of the flesh is flesh; and that which is born of the Spirit is spirit. Book of Wisdom, 43:3-6." Surprised at her own utterance, she clamped her mouth shut, and her heart pain left.

Beast reared back, and a simultaneous flash of brilliance split the air. A dark, twisted shadow shot upwards from his form and flew away howling and screeching. Violent coughing and guttural sounds came from the remaining jerking torso in the chair.

She pressed the alarm for help.

The therapist rushed in. "What happened?"

"I don't know. We were talking, and all of a sudden he shrieked and started trembling."

Beast's body slumped over and became still, and the therapist yelled for help.

Attendants rushed in. Most swarmed around Beast, but one grappled with her chair, programmed it to return her to a standing position and then escorted her back to her room.

When her escort left, SJ exhaled. Something besides adrenaline coursed through her veins. She placed her hand on her heart and remembered Michael's words about her gift.

Was that it? Speaking gibberish? From an ancient book?

Even if the words held truth, if she spewed them in random fashion in the house of science, she'd become even more of an idiot. She needed substance. Study. Observation. Taking notes. Learning. A copy of the Book of Wisdom would be a good start.

The sound of child's laughter came from behind her. Turning her chair, she strained to identify the small form dancing in front of her.

"You were hiding, but I found you." Girlish laughter came again. "Mr. Chris brought me here."

"Bow?" SJ's astonishment turned to unexpected tears. She brushed them away but then remembered the child could not see.

"I hope we aren't intruding." A tall figure moved in the opening of her door. "We came for Bow's annual evaluation and to visit another student. Bow insisted we stop and bring you a present." Chris's voice held a hint of amusement.

"His name is Damien, and he's a thief. He stole a cyclobike." Bow's soft hand patted hers. "We brought him some paper and colors, so he can be an artist like me and not steal."

A rustling noise came, and then an oblong weight dropped in SJ's lap. "Open it."

She patted the wrapped object, but then Bow took over and ripped it open.

"It's the Stick Healer book. It's so you can practice the stories and help people get better. Remember the name? B.O.W. like my initials only it means Book of Wisdom." Bow pushed SJ's hand across the smooth surface.

Emotion bound her tongue, but she eventually managed a whisper. "Thank you, Bow. Thank you very much."

"Bow wanted you to have it," Chris said.

"Yep. 'Cause you gotta get better and come be a teacher at the school. There's lots of us, and we have to learn stuff."

Chris laughed. "Dr. SJ has a job here, Bow."

"Actually, I don't think I do. I'll be hunting for a new one just as soon as my eyesight improves. They think it's something that's reversible, but so far not much has changed."

"Did you ever get your name back?" Bow's tiny hands stroked her arm.

"I sure did." She smiled. "It's Selah. Selah Joy."

"Selah Joy? I like it. I'm gonna pray right now about your eyes. It's for a miracle. Then you can pray for mine."

"Bow, miracles don't always come," Chris said. "And Dr. Selah might need to rest now."

"It's okay. Really. It would be lovely." SJ converted her chair to *Sit* mode and allowed Bow to climb into her lap.

"Close your eyes." Bow touched SJ's eyelids. "Please, Stick Healer, make my Selah's eyes all better again, and take out the shadows from mine too. Amen."

Selah opened her eyes and stared into the face of a tiger. “Bow, why is your face painted that way?”

“It’s animal day at school, and I’m learning to roar.” Bow pranced around the room and clawed at the air, then she came to a sudden stop. “How did you know about my face?”

Tears welled in SJ’s eyes. “I can see.”

THE MESSAGES

A pelican drawing appears before each chapter where SJ finds one of her five messages. Pelicans are one of the oldest living bird species and found on all but one continent. In history, pelican art is a symbol of focus, persistence, and self-sacrifice, and on Egyptian tomb walls as protection from snakes.

The messages appear to SJ in various ways, and all come from the 43rd book of the Bible, the book of John.

In Chapter Three, Evie's letter contained the first message. "The thief comes to steal, kill, and destroy. I come that you may have life to the full. Book of Wisdom 43. 10. 10"

In Chapter Five, Kate's End Tablet held this one: "Believe and live. Book of Wisdom 43.11.25"

In Chapter Eleven, this message appeared as Kate's garden stone inscription: "Love is. Book of Wisdom 43.3.16"

In Chapter Seventeen, Ben retrieved a paper from inside Kate's empty microtherm cylinder. "Choose truth. Book of Wisdom 43.14.6"

In Chapter Twenty-six, Bow's drawing contained this one. "Be healed. 43.3.14.15"

Imagine a world one hundred fifty years from now where book banning, including religious texts, has been the norm for decades, and existing copies of banned works are often lost due to age and lack of interest. If these verses, or the first fourteen chapters of John, were re-discovered in some form, then readers would still be able to piece together basic tenets of the Christian faith. The message topics include words about life, afterlife, resurrection, and the presence of good and evil.

AFTERWORD

I've thought about death a lot. It's a regular topic in my life, as I am married to a physician. In my years before writing, I worked as a nurse in a hospital and served as a caregiver for the elderly in a nursing home.

The topic of death is also personal. My father, a writer and teacher, died just before I started writing this story. Then, the second week after I began the rough draft, a close friend died unexpectedly.

Initially after someone dies, memories are recalled and attempts are made to preserve them, but as years pass, all evidence of a person's time on earth disappears. If the deceased is memorable enough, a person living two generations past their death might recall details about them. If they have a family, child, or grandchild, they might be remembered longer. Most of the time by the third, fourth, and fifth generation, any evidence of a person's existence is long gone.

So I began to wonder. Is it possible for an ordinary person to touch generations in the future by purposeful words, stories, and actions?

Theoretically, it can happen. If I live to tell my great-grandchild something important, and they live to tell it to their great-grandchild, then the "something important" travels forward about five generations, perhaps one hundred fifty years or more.

The idea compelled me, birthed this story, and made me think.

What can a person say, do, or strive for today that will impact generations to come?

Muse with me more on this idea and others at:

CLARKMCFARLANDBOOKS.COM

ACKNOWLEDGEMENTS

I'm deeply grateful to the following beta readers who slogged through various drafts of this story that began so long ago.

To my siblings, the Clark brothers, sister Eileen, and our beloved sister Heather, the middle sibling who has run on ahead of us into eternity. (We miss you so much, Heather.) All of you knew my imaginative ways from the very beginning and might have guessed I would turn out this way, but you still keep my company. I am blessed.

To Dr. C. Brock, my ever supportive and inquisitive educator. You are a true inspiration and instigator of many great discussions.

To Greg Scott and Ted Atchley, my fellow partners in the crimes of writing books. I am undeserving of the time and dedication you put into reviewing my literary ramblings. It was very kind of you. You helped me understand so many things. I wish I could repay.

To visual artists Isabella and Krista. Thanks for joining this merry band and adding your art originals to the concepts for cover and interior art design.

And to my dear husband, Dr. Tim McFarland. You have supported my creative endeavors through all forms and phases over all these years. You bring balance and humor to my life. You listen to all the details of the worlds I've created and gently remind me not to obsess too much when I'm stuck on a detail. (After all, I'm writing fiction, and the detail I'm obsessing over is made up.) You have also become quite the editor, and I appreciate all the errors you catch and your ever present enthusiasm for my story. "Hurry up and publish," you said. And so, minus the hurry, I finally did. (Next time I'll be faster.)